PREY DRIVE

TOPAZ TRILOGY BOOK TWO

VICTORIA JAYNE SAUNDERS

VJS Books

This one goes out to my fellow anxiety babes as a reminder that you can still kick ass while having a panic attack.

CONTENTS

THE CHEHWINOO

Sit down, gather 'round, have a drink or two.
If you wait and fill your plate, I'll tell you 'bout the Chehwinoo.

The night is young, the wind is calm, the sky is still light blue.
If you think you're tough, then you're in luck. I'll tell you 'bout the Chehwinoo.

Long before we settled here before this town stood high,
A family man traversed this land, his pack heavy with wares.
He traveled with his wedded wife, with locks the colour of rye,
On her hip, her son did sit, sporting his father's raven hair.

The father, the mother, the son, the troop,
To Devil's Lake, their path would lead.
But misfortune fell on their little group,
On their sorrow, it would feed.

Quiet now, little ones, don't tell the flies to shoo.
If you're loud and make a sound, you might call the Chehwinoo.

Ten feet tall and made of ice, his claws turn your skin blue.
The air grows cold and you hear a scream- it must be the Chehwinoo.

Winter came before the frost, harder than ever before,
The father grew scared with every gust, as their store of food grew bare.
I must go and hunt, he said, one hand on the door,

The other reached for his young son, who screamed it isn't fair.

I'll be back before the sun,
The father unknowingly lied.
He tied his boots and took his gun,
While his wife and young son cried.

Hunger is a powerful foe, can leave you with nothing left to do.
Just be smart and play your part. Don't anger the Chehwinoo.

Where darkness lurks, where spirits hide in shadows of every hue,
Have no doubt it's lurking about. You'll find the Chehwinoo.

The father searched high and wide for signs of doe or buck,
He wandered far into the woods, where the rays of sun wouldn't touch.
He wandered as far as he dared, and when he thought he'd run out of luck,
The father came across a man, dying in a little hutch.

I have no food, he wept
I need your help, please.
From his cheeks, the tears he swept
Dripped on the father's knees.

I'll whisper now as the night goes on and the moon rises new.
It shuns the sun and fears the light, that sneaky Chehwinoo.

Quickly now, we must make haste, we have no time to lose.
Finish this tale and get inside where it's safe from the Chehwinoo.

The dying man knew not his fate as he begged for help,
The father had a terrible thought as his hunger screamed for blood.
The dying man could feed his wife, his strapping little welp.
With his gun, he shot the man and watched as he fell into the mud.

But the father had failed,
He wouldn't see his wife this night.
For if she knew, her skin would pale,
She'd stare at her husband in fright.

Hunger is a powerful foe, but you cannot let it win.
You'll lose yourself along this path, your humanity will grow thin.
What would you do to survive?
Would you sin so too?
The beast inside will come alive.

You are the Chehwinoo.

INTERLUDE

The Basin

When Malcolm Diamond accepted a contract position with Blunden Construction, he wasn't prepared to end up in the middle of backwoods Wisconsin for two months. All he'd wanted was an escape from his obnoxious roommate, then he'd gotten stuck with more than he bargained for.

Mac lived in Madison, which was over an hour's drive from the new Stamkos & Stein pharmaceutical factory that formed the basis of his contract. His portion of the work was due to wrap up over three weeks ago and here he'd barely made a dent in his assigned duties. It was frustrating, especially because the commute home was too long to make twice a day for 12 weeks. His mom wanted him to come back to Madison over the weekends, but Mac physically recoiled at the thought. His roommate, the reason he'd accepted the contract in the first place, was a full-time student and spent all of his off time at the apartment. Normally, that wasn't much of an issue. Mac worked odd hours, so even if he was home, they rarely crossed paths.

In the few weeks before his contract began, their alternating schedules didn't matter. Kyle had a new girlfriend and the two of them were firmly in the honeymoon stage of their relationship. That meant humping like rabbits at any opportunity, and always at Mac and Kyle's place. Apparently, Kyle was allergic to Ariana's cat.

Yeah, Mac was much happier lounging around a dust-covered work camp than subjecting himself to nights of poorly muffled mattress springs squeaking out an embarrassing rhythm from across the hall.

Mac Diamond was a resourceful guy. While Somerton wasn't the height of social opportunity, all Mac needed was an open space and a boatload of booze to make a memorable night. Technically his open space of choice wasn't *his* per se. If he was caught hosting a party on the recently-leveled ground for the new factory, he'd undoubtedly be fired. The knowledge tickled his conscience, ultimately fading behind the surge of determination and boredom that permanently occupied his chest in these woods. How would his bosses find out, anyway? They were all corporate-born nepotism babies, with three houses and as many wives spread out over the country. None of them would be caught dead spending their weekend within spitting distance of their lower-class employees.

Besides, half of his coworkers were *here*, toting full cases of beer and filling their rolling papers with more than plain tobacco. If word did get back to the higher-ups, they couldn't fire *everyone*.

At least, that's what he told himself.

Originally, Mac wasn't expecting much of a turnout. Aside from the men sharing the camp, he didn't know many people in Somerton. He couldn't exactly post about the party on social media— talk about asking to get caught— so he was a little concerned about the attendance rate. Not to mention, it was Halloween weekend. He wasn't into themed parties, so he hadn't put any effort into reflecting the holiday in his spur-of-the-moment gathering. He assumed everyone interested in going would already have other plans.

Luckily, he'd forgotten about small-town rules. Within a few hours of sending out the first text, every person under the age of 25 in Somerton and the surrounding area knew there was a party happening and that they were invited. Any smaller Halloween bashes happening at the same time had merged into this larger get-together, with the only evidence of them ever existing independently being the scattered guest wearing a half-assed costume and face paint.

S&S had chosen the perfect building site for illicit activity. Mac would've felt bad taking advantage of his employer-by-proxy, if not for their laughable decision-making skills. If they'd been smarter with their location scouting, they wouldn't have to worry about trespassers in the first place. If anything, Mac was helping them out. Let them learn their lesson now, well before they started producing actual products that would be worth stealing, like painkillers or pseudo-psychedelics. A little property damage was nothing compared to narcotics theft.

"MAC!" Graham's drunken voice slurred through the pounding EDM shaking the leaves of the surrounding firs. "WHERE'S THE KEY TO THE GENERATOR?"

Mac reached into his pocket, retrieved the key, and tossed it to Graham. Given the obvious absence of Graham's sobriety, that wasn't the smartest move. The key thumped to the dirt with three bystanders plus Graham scrambling to find it. Mac shook his head and walked away without offering to help; the generator belonged to someone's uncle. He didn't care what happened to it.

With only rudimentary planning and a few volunteers, they'd managed to turn the construction site into something akin to an outdoor music festival. The generator was powering strings of yellow lights that skirted the edge of the clearing, marking the start of the treeline and unmonitored territory. It was also powering an impressive number of speakers, which blasted music from Mac's own phone. No less than ten coolers were scattered around, housing partially-melted ice cubes and chilled bottles of cheap alcohol. Mac had really outdone himself with this one— even the weather seemed to be praising his ingenuity. For the end of October in Wisconsin, the temperature was shockingly mild.

A shrill laugh caught Mac's attention, souring his mood instantly. Lisa. He knew she'd be here, but that didn't mean he was any less bitter about it. The sudden and intense urge to take a piss overwhelmed him, and the timing couldn't have been better. He'd take any semblance of an excuse to hightail it before his ex's sister spotted him.

"I gotta empty the tank," Mac said to no one in particular, waving to Graham before jerking his thumb over his shoulder when he had his attention. "Be back in a sec."

Graham nodded, though he was too far away to have heard what Mac said. Context clues would help him figure it out if he needed to.

The Basin, the forest that was home to their agonizingly drawn-out construction project, wasn't the most interesting place to work. It was a nice enough forest, as far as forests go. Mac could understand why someone would really enjoy spending time here, just not him. He wasn't a nature guy, so without work to do, he was bored out of his damn mind. With towering trees, dense foliage, a myriad of wildlife, and a thick coating of bugs, Somerton and its adjoining wilderness were the kinds of places where a person could live their whole life and never see anything interesting, not once. Mac never saw the appeal of places like that. Even less so now that he was plunged into the untamed void of the Basin, looking for a place to piss.

As he stumbled through the darkened woods, the temperature plummeted. Maybe it had been mild earlier, or maybe he'd had more alcohol than he realized, but Mac couldn't deny that winter weather hovered in the shadows around him. The combination of heat from the string lights, the people milling around, and the whirring of the electronics must've warmed the air at the construction site more efficiently than he'd assumed. Mac wished like hell he'd brought his overcoat.

Sound didn't carry well through the dense trees, so Mac only had to walk a brief distance before the music faded to a soft hum barely loud enough to drown out his own labored breath. He was *definitely* drunker than he thought he was, the imposing tree trunks swaying in his vision and making it look like the forest was gently dancing to the far-off chords. Mac chuckled at the ridiculous thought, unzipped his jeans, and began relieving himself.

"*...Malcom...*"

The words tickled his ear like the gossamer threads of a spider web caressing his skin. Mac jolted, stumbling back against the weathered oak he'd just doused in beer-scented urine.

He waited for the voice to sound again, but the forest remained stubbornly silent.

"Graham?" Mac growled, shaking his head to clear some of the drunken haze clinging to his vision. The cold was sobering him, turning the tips of his fingers red and clouding his shaky breath. "Stop messing around, Graham!"

Mac waited again, to no avail. The woods were silent.

He hastily zipped up his jeans, pulled his hoodie back down over his hips, and stomped loudly back in the direction he'd come from. The Basin may have bored him to death in the daytime, but it was creepy as hell at night. Suddenly, the prospect of being accosted by Lisa wasn't the worst fate he could imagine.

As he rushed to return to the comfort of the light, Mac could've sworn he heard someone creeping through the underbrush somewhere behind him. The sound was muddled by the fabric of his hood against his ears and the ruckus of his own movement, but the longer he listened, the more certain he was that someone was there. The rest of the forest had gone eerily quiet, allowing him to hone in on the rustling of leaves ten paces away.

It wasn't Graham. Mac had no idea why, but he was absolutely sure that whoever was tailing him, wasn't his friend. He slowed his step then quickened it again, trying to trick his pursuer into fumbling their walking pattern. He made it only a few feet before realizing how ridiculous he was being. He was in the *woods*, for Christ's sake. There were animals everywhere. All this fuss and Mac's stalker was probably a stupid squirrel.

He needed to get back, and he sure as shit needed another beer.

Jesus, it's cold. It was like the entire forest had frozen to a standstill, with not even a whisper of wind to dispel the quiet. Should that be peaceful? Mac didn't know. The feeling in his gut was anything but pleasant, whether from booze or paranoia he didn't much care. How far had he walked, anyway? He didn't want Lisa following him, so he'd moved a bit further away from the crowd than he'd needed to. Still, he didn't think he'd gone *that* far. He should be back by now.

"*Malcolm.*"

The voice again, louder this time. Mac stumbled from the shock of hearing it, close enough that it could be coming from his own mouth, and he wouldn't be able to say differently. *What the hell?*

"Who are you?" Mac demanded, not sure that he wanted an answer. The Basin remained silent, teasing him with its refusal to answer his question. "Fuck off."

It was a childish thing to say, but it did make him feel better. Mac started walking again with renewed vigor only to collide with a wall of shadow that knocked him clean off his feet.

He flailed on his way to the ground, trying to catch himself before he hit his head on a rock. His hands grasped the air, finding nothing with purchase, and Mac felt the somersault of gravity in his stomach. He was falling for what seemed like a lifetime, and then the shadows grabbed him.

He didn't understand, but it was true. The shadow that he'd walked into, the swirling mass of darkness in front of him clutched at his arms first, then his shoulders, and suddenly Mac was lifted from the ground. He tried to fight the shadow's hold on him, but it was no use. The darkness remained intangible to him, with the grip on his body as solid and cold as glacial ice. The shadows pulled at him, yanking him in every direction until he felt like his skin would tear. The touch of darkness on his body was like nothing he'd ever experienced before, as though the absence of light had manifested into a corporeal form and latched onto him, injecting icy terror into his veins.

And then it entered his mouth.

Mac didn't know he was screaming until the shadow plunged an undulating tendril into his mouth, choking him. His scream died in a guttural gasp as saliva pooled in his cheeks, tears flooding his eyes. The shadows funneled into his mouth until Mac couldn't breathe, his lungs straining against the intrusion and clawing for oxygen all at once. Mac grabbed his own throat, his hands now free, and clawed at his taut skin. The shadows pulsed in his mouth, gagging him, until he felt like he was freezing from the inside out. He was so cold— it felt like his heart was stilling in his chest, weighed down by fractals of ice mounting behind his ribs. If not for the fear and panic powering his body, Mac was sure his heart would've stopped by now.

His vision darkened, the shadows filling him so completely that he could now see them from the inside of his eyes. Mac was going to die. In a sharp moment of inescapable clarity, he knew it. He also knew there was nothing he could do to stop it.

Then, just as abruptly as it began, it was over.

Mac collapsed to the ground, sucking in breath after precious breath. His lungs burned with gratitude, pumping oxygen through his blood with frantic speed. For a split second, he wondered if he'd imagined the whole thing. Maybe he'd accidentally ingested LSD, or maybe he was in the middle of a psychotic break. Both of those theories vanished when he stood, and the echo of the shadows thrummed in his limbs. They were still there, writhing under the surface of his skin, worming into his flesh. He retched, steadying himself on a nearby tree.

Help. He needed help.

Mac spun, searching for his trail, grasping for his bearings. The forest pressed in on him, distorted faces against carnival glass, mocking him. Mac tried to ignore it, to focus on choosing the right way back. He couldn't risk choosing wrong and getting himself even more lost. Whatever was happening to him, he wouldn't survive it alone.

The inky blackness of the night swelled and mottled before his eyes, squirming in a thick, viscous boil, like sauce simmering on a stove. Mac ground his palms into his face, shaking his head to dispel the illusion. The Basin was alive and breathing, clinging to his cold skin, and dragging him deeper into the darkness. Where were the others? Could they see what he was seeing?

With his eyes squeezed shut, he had no way of knowing.

Mac didn't understand that he was moving until the sounds of laughter and drunken cheers pierced his hammering skull. He gagged against the bolt of pain, jerking as it spasmed along his spine and down his legs. He thought he must've screamed because everything was silent in the next instant, save for his gasping breaths.

"Hey, Mac? You alright, buddy?"

Did it *look* like he was alright?

The bitter retort ignited and fizzled in the same second, smothered by the electrifying pain in his throat. Why were they still here, partying? Mac would've been long gone by now if it weren't for the lead weight in his aching limbs. They should run, get back to their cars, to their homes, to safety. From what, he didn't quite know. Urgency and panic coupled in his gut, alerting him to the presence of danger. He cracked his jaw open to warn them, but only a screech came out.

"Christ, Mac!" That was Graham's voice, he was almost positive. "What happened? Someone call somebody! An ambulance, the police, shit, *anyone!*"

Rage surged in Mac's chest. How the hell was *he* supposed to know what happened? It's not like he planned this. Did they think he was doing it intentionally? Shoving away the insult, Mac tried again to speak.

"Do you see it?" he rasped, doubling over with the effort. Every breath felt like fire in his lungs despite the chills consuming his body. Graham didn't answer, but Mac couldn't look at him. He refused to open his eyes, not again, not while the world taunted him with its wrongness.

"See what, Mac?"

Graham's voice again, right next to him and yet also distant and echoed, like he was speaking through water. How could he not see it? Mac retched when he tried to answer, a mixture of stale beer and gas station nachos souring the back of his tongue. He couldn't take this anymore— the agony in his head, the burning in his veins, the all-consuming cold— it was too much. Mac's knees buckled, and he fell to the dirt with a painful thud.

"Call 911!" Graham was yelling, his voice cracking in desperation. Mac had never noticed how... melodic Graham sounded when he was afraid. It was sooth-ing, almost pleasurable. Mac shuddered on the ground, inhaling against the stab-bing pain in his chest. As his lungs filled, Mac felt the knot of tension in him ease. The cloying scent of dirt, pine, and alcohol was strong, but beneath it, something else coated his throat. Something sweet, intoxicating, and new. Something Mac had never smelled before but was immediately addicted to. *Fuck*, it felt good. He thought that... yes, yes, he was. The smell was so good he was getting *hard* for Christ's sake. Somehow, deep in his gut, Mac knew what this smell was.

Fear.

Mac took another deep breath, shuddering at the pleasure that coursed through him with the intoxicating scent of fear permeating the clearing. *God above*, he needed more. Mac let his lips fall open, drool spilling over the pockets of his cheeks and dripping down his chin as he sucked in breath after breath, a clawing emptiness deep inside him desperate to be sated. The commotion of the ruined party faded to a dull roar in his ears, erasing his pain. Mac's limbs were numb, tingling with the aftermath of exposure. He stretched, vaguely confused by the symphony of cracks that erupted from his joints. They sounded strange, like snapping twigs. Why were his eyes still closed?

The ground crumbled under his fingernails as Mac twisted onto all fours— no, not fingernails. *Claws.* He inhaled again, invigorated by the delicious panic seeping through the air. The forest was loud again, invading his newfound peace with annoying clarity. It took him longer than it should've to realize that everyone was screaming. Could they see it now?

Mac had forgotten the reason he'd closed his eyes in the first place. He pried them open now, welcoming the swell of colour that assaulted his vision. The blackness of night hemorrhaged into deep, crimson red, dousing the glitter of stars left in the sky. People swarmed around him, some shocked, some horrified, some angry, all mouth-watering. Mac surveyed them with a discerning glare.

They were trespassers here, he decided. Unwanted. Undeserving. They couldn't see what he did, too distracted by his grotesque appearance to notice the beauty around them. Red, like the rarest ruby on Earth. Red, like a single drop of blood in crystal clear waters. They couldn't see it, but Mac could. He was an ugly scar of shadow on this vibrant scene. Red flowed through the trees, thrumming with life. Red flowed through *them*, fueling the air with the delectable taste of terror. They couldn't see it, but he *needed* it.

Mac flexed his new claws, picturing them coated with blood as thick as paint, satisfying his darkness with shimmering life.

They couldn't see the glorious red pumping through them now, but they would. Mac would make sure of it. By the time he was done, they would see everything. By the time he was done, the *world* would see everything.

By the time he was done, everything would be red.

Chapter One

AMELIA

As the front door of LJ's Diner slammed shut behind her, muffling the abrasive shouts of Derek Harris, Amelia was decided. Dating in Pennsylvania was *way* worse than dating in Illinois.

The early autumn air was a bracing relief after the oppressive heat of the diner. Amelia loved LJ's for its open kitchen and family-oriented atmosphere, but eating next to the bustling grill always left her with a thin sheen of fry oil and sweat over her entire body by the time she'd settled her bill. Not this time, at least. This time, she hadn't made it past the appetizers before storming out.

Something crashed inside, and Amelia felt anger surge in her chest. She reached for the door handle with every intention of dragging Derek outside herself, stopped only by the stern look Matt shot her through the tempered glass. For a line cook, Matt was terrifyingly large. Determination and spite would only get her so far when the man could easily lift her off her feet with one hand. Annoyed, she settled against the yellowing brick with her arms crossed over her chest.

Derek Harris threw an impressive tantrum, she'd give him that much. At 34 and a chronic smoker, he was screaming with the lung capacity of someone half his age. The muted insults she could hear left her vibrating with fury; *she* was the one who'd ruined his shirt, not the staff. Who the hell was he to berate them like that? Again, the urge to burst back inside and haul Derek out by his ear surfaced in her gut. If Matt wasn't keeping a close eye on her, she would've. The seasoned line cook would never let her put herself in harm's way, even if it was her colossal mistake of a date that was causing the ruckus. Maybe especially then.

All Amelia could do was wait, seething against the weathered brick wall of LJ's, until a familiar red truck veered into the parking lot.

The dirt-spattered Tacoma screamed to a stop just feet from her, the engine hissing in protest at the abrupt shift from Drive to Park. Before the truck had fully settled, the driver's side door crashed open, and Sam launched himself onto the asphalt. He rounded the vehicle in four determined strides, quickly assessing her for any injuries. Seeing none, Sam nodded toward the diner.

"He still here?"

Amelia loosed one arm and cracked open the diner's door. Derek's rough threats tripled in volume, startling a nearby group of schoolgirls sharing a basket of onion rings at a splintering picnic table.

"Unfortunately," she confirmed, letting the door close again. Sam's expression darkened, shrugging out of his jacket, and tossing it to her.

"Get in the truck," he commanded, disappearing into the diner before she could protest. Amelia had absolutely no interest in listening, although she did move to the driver's side in case someone tried to make off with the still-running vehicle. She was only alone for seconds before LJ's front door slammed open, spitting out a stunned, sputtering Derek Harris.

"Who the fuck do you think you are?" Derek cursed, catching his balance before he fell face-first into the pavement. "Mind your own damn business!"

Sam followed behind Derek, shutting the door behind him with deliberate finality. He sank his hands into his jeans pockets, planting himself between Derek and the establishment.

"I think you've caused enough of a scene," he said, raising an eyebrow challengingly. "How about you sit in your car and cool off until the cops get here."

"Oh, you called the cops, huh?" Derek sneered. "Good. I want to press charges!"

"For what?"

"Assault!" Derek whipped his head in all directions, suddenly searching for something. When his eyes landed on Amelia, he grew incensed. "*You!* I'll sue you both! And this dumpster of a diner!"

It was almost comical, the way his eyes bulged, and his face reddened. Amelia briefly wondered if it was possible for a person to actually explode from anger.

"What do you think, Am?" Sam asked her, bitter amusement easing the severity of his anger. Amelia felt a small pang of pride— Sam wouldn't typically be so composed. She pretended to think for a moment, smirking.

"Would a strawberry milkshake count as a deadly weapon?" Derek reeled back like he wasn't expecting her to speak. The front of his shirt was horrifically stained with the sugary, dairy-filled evidence of their disastrous first (and only) date. Otherwise, he was unharmed. Dumping a milkshake on a misogynist was hardly a crime. Uttering threats and destroying private property, on the other hand, certainly were.

"Face it, Harris," Sam growled, drawing Derek's attention back to him. He cut an imposing figure silhouetted by the residual glow of LJ's interior fluorescents. "When the police show, you're the only one getting a record out of this."

"You threw me into the street!" Derek screeched at Sam, taking an aggravated step toward him. Sam didn't flinch but Amelia did, ready to throw herself at Derek if he even *thought* about flinging a cheap shot at Sam. "You fucking man-handled me, asshole! I could've broken something!"

"You did," Sam said pointedly. "A table, two chairs, and at least six dishes. Also, any dignity you had left, but I'm guessing that wasn't much."

Derek's jaw snapped shut. He simmered for a long second and then, realizing he was already in deep shit, decided to go for broke. He pulled back his right arm, throwing a punch at Sam with the full force of his stocky frame. Amelia snapped out a warning, but Sam didn't need it. He caught Derek's punch and cranked his arm behind his back in the same motion, dropping Derek to the ground. He howled indignantly, trying in vain to break Sam's hold.

"Aggravated assault, destruction of private property, making threats... did I miss anything, Am?"

"Not unless being a colossal douche is a crime."

"It's not," Sam shook his head sadly, "luckily for our boy Derek here. Get in the truck."

Sam's tone shifted abruptly, so much so that it took Amelia a second to realize the instruction was for her. She bristled, leveling a glare at Sam that could freeze lava.

"I'm sorry," she said, her words dripping in sarcasm, "just because I'm pissed at him doesn't mean you've got a free pass. Watch your tone."

Sam pulled his gaze away from Derek to meet her defiant stare with ease.

"You're right," he droned. "I wasn't thinking. Get in the goddamn truck *now*."

Outrage filled her. "Excuse you—"

"Amelia, I'm not asking."

This time, urgency undercut the authority in Sam's voice. She paused, willing her temper to settle as she listened. When the blood rushing in her ears quieted, she finally heard it. Sirens.

"Shit," she muttered, momentarily forgetting her annoyance. She yanked open the Tacoma's driver-side door and scrambled across the middle console to the passenger seat. Sam waved to Matt, releasing Derek into the dirt only when the line cook had joined them. Derek didn't try to attack them again or run, just sat on the pavement, huffing like a petulant child. Sam rushed over to the truck, slamming it into Drive, and peeling out of the parking lot at frantic speed. They were barely around the corner when the first police cruiser came into sight, heading directly for LJ's Diner.

***

"I know you just saved my ass back there and all, but if you ever speak to me like that again I'm going to formally introduce my foot to the inside of your colon. Understood?"

"Promises, promises," Sam said dreamily, reclining in his seat as they navigated through the typical evening traffic. "You know, all these empty threats are really starting to take the bite out of your image. Either commit or admit that all your hostility comes from a deep-seated obsession with my asshole."

Amelia gave him a look that could curdle milk.

"I'm just saying," Sam shrugged, "if you want it, all you have to do is ask."

"I think I'm going to be sick."

"Not on the upholstery you're not."

She fought back a laugh, her attention catching on every speck and stain that adorned the inside of Sam's beloved truck. The vehicle had seen much worse than a little vomit in its time, and they both knew it.

"You're not allowed to pick your dates anymore, by the way," Sam said, sighing. "I swear, you have some sort of dick magnet on you. And not the sexy kind."

Amelia rolled her eyes, letting her head droop onto her shoulder and staring up at Sam through her lashes.

"To be fair to me, this is the first time Matt's called you in like a year."

"That doesn't count when this is the first time you've been on a date in like a year."

She stuck her tongue out at him, returning her attention to the window. Sam cranked the volume as *Nickelback* blasted through the speakers, slapping his palms against the wheel in time with the beat. A jerk like Derek Harris could never bring Sam down, not even when he had to unceremoniously eject the scumbag from their favourite restaurant.

Sam and Amelia had been regulars at LJ's ever since they moved to Royersford. Matt was the owner's nephew, so he'd been on staff the first time they'd stumbled across the place, lost and in the wrong neighborhood after a drunken night at the college bar. While they didn't see much of each other outside the diner, Matt always made time for them whenever they stopped in. In fact, it was his idea for Amelia to start bringing her dates there, so she'd have backup if things went sour. It didn't happen often, but it did happen. Despite Matt's kindness, Amelia was typically able to handle things herself. Still, it was nice knowing that the staff at LJ's were looking out for her when a situation came up that she *couldn't* handle alone. Like Derek Harris.

They'd met only a couple of weeks prior at the Ursinus College student services office. Amelia was Derek's little sister's assigned admissions counselor, and he'd asked her for her number after crossing paths when he came to pick up Aretha after her appointment. He seemed charming enough, so Amelia had given it to him. Only five minutes into their date, she knew she'd made a mistake.

"Are you going to get one of the other counselors to take on Harris's sister?" Sam asked conversationally. Amelia knew better; he wasn't asking, he was telling her what he wanted her to do. She had no intention of listening, of course.

"What? And rob me of the chance to watch him squirm every time he comes in?" Amelia gave him a sly grin. "Not a chance."

"Why did I know that?" Sam shook his head disparagingly. "Fine, but I'm walking you to your office for the next few weeks. I don't trust that guy."

"Aye-aye, Captain."

Amelia watched Sam discreetly out of the corner of her eye, looking for any sign that Matt had told him what caused her date with Derek to blow up in the first place. She decided he hadn't. If he *had*, Sam would never be this calm.

As if reading her thoughts, Sam glanced over at her.

"So, tell me, Milkshake Molly," he teased, backing into his preferred parking spot at their apartment building. Spots weren't formally assigned, but the residents had formed their own loose system. "What exactly did Harris say to incur your wrath?"

"Oh, you know," Amelia shrugged her shoulder, elbowing the Tacoma's door open and easing her legs out, "typical sexist bull. I believe it had something to do with the fact that I ordered a cheeseburger instead of a salad."

It didn't. Ginny, LJ's veteran waitress, had pulled Amelia aside to tell her that she'd seen Derek slip something into her milkshake. She wasn't going to tell Sam that, though. She wouldn't be able to stop him from committing a felony.

"That's so fucking stupid," Sam said, clicking the lock on his key fob and looping his arm around Amelia's shoulders in the same motion. She fell into step beside him, retrieving her apartment key from her back pocket. "I can't believe some men still think that way."

"Women too," Amelia grimaced, "I've had more than one teenage girl give me the stink eye when I ask for large fries."

"I take it Harris showed his true colours before you could eat?" Sam guessed. Amelia nodded regretfully. "Well, you're in luck. I'm making Sammy's Spicy Spaghetti."

Amelia made a face that was equal parts intrigue and concern.

"You're not putting the same sauce you used last time in there, are you? That Devil's Pepper stuff? You couldn't get off the toilet for an hour."

"No Devil's Pepper this time," Sam vowed. "Scout's honor."

"In that case," Amelia jiggled the handle to their apartment door, lifting as she inserted the key. It was a finicky lock that needed a bit of finesse to conquer, but they'd found their system over the years, "to the kitchen with you, Fisher. I'll get the garlic bread out of the freezer."

"Way ahead of you, Amy Baby."

Chapter Two

AMELIA

"Oh, come *on!*" Sam yelled, sitting bolt upright and jostling Amelia's nearly empty bowl of spaghetti. It made a valiant effort to reach the floor, but she managed to wrangle it back into the safety of her grip. "That was offside!"

"Stop screaming," she said, shoving her back into Sam's chest, forcing him to relax into the couch cushion again. He did, albeit with some adamant grumbling. "Mrs. Schwartz is going to call the building manager on us again."

"It's not even eight!" In lieu of lowering his voice, Sam shoved an entire half-slice of garlic bread into his mouth— *her* half-slice of garlic bread, no less— and used his free hand to tug Amelia further into the clutches of their deteriorating sofa. She was already practically on top of him. He'd be using her as a blanket if she fell any more. "Besides, it's not my fault. Blame the officials."

Yeah, she'd heard that one before.

Gently placing her now-finished bowl on the coffee table, Amelia relented and settled against Sam's torso. He hummed in contentment, squeezing her just enough to dispel any remaining distance between them. She huffed in exasperation, knowing there was no use in trying to worm her way out of this. Sam always was a terminal cuddler.

He was also an obnoxious sports fan.

As much as Amelia resented Mrs. Schwartz and her strange habits, she couldn't blame her for the occasional noise complaint. All through high school and college, Sam was a dedicated football player. And he was good. So good that, after graduating from Ursinus with the appropriate degree, he was hired on as an associate athletics trainer. Sam lived, breathed, and bled sports; not just football, although that was his favourite. It was a rare evening that the Fisher-Bradley apartment wasn't streaming a game of some kind. Today, it was hockey. And Philadelphia was losing.

"I knew I should've cheered for the Pens," Sam muttered, downing the rest of his beer in two large gulps. Amelia took the empty bottle from him and put it on the table next to her bowl.

"We live too close to Philly for you to start walking around in black and yellow," Amelia reminded him, though she knew he was bluffing. Growing up just outside of Chicago meant that the Blackhawks were his true team. Going to school in Philly has given him a soft spot for the Flyers.

This late in the year, the world outside of their living room window was stained with black despite that it was only seven in the evening. As much as Amelia appreciated the beauty of fall, she hated how early everything turned to darkness. It was unsettling, and by mid-November, she'd already be longing for the soft light of summer. She didn't like the dark, especially when it was cold.

Her phone buzzed, distracting her from the fight that had broken out between two of the teams' third-liners.

Derek Harris was arrested. The milkshake on his shirt tested positive for Rohypnol.

The text was from an unknown number, but that didn't matter. Amelia knew who it was.

You okay?

The question seared her, dredging up instant and festering anger. Terrence didn't care if she was okay. He knew it, and she knew it. The only reason he'd texted her at all was to ease his own guilty conscience, and Amelia wasn't responsible for making him feel better. Especially when his inaction had almost cost her her life.

She almost told him as much, letting her anger dictate her words with stinging vehemence. Before she hit send, Amelia forced herself to pause and take a deep breath.

Cussing Terrence out wouldn't help anything. She'd already tried that. Many times.

Instead, Amelia deleted her message and sent back a simple: *Yes*. Then, she blocked his number.

He wasn't the first person from the Chicago PD to reach out to her in the last year, and she was sure he wouldn't be the last. At first, she'd wondered how they were getting any information on her at all. She wasn't in Illinois anymore. It took her screaming into the phone at three different officers to find out that someone had a contact in the local precinct and forwarded anything that bore her name directly to Terrence. She'd filed a complaint, but it didn't go anywhere. Her only option was to avoid the cops altogether, and she was pretty good at it.

Except, of course, when disgusting pigmen tried to drug her.

"Hey, I can see steam coming out of your ears," Sam said jokingly, jostling her. "What's going on?"

"Just a text from Terrence," she said, knowing there was no point in lying to him. "Checking in about Derek."

That was the one benefit of Chicago PD's collective guilt about the way they'd treated her; Amelia frequently avoided the more tedious aspects of interactions with law enforcement. She had no doubt that Derek Harris sold her out immediately— how else would Terrence know she was involved? Yet, she hadn't been contacted by her local officers. Not once. And she knew she wouldn't be. Whatever contact Terrence had with the local precinct, they'd keep her out of whatever they could as part of some ill-driven act of repentance.

"Did you tell him where he can shove it?"

"More or less."

Sam was satisfied with that, tilting his head back and closing his eyes. He'd lost all interest in the hockey game; with a score of 5 to 2 in favor of the Tampa Bay Lightning and only 45 seconds left in the third period, the Flyers wouldn't be taking home the win on this road trip. He yawned, drawing her into him like he was clutching a teddy bear.

"Remind me to grab my shower stuff in the morning," Sam said, already sounding half-asleep.

"Why don't you pack it tonight?"

"I want to shower before we go to the airport."

"It's not a long flight, Sam," Amelia said disparagingly. "Can't you just shower when we get there?"

He cracked open an eyelid to peer at her, his disbelieving expression telling her that he thought her suggestion was utterly insane. Amelia raised her hands in surrender. She knew better than to argue with Sam over the seemingly nonsensical decisions he made, particularly when the topic was mundane.

Excitement and trepidation plagued her at the thought of their morning flight. She was looking forward to visiting the Somerton cabin again, of course. It had been years since they'd made the trip. Now, though, they were traveling in the middle of a municipal politics warzone and the aftermath of a tragedy.

As much as she'd pestered Sam about his reluctance to go, their roles had reversed over the past week.

Speaking to Tyler about the bear attacks in Somerton had the dual effect of triggering Sam's desire to do whatever he was told explicitly *not* to do, and making Amelia wonder if there was more to be worried about than she initially thought. Tyler wasn't as foolhardy as Sam, but he definitely had a defiant streak. If he was warning them away, there must be a serious reason. If Sam hadn't called Tyler the next day and talked it over, deciding that a short visit would be totally fine, Amelia would've canceled their tickets already. Not that that would've stopped Sam. Her stubbornness was no match for his enthusiasm or for Mrs. Fisher's anxiety over her investment.

The cabin was worth a lot of money, more money than Amelia could fathom. Construction going on around cabin county was a serious cause of concern for the status of their property value.

With no reasonable out in sight, Amelia instead set to doing her research.

She was good at that. Her first therapist had referred to her unique talents as a result of her 'delinquent behavior' as a youth, but Amelia preferred to think of them as finely honed survival skills. So did her new therapist, who was much more understanding about her upbringing than the first guy. Amelia wasn't surprised when she later found out his family boasted multiple Boys in Blue.

Information came readily to her when she wanted it. Amelia wasn't nearly adept enough to call herself a 'hacker,' but she could work her way around some rudimentary firewalls. Simple maneuvers that she picked up from a combination of YouTube videos and practical experience. After their trip had been finalized, Amelia began gathering whatever information she could about the bear attacks.

Unfortunately, it wasn't much. Even bypassing some region blocks and password-protected webpages, the most she could find was a snuffed article about evidence of Native American artifacts being found near the bear's den. Finding nothing more of value, she'd turned her attention to rabies research. That hadn't helped either, in fact, it raised more questions than answers. The situation in Somerton didn't fit any kind of previous rabies outbreaks Amelia could find. Rabies was present year-round in some locations, the residents relying on local news to inform them if any diseased animals were seen wandering near town. Nothing like the Somerton killings had *ever* been reported before, not that Amelia could identify. And yet the media attention had faltered after only a few weeks. Something wasn't right about that.

Then again, a wilderness expert she was not. When Amelia caught herself starting down a conspiracy theory rabbit hole at two in the morning the night before, she'd decided to let the whole thing go. She was confident in her intelligence, but she couldn't ignore the fact that she had diagnosed anxiety. Sometimes, she struggled to separate the instinct from the illness, and when the tinfoil hats broke out, that was a good sign that she was in too deep.

"You know, I don't want to hear you complain about how forgetful you are anymore," Amelia said in a grumble, elbowing him in the ribs. Getting Sam to finish packing tonight wasn't a task she was prepared to undertake. She didn't have the energy. "Every time I suggest something to help you, you never listen. At this point, you're your own worst enemy."

"Maybe I just like making you feel useful."

"My middle finger feels pretty useful right about now."

Sam laughed, adjusting his grip on her until she was both uncomfortable and completely trapped by him. Amelia shoved her palm into his stomach, making him gag and release her just as her cell phone buzzed again.

"Tell Terrence to focus on his own jurisdiction," Sam growled, reaching for her phone. She didn't give it to him, furrowing her brows in confusion.

"I blocked his number," she said absently, unlocking her phone screen. When she saw the name, her stomach sank. "Oh, for fuck's sake."

"What?"

"It's Derek."

"*What?*" Sam sat up, bringing her with him. Amelia opened the message with a grimace, not knowing what to expect. "Why is he texting you?"

"Probably to tell me to go fuck myself," she guessed, planning to block his number as well without even reading the message. It wasn't a text, though. It was a photo.

Specifically, it was a photo of Derek's fully erect penis.

Amelia gagged dramatically, turning the phone screen so Sam could see what she was dealing with. He mimicked her reaction, snatching the phone before she had a chance to stop him. Amelia lunged for it, worried about what he might say or do.

"Let me handle it," he begged, holding the phone out of her reach. "Please? I swear I won't do anything illegal. Honest."

"Illegal *or* borderline?" She regarded him with suspicion.

"I swear. I'm just going to... match his energy."

Amelia was still trying to work out what that meant when Sam bolted for the bathroom, slamming the door shut behind him and clicking the lock into place.

From the brief look she'd gotten, Derek must've posted bail and was back at home. She didn't think he'd get away with sending a dick pic in a jail cell, no matter how rich and white he was.

Sam was in the bathroom for enough time that she was beginning to wonder if he'd called Derek and was in the middle of a heated verbal battle. Amelia braced her arms on the edge of the cushions, preparing to stand and knock on the door when Sam finally emerged.

"Done and done," he said cheerfully, holding out her phone to her. "Derek Harris has been thoroughly put in his place."

"What did you do?" Amelia demanded, rushing over to him. She grabbed her phone out of his hand, looking for Derek's conversation, only to find it deleted. "Sam! What did you *do?*"

"Relax, Amy Baby," he said, appeasing her. "I told you. I matched his energy."

When she still didn't get it, Sam clarified.

"I sent him a dick pic."

"You... sent him a dick pic." Amelia blinked at him in amused shock. "Like, an *actual* dick pic, or did you Google one?"

"No, it was mine," Sam assured her proudly. "With the caption 'she already found a bigger one.'"

"Sam!" Amelia fell into a fit of laughter, shaking her head in amusement and shock. "I hope for your sake you're not bluffing. He has the photo to compare."

"Do you want proof?" He eyed her mischievously, waggling his eyebrows. She gave him a withering look, communicating her exasperation through a multitude of slow blinks. Suddenly, Sam's expression shifted to one of surprised delight.

"Did you just *glance down?*" He asked her, an incredulous smile stretching across his face. Amelia's face blanked, opening her mouth to protest, just not quickly enough. "Holy shit, you totally did. You looked."

"I did not!" She had. As much as she wanted to be telling the truth, she'd instinctively flickered her attention to Sam's jeans for a fraction of a second.

"You're curious," Sam said, a triumphant smirk overtaking him. "You want to know what I'm packing."

"Samuel Peter Fisher, if you don't shut the fuck up immediately—" Amelia let the end of her threat hang unfinished in the air between them, only because she *had* looked, however briefly.

"Hey, hey, a little curiosity is natural," Sam mused, strutting through the living room and spreading himself out over the couch. He crossed one leg over the other, hooking his elbows over the back of the couch, and vaguely gestured toward his crotch. "If you ever want to take it for a test drive..."

"Oh my God," Amelia propelled herself into the hall, giving him the middle finger over her shoulder, "I can't deal with you right now. I'm getting a shower, tonight, *before* we have a plane to catch."

"A cold shower?"

She didn't need to look to know that her projectile made contact. Sam's grunt as her sweater walloped him in the face was more than enough confirmation.

Safely tucked away in the bathroom, she sent a text to Roxy.

Your brother's being insufferable again.

Less than two minutes after the text was sent, her phone rang.

"*I can give you ten minutes,*" Roxy breathed into the phone. She was panting from exertion, crowded voices marring the clarity of their connection. "*I'm in between runways.*"

"I just need you to convince me not to murder him," Amelia said, crouching to examine the cupboard beneath the bathroom vanity. She was mostly packed, but a few things still needed gathering. "He sent Derek a dick pic."

"*What?!*" Roxy's astonished laughter crackled through the phone. Her university's auditorium didn't have much in terms of reception, so Amelia wasn't surprised to only catch half of her cackling. "*Okay, context. Now please.*"

She explained, in complete detail, the events of her disastrous date and the fallout from it. Roxy listened intently, adding the occasional distressed noise to convey her attention, pausing to answer questions from the models and seamstresses milling around her. By the time Amelia was done, the line was much quieter. Roxy had probably moved to the bathroom.

"*What a douche,*" Roxy said, sniffing in disgust. "*And a really unfortunate return to the dating scene for you.*"

"Tell me about it." Amelia sat down on the vinyl tile, crossing her legs. "First date in a year and the guy tries to drug me."

"*Maybe you shouldn't have broken it off with Ben after all,*" Roxy said drily. "*He was a saint compared to that guy.*"

"I'm not sure anyone could make Ben look like a saint."

"*You're right. You should have stayed with Alex.*"

"If he hadn't moved to Paraguay, I might've." Amelia leaned back until her shoulders touched the wall. Their bathroom was tiny, even by apartment standards. She couldn't stretch her legs out at all without kicking the vanity, the toilet, or the shower. "Your sympathy for me is truly touching, by the way."

"*Oh, come on,*" Roxy laughed. "*We both know this was a pity date. You weren't actually interested in the guy.*"

"It's the last pity date, that's for sure." She almost left out 'pity,' but she didn't want to have that conversation again. Not that it mattered; Roxy picked up on her meaning anyway.

"*Amelia, what Ben did to you was beyond fucked up,*" she said, and Amelia could hear the anger behind her words. "*You don't have to force yourself if you're not ready. No one is going to blame you for taking a break from guys.*"

"I've *been* taking a break," she argued. "I'm pretty sure a year is more than enough time to get over it."

"*It's not even half the length of your relationship.*"

"Don't say it like that, it makes it sound like..."

"*Like I'm right?*"

Amelia laughed, conceding the point. This time.

Truth be told, her lack of interest in dating had nothing to do with Ben anymore. Yes, Ben had messed her up for a while, and his timing couldn't have been worse considering the news she'd received not three weeks later, but all of that pain had faded a long time ago. She hadn't forgiven him- she didn't know if she had that in her- but she wasn't letting him dominate her life.

No, her reluctance to get back on the horse was a lot simpler than that.

For the first time in her life, Amelia was *happy*. There were no oppressive clouds hanging over her head, at least none that bore an oncoming storm. Her past lingered, as it always would, but it didn't control her anymore. She was free to do whatever she wanted, and she wasn't sure she was ready to risk her contentment just yet.

And then there was Sam, but she couldn't talk to Roxy about that. Not without too much squealing and I-told-you-so's.

"*Sam told me you started your medication again.*"

Roxy's tone was cautious as if she didn't know Amelia's feelings on the matter. She hummed in confirmation, sizing up the open make-up bag on the counter.

"As a precaution. I was feeling a little on edge after the funeral. I've been thinking about going off them again, but I don't want to jump the gun."

"*So soon? Really?*"

"It's been months." Amelia heard Sam walk by the door and into his room, singing off-key to a song she didn't recognize. "Things have been calm lately. I think I can handle it."

"*Whatever you think is best, I trust you,*" Roxy paused, listening to someone else in the room. "*Shit, I gotta go. They need me. Text me later though, okay? I want to talk about you guys coming to visit, and I* need *to know if Derek responds to Sam.*"

"Of course," Amelia said, smiling. "Break a leg."

"*Always!*"

When she found him after her shower, Sam was sprawled comfortably in his bed, eyes closed, sweatpants on, and his hands folded beneath his head and pillow. Amelia knocked on the door frame, and he cracked an eye open to look at her.

"There you are," he mumbled sleepily, loosing one arm to beckon her over. She crossed the room in three strides, crawling into the mountain of blankets on Sam's bed and curling against his side. He wrapped his arm around her, securing her to him. "How's Rox?"

"Good, busy." Amelia tilted her head back to look up at Sam, still hovering on the edge of sleep. "She wants us to visit."

He hummed noncommittally, adjusting his position so there was no space between her body and his. They stayed like that for a while, Amelia listening to the slow pace of Sam's breathing until she too felt her lids growing heavy.

"Hey, Sam?"

"Mm?"

She paused, choosing the right words.

"Dating is overrated," she settled on after a time, releasing her pent-up stress in one long, bone-weary sigh. "Single living is a lot less complicated."

"You got that right," Sam mumbled, squeezing her. "Seriously though, I'm sorry about Derek."

"Fuck Derek," she said, rolling her eyes. "Honestly, I didn't want to go on the date anyway. After what happened with Ben, I'm more than happy spending the rest of my life with you in this shitty little apartment."

"Well, we both know that's not going to happen," Sam snorted. "We'd get a house eventually. A condo, at least. I can't handle living here for another 60 years."

"Fair point." Amelia laughed, fixing her gaze on the ceiling. "I'm not really joking, you know. If this is what my future looks like, I'm good with that. As long as your wife-to-be is fine with me third-wheeling for eternity."

"If she's not, then she wouldn't be my wife," he said. "Am, everyone in my life, past, present, or future, comes second to you. You know that."

"I don't think that bodes well for your relationship status."

"Then I guess we'll be single together."

Amelia fell silent, chewing on her emotions. They were tangled, as they always seemed to be with Sam.

"If you wanted to put some space between us, you'd tell me, right?"

Sam opened one eye to glare at her, warning her off of this particular line of thinking. Amelia ignored him, stubbornly wanting to say her piece.

"You can't tell me that this," she gestured to their position, cuddled together in his bedroom, "would fly with most women. When you were dating Dee, we barely *hugged*, and she was still jealous of how close we were."

"Dee was jealous of how close I was with the cashier at Dollar General," Sam scoffed. "She's not a great frame of reference."

"Okay, but the point stands. I can't see many women being comfortable with their boyfriend lying in bed with another woman, friend or not. I wouldn't be. And I *don't* want to be the 'girl best friend' that everyone hates."

"Are you telling me you want to start using your own room again?"

"I'm saying that I'm more than happy to take a step back if it makes things easier for you. The most important thing to me is being respectful toward you and any girl you date. You know, other than Dee. But that was different." Amelia propped herself up so she could read his expression. "I don't want your relationships suffering because you're too afraid to tell me the truth."

Sam opened his eyes to look at her properly, scrutinizing her face.

"Am, I'm single right now because I want to be. I'm here right now because I want to be. My relationship with you is more important to me than any hypothetical girlfriend, so, no, I don't want you to put any space between us. That's the last thing I want."

"Are you sure?"

"Absolutely."

She raised an eyebrow at him.

"And if anything changes?"

"I promise, you'll be the first to know. But as of right now, I'm probably going to end up marrying you anyway. Unless you find someone else before we turn 40."

They'd made that pact long ago, as a joke, but now she wasn't so sure. The thought of spending the rest of her life with Sam was exactly what Amelia wanted, married or otherwise. She wasn't about to give him the satisfaction of saying that, though.

"Well then I'd better rethink my plans," she deadpanned. "I'd rather be married to a Rangers fan than you."

"*YOU TAKE THAT BACK!*" Sam cried in outrage. "Amelia Geraldine Bradley, if you think for one FRACTION OF A SECOND that I would *ever* let a fucking *Rangers* fan anywhere near you, you're out of your damn mind!"

She laughed, fully, her belly hurting with the effort. One surefire way to get under Sam's skin was to throw around some rival teams.

"Relax, Sammy Honey," she said teasingly. "I promise that if I ever date another sports fan, it'll be from a Western Conference team."

"If you ever date another sports fan, he'll be cheering for the Bears, the Eagles, the Blackhawks, or the Flyers. No exceptions." Sam reached over her and yanked on the chain switch of his bedside lamp so hard that it teetered. "Now, *goodnight*. This conversation is giving me heartburn."

With another poorly-contained laugh, Amelia relented, snuggling into Sam's embrace like she had so many nights before. For a long time, this was her only safe space. Now, it was merely her favourite.

It wasn't long before they were both sound asleep, oblivious to the symphony of city noise outside their cramped apartment.

Chapter Three

SAM

"Alright, get it together Sammy. You can do this."

He kept his voice low, not trusting the roaring showerhead to mask his words on the off chance that Amelia woke up before he roused her.

"This is it. No more fucking around. It's time to tell Amelia that you love her."

Even saying it alone in the shower with no one else to hear him made Sam's stomach somersault uncomfortably. How the hell was he going to do this in reality when the thought alone made him want to vomit in fear?

He needed a plan. A smart plan. Unfortunately, all of his smart plans usually came from Amelia.

"First thing's first," he coached himself, massaging his shampoo determinedly into his scalp, hoping it would encourage his brain to work faster. "The five W's. Start there."

The *who* was pretty obvious— him and Amelia— he could skip that one.

The *what* was simple enough in concept. He had to tell her he loved her.

The *why* was too complicated to think about before 8 am.

That left *when* and *where*. Sam had a few options, and none of them jumped out as being particularly smart.

Option one: he could tell her right now, before they even left for the airport. Pros: he'd get the conversation over with before his nerves completely overtook his cardiac system and sent him to an early grave. Cons: if it went poorly, Amelia would just stay home, and he'd be left to stew in his own anxiety for a week in Somerton. Option one was a no-go.

Option two: he could tell her on the plane. Pros: she couldn't go anywhere on the plane, so they'd be forced to talk about it. Cons: Amelia wasn't afraid to make a scene, and Sam wouldn't put it past her to call security and accuse him of having a bomb shoved up his ass for putting her in an awkward position. Since he didn't feel like going to jail, option two was out.

That left option three: telling her while they were at the cabin. That was his plan all along, but as the trip got closer, the more he began to doubt himself. Sam wasn't eloquent, nor was he observant. Confessing his feelings to Amelia while they were alone in one of their childhood retreats seemed like a sweet idea to him, but would it feel claustrophobic to her? Like he was giving an ultimatum and cornering her into giving him an answer? The last thing he wanted was to approach the issue with serial killer energy. Maybe he should call the whole thing off.

Nope. No. No way, Sammy boy. Stop right there. You're not chickening out again. Not this time.

Sam shoved his head directly under the stream of hot water, shaking the negativity from his mind. This was the moment he'd been working towards for the better part of ten years. After countless plans, panic, and thousands of opportunities, it was finally time for him to trust himself. To trust *her*. If there was one thing Sam never doubted, it was that the strength of their friendship could overcome anything. Even his own stupid, lovesick heart.

He may not know exactly how Amelia was going to react to his feelings, but he knew that she'd listen. However atrociously he mangled the moment, she'd listen, and she'd make sense of his nervous blabbering. And if she rejected him? Well, then she rejected him. He'd recover. Eventually. First, though, he needed to get them to the airport on time.

The shower screeched to a slow drip as he flicked the tap off with his elbow, grabbing his threadbare towel from its hook. They had nicer towels in the linen closet, but Sam needed the luck worn into every rip of his old post-football-game-shower staple. He thought the towel was white at one point, but now it was a dank and inconsistent grey. Amelia hated it and had tried, more than once, to throw it out without his notice. It never worked, but he had to give her credit for the creative effort.

The mirror was clouded with steam, useless to him. Sam pushed his hand through his damp hair, shaking his soft waves into place. Amelia always pestered him about styling it, but he'd learned that if he didn't do it himself, she'd offer. He much preferred her refined touch over his rough one.

Sam couldn't hear much over the drone of the bathroom fan, the rest of the apartment fading to background noise. Given there were four hours before they were due to board their flight, Sam was confident that Amelia was still sound asleep under the mountain of blankets he kept on his bed. She'd stay there until the last possible moment when he'd have to practically drag her from the warmth and comfort of her cocoon. Sam smiled to himself; he could already hear her half-conscious disgruntled murmurs of complaint followed by a frenzy of panic when she realized the time and berated him for not waking her sooner. He probably *should* give her more time to get ready, but he couldn't help himself. Amelia's flustered bumbling filled him with a deep sense of affection that warmed him through. God, he loved her so much. He just needed to summon the balls to tell her.

Today, he decided resolutely. *It's happening today.* Come hell or high water, Sam was going to tell Amelia how he felt about her.

Sam took his time drying off, getting dressed, and doing his final sweeps of the bathroom. If he left something important behind, Amelia would never let him hear the end of it. Shampoo, toothbrush, deodorant, comb, all of that he could easily replace once they arrived. His medicated muscle relaxant cream on the other hand, not so much.

When he was satisfied, Sam decided it was finally time to wake the dragon.

Just as he'd suspected, Amelia was curled into a tiny ball beneath a heap of four blankets, two of which were hand-sewn quilts from his grandmother. How she didn't overheat under all that was beyond him. Sam cleared his throat, kicking the already open door and flipping the light switch in the same dramatic display.

"*Goooooooood morning Royersford!*"

With a horrendous imitation of a military trumpet call, Sam grabbed and yanked the top blanket on the pile. It came away easily, so he pulled at the second one. An annoyed groan accompanied some resistance on that one, so Sam pulled harder and trumpeted louder.

"Oh my God, would you *shut up?*" Amelia hissed from the depths of her cave, wrapping the remaining two blankets tighter around her. "You know some people wake up to breakfast in bed."

"I can throw some toast at you if you'd like."

Muttered curses answered him, followed by something that sounded suspiciously like a death threat.

"Come on, Amy Baby!" Sam bounced on the bed next to her, draping himself over the pile of blankets and Amelia's still-huddled body. She complained, loudly, burying her head further into the mattress. "The sun is shining, the birds are singing, the crackhead outside is selling matches to the local squirrels, and our plane leaves in about... two and a half hours."

"WHAT?"

In an instant, Sam was thrown off of Amelia and bombarded with tangled blankets. She scrambled to her feet, sprinting out of his room and into her own, all the while yelling over her shoulder about how he should've woken her sooner. Sam grinned, hooking his arms behind his head, and reveling in the chaos Amelia was spreading throughout their apartment.

"You always do this," she said in a huff, tossing her bag onto the bed. She was mostly packed already, but Sam knew that wasn't going to stop her from triple-checking before she was satisfied enough to leave. "*Why* do you always do this?"

"*Why* don't you set an alarm?"

"I do!" She shoved her phone charger into her purse with more force than necessary. "*You* always turn it off on me!"

"You never wake up to it anyway."

"I would if you *let it go off for once.*"

"Where's the fun in that?"

The look she gave him was murderous, and Sam couldn't help his smirk. He idly wondered if Amelia was the kind of girl that he could sway to forgive him by interrupting her ire with a passionate, ill-advised kiss. He decided she was, and the thought of (hopefully, maybe, possibly) finding out soon made his heart do Olympic-level gymnastics in his chest.

As a friend, he knew Amelia better than anyone else. As a *girlfriend*, there was still so much he had to learn. The prospect, and the uncertainty, were both terrifying and thrilling.

"Okay, I think I have everything," she said with a relieved sigh. "Come on, we have to leave now or we're going to be late."

"We still have two hours."

"It takes an hour to get there!"

Sam didn't quite understand why waiting around the terminal for an hour was the goal, but he decided he'd pestered Amelia enough for one morning.

"Have you talked to Ty today? Is he meeting us at the airport?"

Sam froze. Right. He'd forgotten about that part.

"Uh, no," he said quickly, reaching for his leather jacket to avoid looking at her. "No, we're going to meet up with him later."

As soon as Sam told him they were there, that is.

Amelia was too frazzled to notice his lie, much to his relief. Sam was never good at keeping secrets from her, bar one major one. He didn't know how she'd react to finding out Tyler hadn't *actually* given them his blessing to travel, but he could imagine it wouldn't be good.

To ease some of Amelia's anxiety about visiting Somerton so soon after the tragedies of the summer, he'd lied and told her that he'd talked to Tyler again, and they agreed that it was safe for them to come after all. He didn't like lying to her, but he also knew that if he didn't, she'd have been stressing herself out over their trip for the entire time building up to their departure. Besides, it *was* safe for them to visit. Sam didn't know what had made Tyler so paranoid all of a sudden, but it was *Somerton* for Christ's sake. Nothing ever happened in Somerton. The rogue bear situation was just that, rogue. The chances of anything even remotely close to that level of danger again in their lifetimes were slim to none.

Once they were at the cabin, he was sure both Tyler and Amelia would see that they were being unreasonable.

Hoisting both of their bags onto his arm, Sam gestured for Amelia to lead the way.

"Well, it's still standing."

Sam parked the rented Tacoma halfway down the gravel driveway, begrudgingly noting the smooth transmission and gear shift. The front desk agent at the car rental kiosk had looked at him strangely when he specifically requested a red Toyota Tacoma, preferably pre-2010, but Sam didn't care. He had his preferences, and he wasn't ashamed of them. While they *did* have a Tacoma available for rent, it was black and practically brand new. Still, it was better than settling for a sedan, so Sam signed the contract and he and Amelia began their journey from Madison to Somerton in the dazzling truck.

His own truck was ancient in comparison to the modern monster, and there was a definitive thump whenever he changed gears that wasn't present in the newer model. The rental may outperform his beloved rig, but Sam wouldn't give it the satisfaction of admitting so out loud.

"Looks like a tree fell near the tool shed though." Amelia interrupted her post-drive stretch to lean forward, squinting out the front window. Sam followed her attention, spotting the splintered stump with little difficulty. "I can't tell if there's any damage from here."

"Let's get everything up and running first, then I'll do a walk-around while the place heats up." Sam reached for the keys, remembering at the last moment that this model had a push start. He pouted, grabbing the key fob from the cupholder he'd dropped it in. Then, he stepped into his childhood.

The Somerton cabin had been in his family for 30 years. He was barely three months old when his parents signed the deed, so he had no hope of remembering his first trip here. That didn't lessen the wave of nostalgia that washed over him when his boots sank into the crisp, off-white gravel. The bluish tint to the small rocks looked extremely out of place in the myriad of browns and greens colouring the rest of the scenery, so Sam guessed it was imported and newly laid. He rolled his eyes— leave it to his parents to *buy* rocks. Sam loved his family dearly, but they weren't the most conscientious spenders.

"Is the water on?" Amelia asked, hopping from the rental truck and stretching properly. Sam pulled out his phone and skimmed the email he'd received from the electric company two days earlier.

"We should be good to go," he said. "I need to flip some switches on the electrical panel, and then we'll be in business."

"Well, hurry up," Amelia teased him, bumping into his hip with hers. "You may have showered this morning, but I didn't. I need to wash the plane gunk off me."

"Right away, your majesty," Sam saluted her with an exaggerated mask of professionalism on his face that neither of them believed, "whatever your heart desires!"

He was already laughing when the wadded napkin struck him, deflecting off his shoulder as he headed for the cabin's back porch. He fought the urge to pester Amelia about littering, wanting to at least survive one night of their vacation.

The front door had a keyless PIN-pad entry, which he knew Amelia had long since memorized the code for, so Sam set straight to preparing the building for their brief stay.

Calling the place a 'cabin' was a gross understatement. His parents never did anything by halves, so the Somerton *Cabin* was really more of a Somerton *Second Home*. The house was fully equipped with electricity, indoor plumbing, internet, heated floors, a security system, and any number of gadgets that had been popular over the years. At one point, Sam distinctly remembered an early 2000s-era satellite dish perched offensively on the roof, providing him and his friends with Pay-Per-View WWE specials. Now, the bulky grey dish was gone, and the cabin was outfitted with multiple Smart TVs and an extensive list of streaming service subscriptions.

No, his parents were quite the opposite of conscientious spenders. Luckily, their investing prowess outweighed their expensive tastes.

Sam had to clear some intricately woven spider webs from the back door before he could put his keyring to use. He suspected the lock would've rusted from disuse long ago if his parents didn't hire maintenance workers to regularly visit the property. Soon enough, and with minimal effort, he was stomping the dust from his boots on a sleek, dark grey floor mat in the back entryway of the house. The electrical panel was hidden behind a massive canvas print that Sam always hated— it was gaudy, splattered with obnoxious colours and intersecting lines that looked random at best and intentionally chaotic at worst. More than once, he'd considered tossing the thing while his parents were away, but he'd always changed his mind. He had no idea how much that canvas cost and, with his luck, it would turn out to be an original from some famous artist. So, the ugly painting remained.

The panel creaked as he opened it, surveying the breakers for damage. Seeing none, Sam flipped them. With an electric groan, the Somerton cabin flared to life.

"It's alive!" Sam cackled, wavering his voice in cartoonish excitement as he burst into the kitchen. Amelia paid him no mind, dropping their bags in the middle of the hall with a decisive thwack. "Anything left in the truck?"

"Nope, I She-Hulked it." Amelia flexed her biceps animatedly, striking a poor excuse of a bodybuilding pose. "All bags present and accounted for."

"Woah, put those guns away soldier!" Sam took an exaggerated step back, holding his hands in front of him protectively. "You need a permit if you're gonna wave 'em around like that!"

She eyed him with comical disdain, rummaging through the bags until she found her toiletry kit.

"Do you need help with anything before I shower?"

"Nope," Sam said confidently. "I'm going to do a full walk-around while you clean up. Take some pictures for Mom, look for less obvious damage, that kind of thing. We'll figure out the food situation when we're both finished?"

"Sounds like a plan to me."

In truth, Sam wasn't overly worried about the property. His parents spared no expense in the companies they hired to tend the cabin while they were gone. The fact that the building wasn't already overrun with underbrush was a testament to their attention to detail.

He used the last of the three exterior doors to go back outside: a sliding glass patio door that opened onto a ground-level deck. The built-in barbecue and stone pizza oven were covered with thick, army-green tarps to protect them from the elements and, after a quick once-over, seemed to be in working order. Sam gave each piece of patio furniture a swift kick to dislodge any insect residents, paying particular attention to the wooden sunchairs. He and Amelia liked to sit on those in the evening and if a creepy-crawly made its way onto her arm when she wasn't looking, Amelia would no doubt spend the rest of the trip inside. Sam made a mental note to retrieve the cushions from the storage shed before nightfall so he could inspect them as well.

It was cold in Somerton, much colder than in Pennsylvania. Sam shook his arms and legs to get his blood pumping before venturing further from the cabin, tapping the solar-powered garden lights that lined the stone path from the deck to the sheds as he went. Two storage lockers stood at the very edge of the trees, one for tools and equipment, the other for everything else. Sam checked the padlocks on both, finding them secure. He'd need the keys to get in, which he didn't have. They were still in the kitchen, or they should be anyway. He'd have to remind himself how to open the secret compartment in the utensil drawer where they normally lived.

His breath clouded in front of his face, billowing in the brusque mountain air. Sam scowled at the sky, wondering why the sun wasn't doing its job. He'd need his jacket before he came back out to inspect the sheds.

From this distance, Sam could clearly see the tree that Amelia spotted upon their arrival. It hadn't damaged the shed from what he could tell, but the thinned section of the trunk rested precariously on the shingled roof. He gave the branches a cursory tug, the tree shuddering in protest at his invasion. He gave up after only a few yanks, realizing quickly that the trunk wasn't as precariously placed as he thought. His dad kept a wood saw in the tool shed, that would have to do. Sam rounded the shed from the opposite side, looking for the source of the felled tree. The forest pressed against the pair of small buildings, crowding the property line like paparazzi at a red-carpet event. He shouldered some of the more intrusive boughs out of the way, ducking under others and stomping saplings into the earth until he was clear of the initial thicket.

It was much darker underneath the tree cover, but at least he could see the stump now. The fallen tree barely clung to its roots, the exposed wood splintered and jagged with tendrils of moss snagged on the jutting splinters. Sam pressed his lips into a thin line, assessing the situation. He'd need some gloves before he tried touching the trunk, which were also in the tool shed. While the tree looked to be nearly severed from its base, Sam didn't bother trying to dislodge it a second time with his boot. He knew from his prodding that the tree was caught on something.

What toppled it, anyway?

Sam felt the realization spark and fizzle in his chest in less than the span of a full breath. This tree was shorter than the others surrounding it, meaning it was sheltered from the elements. He couldn't see any signs of a lightning strike or rot, and the splinters were too large to be from a critter burrowing its new home into the winding trunk. Between the two sheds and the enclosed grove of healthy trees, Sam could barely feel the cold tickle of wind grazing the back of his neck. It was freezing in the shadow of the branches, but it wasn't exposed. Not weather-related, then.

The chaotic state of the tree trunk would've never come from an ax or saw, so that left... an animal, maybe? An image of a bear slashing wildly at the tree flashed through his mind, making his heart stutter. Sam shook himself with a self-deprecating smirk. He was letting Amelia's worrying get to him.

His knees cracked as he crouched to get a better look, squinting into the darkness. The trunk didn't look damaged below the split. The large gouges in the wood weren't unnaturally straight or tinged with grease, ruling out any other kind of tool. He was about to give up when the sting of cold-induced numbness spread up his fingers, and Sam's attention caught on something he'd missed in his initial perusal. Frost tickled the edges of the splintered cracks, sheltered from the sun and thriving into a thin sheet of proper ice. That must've been the cause, Sam decided. Water had seeped into the trunk and frozen, expanding to the point of snapping the tree. It was about as plausible an explanation as he could come up with. Sam stood, stretching his tired limbs. Travel always exhausted him, even trips as short as the flight they'd taken from Pennsylvania to Wisconsin.

"Uh, Sam?"

Amelia's call was quiet, but the uncertainty in her voice had concern lancing through his chest. Sam quickly backed out of the trees, still shivering from the absence of sun.

"What's up?"

"Have you been to the garden yet?"

No, he hadn't. Sam didn't bother thinking to check the garden; it was the most open area on the property, cleared to the very edges of the trail to give his mother room to build her obnoxiously large, raised flower beds. Her interest in gardening lasted for two months, and the beds had remained untouched by her ever since.

Amelia was waiting for him at the patio door, leaning against the frame and watching him with growing wariness. Sam jogged up to the deck, stopping just short of where she was standing.

"Why? What's wrong?"

"I hate to be cliché about it, but I think it's better if you look for yourself."

He gave her a questioning frown before doing just that, following the edge of the deck to the other side of the cabin, the one fully hidden from the access road. At first, he couldn't understand why she'd asked him about it. The garden looked the same as it always had, albeit with a few more wild shrubs inhabiting the abandoned beds. Sam was about to give up and ask her when something caught his attention on the horizon.

"Oh, hell."

One of the reasons his parents were reluctant to part with the cabin, other than Sam's insistence, was the unparalleled view of the mountain and Basin Lake. His mother had wanted the garden built facing the lake, which they could just see poking through the sparse trees scattered along the bank. With the picturesque mountaintops serving as a backdrop, one of the most valuable features of the Somerton cabin was the sprawling wilderness in its backyard.

Sam saw none of that now.

Barely a mile from the edge of his parents' property, the beautiful views were crowded by a sea of yellow, grey, and blue.

Stamkos & Stein were building their new factory a stone's throw away.

Chapter Four

SAM

"Mom is going to lose her fucking mind," Sam said with a groan, pinching the bridge of his nose between his thumb and forefinger. "How did this even happen? Construction isn't supposed to be anywhere near here!"

"You know what big corporations are like," Amelia soothed, gently rubbing his arm as Sam measured his breaths. "They're never satisfied with what they have, they always want more, and they'll take it wherever they can get it. Someone must've adjusted the agreement to give them more land."

That was the only explanation that made sense, but it didn't seem to capture the outrageous imposition of Stamkos & Stein's latest work. Sam stared in open shock at the severed trunks laid bare from clear-cutting, the flashes of yellow construction equipment peeking between evergreen boughs, and the bright, electric blue of what he could only assume was a portable outhouse. While the production facility wouldn't be *directly* in their backyard, it certainly wasn't far off. How long until S&S decided to demolish the remaining sprinkle of trees that was the only thing providing his family a shred of privacy? When would they proposition his parents to buy their land and expand the parking lot? What about the noise? The smell? The pollutants? No amount of money could convince Sam to step foot in the manmade river skirting their apartment complex back in Royersford; the number of used condoms, take-out wrappers, and discarded drugs that littered the concrete banks was enough to make him sick to his stomach. Would Basin Lake suffer the same fate?

"Christ." Sam didn't know if it was the jarring revelation or the travel, but suddenly he was exhausted. The sooner the heat kicked in and the cabin became livable again, the sooner he could take a nap and pretend life was okay for a little while.

"What are you going to tell Sandy?"

Sam didn't want to think about it.

"I'm not," he admitted, resolve settling into the pit of his stomach like a dense rock. "Not yet. I want to find out more about the situation first, see if there's anything we can do. If not, then I'll call Mom. I'll just take a few shots of tequila first."

"Going straight for the hard stuff," Amelia said, smiling. "You really are stressed."

She gave him a reassuring hug, squeezing his ribs with unnecessary tightness. Sam wrapped his arms around her automatically, letting her calm his fraying nerves.

"Speaking of the hard stuff," Sam mumbled, trying to shake his mood back into something more palatable. "We don't have any food. Wanna head to the store while we wait for the place to warm up properly?"

"I could go for a grocery expedition," Amelia agreed, giving him one final squeeze before letting go. Sam thought about pulling her back into him for just one more second of peace, but he stopped himself. They had things to do before nightfall; wallowing in his despair could wait until they had full cupboards. "I'll drive?"

"What about this one?" Sam held the box aloft, presenting it like a trophy. Amelia began to nod her head but stopped when the content of the box caught her attention.

"You're allergic to pomegranate," she reminded him with a doubtful stare. "You can't eat that."

"There's no pomegranate in this, is there?" Sam furrowed his brows, flipping the box over to search it for any mention of the offending fruit. "It says 'mixed berry flavor.' That's like... blueberries and strawberries and stuff, isn't it?"

"Samuel," Amelia veered the cart back toward him, blinking in stunned fascination. "There is literally a pomegranate on the box."

He stared at the image again, zeroing in on a round, red fruit with what looked like bright ruby seeds amidst a white pith.

"Huh. I never knew that's what a pomegranate looked like."

"You—" Amelia stopped herself, shock dropping her jaw. Inhaling, she tried again. "You didn't know what a pomegranate *looks like?* How the hell have you survived 32 years without knowing what your *deadly allergy* looks like?"

"I knew it was a red fruit," he shrugged, "so I just don't eat unidentified red fruit."

"Unbelievable." Amelia shook her head, a hopeless smile spreading across her face. "Darwinism should've claimed you years ago."

"That's why I have you to keep me alive."

Amelia gave him a pointed look that screamed 'right, and don't forget it' before scanning the shelf again. She plucked a black bag of Doritos from its place, dropping it into the cart. Sam frowned.

"I like the blue one, don't I?" he argued, pointing to the bag closest to him on the shelf. "I feel like I like the blue one."

"You don't," she insisted. "You *think* you like the blue one, but you like the black one. We have this conversation every time."

Sam's memory crackled. The disagreement was familiar, but the outcome was blurry.

"But... it's blue. I love blue."

"Sam, we're not doing this again," Amelia groaned, dropping her head forward in exasperation. "Just because the packaging is a colour you like doesn't mean it's a *food* you like."

"Then why bother adding colour?"

"If you need me to explain marketing to you as an aspiring team manager, you can kiss your promotion goodbye."

She had a point. He slid his attention away from the blue bag of Doritos, just barely smothering his cringe when he finally saw the word 'ranch' in big bold letters for the flavor, and moved on to the endless array of chocolate bars in the next aisle.

Somerton's supermarket confused his nostalgia for the small town. It was the same grocer that had always been there, Binky's Bins, and the layout was almost identical to his memories of their first visit, but the contents were offensively modern. Organic, vegan, gluten-free, non-GMO, and an endless list of increasingly nonsensical buzzwords littered the produce aisle as a sad justification for the inflated price tags. Sam tried not to roll his eyes. He could understand the necessity of gluten-free, vegan, and similar options, but he also knew from experience that these labels were pandering to a trend of clean eating that was often more harmful than helpful to people who didn't actually need them. He couldn't count the number of young players he'd escorted to the nurse's office because they'd tried to play a game on a stomach barren of carbs or protein.

As they moved through the store, Sam paid careful attention to Amelia's body language as he'd taken to doing whenever they went shopping. When she showed interest in something, inevitably walking by it with the intention of leaving it behind, Sam plucked it from the shelf and dropped it into the cart before she could complain. They'd been friends for so long that it was easy to forget the differences in their upbringing, but every now and then Sam was sharply reminded. For the first dozen or so grocery runs they'd made after moving in together, he'd all but physically restrained her from putting items back on the shelf that she wanted but didn't need. She wouldn't argue with him anymore, just squirm uncomfortably as the cashier rang them up and their total climbed. Sam knew better than anyone that Amelia was used to going without; he wouldn't let her do that around him. Especially when he could easily afford it.

They were making their way to the check-out counter when Amelia paused. At first, Sam thought she'd spotted something else they needed and he prepared himself to go get it, whatever it was.

"Is that Tyler?"

The question had no sooner left Amelia's mouth than Sam spotted him too, deeply engaged in a conversation on his cell. Panic gripped his chest— he hadn't thought up an excuse yet, he needed more time, Tyler shouldn't be here— he tried to grab Amelia before she approached him, but he was too late.

"So, you have time to shop but not to meet us at the airport?" Amelia greeted with a smile, oblivious to Sam's floundering. "Pretty rude of you, Pratt."

He prayed that this man was somehow not Tyler, that he was just a carbon copy, a doppelganger, a clone, something, but all hope drained from him the moment their eyes met. Tyler turned at the sound of Amelia's voice, blinking in shock, then confusion, and finally settling on outraged understanding when he registered Sam's guilty expression. Amelia looked between them, struggling to figure out what caused the strained reaction. Tyler muttered something into the phone, trying to end the call quickly, as Amelia slid the puzzle pieces into place. She whirled on Sam, fire burning in her gaze.

"You didn't tell him we were coming, did you?"

It wasn't a question so much as it was an accusation, one that Sam didn't need to respond to. She knew.

"Oh my god, *Sam!*" Amelia snapped, rubbing furiously at her eyes in aggravation. "You *told me* that Tyler said it was okay to visit! Why did you lie?!"

"I said it wasn't *safe*, you idiot!" Tyler slipped his phone back into his pocket, crossing his arms over his chest. Sam knew better than to argue with either of them at this point.

"We decided that we wouldn't go if Ty didn't think it was a good idea," Amelia reminded him, although it was more for her sake than his. "So, what? You wanted to come regardless of what he said and just booked the tickets anyway? To hell with what either of us think?"

"Fisher, you're completely insane, you know that, right?" Tyler huffed, pushing his hand through his golden hair. Sam could never get used to seeing him as a blond, but now didn't seem like the time to bring that up. "Why did you bother to call if you weren't going to listen to what I said?"

"Because he can't help it, Ty," Amelia said. "You know what he's like when he gets an idea."

"You'd think he'd have grown out of that by now."

"You have more faith in him than I do."

Sam waited patiently for the steam to dissipate from their ears before he even entertained the thought of defending himself. Once the initial shock had worn off and their trio fell into silence, he risked opening his mouth.

"In my defense," he began slowly, acknowledging the warning glare Amelia gave him. "You knew I bought the tickets against Ty's advice."

Anger sparked and ignited in Amelia's expression before he could utter another word.

"*You said—!*"

"I know, I know!" Sam held up his hands to interrupt her. For Tyler's benefit, he added "I told her that we'd been talking after the first call, and you decided it was fine to visit as long as we stayed out of the woods."

"Why the hell would you tell her that?"

"You know Am," Sam said, chancing a glance at her face. She looked irritated, but not murderous. "She worries. I knew if I didn't tell her that you were on board, then she'd spend the entire week panicking."

"Or, alternative solution," Amelia said in annoyance, "we could've just *stayed home.*"

"Come on," Sam prodded, looping his arm around her waist, and gently tugging her against his side. She resisted superficially, reluctantly letting him pull her toward him when it was clear he wouldn't accept anything less. "Are you honestly telling me you aren't glad to be here?"

She didn't answer him, which was as much confirmation as he was going to get.

"And you're not at least a little excited to see us?" Sam turned to Tyler, putting on his best puppy-dog eyes. Tyler raised an eyebrow at him, but the frustration was gone from his posture. Sam smiled triumphantly.

"Oh, wipe that stupid grin off your face," Tyler jabbed him with his elbow, "and get over here before I change my mind."

Amelia disengaged from Sam and let Tyler sweep her into an enthusiastic hug. Sam was next, encompassing the two of them in his arms before Amelia could step away.

"We missed you," she told Tyler, her feet firmly on the floor again. "Ever since Rox moved, I've had to deal with this buffoon solo."

"I'm shocked he's still alive," Tyler said, laughing. Sam clapped his hand firmly on Tyler's shoulder, squeezing fondly.

"She loves me too much to do any real harm," he bragged. "Her punishments are limited to mild torture, much to my delight."

"Wait, if you're not here to see us, then why *are* you here?" Amelia tilted her head, leaning against their full cart. "Shouldn't you be in Chicago?"

Tyler looked momentarily stunned, like he'd forgotten that strolling around Somerton wasn't a normal part of his routine.

"Right, shit," he reached into his pocket, fumbling for his phone again. "I'm supposed to be meeting some friends soon... uh..."

He looked at his phone, then at Sam and Amelia. Sam could almost see the gears turning in his brain, clicking into place.

"Actually, you know what?" Decided, Tyler offered them a casual smile. "I was going to say I'd meet you at the cabin later, but why don't you come with me? It's lunch time, and we're meeting at Tinny's. Could you guys go for a taco?"

"I'm always on board for tacos," Sam answered before Amelia could, pushing their cart toward the checkout. "We'll get this bagged up, packed into the truck, and then we'll be good to go."

Tyler nodded absently, tapping away at his phone, presumably texting the friends he was meeting. Sam must've been imagining the wrinkle of worry between Tyler's brows, the tense set of his shoulders, and the stress creasing the corners of his mouth. He couldn't be that concerned about their arrival, even if the timing wasn't ideal. No, Sam was imagining things, or else Tyler was focused on a case. That must be it, he decided. Whatever was causing that dark cloud that hovered at the edge of his friend's smile was work-related and nothing that they needed to concern themselves with.

He was still telling himself that as they made their way to the parking lot, teeming grocery bags in tow.

Chapter Five

INTERLUDE

Nyla

Willow Lodge was always a quiet retreat in the mountain forests of Wisconsin. It had to be— as a hunting lodge, proximity to wildlife was of paramount importance. Guests were encouraged to keep the noise level to a minimum, if not by her then by the old guard of hunters who'd been frequenting the establishment since long before it was owned by Nyla Jameson. Lately, though, the surreal silence wasn't the result of strict compliance by her guests, but rather a lack of guests altogether. Nyla had closed Willow Lodge back in July and had yet to re-open, leaving the building completely barren aside from her occasional self-talks, Aaron's investigatory work, and their increasingly frequent arguments with newly-appointed Sheriff George Mason.

"How many more times do we have to have this conversation?" Mason growled at her now, arms crossed over his inflated chest. Nyla was used to his bluster, relaxing in her computer chair with her attention alternating between George and the game of Battle Tetris she was currently losing to someone in Germany. "Tell me what I need to know and let me get on with my day!"

"I've told you everything, George," Nyla said pointedly. She wasn't sure when they'd reached a first-name bases, but she wasn't upset about it. One less person called her 'Jameson,' and that was a win for her. "You're wasting your time here of your own free will, not mine."

"Bullshit," Mason spat, although he was quickly losing gusto. He knew how this would end just as well as Nyla did. "You know something, and you're refusing to disclose your information to law enforcement. I could have you arrested for obstruction of justice."

"Then do it," Nyla said daringly. She abandoned the game, winning long out of the question, and laced her fingers beneath her chin. "You've had months to bring charges on us, so what's the holdup? I'm sure you're not worried about losing the pleasure of our company."

Mason's glare intensified.

"If you're so sure we're lying about what happened to Bill, then arrest us. Go on, I'll wait."

To punctuate her point, Nyla held out her wrists for a pair of handcuffs she knew would never come. Mason took two steadying breaths, reining his temper. Nyla had to admit that he was better at it than Hannaford was. For all the needling she gave Mason, he'd rarely raised his voice at her in outright anger. It was impressive.

"You know if I had even a single shred of evidence, you'd be down at the station already," he muttered. Nyla lowered her wrists, folding them neatly in her lap. "I can't prove you're lying, Nyla, but I know it. Deep in my bones, I know it."

He was right, of course. Nyla and Aaron had been lying through their teeth since the night Bill Hannaford met his gruesome end. She just couldn't tell Mason that.

"We didn't kill Sheriff Hannaford." That much was true, and for the first time, a look of resignation passed over Mason's face that made her think he believed her. "We don't know where James Carver is." Also true. After retrieving Pratt from the Hovel of Horrors, as she'd taken to calling it, the three of them returned to their crude battlegrounds only to find them deserted. Carver's body had vanished, leaving nothing but slush and melting ice behind. "I'm sorry George. I don't know what else to say."

Nyla didn't know if the apology lessened the sting or poured salt in the wound, and Mason's reaction didn't clarify. He turned on his heel, storming through the Willow's front door and into the fading sun. She wanted to call after him, to remind him to stay inside after dark, but she stopped herself. Her warning would only invite more questions she couldn't answer. If he was going to listen to them, he'd already be conscious of the dark.

When the door stopped swinging, Nyla flopped forward on the desk, smacking her forehead harder than she'd intended. The sting echoed through her skull, and she found herself wondering why she hadn't already packed up shop and moved to the tropics. Add that to the list of questions that held a permanent residence in her mind, making it difficult to sleep.

Where had the creature come from?

Why did it show up when it did?

Was it actually dead?

Would it *stay* dead?

What would they do if it didn't?

What would they do if it did?

Nyla felt the uncertainties pulse in her brain, adding pressure to her already mounting headache. The forest had been quiet since they took care of the Chehwinoo, at least until Halloween weekend. Until the party massacre, not a single person was reported missing, no strange weather events, no vanishing pets, nothing. The Basin was calm, but Nyla hesitated to say that it was normal. The Basin had always been cloaked in a peaceful sort of quiet, the kind that wasn't truly silent, but filled with the subtle, indistinguishable noises of life. Now, the quiet was... different. Expectant. Like it was waiting for something.

She'd long since decided that she didn't want to find out what that might be.

As Nyla wallowed in her thoughts, she heard a door open down the hall. Her attention followed Aaron as he walked from his temporary office to the front desk, pausing at the mouth of the hallway to no doubt process the scene in front of him. After a beat, he stepped behind her chair and gently slid his hands over her shoulders, pressing a soft kiss to the back of her neck that sent shivers exploding down her spine.

"I take it George just left?"

Nyla grunted a response, still refusing to lift her head from the desk. Aaron breathed a chuckle, gently kneading the bunches of stress gathered along her neck and spine. She let him coax her into relaxing, turning her head to rest her cheek on the desk in a more comfortable slouch.

"He's on edge," she said, sighing as Aaron's palms worked magic that she couldn't replicate no matter how hard she tried. "That's the third time he's been here since Saturday."

"I can't imagine the pressure he's under," Aaron mused. His voice was laced with concern more than sympathy, and Nyla could almost hear the gears whirring in his mind. "He's done an admirable job keeping the press quiet, but it won't last. Disasters are like a disease. You can only manage the spread for so long. Something is going to leak, and the public isn't prepared for it."

Yes, Nyla had said as much to George. So had Aaron. And Pratt. None of them had gotten through to the fledgling sheriff.

They could only speculate as to why Mason decided to keep the party massacre quiet for the time being. Nyla thought it was a case of selfishness on the part of the Somerton Sheriff's Department, hiding the fact that they had nothing to go on when a classroom-worth of teenagers had been slaughtered. Aaron thought it was to let them investigate in peace, to keep people from flooding the woods and accidentally contaminating evidence. He was probably right, but that didn't stop Nyla from being bitter about the whole thing.

Not to mention, she wasn't sure they'd find any evidence at all. Not if her theory was right. She *hoped* it wasn't right, because she didn't know what to do about it if it was.

"Stop it," Aaron whispered in her ear, nudging her with his nose. Nyla looked at him out of the side of her eye.

"What?"

"I can almost hear your thoughts," he teased, wrapping his arms around her and hugging her tightly from behind. Nyla melted under his comfort, still not used to open displays of support. "What happened last week was tragic, but we don't know anything yet."

"We know enough, don't we?" Nyla argued, wanting desperately to be wrong. "A bunch of contractors killed in the Basin woods, with no trace of foul play?"

"A bunch of *out-of-town* contractors threw a party in the woods with no safeties in place. Who knows what kind of animal they accidentally pissed off?"

Before Nyla could interject with a list of native predators, Aaron continued.

"That doesn't mean there's another creature out there. As soon as Pratt gets us clearance, we'll go to the site, check it out, and put this to rest once and for all."

"And if we can't?" Nyla challenged, reaching down to twine her hand with Aaron's, clinging to it like a lifeline. "If there *is* another one? Then what?"

Aaron thought for a moment, gathering his conviction.

"Then we'll deal with it," he promised. "We've already killed one Chehwinoo. What's one more?"

"I can't decide if your confidence is hot or irritating," Nyla said, sinking further into her desk. It wasn't a comfortable position, but getting up would require far more commitment than she had the energy for.

'Then what' was a far more complicated question than Aaron was giving it credit for.

They hadn't talked much about what life would look like for them after the Chehwinoo situation was put to rest. She'd thought about selling the Willow, but her heart revolted every time she considered it. Aaron was experimenting with different clientele while he was staying in Somerton, finding a deep-seated interest in corporate espionage that he'd never known about himself before. If he pursued that sector of private investigating, he couldn't stay in Somerton. He'd need to go back to Chicago, at the very least. Nyla wasn't against long-distance relationships, but could she really stay here after everything she'd been through?

On some level, she *wanted* the party massacre to be the work of another Chehwinoo, if only so she could put off making any life-altering decisions for just a little while longer. That thought made her feel sick, so she shoved it violently aside. She *didn't* want another creature. No, she just wanted an excuse.

"Come on," Aaron said suddenly, tapping her on the shoulder. "We're meeting Pratt at Tinny's in 15 minutes. We should get going."

"It only takes 10 minutes to get to Tinny's," Nyla said, stretching the kinks out of her back. "We don't have to leave yet."

Aaron's expression went blank, staring at her in blatant and distraught confusion. Nyla could almost see his brain short circuiting as he tried to understand her lack of urgency.

"Right," Nyla smirked, rolling her eyes at him, "I forgot who I was talking to. Forgive my egregious indiscretion, oh Punctual One."

"What's wrong with being punctual?"

"Nothing, my love," Nyla teased, scrunching her nose at him. Aaron ignored the mocking lilt of her voice, grasping her hand and all but lifting her from her chair. "Let's go before that vein in your neck gets any bigger."

Chapter Six

AMELIA

Amelia really should've known better.

While Sam's trickery was a shock to her at the time, she only had herself to blame. If she'd been paying proper attention, she would've figured out that Sam had flubbed the truth. He was never a good liar. She'd just been so overwhelmed with the Derek situation that she hadn't thought to actually check in with Tyler after Sam claimed they'd worked things out.

It was too late now, anyway. They were in Somerton for at least the next week, so her anxiety would just have to deal with it. Sink or swim, Amelia's home for the foreseeable future was in the Basin.

After loading up the rental, they followed Tyler's black sedan to Tinny's Taco Truck where it was parked in the gravel lot next to Jesse's Grill which, despite its name, was not a restaurant but a bar. The food truck took up the far corner of the lot, with wooden picnic tables scattered along the perimeter. Tinny's itself was a bright aqua blue with a neon-orange goldfish plastered on the side, wearing a sombrero, and wrapping a tortilla around itself like a blanket. Amelia didn't let herself think too much about the implications of that.

Half of the tables were occupied when they finally parked the Tacoma in what they were pretty sure was an official parking spot. Tyler alighted first, clicking the alarm on his sedan, and staking his claim on a picnic table at the exterior of the lot. Sam and Amelia followed him, dropping their jackets on the bench before approaching the window to order. Amelia couldn't remember if she'd ever eaten at Tinny's before. She'd passed by it countless times— the truck was almost as old as the rest of Somerton— but her memory failed her on the food. Either it was forgettable, or she'd never had it.

Orders placed and drinks in hand, they wandered back to their table to wait.

"Not much has changed around here, huh?" Sam offered, dropping onto the bench so hard it nearly tipped the table. Amelia waited for Tyler to seat himself on the opposite side before taking her place next to Sam. "I mean, aside from serial killer bears. That's new."

"And not intimidating enough to keep your ass in Philly," Tyler said, rolling his eyes. "To be honest, I haven't seen much of town. This is only my second time here since the last summer we spent at the cabin."

"I suppose you don't get much work this side of the State line," Sam said with a smile. "The Illinois field office still tied up with Canada?"

"No, they clued that up last month." Tyler took a long sip of his soda. "Honestly, they didn't need much help. The Canadian border service agents are a force to be reckoned with. I'm starting to think we should all be doing maple syrup shots before work."

"How's Chia?" Amelia's ears perked up at the sound of their names being called and waited patiently as Sam and Tyler went to retrieve their food. When they returned, she repeated her question around a mouthful of chicken quesadilla. Tyler's grin turned goofy, and suddenly he was 16 again and they were all hanging out on the soccer field, praying the lunch bell didn't interrupt their very important debate on the best movie snack.

"She's glowing," he said, flinching like he wanted to pull out his phone to show them a picture, but his hands were covered in bright orange grease. "Miserable, but glowing. I wish I could make it easier on her. I know how much she wants a boatload of kids."

"Is Izzy excited to be a big brother?" Amelia smiled until her cheeks hurt. She didn't want kids of her own, she didn't even really *like* kids, but she loved Tyler's. As shocked as she'd been when he first told them Chia was expecting, now she couldn't picture Tyler as anything but a natural-born dad.

"Izzy is... something." Tyler shook his head. "He wants to meet the baby, but he somehow got it in his head that the baby isn't *staying*. He thinks we're preparing for a sleepover and then the baby will go find new parents and the new room we're painting is going to be his 'second bed.' Jabulani is trying to explain it to him, but he's not getting it."

"He'll figure it out pretty soon," Amelia grimaced, "you know, when the baby *doesn't* leave."

"I'm a little worried about that realization." Tyler took another bite of his taco, chewing carefully. Despite his words, he was fighting a smile. "We're going to have our hands full; I know that much."

"Who are we meeting here again?" Sam interrupted, his attention caught on a vehicle pulling into the lot. "Someone we know?"

"Kind of—" Tyler stopped, also catching sight of the vehicle. Sam's instincts must've been right on target because suddenly Tyler was shoving his unfinished taco back into its aluminum wrapper. "Hang out here for a second, okay? I'm just going to…"

He never finished, the sentiment hanging open in the air. Tyler then stood abruptly, almost vaulting from the picnic bench. Casting them a mildly embarrassed smile, he hurried to intercept the two people exiting the SUV and she was reminded of the uneasiness that tickled the back of her mind at the grocery store.

Tyler was only marginally better at keeping secrets than Sam, and Amelia had gotten the impression that, while he wasn't *lying* exactly, Tyler was leaving a lot of things unsaid. What that meant, she had no idea, but she guessed it had something to do with the people Tyler was nervously rushing to meet.

The first person that Amelia could see was a woman emerging from the passenger side door. She greeted Tyler with a worried, almost anxious smile before the expression faded to confusion and finally understanding. While she didn't glance toward them, Amelia had a feeling Tyler was warning her about her and Sam's intrusion on their meeting. A bubble of suspicion filled Amelia's stomach; Tyler had been tense since they'd met him at the grocery store. Now, he was meeting a mysterious woman and going out of his way to speak to her before she met Amelia and Sam. She hated to even consider it, but… was it possible Tyler was cheating on Chia?

No. No way. Tyler wasn't like that. If she didn't know it deep in her heart, the dreamy-eyed look that came over him whenever he talked about his family was enough to dispel any lingering doubt. Not to mention, it was Tyler's idea for them to crash this meeting. Not a secret girlfriend, then. So... why the nerves?

Amelia had to admit that the woman was pretty. If she *was* an extramarital affair, Tyler at least had good taste. She looked like she belonged in Somerton, sporting fitted blue jeans and a loose, knitted blue sweater that lightly obscured her ample curves and complimented the pink hue of her blonde hair. She was also short— much shorter than Amelia had thought at first. The woman stepped closer to Tyler and wrapped him in a hug, clearly demonstrating the stark contrast in their height.

"Do you know her?" Amelia asked Sam, trying, and failing to keep the concern from her voice. Sam looked just as troubled, which only solidified Amelia's worries. Sam was oblivious on the best of days; if he was picking up on the same strange details that she was, then something was definitely off. Tyler may not be cheating, but there was *something* he wasn't telling them.

"Probably a co-worker or something," Sam said, shrugging. His nonchalance was about as believable as the 'all-natural' labels adorning Tinny's Taco Truck, but Amelia didn't bother pointing that out.

The driver's side door opened, revealing the second of their guests. As he rounded the SUV, Amelia could've sworn she felt a spark of familiarity that she couldn't quite place. Unlike the woman, he didn't fit in with Somerton's style. The man wore a tailored, clearly expensive, slate-grey suit jacket over a pair of dark denim jeans. The jacket was open, revealing a crisp red dress-shirt buttoned to the hollow of his throat, leaving the top two buttons undone. He approached Tyler with confidence, grasping his outstretched hand and using his other arm to reach out and squeeze Tyler's shoulder. Amelia couldn't read his expression like she could the woman's. He was professional, calm, and collected, at least on the surface. His thick, brown hair was styled in an intentionally mussed more-on-top cut, with no hint of adjoining facial hair marring his dark skin. While Amelia would have trouble believing the woman was a co-worker, the man on the other hand was almost certainly FBI. Maybe she was being unfair— if this man was a co-worker, why couldn't the woman be one too?

In the next instant, Tyler was leading the duo to their picnic table. Amelia schooled her features, donning a polite smile as they got closer. She was being paranoid, she decided, questioning everything because they were visiting on Sam's lie. There was no need to lump Tyler in with her annoyance at her best friend.

"Sorry about that," Tyler said. He chuckled to dispel his lingering tension, clapping a hand on the man's shoulder. "I had to make sure Klein wasn't going to start spouting trade secrets in the presence of civilians."

The man rolled his eyes, somehow managing to look composed in the midst of an exasperated sigh.

"You say that like *I'm* the one who had to redo the discrepancy seminar. Twice."

"Sam, Amelia," Tyler cleared his throat, trudging forward over the woman's stifled giggles. "This is my good friend Aaron Klein. We went through the Academy together."

"We've met," Aaron said, smiling at them. He reached out to shake Amelia's hand, then Sam's. "Isaiah's first birthday, right?"

"Oh yeah!" Sam grinned, snapping his fingers loudly in recognition. "That's right. I knew I'd seen you somewhere before. Sorry it didn't click sooner, my memory is shit."

"That was also two years ago." Aaron eased back onto his heels, sinking his hands into his pockets. "If you can believe that Izzy is three now."

"You're making me feel old," Amelia complained, turning her attention to the woman. "Have we met before, too? My memory is only slightly better than Sam's."

"Nope, I'm the new kid on the block," she chirped, "which you would know if Pratt bothered to introduce me. Alas, I'm so low to the ground that people usually forget I'm here."

"And this is Nyla." Tyler shook his head, the fondness in his smile showing through his exasperation. "Owner of Willow Lodge, certified pain in the ass, and way out of this guy's league."

Aaron hooked his arm around Nyla's shoulders, pulling her comfortably against his side. The gesture was so natural, so confident, Amelia knew that Nyla and Aaron were happily committed to one another, further confirmed by the look they gave each other. Whatever Tyler was worried about, it definitely was *not* the exposure of a clandestine affair with the local lodge owner. She'd decided as much already, but she couldn't deny the relief she felt unfurling in her stomach anyway.

"You're one to talk," Nyla said with a scoff. "There's no way you and Chia are even in the same sport, let alone league. I've seen pictures."

"She *is* too good for you," Amelia agreed. "You're like one of those average-looking guys dating a supermodel in a comedy."

"You mean every Adam Sandler movie ever made?" Nyla dropped into her seat next to Tyler, while Aaron went to order for them. "Or *Superbad*?"

"Hey, leave *Superbad* out of this," Tyler grumbled. "That's my favourite movie."

"*Superbad* isn't even in the top ten of best comedies," Sam argued around a mouthful of curly fries. "It's mid, at the *most*."

"This coming from the guy who thinks *Tenacious D* is the height of cinema," Tyler jabbed, to which Sam released a shuddering, dramatic gasp.

"How *dare* you disrespect the D?" he demanded, clamping his hands over Amelia's ears and muffling the sounds of people milling about. "And in front of the women? Have you no *shame*, sir?"

It was at that moment that Aaron returned, placing their food down with a look of horror-tinged wonder.

"Dear God, there's two of them," Aaron said under his breath, making Nyla laugh. She patted her boyfriend's arm comfortingly, taking a long sip of her horchata.

"He started it," Tyler said in his defense. Sam started to rant, but Amelia beat him to the punch before he could get too invested and she was stuck listening to the rest of the conversation through his hands.

"Would you get off me?" Amelia shoved him with her shoulder, nearly knocking Sam off the bench and succeeding in dislodging his palms from her ears.

"See? Now you've gone and upset her," Sam said, shaking his head. "Apologize, right now."

Tyler turned his attention from Sam to face Amelia, his expression comically serious.

"I'm sincerely sorry that you have to deal with him. My condolences, truly."

"It's a burden," she agreed, "but it's one I bear for the sake of the people."

"So, I gotta ask," Nyla interjected suddenly, wearing her amusement openly. Aaron watched with more reservation, but Amelia could tell he wasn't shy. It was more like he was observing, filing information away for later use. It made her a little uncomfortable, but she wasn't sure why until she realized it was the same look that she'd seen on so many of her father's co-officers. A cop's look. Panic began to bubble in her stomach before she could stop it. But Aaron wasn't a cop, he was FBI. She found that knowledge and clung to it so hard she almost missed Nyla's question. "How long have you two been dating?"

"We're not," she answered, to which both Nyla and Aaron were visibly surprised. Nyla's gaze darted between her and Sam, finally landing on Tyler for confirmation.

"Yes, she's serious," he said in response to her unspoken questions. "And before you ask, yes, they're both that delusional. Sam's sister and I have a running bet on how long it'll take for them to fold."

"Who's winning?" Amelia asked, unfazed.

"It was Roxy until a few weeks ago." Tyler turned to look at Nyla again. "She bet that they'd at least bone before they were both in their thirties, but Am's birthday was last month. My cut-off is when Sam turns 40."

"Not when we're both 40?" Amelia prompted, fighting a smile at the bewilderment on Nyla's face. Aaron had composed himself, returning to an expression of polite interest.

"That would've been cheating," Tyler said. "I know you guys have that marriage pact. The two years between Sam turning 40 and you turning 40 is my fail-safe." He looked at Sam then, his gaze sharpening into a glare. "You have eight years to get your shit together and win her over, Fisher. Don't let me down."

The conversation derailed quickly after that declaration, with Sam arguing in his own defense and Tyler providing an extensive list of wasted opportunities for Sam to bite the bullet and make a move. The topic barely registered for either of them anymore, having been subjected to a vast number of interrogations about their non-relationship over the years. Amelia and Sam had learned that it was best to roll with it.

All the same, she couldn't stop the occasional fleeting thought that made her wonder *why* Sam had never made a move on her. In all of the conversations they'd had, both with each other and their friends, Sam had never actually *denied* interest in her. Nor had she. She'd always assumed it was as simple as the fact that they were just friends. Lately, though, Amelia found herself wondering if that was entirely true. If it had *ever* been true.

Tyler was clearly getting to her.

A police siren interrupted her thought, making Nyla, Tyler, and Amelia jump. Despite there being two other people who'd startled, Aaron's attention fixated immediately on Amelia, scrunching his brows in the barest display of confused curiosity. She offered him an abashed smile, trying not to read too much into him singling her out. He was dating Nyla and was close with Tyler, likely able to guess their respective reasons for jumping at the sound of sirens. She was the anomaly here, of course he'd be curious.

"I'm not a big fan of cops," she explained, confusing the others who'd missed the subtle exchange. "I get nervous when I hear them."

"Had some trouble before?" Aaron guessed, and she wasn't sure if he was making conversation or fishing. Perhaps both.

"You could say that," she said. "I—"

"It's a personal thing," Sam interjected. "No offense—"

"It's okay, Sam." She laid her hand on his arm, stopping him from jumping to her defense. "Honest. I'm fine."

He gave her a worried look but didn't stop her when she started speaking again.

"My dad was with Chicago PD," she said, directing her attention at Aaron. "He died last year."

"I'm so sorry to hear that," Aaron's expression softened in understanding. Amelia snorted.

"Don't be," she insisted bitterly. "He was an alcoholic, abusive piece of shit. I cut contact with him when I was seventeen."

Most people reacted in awkward embarrassment after that admission, but not Aaron. Aaron gave her a minute nod, something in his eyes akin to sympathy. He'd probably seen similar situations throughout his career, no doubt guessing how her story ended without her having to say a word. She did, for Nyla's benefit.

"His precinct covered for him all the time," she said to Nyla, who was putting the pieces together now. "To say I don't trust most officers is a bit of an understatement. The sound of sirens sent me into a panic attack right up until Sam and I moved to Philly."

"You live in Philly?!" Nyla gasped excitedly, effectively steering the conversation in a lighter direction. Amelia was grateful, and though she couldn't be sure, she thought Nyla had done so on purpose. "I was born and raised in Dickinson Narrows!"

"We're in Royersford," Amelia said, smiling. "Not technically Philly, but close enough. I've never been to Dickinson Narrows. Is it North?"

"South," Nyla corrected. "You should go sometime. It's nice."

"Royersford..." Aaron mused, thinking. "You must've gone to Ursinus, then?"

"We did." Sam nodded, more relaxed now that they weren't talking about Amelia's homelife anymore. "Class of 2017, whoop-whoop!"

"You didn't go to college right away?" Nyla asked Sam, squinting as she did the math in her head. "You're older, right?"

"I worked for two years after high school," Sam explained, discreetly squeezing Amelia's thigh under the table. The warmth of his hand made her smile. "I wanted to save some money so I wouldn't be living in a water-logged box on the UC campus."

Nyla and Aaron nodded, but Amelia knew that wasn't entirely true. Sam's parents had offered to pay for both his and Roxy's tuition in its entirety, along with the first year of their rent. Roxy accepted after she was passed over for a fashion scholarship, but Sam had adamantly refused. He'd never said as much, but Amelia knew he'd stayed for her.

Before cutting her father out of her life, Sam was the only one who'd known about the situation. He wouldn't leave her, even if it meant delaying his education for a few years.

"We actually work there now," Amelia added. "Sam's in the athletics department. I'm an admissions counselor. We're just getting over the start-of-semester rush, which is the only reason we were able to make this trip at all."

"About that..." Nyla looked at Tyler first, then Aaron, as though she were gauging their reactions. Amelia sat up a little straighter.

Friendly conversation was great and all, but she'd been praying that the conversation would veer in this direction eventually.

"I'm kind of surprised anyone is coming to visit after this summer," Nyla ventured cautiously, finally addressing the elephant in the room. "I was sure tourism would drop to a standstill until at least next hunting season."

"A bunch of butchered hunters doesn't exactly scream 'vacation,'" Sam agreed, downing the last mouthful of his vitamin water. Amelia thought she saw Nyla flinch, but the action was so slight that it could've been a mistimed blink or a trick of the light. "But Mom wanted to check on her investment, and it's not like we can wait until there aren't any bears in the Basin."

"Besides, it was just that one rogue, right?" The statement came out as more of a desperate question twined with a challenge. Despite all of her logical reassurance, Amelia had never been able to shake the sense of dread clinging to this trip, even when she was under the impression that Tyler was on board. Maybe Sam couldn't feel it, but she could. "A random bear got a taste for human flesh and went on a rampage? What are the chances of something like that happening again?"

Nyla and Aaron shared a look.

"Still," Nyla began, skirting the question. "It's possible the bear was sick and passed it on before it was killed. Just to be safe, I'd stick to the more populated areas of town."

"And don't go outside at night, if you can help it," Tyler added, looking to Nyla for confirmation. She nodded.

"Bears are nocturnal?" Amelia scrunched her nose in confusion. "I thought they were active during the day?"

Tyler froze, his expression carefully neutral as he processed the question.

"They're getting ready to hibernate," Nyla cut in helpfully, giving them a shrugging smile. "This time of year, they tend to be pretty territorial about their nesting spot. You wouldn't want to accidentally stumble across one bunking down for the night. People have been mauled for less."

"Duly noted." Amelia shivered, shooting Sam a sideways glare to make sure he was listening.

Silence fell over them, thick and uncomfortable. Amelia watched Tyler, Aaron, and Nyla as discreetly as she could, the sense that they were hiding something spreading like smog through the air. Eventually, Aaron ended the stalemate.

"Pratt, did you get those papers I asked for?"

Tyler blinked, visibly processing Aaron's question.

"Yes," he said after a beat. "I... I'll email them to you."

"Great." Aaron smoothly extracted himself from the picnic bench, his hand pressing gently between Nyla's shoulders to get her attention. "We should go, *mi tesoro*. We've got a few more things to finish up before we head home."

"Right," Nyla allowed Aaron to help her up, taking his proffered arm gratefully. "It was really nice to meet you two! I hope you have a good trip. Maybe we can meet up again later this week?"

"That'd be nice," Amelia smiled, hoping she'd succeeded at hiding the tension in her face. "Tyler can give you my number."

"Give her mine, too," Sam said, either oblivious to the unspoken suspicion or choosing to ignore it. He nodded at Aaron. "We'll have you over for a barbecue before we head back to Philly."

"Make sure Pratt gives you our numbers too," Nyla insisted almost worriedly. "And call me if you need *anything*, okay? I mean it. I'm a wilderness guide, there isn't much I haven't dealt with. No matter how stupid it seems, I'd rather you be safe than sorry."

The urgency in her plea gave Amelia pause. It could be as simple as Nyla having seen more than her fair share of people getting into trouble in the woods because they were too stubborn or embarrassed to ask for help. Or...

"We'll reach out if we have any questions," she said. "I promise."

Looking mildly relieved, Nyla and Aaron made their exit.

They sat in silence for another minute after the SUV left the lot, and then Amelia remembered they had groceries in the back seat of the Tacoma.

"We gotta go too." Sam seemed to remember their food at the same time she did, gathering their garbage in one hand and scanning the lot for a trash bin. "But stop by the cabin before you go back to Chicago, alright?"

"When are you going back?" Amelia asked, helping Sam with the garbage. Tyler hesitated.

"I'm not sure," he said honestly. "I have some things to take care of here first. I'll see you again before I leave, I'll make a point of it."

"Good," Sam clapped a hand on Tyler's shoulder. "Then it's a date."

They were only a few steps away from the table when he called after them.

"Hey, guys?" Tyler paused, unsure if he wanted to continue. "I know it might seem stupid, but... please listen to Nyla, okay? She's the best outdoorsy person I know, and if she's telling you to do something, or not to do something, well... I have it on good authority that not listening to her advice has gotten people killed."

Amelia frowned, her eyebrows knitting as she took in the gravity of Tyler's voice.

"I get that we're in the woods, and there are always going to be dangerous animals out there," Tyler hurried on as if he was forcing himself to speak before he changed his mind. "But if Nyla says to stay inside after dark, stay inside after dark. Alright?"

Chapter Seven

SAM

By the time they returned to the cabin, Amelia had forgiven him for lying about Tyler. It was begrudging forgiveness, but Sam would take what he could get. He hadn't meant to lie about the situation, not at first. Amelia was just so stressed about Tyler's reaction to their visit that Sam flubbed the truth a little, easing her concerns enough that she could enjoy their trip and not be afflicted with anxiety for the entire week leading up to their departure. She hadn't had a panic attack since she'd started her anxiety medication again; Sam didn't want to set her back over Tyler's oddly cryptic paranoia.

And cryptic it was.

Sam wasn't suspicious by nature. Every fiber of his being wanted to trust people, to believe in the good in the world. It rarely crossed his mind that people *could* be misleading him. Sam had always lived his life with a What You See Is What You Get mentality, and he frequently forgot that most others didn't. Amelia sometimes called him naïve, and he supposed he was, in a sense. He could spot a jackass in a crowd with ease, but he struggled with the sneakier, hidden rottenness that skulked behind a friendly face. Amelia was much better at identifying those people than he was, thanks in no small part to her upbringing.

His fists clenched, muscle in his jaw twitching agitatedly as he thought about the first man who'd proven to him that not all people were good by nature.

Howard Bradley, Amelia's son-of-a-bitch father.

Sam felt his pulse rise immediately, undirected rage simmering in his veins. Sam had never hated anyone before Howard, and he'd only hated one person since. It was pure coincidence, probably, that they were both men who'd hurt Amelia so deeply that it became a part of her identity.

Howard had hated Sam too, of course, even before Sam discovered the extent of his cruelty towards his daughter. He remembered the night vividly, etched into his memory, resurfacing at random and refreshing his anger. It was late August, the summer after his senior year, and he was on his way to pick Amelia up for a party his friend and teammate was throwing. It should've been a normal Saturday night for them, but when Sam's motorcycle crunched onto the packed gravel of the Bradleys' driveway, everything changed.

Sam would never forget the sound of Amelia's crying, the frantic and unfiltered fear on her face as she sprinted to him, clinging to his jacket like he was her only lifeline in a vast ocean of danger. He'd never seen her afraid before, not like that. The panic that gripped his lungs at that moment would never leave him— Sam had never felt so scared before, like he'd forgotten how to breathe and was quickly suffocating. Before he'd had a chance to ask Amelia what was going on, Howard thundered out the door after her, raising his hand in a clear and unflinching threat. Not only was it the first of many nights he'd spent with Amelia safely tucked away in his room, it was also the first time Sam had punched someone.

After giving her father a nosebleed and bringing Amelia back to his house to pack make-up over her bruises, Sam knew he wasn't going to college in the fall. He couldn't leave her, not with that man. For the next two years, Sam took care of Amelia however she'd let him, sneaking her into his house at night so she could get a full eight hours of rest, using his allowance to buy her basic necessities that her father deprived her of, and engaging in more than one physical altercation with Howard Bradley when his temper got out of hand. Sam was glad to do it, and Amelia begrudgingly accepted his help after he'd been rejected from Ursinus with his first two applications.

Except, he hadn't. Sam would never tell Amelia this, but he'd been on his way to her house that night well before their scheduled pick-up time to tell her that he'd been accepted into college and that he'd be setting up apartment viewings the very next week.

If she knew, Sam had no doubt she'd blame herself. So, it was a secret he'd take to his grave. He'd made his choice, and he didn't regret it for a single second.

The underhandedness, the secrecy, and the unspoken weight of Howard Bradley and his abuse toward his daughter was a truth that poisoned everyone it touched. After Amelia confessed everything to him, Sam saw Howard for what he really was: a righteous prick with a badge and a god complex. He saw it in the way the man held himself, the way he looked down his nose at everyone like he was better than them. He saw it in the way Howard never fully relaxed like he was tensed for violence at any given moment. Sam saw it, but only after the fact. Only after he'd been slapped in the face with the reality.

Sam felt sick with dread as he wondered what sort of life Amelia would've lived if he *hadn't* tried to surprise her that day. Would he ever have figured it out on his own? Amelia wouldn't have said anything, he knew that. She'd convinced herself long ago that she wasn't worthy of the same grace she gave others. It was bullshit, and Sam reminded her of that every single day.

Yeah, he was naïve. But he vowed to never make that mistake again.

The problem now, then, was what to do about Tyler.

Amelia picked up on whatever secret he was harboring well before Sam did, but he *had* picked up on it, which meant it must be pretty hefty. Sam and Tyler had been friends since grade school, crossing paths constantly because they were both involved in sports. Tyler was on the hockey team, and Sam was on the football team. They never played together, of course, but their circles mingled, and they became fast friends. Tyler wasn't much for secrets, more so than Sam was but not as much as Amelia, so it was easy to pick up on his discomfort. What it meant, Sam didn't know. He also didn't know if it mattered.

Whatever was going on, was it really his business? Tyler was with the FBI, who knew what kind of crap he dealt with on a daily basis? In truth, since he'd joined the bureau, they hadn't spent much time together. It was a lot more difficult now than when they were in school and lived down the street from one another. Now, they were adults. They had jobs. Responsibilities. Not to mention the fact that they were in different states.

Maybe this was what it was like being friends with a federal agent. Always feeling like there was something lurking between words, an ugliness coiled and ready to spring to the forefront with just the right prodding. Like they were outsiders, cared about but not invited into the heart of the issue. It stung, just a little. Not that Sam expected Tyler to start spouting classified information just because his childhood friends were worried about him, but that didn't lessen the feeling of 'otherness' that gripped him.

Was this how Amelia was feeling too? Or was she more suspicious than him?

Sam glanced over at her, hunched over the kitchen island, staring into space. No, Amelia wouldn't look at this the same way he would. Her heart was more hardened than his. She'd be looking at this objectively, convincing herself that there was something wrong, that Tyler might be in some kind of trouble. She'd work herself into a frenzy over it if left to her own devices. It was Sam's job to prevent that from happening.

Amelia had been quiet for longer than Sam realized. It was well into the afternoon now, and their homemade pizza was just about finished cooling. When was the last time she'd spoken? He couldn't remember, which meant it was too long. He was about to ask her if anything was wrong, redirect her thoughts to her irritation at him maybe, when she suddenly broke the silence without prompting.

"Why is Tyler here?"

"What?"

Of all the questions she could've asked, that one surprised him. Sam took a seat next to her at the island. Neither of them liked using the large, ornate dining table in the adjoining room. Amelia once likened it to a museum piece. She wasn't wrong.

"He wasn't expecting us to visit," she continued, poking the pizza with her index finger. When she didn't flinch away at the heat, Sam surmised it was safe to grab a piece. "The bear incident was months ago. Anything that needs doing is probably paperwork, which can be done from his desk. Not to mention, nothing criminal happened. The FBI's involvement should've ended when they caught the damn thing, shouldn't it? And Chia is heavily pregnant and miles away in Chicago. So, why is Tyler here?"

Sam took a bite of his pizza slice, chewing hard in contemplation. As he suspected, she'd put more thought into the sinister side of things than he had.

"Maybe he's just here to visit Aaron and Nyla?" He forgot to swallow before speaking, earning a scowl from Am.

"Aaron lives in Chicago too," she said with a frown. "Ty wouldn't leave Chia to visit someone he could see at home. I doubt he would've come to see *us* for more than a day or two if she and Izzy couldn't travel with him."

"Then he's here for work. Doesn't have to be the bear thing. Could've had another case."

Amelia crossed her arms over her chest, leaning back on the silver bar stool until the front legs lifted from the ground. Sam jolted to put his arm behind her instinctively, but she'd hooked her legs under the stability bar beneath the table.

"In Wisconsin?" Amelia pursed her lips. Tyler's assignment on the rogue bear certainly should've been a one-off, but that didn't mean it was impossible. It also didn't mean Tyler wasn't here for other reasons, perfectly logical ones.

"Maybe he's just doing some unofficial follow-up." He shrugged indifferently, knowing that wasn't a good enough answer to keep Amelia from fretting. Unfortunately, he didn't have a better explanation.

She didn't look convinced, rocking thoughtfully on the back legs of the stool and saying nothing.

"Something's off," she insisted, finally taking a bite of her pizza. "I can't put my finger on it, but something isn't right."

"Come on, Am. This is Tyler we're talking about, remember? The guy who couldn't get into the DEA because he didn't think there was a difference between cocaine and heroin? What could he possibly be involved in?"

"I'm not saying he's involved in something, I said something was off." Amelia gave him a hard look. "Believe me or don't believe me, but my gut has never been wrong before. Between the weird resolution to the bear thing, Tyler's sketchy attitude, and how jumpy everyone is, I'd bet anything that there are some secrets in this town that aren't going to stay secret for long. I just hope it's nothing dangerous."

"Tyler would never risk leaving his kids without a father," Sam assured her, knowing that, if nothing else, that much he was certain of. "Whatever is going on, I have every confidence it'll all blow over before Chia's next baby shower. Which I hope you bought a gift for, because I have no idea what babies like. If they like things. I've never thought about it before, but can a baby like something? Or do they just kind of... roll with it? Am?"

After the third noncommittal mumble, Sam knew that Amelia was fully absorbed in her own mind. Time for an impromptu intervention.

Sam hooked his heel behind the raised bar stool leg closest to him, giving her chair a swift kick. The stool teetered, startling Amelia from her reverie. She screamed and jerked forward to catch herself, but Sam had it covered. He grasped her forearms as the stool twisted her toward him, steadying her until all four legs were firmly on the floor.

"What the actual fuck, Fisher?" She gasped, shaking the fright from her limbs. Sam maintained his hold on her arms, relaxing his grip from steadying to soothing.

"Sorry," he smiled apologetically, "but I could see the steam coming from your ears. You're thinking too much."

Amelia didn't deny it.

"Look, we came here to get away for a few days, right? We can't do that if you're driving yourself crazy worrying about Tyler. Whatever is going on with him, he'll tell us when he's ready. Or, if not, then we'll drag it from him the next time we get a chance."

He meant that. Sam and Tyler had been best friends since they were in pre-k, so FBI or no FBI, Sam knew how to pry a secret from him. Amelia was slightly mollified with that notion, some of the tension leaving her shoulders.

"You're right," she admitted. "Sorry. I'm not trying to bring you down or anything."

"Oh, shut up," Sam snorted, pulling her forward until she was forced to stand up, her hips settling just between his knees. "A bull elephant couldn't bring me down. I'm just worried about you."

For many reasons, most of which were completely unrelated to their vacation. Sam didn't need to specify; she knew.

"I'm fine, I promise," she assured him, offering a small smile. Sam returned it, wrapping his arms tightly around her middle and squeezing until she laughed. "Okay, no more moping. I think I saw some of our old DVDs in the movie room. In the mood for a horror movie marathon?"

"Always," Sam released her, taking their dirtied plates and stacking them in front of him, "as long as you think you can handle it."

"When have I ever *not* been able to handle a scary movie?"

"You looked pretty pale when we watched *Hide and Seek* with Roxy and Ty."

"I had the stomach flu, you idiot," she said, smiling. "Besides, I was amping up the tension for Roxy's sake. She didn't want to look like a wimp in front of her *big crush*."

Sam scowled, grumbling at that particular part of the memory. While Tyler and his sister had never officially dated, he knew they'd hooked up a few times before Tyler was accepted into the FBI Academy. The thought still made his skin crawl over a decade later.

"You're so easy to rile up." Amelia shook her head at him, chuckling, and started to make her way to the movie room. "Come on, Sammy Honey, let's find something on theme. I'm thinking... a cabin, in the woods, with... ghosts?"

"What, no bear attack?" Sam bounded across the room to sling his arm over her shoulders, steering them both down the hall. "I'm sure we could find something. *Grizzly*?"

"I think that's a little too close to home," Amelia said, pursing her lips in thought. "Let's go for something less plausible, like a bigfoot or a demon."

"Amy Baby, I have the perfect choice."

Chapter Eight

AMELIA

The Fishers' movie room was like something out of a snotty rich kid's wet dream. There was a projector that consumed the entire back wall, with six plush recliners spaced along two-tiered platforms so everyone could see. Amelia always loved the movie room, even though it was smaller and less lavish than the one in the Fishers' main house in Illinois. The Fishers weren't shy about their wealth, and the blatant extravagance still made her squirm. The Somerton cabin was a good mix of upper-middle-class and rustic, which made the entire property more palatable for her terminally broke self.

To her delight, Sam had chosen one of her favourite movies, aptly titled *The Cabin in the Woods*. It wasn't the scariest movie she'd ever seen, but it was one of the most fun, and it effectively distracted her from the confusing blend of worry and suspicion roiling in her gut after their lunch date with Tyler and his friends. She'd only thought about them twice since the start of the film, which might've been a record for her.

They were well into the third act now, and Sam was sound asleep. That was typical; Amelia couldn't remember the last time they'd watched anything without Sam's snores interrupting crucial bits of dialogue. It was kind of amazing, really, the consistency with which he was able to nap no matter what screeching horror was on the screen. Amelia almost envied him.

Despite there being five other available chairs, the two of them were huddled in one directly in front of the screen in the first row. Sam lounged across the entire length of the recliner, one arm folded beneath his head, his ankles crossed, and his mouth hanging open just enough to release the occasional ear-shattering snort.

Amelia would've moved to another chair, but Sam's other arm made that impossible. He'd wrapped it around her waist, pulling her flush against him, her head resting in the junction between his neck and shoulder. It was cramped, but also annoyingly comfortable which, she supposed, described her entire relationship with Sam pretty succinctly.

Amelia didn't actually *like* physical affection, not that anyone would ever be able to tell. After growing up around a man who doled out slaps like candy on Halloween, any kind of touch made her deeply uncomfortable. Even as a young girl, she'd understood the concept of boundaries well enough to communicate to her friends that she didn't want to be hugged, or pushed, or high-fived, or anything that brought her within breathing distance of someone without explicit and direct permission. Maybe the other kids were smart enough to sense that there was something more than simple preference to her request because they all listened without incident.

All of them except Sam.

She didn't blame him. Sam was always oblivious, so he probably didn't think twice about pushing her buttons by crossing lines she'd clearly drawn in the sand. Add that to the fact that he was young, and in his defense, she didn't put much energy into trying to correct him. He was Roxy's older brother, wasn't he *supposed* to be obnoxious and irritating? Whatever her immature reasoning, she didn't stop Sam's quest to annoy her with his mere presence, and, over time, she got used to his ambush hugs and playful tackles. She even came to anticipate them, missing his warmth when he wasn't in a teasing mood and decided to leave her alone. Slowly but surely, Sam had wormed his way into her bubble of comfort, and Amelia found that she, surprisingly, didn't mind.

It was late, just past midnight. The movie room was mostly soundproofed, so Amelia couldn't hear the typical sounds she associated with Somerton— rustling leaves, whistling wind, and crackling twigs thrumming through the mountain air. With the movie nearing its end, she found her attention drifting to her phone, the conversation at Tinny's still ringing in her ears.

Sam told her to stop worrying about it. She should.

Her phone screen blinded her as she unlocked it, opening her web browser. Amelia knew that Sam was right, Tyler would never risk leaving his children without a father if he could help it. That didn't mean that *nothing* was going on though, and Amelia couldn't let go of the squirming suspicion without at least trying to figure out what they'd stumbled into. *If* they'd stumbled into anything.

She started with Nyla.

It felt a little sleazy researching Tyler's friends. Nyla and Aaron had been nothing but nice to them over lunch, and Amelia's conscience briefly delayed her. Briefly. It occurred to her that in all of their chatting, very little had been said about Aaron and Nyla. She wasn't even sure what Aaron did for a job now—Tyler made it sound like he wasn't in the FBI anymore, but he certainly looked like a Fed. Pushing aside the twinge of guilt, she began scanning through whatever information she could find on Nyla Jameson and Aaron Klein.

Information popped up readily. Aaron had a decorated history with the FBI, highly respected and recognized for his accomplishments. His business now was private investigating, and his website was a clear reflection of him: simple, sleek, and modern. The only thing that stuck Amelia as odd was that he was based in Chicago.

So why was *he* here?

Amelia had assumed that Aaron lived in Chicago, but she hadn't really considered the implications of that until now. Obviously, he could be here visiting his girlfriend, but how had they met? Was it a coincidence that he happened to be seeing someone in the same town that made national news for a rabid bear? Had he been involved somehow? PIs didn't take cases pro bono very often. If he was here to investigate, he must've been hired. By whom?

Switching gears, Amelia looked up Nyla's place of business: Willow Lodge. Nothing egregious stood out to her there either, until she noted the banner scrolling along the bottom of the page. The Willow was closed for the foreseeable future, despite the fact that Nyla was here and well. As a small business owner, why was she taking an extended break just before the Christmas season? It wasn't peak tourist time, sure, but Amelia guessed that some people would be coming through, wouldn't they?

She made a mental note to look into other lodges in the state. Maybe closing for extended periods during off-season was more common in Wisconsin.

She was about to give up on Nyla's background when she had a thought, scanning through some local gossip pages until she found what she was looking for. Nyla had been one of the witnesses in the bear attacks. And she wasn't very well-liked in town. In fact, she was downright hated in many of the more established groups in Somerton. Amelia felt her stomach twist uncomfortably—the things being said about Nyla in Facebook groups and Reddit forums were nasty, sexist, and, from the little time she'd spent with her, blatantly untrue. Where was all the hostility coming from?

Locking her phone screen again, Amelia considered what little information she had. Aaron, an ex-Fed and current PI based in Chicago, was in Somerton for an unknown period of time. Nyla, a local business owner and key witness in the bear attacks, was hated by the locals and had closed her lodge temporarily. Tyler, Nyla, and Aaron all had some business with each other, the nature of which was inherently cryptic. Adding that information to what she knew already, namely that the mayor James Carver was missing, the Sheriff had recently passed in a freak accident, and none of the details of the Somerton killings matched with any known rabies outbreaks, and Amelia ended up with nothing more than a headache.

So many pieces, and none fit together. Were they even supposed to? For a fleeting time, she was convinced she'd separated her anxiety from her gut instincts. Now, exhaustion and confusion coupled to leave her uncertain. She needed sleep.

The movie was over now, the Smart TV having automatically powered down after a time. The soundproofed room was left quiet bar Sam's snores. Amelia could've fallen asleep right where she was, knowing she wouldn't be disturbed by the morning light due to the lack of windows. They'd left the door open, though, and if not for that decision she may not have heard the distressing thud coming from the kitchen window.

Amelia sat bolt upright, dislodging Sam's arm in one swift motion. She peered into the darkened hall, but nothing looked out of place. That was of little comfort; she couldn't see the kitchen from here.

"Sam?" She nudged him with her palm, whispering urgently. "Sam, wake up. I heard something."

He didn't, which wasn't a surprise. Both Sam and his sister slept like the dead. Amelia couldn't count the number of times she'd had to resort to drastic measures to make sure he made it to class or work on time.

"*Samuel,*" she tried again, louder. He grunted, refusing to wake. Seriously, what was the point of having a best friend (quite literally) the size of a linebacker if he insisted on being unconscious whenever something spooky happened? Amelia hesitated, looking between Sam and the open door. The noise she'd heard sounded distant enough that it was likely coming from outside. She could investigate it on her own.

Unraveling herself from the recliner, making no effort not to disturb Sam and huffing in annoyance when he *still* didn't budge, Amelia made her way swiftly to the hall.

The Fishers had installed motion-sensor floor lights in the main hallway of the cabin that were powered by a solar battery. Power outages were common in Somerton, and the last thing Sandra and Richard Fisher were was unprepared. Amelia resisted the urge to tip-toe like she was sneaking up on someone. It was a thump, on a window, at night, in the woods. Any number of creatures could be responsible, none of which she needed stealth to identify from inside the house.

The kitchen was as they'd left it, the lingering scent of popcorn permeating the air. Amelia did a quick scan of the room, looking for anything at all out of place. Once she was confident that she was alone, as she should be, she made her way over to the large bay window that consumed most of the dining area wall. There were heavy, intricately woven art-deco curtains covering the glass, along with a layer of gossamer sheers separating her from a proper look into the outside world. Amelia pulled back the corner of both curtains, squinting into the dark.

The fact that it *was* dark soothed her. The Fishers had motion-sensor lights on the patio too, so whatever had disturbed the silence was either too far away or too small to trip the lights. She continued her perusal anyway, if only for the sake of satisfying her curiosity. The moon was only half full, not enough to properly illuminate the ground, but Amelia still managed to zero her attention on the source of the disturbance.

An old birdhouse, usually mounted on a towering pine near the side of the cabin, had been knocked free from its perch. Given its location on the ground, it was likely that it hit the side of the house when it fell, glancing off the window and alerting her to its plummet. Amelia sighed in relief, dropping the sheers from her grip, but something stopped her from letting go of the curtains too. Something about the birdhouse snagged her attention, and it wasn't until she peered at it again that she realized what. The poor art project was shattered, shimmering in the low light like shards of glass, every inch frozen in a solid mass of ice.

Amelia frowned. Was it that cold out? She wouldn't dream of checking, not now, not when it was late and Nyla's warning rang fresh in her ears, but she couldn't deny that she was tempted. In all her years of visiting the cabin, she'd never seen a frost like this. If not for the evidence in front of her, she wouldn't have thought it possible at all. How cold did it have to be to freeze solid wood and break it like a crystal champagne glass?

As she pondered, the feeling of someone watching her inched along her spine. Amelia froze, her breath stilling in her lungs, her muscles seizing in a long-instilled fear response. She counted to three, willing her body to relax. She wasn't in danger. She wasn't.

The woods loomed around the edge of the cabin's property, dark and blurred. There wasn't enough light to make out defined shapes in the branches, but something told her that she wasn't the only one surveying the surrounding grounds. Swallowing her reflexive panic, Amelia squinted into the dark, trying to pick out anything that might be a creature or, worse, a human.

God, what if it's a human?

Anxiety was a cruel beast. Amelia was used to her mind making admirable leaps to the worst possible conclusions, and she'd gotten pretty good at sorting the genuine concerns from the mental illness. If they were back in Royersford and she'd felt like something was watching her from a window, she'd know for a fact that it was only her anxiety screaming at her that there was a murderer or, more likely, her father stalking her from the shadows of their apartment. The notion would unsettle her, but only for a second. She'd recognize it for what it was almost instantly and dismiss it accordingly.

Now, she hesitated.

Was it her anxiety making her think that someone or something lurked beyond the trees, assessing her? Or was it her instincts, charged and sensing danger even when she couldn't explain it? Normally, she could tell. Tonight, she couldn't. The realization made her uneasy. *If* someone was out there, she'd see them well before they reached the cabin. She'd scream and Sam would hear her, asleep or not. She'd be alright.

But what if she was wrong? What if the noise she'd heard *wasn't* coming from outside, and her senses were confused? What if the sense of being watched was coming from inside the house.

Impossible, she reminded herself. *The alarm is set. The locks are turned. There's no way anyone else is in this room—*

"Am?"

The curtain dropped from her grip with a soft flutter that contrasted with the panicked spike in her heart rate. She stumbled back from the window and whipped around to face the intruder, realizing immediately who it was but not quickly enough to stop the knee-jerk reaction of taking a swing. Sam caught her fist with ease, rubbing the sleep from his eyes with his other hand.

"Are you trying to give me a heart attack?" Amelia demanded, yanking her closed fist out of Sam's grasp. "What are you doing here?"

Sam shrugged his bare shoulder, shaking his sleep-mussed hair out of his eyes.

"I woke up and you weren't there. I thought you went to bed, so I was getting ready to join you, but you weren't in the bedroom either. What are you doing here?"

She opened her mouth to answer, but the words wouldn't come. An invisible gag clung to her throat, some psycho-somatic instinct to lie about what she hadn't seen. Sam watched her, clarity returning to his face as he woke fully. He glanced at the window, and Amelia knew she had to say something.

"I heard a noise, that's all," she said as casually as she could manage. "I was trying to see what it was, but it's dark. I didn't want to turn on a light."

As the explanation left her lips, it suddenly occurred to her how stupid she'd been. The Fishers had security cameras all over the property. If she was thinking straight, she would've checked them.

Sam was clearly thinking the same, judging by the odd look he was giving her.

"I was going to check the cameras," she added untruthfully, "but I don't have the passcode."

"My birthday," Sam answered easily. She knew that, and he knew she knew that. Still, he didn't push the topic. Instead, he reached around her toward the window. Amelia caught his forearm just as he took the curtain in his hand, too late to stop him from looking for himself. "Did you see anything?"

"Uh..." From the curious expression on Sam's face, he wasn't picking up on the same sense of wrongness that she had. Amelia relaxed. Anxiety it was, then. "Something knocked over the birdhouse. It was probably a raccoon."

"Little bastards," Sam huffed, marching away from her. He passed the route to the bedroom, veering instead for the back door. Amelia's heart lunged into her throat. "Do Mom and Dad still have a broom here? Or is it just the Roomba?"

"Why do you need a broom?" Amelia had barely gotten the question out when Sam reached for the lock, and then she couldn't hold back her panic anymore. Her voice came out in a sharp yell, stopping Sam in his tracks. "Wait!"

"What? What's wrong?"

"Nyla said not to go outside," she reminded him. "It's not safe."

"I'm not going outside. I'm just going on the deck."

"Sam, the deck *is* outside."

"Okay but it's not *outside*, outside. I don't want to clean up after a gaggle of trash pandas tomorrow morning."

"Then I'll clean it up," Amelia said, crossing the room to grab his arm and pull him back toward the bedroom. "Please, Sam? Just forget about it, okay? I don't like the thought of you going out there right now."

"Careful Amy Baby," he smirked, soothing her with his easy confidence, "I might start thinking you care about me."

"I wouldn't go that far."

Sam paused, considering her request and his desire to investigate. Amelia waited, torn. If she pressed him, his reaction could go either way. He might take her seriously upon seeing how distressed she was, but he might also go full Sam-mode and do the exact *opposite* of what she wanted. She couldn't risk it, so she stayed quiet. After a painfully long beat, Sam relented.

"Alright, alright. Who am I to turn down a beautiful woman's request?" He gave her his most over-the-top wink, engaging his entire face. The tension drained from Amelia's body in one fell swoop, an amused smile fighting to break free. "Let's get some sleep and we'll assess the damage in the morning. Deal?"

"Deal." She ducked gratefully under Sam's arm as he slung it over her shoulders, pulling her against his side. "Let's go, I'm exhausted."

"If all you wanted was to get me into bed, you could've just asked."

Amelia didn't dignify that with a response, instead breathing a sigh of relief as they made it to the bedroom without any of the exterior motion lights flickering to life.

Chapter Nine

INTERLUDE

The Basin

There was something eerie about the woods at night, even from the comfort of his own backyard. Wanda had always hated coming to the cabin this late in the year when the sun fell early, and the temperature dropped with the hour. Ned didn't want to admit that he missed his ex-wife's nagging because it would mean he'd made a mistake by signing those papers. He couldn't admit that even to himself.

Still, the night was quiet without Wanda's commentary. Ned used to wish she'd shut it for just a minute, long enough to let him bask in the sounds of the forest. He begged for it, pleaded with her to just sit and *relax*, stop worrying herself into a frenzy over their car payments or the kids' grades. Ned loved the isolated calm of the cabin, but Wanda could never pull her mind from their everyday troubles long enough to enjoy it as he did. They never really understood each other, not from day one. Their first date was a misunderstanding at the bar; he'd wanted to ask her friend for a dance, but she'd heard something about buying them a drink and the whole thing got muddy fast, due in no small part to the amount of alcohol they'd both already consumed. Somehow, to this day he couldn't remember how, he'd ended up taking Wanda home despite the fact that she wasn't his type. From their very first meeting, Ned and Wanda were never on the same page.

He shouldn't have been surprised when their marriage fell apart. Their relationship was built on what was fundamentally a lie.

It was hard to believe that they'd been separated for over a year. Ned felt like he'd just seen Wanda that morning, reminding him to take the garbage out on his way to work, which he would inevitably forget anyway. No, he'd come to the

Somerton cabin alone, free from company in all forms. Even his kids hated it. They were all into tech and video games now, things Ned couldn't quite wrap his head around even when he tried. He'd woken to an empty room, made himself a slice of plain toast, and cracked open his first beer of the day.

He was on his twelfth now, he thought. He'd stopped counting when he moved from the couch to the lawn chair, watching the crackling embers of his campfire reflect off of his emerald-green bottle in miniature explosions of light. Gerald said something about dropping by, but he didn't specify a time. It was fully dark now, well into the night, with nothing but gas stations and fast-food restaurants still open. If Gerald didn't show up soon, he wouldn't show up at all.

That wasn't the oddest thing. Gerald and Ned used to work together on the oil rigs before Ned developed a bum wrist and made the enthusiastic switch to living off of disability cheques. They'd remained friends for nearly twenty years, the only one of his friends that didn't abandon him in favor of staying in Wanda's good graces. Gerald was loyal if a bit dull.

Ned took a swig from his beer, finding it empty. He sighed, dropping it onto the damp grass with a satisfying *thunk*. There weren't any more bottles outside. He'd need to get one from the fridge.

His bones creaked and crackled as he stood, echoing the noises coming from the ancient lawn chair. He'd won it at a work function back before he was married, and the janky piece of furniture was holding up far better than his joints. Ned shook himself, stretched, and meandered through the back door.

Admittedly, he'd let the cabin fall into an embarrassing state of disrepair since the separation. He didn't remember the last time he'd picked up a broom, or a mop, or thrown out anything. The living room was cluttered with all manner of useless junk, none of which he intended to keep but wasn't quite offensive enough to make him throw it out in a hurry. Wanda would be appalled, and she'd yell something about his father. Ned hated his father, and she knew it. It never failed to come up during their explosive arguments.

The beer was in the fridge, taking up most of the available space. Ned grabbed as many as he could comfortably carry, telling himself he was getting some for Gerald but knowing he wasn't expecting Gerald to actually show up. The beer was for him; he knew it, Wanda knew it, and his kids knew it. Who was he trying to fool? Himself? Yeah, he gave up on that goal a long time ago.

November in Somerton was a strange time of year that manifested in a kind of limbo. It wasn't cold enough to snow, but it wasn't warm enough to enjoy the outdoors. Tonight, though, was teetering more toward winter. Ned almost expected to throw open the backdoor to find a thin sheet of white coating the grass and surrounding trees. No such sight greeted him when he returned to his dying fire, but Ned still felt the urge to pause.

Something was different. He couldn't put his finger on it, but the landscape he'd been nestled in comfortably all evening was disturbed like some wayward creature had darted through the scene and left its footprints scattered in the dirt. Ned did a careful scan, looking for signs that a black bear had wandered into his midst.

One time, Ned wouldn't have been so observant. He had the confidence and stupidity of youth on his side, believing deep in his core that nothing could hurt him. That was idiocy at its finest, and his many years had slowly pushed the invincibility from his bones. He was fragile now, and he couldn't risk letting a wild animal catch him off guard and drunk. He grabbed his phone from his flannel pocket, directing the flashlight in a wide circle. He saw nothing at first, just a collage of trees and shrubs that used to make him feel secure. Now, they were drenched in an element of the unknown that had him hesitating on his back porch.

"Gerald?"

His voice sounded scratchy from disuse, but it rang out clear in the night air. Ned waited, listening for an answer that he wasn't expecting to come. Gerald had likened himself to a bull in a china shop on more than one occasion; he was a man who was difficult to miss. Sneaking around Ned's property wasn't exactly one of Gerald's signature moves.

"Is someone there?" Ned tried again. If it was an animal, hopefully, the sound of his voice would scare them off. If it was a human and they were lost, then they could ask for help. If it was a human that meant him harm, well, then at least they'd know he heard them coming.

He was still on the porch, just three steps from the back door should trouble crop up. He couldn't stay there all night, though. He'd have to move at some point.

"I don't want any trouble," he said, louder this time. "I'm just going to douse this fire, and then I'm going inside."

His foot was nearly clear of the worn wooden steps when the crunch and snap of leaves caught his attention. Ned stumbled, off-balance with alcohol and anxiety, and then he heard Gerald's clumsy laugh bouncing off the tree trunks.

"Getting paranoid in your old age?" Gerald's voice came from Ned's right. He turned just in time to see his old friend rounding the corner of the cabin, following the trail from the driveway. "I just stopped to take a leak."

"Was it the longest piss in the county or what?" Ned snapped, adrenaline making him irritable. Gerald only grinned.

"Took me a while cuz it's colder than a witch's tit out here."

"Jesus." Ned laughed breathlessly, running a hand through his thinning hair. "I must be losing it. I didn't even hear you pull up."

"I parked a little up the way," Gerald answered, reaching for one of the beer bottles still balancing in Ned's arms. "Your drive is too overgrown for the new wheels."

Right. Ned had forgotten that Gerald finally bit the bullet and bought himself a new rig— his dream rig, straight from the John and Horace Dodge assembly line.

"You should come up and take a look at her," Gerald gushed, cracking open the beer with his canine. "It's a bit dark now, but in the morning. I just got her waxed."

"You only got her two weeks ago," Ned said, chuckling. "What are you doing to her that she needs a wax already?"

"That's between a man and his truck. Ain't none of your business, Eddie."

Ned didn't know what quip was about to come out of his mouth— at this point in the night, he'd open his lips and let the beer decide if he was going to move on, or roast Gerald for his questionable relationship with his truck. As the words bubbled in his throat, Ned caught sight of something he didn't quite understand, something that brought all previous thoughts to a full and complete stop. It was like a spot of ink had bloomed on Gerald's shirt, just above his navel. Some feral instinct buried deep in Ned's subconscious stirred warily, knowing that something was wrong with that spot without ever knowing why.

"What—?"

His question drowned in a deafening crack that split the very air around them, electrifying the hair on his arms to rapt attention. Gerald looked down at the stain on his shirt in confusion, his brows knitting the wrinkles on his forehead into an intricate web of taut skin. The cracking sound vanished as quickly as it had come, and the remaining silence was loud enough to make his ears ring. Thunder? This time of year? Ned's first thought, ridiculously, was of the satellite dish. Would it act as a lightning rod, setting the cabin ablaze? His shirt had more than a few splotches of beer down the front; would it be enough alcohol to set *him* on fire? Lost in his momentary panic, Ned only returned to reality when Gerald moved, his knees buckling just enough to make him stumble. Ned looked up, confusion slowly ebbing away to shock and, eventually, fear.

Gerald clutched his stomach, the stain spreading through his fingers. As the fire flickered brighter, Ned could see that the spot wasn't black like he'd assumed, but bright, offensive red. Two beats of quiet followed the revelation, and then Gerald's mouth opened to unleash a horrid, guttural scream from the very depths of his chest. The sound was inhuman, threaded with terror and pain and desperation. He stumbled forward, doubled over, and collapsed to his knees with a sickening thud. Ned stood frozen, transfixed by the scene unfurling before him in a series of incomplete shadows. Gerald was on the ground, his blood seeping into the grass, his torso impaled on the hooked claw of a creature born of childhood nightmares.

The monster regarded him silently, its claws piercing Gerald's writhing flesh. His screams deflated into wet gurgles coughed between gasps for air. Ned had lost feeling in his legs, his armload of beer bottles scattered around his feet in shards of broken glass and globs of foam. He didn't remember dropping them.

With only the firelight illuminating the yard, Ned couldn't see the creature with any clarity. It hovered at the edge of the orange glow, its true shape marred by darkness. All Ned knew for certain was that it wasn't of this world, not as he'd lived it.

The creature broke its held stare, jerkily directing its attention at Gerald's body convulsing in the wet grass. His fingers clutched at the dirt and weeds, desperately trying to free himself from the grip of the creature, but his attempts were futile. One claw had shot clean through his torso, the others were embedded deeply enough that Ned couldn't guess at their length. It watched Gerald struggle for a breath, watched the fight to live consume what little energy remained in him. For a moment, Ned thought the creature would simply wait for Gerald to exhaust himself, but he was wrong. When Gerald's cries gave way to one final bellow, one last plea to the universe to spare him, the creature moved. It was so fast that Ned thought he'd imagined it, and then the grass was splattered with crimson blood and thick, gelatinous chunks of what used to be his friend. The creature's claws sliced easily through Gerald's skin, ripping him apart limb from limb. A terrible, squelching snap sounded as the creature pulled its claws free of the remnants of Gerald's corpse, scattering flesh and bone and blood in a wide arc that stained Ned's back porch.

He should've been running. Ned knew he was kissing his life goodbye by standing here and watching the show, but what else could he do? He couldn't outrun this demon, that much he knew for certain. He couldn't block him out or barricade the door. For Ned, death was as certain as the moon hovering just above the distant tree line.

As the creature stalked toward him, bored now with the dismembered, lifeless carnage that had once been Gerald, Ned knew his time was up. Death had found him, and all he could do was close his eyes and welcome it.

Chapter Ten

SAM

Even in the fall, the sun rose too early.

Sam wasn't shy about being a morning person, but today he wished the night would drag on just a little longer. He could feel the chill in the air, see the condensation on the bedroom window, and he knew the lawn would be crusted over with frost until at least noon. The urge to make himself a coffee and wait for Amelia to rouse on her own was overwhelming. On a normal day, he could extract himself from the bed without worrying about disturbing her. This wasn't a normal day, though.

Amelia had a nightmare last night.

It was maybe four in the morning when he woke to her screaming, struggling beneath the blankets like she was fighting for her life. In her mind, she probably was. Sam moved quickly, the entire process so deeply ingrained into his muscles that he was acting before he was fully conscious. He removed the blankets from her, freeing her, and began the slow process of calming her down with gentle, unrestrictive touches to her arm, her hair, her face, all the while speaking in low, soothing murmurs. Eventually, her breathing slowed, and she reached for him, huddling into the safety of his arms as she settled back into a dreamless sleep.

Sam hated her nightmares.

Not the process of helping her through them, that was second nature to him by now. No, he hated what they did to her the following day, draining her of her usual energy and leaving her a husk of her normal, lively self. Amelia rarely remembered her nightmares and even more rarely woke up during one, her only clue to her interrupted sleep being the exhaustion she felt the next day. She'd seen a sleep therapist about it once, but his only advice had been to target the trauma that caused the night terrors in the first place. As if she wasn't already doing that.

He sighed, hugging her a bit tighter.

Amelia was nowhere close to waking, as long as he didn't move. Sam had already decided that he wasn't going to tell her about the nightmare, and if she asked, he was going to do his damnedest to feign ignorance. Amelia was always horribly embarrassed by her night terrors, and she was relieved when her medication seemed to deter most of them. Sam couldn't remember the last time he'd woken to her screaming before now. No matter how often he heard it, the sound of Amelia's fear still ruthlessly lanced through his chest, even knowing she wasn't in danger. As badly as he wanted to help more, the best he could do now was make sure she made up for as much sleep as possible before he had to wake her and start their day.

Getting her to accept his help in the first place had been a long, slow-moving process. Sam was constantly battling with everyone in Amelia's past that convinced her she was undeserving of grace, and he'd made a lot of progress over their years of friendship. Convincing her to start sleeping in his room at the apartment so she wouldn't be alone during an episode was his hardest-fought battle to date, and every incident just reminded him how grateful he was to have secured that win. Even before he was in love with her, Sam couldn't stand to see Amelia in pain.

With nothing else to occupy him, the peculiarity of their relationship started playing out in his thoughts.

It *was* strange, he supposed, how close they were without ever crossing that line into a romantic entanglement. Things were just never that simple with Amelia. When they first met, they were kids. Sam liked her because she'd lob his teasing right back at him as opposed to his sister who'd just cry and tattle to their parents. By the time they were in high school, she was his little sister's best friend. She couldn't be *his* best friend, because he was a guy and a junior and she was a girl and a freshman. Sam rolled his eyes at himself. Adolescent social rules notwithstanding, Amelia had been his best friend since the day they met.

When he graduated, he thought things would be easier. Sam's feelings for Amelia hadn't emerged until that summer, but his timing couldn't have been worse. The night he realized he loved her was the same night he found out about her dad, and that changed things for him. *He* changed, something fundamental in his psyche shifted into place and it was like he could see clearly for the first time. Sam was in love with Amelia, and he wasn't anywhere near good enough for her. She deserved the world, and all he had to offer was his small corner of it.

Amelia groaned into the crook of his neck, where her face was buried. Sam squeezed his arms around her, easing her awake.

His small corner of the world was a lot bigger now, he'd been building it up for a long time. It wasn't *everything*, but Sam felt like he had turned himself into *something* worthy of fighting for her heart.

"Why do I feel like I was hit by a truck?" Amelia mumbled, stretching and rolling away from him. He mourned the loss for the few seconds she had her eyes shut, and then he donned his normal carefree smile.

"Sleeping with me does have a tendency to do that," he cajoled, giving her an exaggerated wink. Amelia scowled at him, rubbing the sleep from her eyes.

"Please," she scoffed, "if we ever fooled around, you'd tap out way before I would."

"Wanna bet?"

"You'd lose," she said with a smirk. An image of himself kissing the smirk right off her face flashed through Sam's mind, but he shoved it aside before the evidence of his whims disturbed the sheets. "Did I have a nightmare?"

"What?" Sam blinked, trying to look innocent. "I have no idea. I was asleep."

Amelia let her head tip to the side until she was staring dubiously up at him.

"You are such a shit liar," she said, laughing. "It's fine. I forgot to take my pill yesterday morning. I realized it when I got up to pee last night."

Sam breathed a sigh of relief. At least her night terrors weren't beginning to break through her medication.

"Besides," Amelia yawned, "it's been a weird couple of days. It's not totally unexpected for me to have an episode, right?"

"Right," Sam agreed quickly, delighted that she was assuring herself. Usually, he'd have to tell her all of these things before she'd believe them. *If* she'd believe them. "Don't tell me you've finally accepted that your mental illness isn't a failure of willpower?"

"I'm working on it," she said. Her expression turned pensive. "I *am* sorry I woke you up though. And thank you, for guiding me through it. Don't bother trying to deny it. I only ever go full koala bear when you help me."

Yes, and Sam loved it. The way Amelia clung to him in her sleep, curling into him for comfort, felt more right than anything else in his life.

"Don't be sorry," he reminded her, wrapping an arm around her waist, and hauling her against him again, jostling her until she laughed. "If I didn't have you, I'd be wrapped around a body pillow. Probably one with a questionable image of an anime woman that everyone pretends isn't underage. You're saving me from scaring every girl I bring home out of our apartment."

"That might be more relevant if you actually *brought* girls home anymore." Amelia removed herself from him with an unceremonious shove. "If I didn't know any better, I'd say you lost your game."

"But you know better because I'm dripping in game?"

"I know better because you've never *had* game."

Sam laughed, reaching for his jeans that were thrown over the nightstand.

"I walked into that one," he said, twisting his torso until he felt a satisfying crackle along his spine. "I guess I'll just have to prove to you that I've got game for days. Starting with the best cup of coffee you've ever had."

"I'll believe it when I see it." Amelia tugged his hoodie on over her pajamas and Sam's heart skipped in his chest. He loved seeing her in his clothes. After years of Amelia helping herself to his wardrobe, the sight never failed to appease that primal part of his brain that wanted to stake his claim on her. "Come on Fisher, I need caffeine."

Once they were fed, caffeinated, showered, and properly dressed, Sam revealed to Amelia that he wasn't kidding about subjecting her to the full force of his aforementioned game. Which was all about proving a point, of course. It had nothing to do with his plan to confess his feelings for her on this trip. Nothing at all.

"You want to go out on the lake?" Amelia repeated his suggestion back to him, blinking in open horror. "Sam, it's *freezing!*"

"Barely." He shrugged, nodding at the thermometer suction-cupped to the kitchen window. "Come on, it'll just be for a few hours. The sun is defrosting the place already, and we'll bring a couple of blankets. It'll be nice to hang out on the water for a while."

"You remember that you don't actually like fishing, right?" Amelia said pointedly. "What do you plan to do in a boat for a few hours? Nap?"

"Maybe." Sam thought for a moment. "You can bring a book, and I've got some emails to take care of for Leland. It'll be a nice, quiet afternoon."

Sam could practically see Amelia's resolve cracking. She loved to read, even more so when he was too preoccupied to bug her every five minutes. Leland, his boss, needed some information from the talent scouts he'd been coordinating with over the summer. They were quick, simple emails, so Sam offered to take care of it while he was on vacation.

He also intended to do some snooping about the local regulations on building permits before his mother got impatient with his half-hearted replies and asked him outright what was wrong with the cabin.

"And we'll be back before dark?" Amelia pushed, eyeing him suspiciously. During breakfast, Sam remembered the incident with the birdhouse the night before. He didn't have much to clean up, but the sight of the shattered wood puzzled him. It reminded him of something he couldn't place, and he'd had to shelve it in his mind for the time being.

"Scout's honor."

"Fine," she said reluctantly. "As long as you're driving."

He'd planned on it. Amelia knew how to operate his family's speedboat, but she wasn't a big fan. In the same way, she knew how to drive Sam's motorcycle, but she rarely did so. Sam only insisted on teaching her in case of an emergency.

A short while later, laden with supplies from the tool shed, Sam and Amelia were making their way from the Fishers' cabin to the wharf at the end of cabin road. The docking point wasn't owned or maintained by the town; it was more of a collaborative effort by the owners of the surrounding properties. On their last visit, Sam had replaced several of the deteriorating boards.

They'd just crested the ridge of gravel that divided the lake from the road when Sam felt his phone vibrate in his pocket. He extracted it as carefully as he could, squinting at the message filling his screen.

"Oh shit," Sam said, coming to a sudden stop. Amelia walked right into him, catching herself by grabbing his waist. "Tyler's going back to Chicago."

"Is everything okay?" Amelia demanded, immediately picking up on the worry in Sam's voice. He shook his head, choosing his words carefully.

"Chia had to go to the hospital. She's okay," he added quickly before Amelia could descend into full panic, "she's just been feeling really faint. They're bringing her in for tests. Ty's gone to be with her."

"Do they need anything?" Amelia circled to look up at him, ignoring the weight of the ropes she was carrying. "We can make the trip. Do they need a sitter for Izzy?"

"Chia's mom is there," Sam assured her. "I told Ty to let us know if he needs anything. Right now, I'm sure they don't want to be crowded. You remember how miserable Chia was in her third trimester with Izzy."

Amelia nodded silently. Poor Chia was riddled with aches and pains, heartburn, insomnia, severe mood swings, and intense food aversion during the last months of her first pregnancy. As much as they wanted to help, Sam wasn't sure their presence would be much comfort. Better to let Tyler dictate their involvement.

"Maybe we can order some food to their place?" Amelia said, continuing her walk to the boat. "Ask Ty what Chia's been eating lately. We'll get it delivered. And maybe some groceries? They've got a few food delivery services there, don't they? *DoorDash* or something?"

Sam agreed that was a fantastic idea and he gave Tyler the heads-up before sliding his phone into his pocket and hoisting his bag higher on his shoulder.

"Come on," he nudged her, harder than was strictly necessary, "let's get moving. Ty is going to text as soon as he knows anything."

He'd also sent Sam two cell phone numbers, one for Aaron and one for Nyla, along with the landline for the Willow. For emergencies, he'd said. Sam hoped that wouldn't be necessary.

Amelia stumbled under the force of his shove, nearly dropping the ropes. She glowered at him, puffing air from her cheeks to blow her displaced hair from her face. Sam bit back a smirk, deliberately avoiding her gaze as he made his way casually to the pier. Taunting Amelia was one of his favourite pastimes, no matter how disgruntled she got with him. He was sure she'd get her revenge later, when he'd forgotten her irritation and let his guard down.

What he *wasn't* expecting was the shock of cold that assaulted his ass cheeks as he was bending over the edge of the boat, dropping their backpacks onto the waterproof tarp that shielded the vessel from the weather while not in use. Sam yelped in surprise and discomfort, lurching forward and tumbling into the hull. It rocked violently, making it almost impossible for him to remove the frozen water bottle Amelia shoved down his pants.

"Serves you right," she said, looping the ropes over one of the dock's posts. Sam finally retrieved the ice-cold bottle, dropping it onto the pile he'd made near the boat's bench seat. Wickedness flashed across his face, an expression that Amelia caught way too late. Her eyes widened in fear, taking a hurried step away from him, but he was faster. Sam lunged from the boat back onto the dock, hooking his arm around her midsection and hoisting her into the air.

"Sam! Don't!" Amelia screamed, flailing in his grip. Sam ignored her, waltzing to the edge of the pier and dangling her over the choppy water. "*NO! SAM!* Don't you dare! I—"

He jostled her, her desperate reprimands dissolving into another terrified scream. Sam bit back a laugh.

"You really need to watch who you pick fights with," he said smugly. Amelia's fingers clutched his bicep fiercely, almost bruising. Sam didn't mind. Another time, he absolutely would've dropped her into the frigid lake. Her fear and distrust of him were warranted. Now, though, Basin Lake had shrunk slightly since their last visit, and he couldn't be sure she wouldn't hit her head in the shallow water if he let her go. Instead, Sam loosened his grip and spun in the same motion, sending Amelia flopping into the hull of the boat. She grunted as she collided with the tarp, pushing her hair out of her eyes, and glaring balefully up at him.

"That hurt, you dick."

"Come on Amy Baby." Sam thumped into the boat after her, making it lurch in the water and ignoring her protests. "We're losing daylight."

Chapter Eleven

INTERLUDE

The Basin

The sun had barely crested the treeline surrounding Basin Lake when Aaron's SUV crunched to a stop in front of the bright yellow police tape cordoning off the driveway. From here, the scene looked innocuous enough, but Aaron knew better. He'd seen too much death not to recognize it even in the most unlikely of places. There was something in the air, something intangible that made the world feel *wrong*. Like the sky was tilted, or sounds whispered too quietly through the maze of investigators and morbidly curious onlookers.

Nyla fidgeted in the passenger seat, and he felt a pang of sadness that she'd come to recognize it too.

Aaron surveyed the crowd, looking for anyone he recognized. Not a single suit stood among the uniforms, and he breathed a tentative sigh of relief.

He hoped— no, he *prayed* that Kelley hadn't arrived on the scene yet. Her ice-cold reception of them at the party massacre crime scene the day before had been more than enough to confirm that she was still angry at him. Aaron couldn't blame her, and normally he'd give her space to cool off before attempting to push more of her buttons. He didn't have that luxury, not after what they'd seen.

Neither he nor Nyla had said as much out loud, but they both knew. The sense of dread settling over them was palpable.

There was another Chehwinoo.

He'd known the moment they manipulated their way into the clearing before Kelley spotted them and all but pulled her gun and threatened to shoot Aaron if he didn't get the hell off her crime scene. The bodies had long since been moved, but there were other signs. The plunging cold that coated the scene, the layer of frost that was permanently bonded to the surrounding trunks and packed dirt.

And the destruction. He couldn't forget that.

Over the summer, Aaron had inspected a trailer that was torn apart by the Chehwinoo. It was pure chaos, like a tornado had speared a tree limb through the roof and left nothing but scars as evidence. The clearing was worse. Much, much worse. A natural disaster was the only way he could explain the carnage, even knowing that wasn't the case. Trees were slashed almost in half, splintered branches and trunks littering the ground, and deep gouges in the dirt making the terrain treacherous. Aaron had never seen anything like it. It was as if a giant spinning top was dropped from the sky, outfitted with jagged blades and fractured metal, and wreaked havoc on the clearing. It was both beautiful and terrible at once.

This crime scene didn't appear nearly as dramatic, but they hadn't made it to the backyard yet.

It was a stroke of pure luck that they were here before Kelley and her team. Pratt stopped by the station in the early morning hours to inform Sheriff Mason that he'd be unavailable for the next two nights, and that was when the call came in about Edward Bolt and Gerald Dannie. Mason was too flustered to explicitly tell Pratt not to contact Aaron with the tip, so he and Nyla arrived just after the sheriff himself, alighting from his squad car just as they came into view.

Nyla wasn't overly happy about having to deal with George again so soon, but Aaron was just glad that they weren't faced with a standoffish Mason *and* a vindictive Kelley.

"Do you think he noticed us?" Nyla asked, staring hard at the front door of the cabin where Mason had vanished. Aaron shook his head.

"He would've waited if he did," he said with confidence. Pushing open his door, Aaron stepped purposefully out of the X5. "Wait here. I'm going to walk around the side of the building."

If Mason was inside, then that was where Aaron *didn't* want to be. Nyla nodded, scanning the onlookers for someone she could probe for information. He fought back a smile. He may have convinced her that he was more likely to successfully infiltrate a crime scene on his own, but that didn't mean she was going to let him do all the heavy lifting. Aaron had no doubt that when he returned, Nyla wouldn't be in the SUV.

As he carefully and determinedly made his way from the driveway to the backyard, Aaron formulated his plan. This early, the bodies wouldn't have been moved. Crime scene analysts were undoubtedly sorting through each blade of grass with a fine-tooth comb, which meant that he couldn't barrel his way into the center of the action. He'd have to start on the peripheral, carefully moving his way in.

At the corner of the back porch, he spotted his first target.

The officer was leaning against the railing, too stiff to be bored but too casual to be at rapt attention. Not a new officer, then, and not a jaded senior. Aaron guessed the man was a handful of years into his position, beginning to toe the line of acceptable nonchalance and outright laziness. He was also sweating, beads of moisture glinting off of his bald scalp in the morning sun. His weathered face was pale, and he was methodically chewing a wad of electric blue gum that was so large, each bite forced his lips open. A nearly empty water bottle perched on the railing near the officer's elbow, and Aaron surmised that, in all likelihood, he'd thrown up at the sight of the scene and was taking a break to collect himself.

Perfect.

"Gravol?"

The officer blinked up at Aaron in surprise, jumping to attention. Aaron held out his badge, too quickly for the officer to notice that it was a PI identification and not FBI, and the officer relaxed.

"How'd you know?" he asked with a shaky laugh, accepting the proffered pill bottle. Aaron smiled knowingly.

"Not my first rodeo," he said, sniffing. "Never gets easier though, does it?"

"You got that right," the officer slumped back against the railing, downing the rest of the water bottle. "I don't know what the sheriff is gonna do. He got damn lucky with those kids, but he's already got an audience for this one. No way this stays out of the news."

Aaron paused, choosing his words carefully.

"I still don't know how he managed the gag order in the first place," he said, shaking his head. "A decade with the Bureau and I've never seen anything like it."

"Luck," the officer repeated. "There ain't no cell service outside town lines. Most of those kids were dead before they reached the road. Couldn't even get a 'goodbye' text out to their folks. Damn shame."

"You'd think the survivors would be more vocal," Aaron shook his head again, emphasizing his disbelief. "A bunch of teenagers and twenty-somethings actually cooperating with the cops? I wouldn't bet the farm on it, that's for sure."

"You and me both," the officer chuckled. "But Mason's smart. People like him, not like Bill, God rest his soul. He sat down with each one and their families, convinced them that it was dangerous to go public about the massacre until the investigation was over. Helps that only a few of them made it out, and none of them were close enough to see what happened anyway."

Fuck, Aaron thought. *There goes that avenue.*

"His luck would've gone further if there were no survivors at all," the officer continued, and Aaron had to stop himself from openly glaring at the man in bewildered shock. Realizing how his statement sounded, the officer rushed to clarify, "those woods looked like a hurricane ripped through it. Mason was going to try to spin it as a natural disaster until the surviving kids showed up."

"Think this is related?" Aaron asked, jutting his chin toward the cabin. He could see more people beginning to shuffle, clearing his view of the yard enough for him to recognize the presence of blood. A lot of blood.

"Beats me," the officer sighed. "Hard to say when we have no leads on either case. Mason's about to pop a blood vessel."

"It's a frustrating position to be in."

"He doesn't help himself," the officer said with a snort. He turned to Aaron with a conspiratorial look. "Jameson has really gotten under his skin. I don't know why he keeps going to talk to her when she obviously doesn't know shit about all this. If she did, she'd be bragging about it all over town. Bunch of the guys think he's getting his dick wet, but I've never met her so I can't say if she's pretty enough for the trouble."

A muscle twitched in Aaron's jaw, the only betrayal of his surging irritation.

"Keep the Gravol," Aaron grunted, clapping the officer on the back with more force than was strictly necessary. His face paled a fraction more, and a placating wave of satisfaction smoothed Aaron's tense expression.

He wound his way through the scene as discreetly as he could, alternating between eavesdropping and engaging. By the time Mason spotted him and thundered in his direction, Aaron had a fairly comprehensive idea of what happened.

"What the hell are you doing here, Klein?" Mason snapped, lowering his voice to a harsh whisper. He no doubt realized that Aaron had already gathered as much information as he could, and drawing attention to the fact that he wasn't supposed to be there would only serve to undermine Mason's authority. Aaron stood his ground, donning a mask of indifference.

"I don't believe I've ever been relieved of my consulting duties, Sheriff," he answered calmly. All the same, his attention shifted to the porch, where German and Andrews were assessing the scene. Kelley wouldn't be far behind.

Her team was loyal to her, but they were still Aaron's friends. He wasn't worried about German and Andrews ratting him out, but he wasn't expecting a warm greeting either.

"That's a crock of shit and we both know it," Mason grumbled. "Look, you got what you want. Now get out."

"I thought you wanted our help?"

Mason's eyes narrowed.

"I want your information," he clarified. Aaron smiled tightly.

"They're a package deal, I'm afraid."

The anger in Mason's eyes simmered and cooled in the span of a few seconds. He opened his mouth to speak, thought better of it, and instead stomped back to the cabin to continue his work.

Aaron extracted himself as quietly as possible.

When he returned to the X5, sure enough, Nyla wasn't there. He found her quickly, engaged in an animated discussion with an elderly woman who was craning her wrinkled neck at every angle to get a glimpse of something. Anything. Aaron cleared his throat just loud enough for Nyla to hear, and then she was joining him in the SUV.

They were silent until the last of the squad cars faded into the background, and then they shared what they'd found. Aaron told her how Mason had managed to keep the Halloween party massacre out of the press, which she corroborated with her knowledge of the survivors. They were local and young. If Mason had impressed the importance of their silence on them well enough, she believed that they would comply. The older woman she'd been talking to was the grandmother of one of the party victims, and she confirmed that Mason had asked all of the families to keep any information to themselves while the police looked into the tragedy. They'd formed a support group among themselves in the meantime, but they were getting restless. Information was starting to leak, and soon it would be a flood.

He also told her what he could of the scene at Edward Bolt's cabin. The ground had been covered in tarps and evidence markers, so he couldn't get a clear view of everything, but he'd seen enough. Edward and Gerald had been eviscerated in the middle of the night, and the chill in the air was enough to confirm that they were dealing with yet another Chehwinoo attack.

"This is getting out of control a lot quicker than last time," Nyla said, whispering. "We need to take care of this before anyone else gets hurt."

"We'll do what we can, *mi tesoro*." Aaron laid his hand comfortingly on her thigh, smoothing the exposed skin below the hem of her shorts with his thumb. "Our job is harder this time. We have more eyes on us. We have to be careful, or we won't be able to do anything at all."

"I know," Nyla bit her lip, staring out the window as they arrived at the Willow.

"We'll figure it out," he promised, lifting his hand from her thigh to gently grip her chin, turning her toward him. "Or, more likely, we'll die trying."

He kissed her even as she laughed, rolling her eyes at him.

They sat in heavy silence for a while, until the X5 was off for so long that the radio cut out on its own.

"So…" Nyla began, averting his gaze. "Sam and Amelia… they seem nice."

"They do," Aaron agreed cautiously.

"You met them before?"

"Once." A toddler's birthday party wasn't exactly a great place to get to know someone, but Aaron recalled their brief conversations being pleasant enough. "Why?"

"Just curious," Nyla said, shrugging. Aaron knew *that* was a lie. "Pratt grew up with them, right?"

"Yes."

"So, he probably trusts them a lot, then."

"I'm sure he does."

They stared at each other, an immovable object and an unstoppable force on a direct collision course.

"Why don't we—"

"Nyla, *no.*" Aaron huffed, dropping his head back against the seat. "We talked about this."

"We could use the help!" she argued adamantly, removing her seatbelt and twisting to face him, crossing her legs underneath her. "Besides, they're in danger! We should tell them the truth!"

"*Everyone* is in danger," Aaron pointed out. "We can't tell the whole town."

"But they're literally in the thick of it." Nyla pouted. "Sam's cabin is *three lots* down from Edward Bolt's! They're practically on top of the creature."

"How do you know where his cabin is?"

Nyla blinked, straightening her shoulders before answering.

"I looked it up."

"You looked it up where?"

"Wherever you look up stuff like that. Town archives or something."

Aaron raised an eyebrow.

"You're telling me you were granted access to the property blueprints for the town? *And* the landowners?"

"I have my connections," she said, nodding matter-of-factly.

"Do I want to know?"

"No."

Aaron huffed a disbelieving laugh, dropping the subject before he was made privy to something he shouldn't be.

"*Mi Cielo,*" he said softly, brushing Nyla's hair back from her face. "I'm sorry. I know you're worried about them, but we can't. We told them to stay inside after dark, and that's the best we can do. There's a reason this whole situation is on a need-to-know basis. As of right now, they don't need to know."

Nyla snapped her jaw shut on whatever she was about to say, settling for looking troubled.

"How about this," he prodded. "Do you want to invite them over tomorrow night? We can ask them to stay over, watch a movie or something. That way we can make sure they're safe for at least one night, and hopefully they'll get to know us better and be more likely to heed the warning. Okay?"

Nyla smiled gratefully at him, leaning her cheek against his palm. Aaron's heart did a small flip in his chest.

"Okay," she agreed, unraveling herself to finally emerge from the X5. "But if anything even *remotely* weird happens, we're telling them. Deal?"

With a chuckle, Aaron followed.

"Deal."

Chapter Twelve

SAM

"Do you think Rox still believes there's a lake monster out here?"

Sam lifted his head from his almost-nap, looking to where Amelia was curled against the poorly cushioned bench with her book hanging limply in her hand. She was staring out into the water, amusement twitching her lips into a nostalgic smile.

"Probably," Sam said, shrugging. "She still believes Mom and Dad's basement is haunted."

"I'd believe in a lake monster before ghosts." Amelia turned her attention back to him, stretching her legs. "Think about how much of our ocean is unexplored. We know more about the surface of Mars than we do about our own planet."

"Sure, but this isn't the ocean. It's a lake."

"I didn't mean *this* lake monster. I was speaking generally."

"Like Loch Ness?" Sam pursed his lips, staring at the sky. They'd been on the lake for hours now, exploring the limits of the shore and relaxing intermittently. Amelia had burned through more than half of her book, and Sam caught more than a few Z's once he was caught up with work. They'd been out there so long that the crystal-clear light of the sun was slowly fading to the brilliant orange of early evening. "What do you think it would taste like?"

Amelia sputtered a surprised laugh.

"You want to *eat* the Loch Ness monster?" When Sam didn't correct her, she laughed in earnest. "What is wrong with you?"

"We eat everything else," Sam argued. "If we ever discovered lake monsters were real, someone would definitely try to eat it. Why not me?"

"You don't like seafood."

"I like some seafood."

"You like fish and chips. That barely counts."

Sam scrunched his nose at her, unfolding his arms from behind his head and stretching until his shoulders cracked.

"Speaking of food," he mused, "I'm starving. Any granola bars left?"

Amelia held up the empty backpack, shaking it to show him their lack of food.

"We should head back anyway," he said, swinging his legs off of the opposite bench. It wasn't the most comfortable place to nap, but Sam had slept in weirder places. "If we stay much longer, we won't make it back before dark."

While he trusted Tyler, and Nyla seemed like she was well-meaning enough, Sam couldn't quite bring himself to be wary of nighttime in the Basin. He'd spent too many summers ducking in and out of shadowed trees, playing hide and seek with flashlights, exploring, and all-around thriving in the Basin Forest to feel any fear from it. Amelia, on the other hand, was more conscientious than him. He often likened her to a guard dog, constantly alert and prepared for trouble. As much as he loved pushing her buttons, Sam would never knowingly make her feel unsafe. That was a hard limit.

He started the motor, lazily bringing the boat back to the wharf. Sam liked to drive just about any vehicle with more reckless abandon than he was exhibiting on their return trip, but the long day and cool sun had left him feeling lazy and content. He eased the boat into position, holding it steady for Amelia to hop out and tie it loosely to the pier. They'd be using it again before they returned to Philly, so he wasn't worried about securing it long-term.

As they gathered what was left of their things and compressed them into the empty backpacks, Sam felt a twinge of unease creep up his neck. A cloud passed over the sun, blocking the bright orange rays for a few seconds. The disruption of light was long enough for him to notice just how late it had gotten. Without the direct beams of the setting sun, the Basin was blue with the onset of night. He shook off the realization, hoping that Amelia hadn't noticed the same.

"Is it really quiet out here, or am I just used to hearing the motor?" Amelia asked from the wharf, drawing his attention to the lack of noise. She was right, it *was* quieter than normal. Sam stepped up and out of the boat, shielding his eyes against the sun that had reappeared on the horizon.

"Weird," Sam said under his breath, shrugging and bending to grab their bags. "Maybe it's just a quiet time of day."

"Feels like more than that," Amelia argued. "I mean, I'm sure I'm just being paranoid, but shouldn't we hear some... I don't know, birds or something?"

Yes, yes, they should. Sam furrowed his brow, scanning their surroundings. Nothing appeared out of the ordinary, no stray animals or people, not even a car could be heard passing on the distant highway.

"I'm sure it's nothing," he said, forcing himself to believe it. Amelia and Tyler were making him nervous, that's all. "Come on, let's get back. If I don't get some real food soon, a quiet forest is the last thing we'll need to worry about."

"Do you ever think of anything other than food?" Amelia sighed, giving a last tug on the mooring line before stepping off the wharf and onto the rocky lake shore.

"Not much." Sam threw his arm around her shoulders in a casual gesture, telling himself he was doing it out of habit and not because the sense of danger washing over him was anything more than paranoia. "Food, sex, and sports. And since I'm not working and you're not offering, I gotta focus on the food."

He winked, making Amelia snort in laughter.

The sound of their footsteps crunching through the gravel echoed noisily through the trees. Sam didn't think he'd ever walked so *loudly* before. While he wasn't ready to admit he was nervous, there was a distinctive lack of the usual sounds that filled the Basin. He wouldn't tell Amelia, but he'd be glad to get them both inside.

Not to mention, he was absolutely freezing.

Seriously, when had the temperature dropped? Sam pulled Amelia closer to his side; if he was this cold, then she would be downright shivering. Sure enough, at the press of her body against his, he felt her trembling. The sun was hanging low in the sky, the orange of sunset fading to the light blue of twilight. The change came with a familiar chill, but this was different somehow. Sam felt like he'd walked into a freezer or had been transported to the North Pole.

And he still couldn't hear anything.

The combination of unsettling cold and unnatural calm put Sam on edge, which made him annoyed on top of wary. The Basin wasn't a scary place, it was his childhood retreat. It was his safe space, his haven. He wasn't going to let a freak accident and a greedy corporation ruin some of his most treasured memories.

He was about to make a joke to alleviate his own tension when Amelia's startled inhale brought his attention sharply to the treeline, where the clear silhouette of a man was weaving between the trunks. Sam immediately abandoned every imagined threat, taking two large steps to place himself between Amelia and the possible, tangible threat in front of them. She pulled out her phone, and Sam knew she was preparing to call for help if things went sour. Normally, he'd think they were both overreacting, but his unease coupled with the strange stillness of the Basin reminded him just how dangerous a man alone in the woods could be.

"Can we help you?" Sam called out politely, making the man jump. He was prepared for trouble, but he didn't want to assume anything until he had concrete reason. The man spun to face Sam and Amelia, tripping over a tangle of underbrush as he tried to free himself from the shadow of the trees.

"I should be asking you the same," the man said in retort, clearing the worst of the terrain and straightening to recover his dignity. Sam performed a brief appraisal of his appearance— he wasn't dressed for hiking. The man wore jeans and a navy button-up with a logo embroidered on the front pocket. Sam couldn't read it from where they were standing, but the radio clipped to the man's belt and the waterproof clipboard in his hand gave him away. This man was undoubtedly a contractor for Stamkos & Stein. "This is private property."

"Bullshit," Sam snorted before he could stop himself. Amelia pinched him, hard, in the elbow. Sam ignored the warning, his irritation at the company for putting his family in a compromising position reigniting all at once.

He'd found only cursory answers during his informal research on the lake, the spotty service making for a difficult deep-dive into Wisconsin permit laws. He'd bounced from state, to federal, to municipal regulations, finding aggravatingly little in the way of options. Without a copy of S&S's contract with Somerton and the specifics of their permits, Sam couldn't do much. The helplessness made him impulsive, and he had the white-hot urge to demand to talk to this man's supervisor and get right to the root of the problem.

Luckily, Amelia knew better.

"Cabin county stretches from route 9 to the other side of Basin Lake," she cut in, sensing correctly that Sam wouldn't remain civil if he took the lead. "If anything, *you're* the one trespassing."

The man puffed his chest indignantly, tapping his clipboard.

"I have a permit here that says otherwise," he slapped the board with more force, "so I'm going to ask you two to move along."

"You're confused," Sam said. Amelia grabbed his elbow again, but he ignored her warning for a second time. "I know the family that owns the cabin over that ridge."

He pointed just behind them, where he knew there was another cabin about a mile into the brush. It was owned by one of his father's business partners, and Sam was certain they wouldn't be quiet about giving up property to a production facility.

"Their land goes all the way to the cabin road." He nodded down at the dirt beneath their feet. "And the road is owned and maintained by the town. So, unless you're the mayor, this isn't your property."

The man bristled, fidgeting with the urge to argue. Sam knew he had nothing, or at least he hoped he did. One of the main components of Sam's job involved dealing with college administration who were used to getting their way through confidence alone. It happened doubly often with him, mostly because his laid-back attitude and friendly demeanor led people to believe he didn't know as much as they did. While that was frequently true, Sam wasn't stupid. He could spot a bluff a mile away and he knew how to call them. This man was definitely bluffing, but he wasn't sure about what. Sam didn't know enough about the bylaws to say for certain that he was in the right, but he was foolhardy enough to try.

"Look, I don't want to have to call my foreman," the man said, clearing his throat uncomfortably. Sam suppressed a grin. Now he was sure that the man had nothing to back up his claims. Threats were always the last-ditch effort to come out on top.

"Please do," Sam challenged, again ignoring Amelia's insistent nudges. They'd become more frequent, but he thought he was doing an admirable job of keeping his cool. "I'd like to talk to your foreman actually. This eyesore of a factory is obliterating the property value of my parents' land."

"Your family owns land here?" The man assessed them again with a more critical eye. Clearly, he'd assumed they didn't own one of the cabins and were just wandering around the lake for fun. "What's your last name? I've been meaning to contact—"

At first, Sam didn't know what happened. One second, the man was talking. The next, the air was vibrating with a crisp, shuddering crack that rattled his bones.

Amelia's now frantic bids to get his attention stopped, and Sam realized she hadn't been warning him to keep his attitude in check. The Basin had gone dark around them, and the night had brought more than an icy chill.

Sam stared, wide-eyed with wonder, as the man was jerked from his feet, his body careening into the dirt 20 feet from where he'd been standing mere seconds ago. Blood arced from a series of jagged wounds on his torso, marking his path through the air before splattering on the earth like thick, red paint. He was dead before he hit the ground.

Amelia screamed, her fight-or-flight taking hold before Sam's. She grabbed his arm, yanking him into action just as he registered the source of the sudden mayhem.

A creature— a *monster*— towered over them from the trees. It was lanky and misshapen, like a child's drawing of a person cast in angled shadows. Sam stumbled backwards, staring in open shock at the monster as it shrieked its displeasure, crimson blood dripping in stringy tendrils from its claws and fangs. It was skeletal, its limbs disjointed, but that didn't seem to slow it down. Sam found his bearings as the creature turned its liquid yellow eyes away from them to the remnants of the man.

"Get to the boat," Sam said under his breath, holding his arm out in front of Amelia and corralling her back the way they're came. "Go! *Run!*"

He didn't wait to see if she'd listen. Sam pivoted on his heel, his grip firm on her upper arm, and tore off down the cabin road. Amelia sprinted beside him, tripping to keep up. Sam wouldn't let her fall, his hold on her compensating for any faults in her balance.

The forest was nearly pitch-black around them, darkness descending with heart-stopping speed now that the sun had dipped below the mountains.

Navigating the road to the lake at night normally warranted a powerful flashlight, but there wasn't time. Sam trusted his muscle memory as the road narrowed to an undefined path through the trees, branches snagging his clothes and hair like bony fingers reaching for him, trying to draw him into their clutches. Amelia screamed as something crashed behind them, followed by a sinister symphony of snaps and cracks.

The monster was done with its last prey. Now, it was after them.

Sam pushed himself harder, drawing on every ounce of strength he had left. Amelia struggled beside him, panting hard, her shoes slamming against the ground and jarring her body so violently that Sam could feel it in his grip. They were almost at the lake now, only a few more seconds—

A tree limb, larger than the average teenager, plunged through the canopy of evergreen branches and barreled towards them. Sam felt the *whoosh* of displaced air with only milliseconds to react, grabbing Amelia by the waist and hauling her into him, both of them tumbling to the ground. He hit the dirt on an angle, rocks and twigs biting into the skin of his hip. Sam swallowed his gasp of pain, focusing on keeping their heads from striking the earth. Amelia scrambled to her feet as they skidded to a stop, pulling her arm free of his hold so that she could help him up.

They were so close. So close to the wharf, he could almost taste it.

He barely felt the gravel shifting under his feet as he skidded down the embankment, landing hard on the wood of the pier. Amelia veered toward the rope to untie the boat, but Sam didn't let her. He grabbed her by the hips and hoisted her into the hull, whipping around to unravel the loose knot Amelia had tied when they docked. The forest shuddered behind him, the creature tearing through the trees at impossible speeds. Sam tried to quickly guess how close it was based on the volume of its approach.

Seconds. He only had seconds.

The rope *thwacked* against the surface of the lake as he pulled it free. Sam positioned himself on the edge of the dock and propped his foot on the engine.

A screech shook the air, stinging his eardrums.

Sam gave the boat a hard shove with his boot, sending it careening into the waves. Amelia caught herself on the steering wheel, pulling frantically at the controls. Even in her panicked state, she remembered his instructions and soon the speedboat was humming to life, ready to take them to the safety of the open water.

At least, he *hoped* it was safe.

"*Sam!*" Amelia screamed, her white-knuckled grip on the throttle hesitating. The boat was drifting away from the dock faster than he'd anticipated, and he still wasn't on it. Sam heard the crunching of the monster's lunging steps loping after him, getting so close he imagined he could feel its icy breath on the back of his neck. He didn't have time to think.

With a three-step head-start, Sam leaped from the edge of the pier.

Amelia abandoned the wheel to reach for him, locking her grip on his wrist as he hit the boat at an angle. The lip of the hull slammed into his ribs, driving the air from his lungs in a strangled gasp. Amelia pulled hard, giving him the leverage that he needed to roll to the bottom of the boat. His legs were soaked through with frigid lake water, but Sam didn't have time to feel uncomfortable. An ear-splitting shriek echoed through the air, and Amelia rushed to take the controls again.

The little boat's motor screamed in protest and smoke, reluctantly dragging them further from the wharf. The creature was on top of them now, its claws stretching from the pier toward the boat. They made contact, tearing a rip through the fiberglass that nearly touched the surface of the lake. Amelia pressed the motor harder, and with a shudder, the boat carried them clear of the creature's grasp.

"Do you think it can swim?" she asked him, her voice fragile in the wind. Sam couldn't answer, stunned into silence for the first time in his life. As he watched, the creature began to pace along the water's edge, plagued by erratic and uncertain steps. Eventually, once it had determined they couldn't be reached without jumping into the lake after them, it turned and skittered into the trees.

From the looks of it, the monster couldn't swim. But that didn't mean they were safe.

Chapter Thirteen

AMELIA

It was a long time before either of them were able to speak. Amelia rarely saw Sam speechless, but his expression was frozen and blank as they both stared back at the shore.

The creature, whatever it was, had run off once they were on the water. It was gone, for now, and Amelia couldn't help but wonder if she'd imagined the whole thing. It was impossible, after all. The creature had been nearly twice her height, emaciated and gaunt, with limbs that stretched and bent like a spider's. Nothing, nothing at all, could explain it.

"What the hell was that thing?" she whispered, unsure if Sam would hear her over the sound of the motor. He shook his head slowly, bringing himself back to reality.

"I— I don't know."

"Was it—?" Her mind shuffled through every possibility, every predator she could name, and none of them bore even a passing resemblance to the creature howling after them as they sped from shore.

"It had to be an animal," Sam huffed, turning off the engine to let them sputter to a stop. They were in the middle of Basin Lake, too far from the shore for any human to swim after them. Amelia didn't know if the same principle applied to the creature chasing them, but it was all they had to go on.

"What kind of animal looks like *that?*" she demanded, harsher than she meant. Adrenaline pulsed through her veins, panic lingering beneath the surface of her skin. *Not now*, she told herself firmly. *Not yet.*

"What the fuck else could it be?" Sam shot back just as harshly, breathing hard. "It's gotta be a— I don't know, something with rabies. Or— or— I don't know, okay?"

"We need help." Amelia pulled her phone from her jeans pocket, pausing on her contacts icon. Her first instinct was to call Tyler, but then she remembered that he was hours away in Chicago with Chia, who needed him more than they did.

"Who are we supposed to call for help?" Sam dropped his head into his hands, taking deep, measured breaths. No doubt, he'd had the same thought process as she had about calling Tyler. "The police will think we're nuts. *I* think we're nuts. So that leaves what, animal control? I think this is a bit more complicated than a stray raccoon."

"We need to call *someone*," Amelia insisted. "A man *died*, Sam. We can't keep quiet about this! Is there... I don't know, is there some kind of wildlife office around here? Do they have an emergency line?"

"I sincerely doubt wildlife usually deals with possessed skeletons with legs."

"All skeletons have legs, Sam."

"What about birds?"

Amelia blinked at him, shock and residual fear slowing the gears in her brain.

"Did you just insinuate that birds don't have legs?"

Sam grunted, crossing his arms over his chest.

"I meant fish. Sue me, I'm not a wilderness expert."

A lightbulb flickered to life in Amelia's mind, hope surging in her chest and flooding her with adrenaline again.

"Give me your phone."

He did without question. Amelia opened his text conversation with Tyler and found two contacts he shared with Sam earlier that day.

"Who are you calling?"

"You might not be a wilderness expert," she said triumphantly, relief coasting through her as the call went through, ringing in her ear, "but Nyla is."

"You think she'll believe us?"

Amelia didn't even have to consider it. Somehow, deep in her gut, she *knew* Nyla would believe them. The ringing continued, driving her anxiety higher with every unanswered tone. It was late, but not *that* late. With any luck—

"This is Nyla! What can I do for you?"

The emotions warring inside her screeched to a halt, tears forming in her eyes as Amelia processed that someone was on the other end of the call. They weren't alone, even if Nyla thought they were crazy.

"Nyla? Can you hear me?"

There was a short pause as Nyla placed the voice. When she spoke again, her voice was thick with worry.

"Amelia? What's wrong?"

The concern only made the tears gather faster. Amelia wrestled her emotions back into place, filling her lungs before even trying to explain herself.

"Uh, that's a bit of a loaded question," she said slowly, glancing at Sam. He was watching with bated breath, supportive but reserved. "Sam and I were out on the lake when... something weird happened on our way back to the cabin."

"Something weird you say?" Nyla's deliberate repetition of her words was clearly directed at someone else in the room, but her tone was still nothing but concerned. *"Is anyone hurt? Where are you now?"*

"We're okay, we're on the lake." Images of the contractor flashed through her mind, and she shoved them down. "There was another man. He stopped us on our way back and while he was talking... I— Nyla, I'm not sure how to explain it and I *know* this is going to sound crazy, but I swear to God I'm telling the truth. Right in the middle of our conversation, this guy was just... he was attacked by something. I don't know what it was. It looked like—" Amelia stopped. She couldn't go any further without really hammering home the insanity of the situation. "He was a contractor for Stamkos & Stein, I think. He was talking about the properties, and he accused us of trespassing, and then there was this loud crack, and he—"

She stopped herself again. She was rambling now; Nyla didn't need to know all of this. She needed the important pieces, and those were the most difficult to spit out.

"Something killed him, Nyla," Amelia whispered, her words catching in her throat. Sam's hand found hers, squeezing reassuringly. "I have no idea what it was. It looked like something from a nightmare, but I know that's not possible. It just happened so fast. One second everything was normal and the next it wasn't. It's like it dropped from the sky."

The line went silent. Amelia cringed, picturing Nyla struggling to process what she was saying, sharing bewildered looks with Aaron and trying to decide if they should call the cops or the psych ward. It was only a few seconds before Nyla spoke again, but it felt like hours.

"*Did it follow you?*"

The quiet seriousness of her tone caught Amelia off guard. She straightened, staring into the waves, and blinking away her surprise. As sure as she was that Nyla would believe them, her immediate acceptance was still jarring.

"The... did it what?"

"*The creature,*" Nyla clarified. "*Did it follow you into the lake? Into the water?*"

"No, no. It stopped at the dock. It wouldn't come into the water." Amelia whipped her head around to look at Sam, who was more shocked than she was. While Amelia had trusted Nyla to listen, Sam hadn't. Her surprise was likely nothing compared to his. "You believe us?"

"*In my experience, people don't generally lie about freaky shit in the Basin,*" Nyla said, sounding bitter. "*Amelia, I need you to listen to me very carefully, alright? How far is Sam's cabin from the shore?*"

"About a ten-minute walk, a little shorter if we beach the boat further up the lake."

"*That's too far to risk. Okay.*" Another short pause, this time with muddled voices in the background. "*I know this sucks, believe me, but you two are going to have to stay on the lake until sunrise. Do you think you can do that?*"

"We don't have enough gas to stay out here all night."

"*Then let the gas run out. Aaron and I will figure out a way to get you back to shore in the morning if we have to, but you cannot under any circumstances leave that lake, do you understand?*"

"I—"

"*Amelia, I need to hear you say it. Say you understand.*"

She felt tears well in her eyes again, faster, and more insistent than before. Nyla believed her, and while that meant they weren't alone in dealing with whatever that creature was, it also meant that they weren't suffering from some sort of joint psychosis. It was real, and Amelia almost wished it wasn't.

"I understand."

"*Good. Okay. That's good.*" Nyla exhaled in relief, more hushed voices coming through the line. "*I'm sorry I can't be of more help right now, but I'll explain everything tomorrow, I promise. Are you wearing jackets? Warm clothes?*"

Amelia took in Sam's water-logged jeans, their meager supplies, and pathetic blankets. She grimaced. It wouldn't be a comfortable night, but...

"We'll manage," she said confidently, trying to convince herself in the process.

"*Call me back if anything changes. I need to go talk to Aaron, but I'll keep my phone on all night, okay? Just hang tight and—*"

"It was never a bear, was it?"

Amelia didn't know where the realization came from, or why she chose now to voice it, but it struck her with such certainty that she knew the answer before Nyla gave it.

"*No. No, it wasn't.*"

The words numbed her, allowing her to ask her next question with an almost eerie detachment.

"Are we going to die?"

"*Not if I can help it,*" Nyla assured her fiercely. "*I'll see you in a few hours. Stay safe.*"

Chapter Fourteen

SAM

Knowing that they were safe on the lake until morning wasn't exactly a comfort, but it did give Sam something to focus on other than his conflicted feelings about what had happened. He'd seen it, felt it, heard it, but he couldn't believe it. With survival on the line, Sam was more than happy to push his existential crisis to the far recesses of his mind and instead fixate on how to keep them alive until the sun rose.

Amelia was several steps ahead of him, as per usual. She operated far better in crisis situations, adapting quickly and stubbornly refusing to falter. He admired that about her, even knowing that the instinct came from unfortunate necessity.

"Take off your pants," she instructed without pausing to look at him. Both of the backpacks they'd been carrying were opened and emptied of their contents, revealing a pitiful assortment of things that would've been more useful if they were stranded and in need of rescue, less that they were stranded and in need of staying put.

"Alright, now we're talking," Sam joked, ignoring his nerves to bring forth his tried-and-true method for dealing with uncomfortable situations. "If I'd have known that a near-death experience was all I needed to get you in my pants I would've orchestrated something years ago."

Amelia paused in her inventory-taking to give him a withering look.

"You're *wet*," she clarified in exasperation. "You can't leave your jeans on all night. You'll freeze."

Sam supposed that made sense, but he didn't see how removing clothes would keep him any warmer. He said as much and was met with a pair of jogging pants hitting him square in the face.

"I always bring a spare," Amelia said. "They're not going to fit you, but they stretch. You can get them on, at least."

"As long as you're alright with getting a full outline of my junk all night," Sam grunted, pulling the jogging pants over his shivering legs. They clung to his skin like saran wrap, the lingering dampness making it even harder to shimmy into the too-small loungewear. "This isn't going to leave much to the imagination, Am."

"I'm sure I'll live," she said, rolling her eyes. "Do you remember if it's supposed to rain tonight? If not, we should put the tarp under us as a buffer from the cold metal. If it is, we'll need it as an umbrella."

"I don't think it's going to rain." Sam finally collapsed onto the bench, eyeing his legs with disdain. It looked like he was wearing tights. "I might prefer freezing to death."

"I think it suits you," Amelia replied with a hint of mischief. "Honestly, this should be your new look."

"You think the guys on the team will be more motivated if I show off the goods?" Sam pursed his lips in thought. "Or is that sexual harassment?"

"If you have to ask, the answer is probably yes."

Cutting off his retort, Amelia stood and set to methodically rearranging the boat, moving things that Sam hadn't even registered they brought. His father wasn't an avid fisherman, but he has some rudimentary gear. Beneath the bench seat closest to her, Amelia pulled out a handful of coarse fibre nets, shoving them into the emptied backpacks to make a sort of cushion. Once that was done, she spread the tarp along the hull of the boat, taking care not to step on it with her wet shoes. They had two blankets from their afternoon of relaxing on the lake, neither of which were particularly warm. They were only throw blankets, meant to fight off the chill in a dark living room, not the Wisconsin wilderness. It was better than nothing, though. Amelia piled them against the bench seat with the cushions, shifting her attention to the rest of the boat. She looked around, growing more confused the longer she looked.

"What?" Sam prompted, standing. "What are you looking for?"

"An oar," she explained. "We should save whatever gas is left so we can dock in the morning, so we'll need an oar to keep us from drifting too close. You have an oar, right?"

He did, secured in a long, padlocked compartment that ran from the steering to the motor. Sam grabbed the key from the console, swiftly unlocking the compartment.

"It's in here," he mused, rattling the lock free from its hook. He flicked the latch, cracking through the layer of rust, and tried to hang the lock back in place while he searched to free his hands. Before he could, Sam heard a sharp inhale behind him.

"Oh god, Sam."

Amelia's squeak startled him into fumbling the lock. Sam didn't bother trying to catch it; the dread in Amelia's voice was familiar and electrifying. The lock clattered to the bottom of the compartment, lost among fishing poles and rusted hooks, as he whirled to face her.

"It's happening again," she said, her words strained and cracking.

She didn't need to explain, Sam already knew what was going on. He abandoned his search for the oar, crossing the distance between them in a flash.

"Sit down," he instructed, keeping his voice low and steady. Amelia dropped shakily to the bench, her eyes squeezed tightly shut against the roiling surges of panic that were undoubtedly making her nauseated. Sam's eyebrows pinched together as he gripped her arms, anchoring her. "Do you have any Ativan?"

"At the cabin," she answered softly, her breath beginning to waver. In a moment, she'd be hyperventilating. "It's expired anyway. I don't— I don't know if—"

Her words cut off with a stuttering gasp. Sam smoothed the goosebumps along her arms, watching her expression for signs of an incoming fit of vomiting. Amelia didn't always throw up in the midst of her panic attacks, but the last one was so long ago that Sam almost expected it this time. He braced his elbows on the outsides of her knees, putting light but consistent pressure on her legs.

"Lean forward, come on," he coaxed gently, reaching behind her neck to guide her forward. Amelia came willingly, dropping her forehead to her knees as she vibrated with each inhale. Sam rubbed soothing circles over her back, hunching forward so that he hovered over her like a shield, keeping her warm and helping her feel secure. He waited, giving her a chance to calm down with her own willpower. After 30 seconds of shuddering, he knew she needed help. The chest pain would start soon, followed by dizziness. He needed to bring her out of the attack before that happened; they both needed a clear head to get out of this alive.

Sam reached over the side of the boat, through the crack that the creature had made with its claw. He scooped icy water into his palm, brushing Amelia's hair from her neck with his other hand. Quickly, without warning her, Sam pressed his frozen hand to the sensitive skin of Amelia's neck, letting the residual water drip down her back. She gasped sharply, jolting her entire body in surprise, her skull driving into his stomach. Sam braced himself, hanging on until the shock passed and Amelia started to breathe normally again.

"Thank you," she murmured into his shirt, still shaking. "I forgot about the cold-water thing."

Sam nodded silently, running his palm along her back in long, firm strokes. It was another long battle to get her to accept his help in the first place, insisting that it was her mental health so she would handle it. Eventually Sam convinced her she was being stubborn for the sake of it, doing his own research on what he could do to ease the burden of her attacks. A shock of cold water to the back of the neck was a last-ditch effort, but these were extenuating circumstances.

Slowly, the tension seeped from Amelia's muscles and Sam felt like he could release her. With the stabilization of her anxiety, Amelia's panic attacks had completely abated. After a brief resurgence following her father's death, Sam had truly hoped they'd seen the last of them. Under the circumstances, he wasn't surprised that another had surfaced.

"Fuck that thing," she cursed, pulling away from him to wipe her nose in the collar of her t-shirt. "As if this night could get any worse."

"You took your meds this morning, right?" Sam was reluctant to let her go completely, leaving his hand resting on her knee.

"Yeah, I took them," she assured him. Sam relaxed at her words, though he knew her daily pills would do nothing to stop another attack if one decided to make an appearance. At least she wouldn't have to combat the more regular symptoms of her anxiety come morning. "This is so stupid. I can run for my life with a giant hell creature chasing me, escape on a speedboat, and set up camp for the night, and I'm all good. The second things actually start to calm down, full panic. What's that about?"

He knew she didn't actually want an answer, but Sam felt compelled to give one anyway.

"Anxiety doesn't make sense all the time, you know that." Now that Amelia was back to herself, Sam resumed his search for the oar. The worst thing he could do was start walking on eggshells around her— it took him years to convince her that her anxiety was nothing to be ashamed of, he wasn't about to ruin her progress by babying her when she didn't need or want it. "To be fair, you kept it together until probably the best time to have an attack."

"Gold star for me."

She stayed silent while he searched, collecting herself or berating herself, Sam couldn't be sure. Amelia broke her silence as he crouched, a snorted laugh meeting his ears followed by the unmistakable sound of a phone camera shutter.

"This is a fantastic angle for you, Sammy Honey," she said, her soft laugh lighter than it was moments before. It eased Sam's own tension, unravelling the knot of stress in his gut. "You weren't kidding when you said those pants didn't leave much to the imagination."

"Want me to show you some moves?" Sam wiggled his hips, bouncing his butt cheeks as much as he could from his crouched position. "I call this the Let-Me-Give-You-Crabs Walk."

He shuffled to one side, then the other, until Amelia was choking on her laughter.

"Stop! You're rocking the boat!" she complained, sinking into a cross-legged slouch against the back of the bench. She unfurled a blanket, wrapping it around her lower half while she waited for him to join her. Sam, oar in hand, made his way over to her with exaggerated movements, making sure to involve his legs whenever possible to emphasize the ridiculousness of his outfit. Amelia started laughing again, and the sound was absolute magic. Sam's heart warmed in the light of her smile, almost making him forget the horror of their circumstances.

"On the plus side," he mused, sinking into the hull next to her. Sam draped his arm around Amelia's shoulders, pulling her snugly against him and wrapping his other arm around her in a tight embrace. Already their shared warmth soothed his nerves, and he knew that everything was going to be fine. "It's not like this is the weirdest place we've slept."

"Good point." Amelia leaned into him, burying her face in his shirt. Sam sighed contentedly, reminded again just how right it felt to have her in his arms like this. Someday, he hoped to hold her like this without reservation, knowing that her heart echoed the longing in his. For now, though, they had much bigger things to worry about. Tucking Amelia's head under his chin and adjusting the blankets so they were as covered as possible, Sam settled in to wait out the night.

"PLEASE TELL ME YOU'RE NOT DEAD!"

Sam shot upright, knocking his phone from his lap and startling Amelia awake. She jumped, bumping her forehead against his nose.

"Ow!" She reeled back, rubbing her reddening skin. "What is your skull made out of, Fisher? Concrete?"

"HELLO? DEAD OR BANGING, WE NEED TO KNOW!"

"*Nyla!*"

Aaron's incredulous laughter, nervous as it was, reminded Sam where they were and why. He leaped to his feet with a chorus of cracks erupting along his spine and knee joints. The boat rocked uncomfortably, making Amelia scramble to catch her balance.

"Not dead or banging, although not for lack of trying!" Sam yelled back, waving his arm in a sweeping arc to prove it. He hadn't slept much, too worried that the boat would drift back to shore in the middle of the night to let himself rest, and he was glad for it. In the span of time that it had taken to sneak in a short nap before daybreak, the motorboat had drifted within swimming distance of the dock. He reached behind him for the oar, which Amelia handed him, and propelled them the remaining distance.

As soon as the boat bumped against the crumbling wooden posts, Aaron was extending his hand to help them. Sam insisted Amelia go first, supporting her with his hands on her hips as Aaron pulled her onto the dock. When she was safely on two feet, Aaron released her to Nyla's crushing hug while he turned to give Sam a steadying hand.

"You two must be starving," Nyla said, frowning as she assessed them like she could see the contents of their stomachs from her perusal alone. She let Amelia go to offer Sam a relieved hug too, which he accepted gratefully. She stifled a laugh when her gaze landed on his pants; he'd almost forgotten he was wearing Amelia's. "Um... maybe we should head back to the cabin before we continue this discussion. Looks like you might need a proper change of clothes."

"What? Does this not look good?" Sam asked, incredulous. He spun, giving them a full 360-degree view of his lower half. Nyla didn't bother hiding her laughter this time, and neither did Amelia. She shook her head, folding her arms across her chest.

"Remember our sexual harassment talk yesterday? This counts," she said with a smirk.

"What happened?" Aaron asked, offering Sam his suit jacket. Sam declined, and he extended the offer to Amelia instead. She accepted, shrugging the warm fabric over her shoulders, and sighed in relief. "Nyla told me the gist last night, but understandably it was all a bit frantic."

"Tell us on the way." Nyla gestured to the trees. "I brought the stuff to make pancakes. Let's get you fed before we bring you up to date on our resident Bigfoot wannabe."

Chapter Fifteen

AMELIA

The walk back to the cabin was quieter than Amelia expected, given the wall of information she and Sam shared with Nyla and Aaron. They talked for the first half of the journey, filling in the gaps in one another's memory, until they reached the more maintained stretch of road. Amelia noticed that Aaron and Nyla had herded them away from the site where they'd encountered the contract worker—Blunden Construction, if Aaron's information was good. She tried several times to ask what happened with him, but her questions were deflected with irritating ease.

By the time they were safely indoors, showered, and wearing comfortable clothing that actually belonged to the correct person, Amelia's curiosity was burning a hole through her chest.

"I wanna start off by saying that I'm sorry you guys had to go through all that alone," Nyla said from the stovetop, opening and closing random cupboards as she oriented herself. "Blueberries?"

It took Amelia longer than she cared to admit to realize she was talking about adding blueberries to the pancakes. Sam answered for her, giving his enthusiastic approval.

"Do we need to call the police?" Amelia asked, looking to Aaron. He was leaning against the counter across from where she was seated at the kitchen island. His collected stoicism had fractured a bit since she last saw him, and Amelia could see stress collecting in the muscles of his jaw and neck. "For the man? The... dead guy?"

Amelia idly wondered if she should be more distressed by the fact that she'd seen someone killed not 20 feet in front of her. As it was, the thought made her uneasy, but it was manageable. That made sense, in a twisted sort of way. All her life, she'd lived in constant fear of the worst-case scenario. Now that it was finally happening, she was as prepared as she could be.

"I would advise against it," Aaron answered her, furrowing his brow in thought. "You *could* report him missing, but that would bring unwanted attention to you. It's best to let his coworkers notice his absence and respond accordingly."

"We're not going to report a body?"

Aaron's gaze flickered to Nyla.

"That's the thing," she said on a sigh, flipping the first batch of golden-brown and purple pancakes onto a square porcelain plate. "There *isn't* a body. Aaron and I searched the area on our way to get you. We found a lot of blood, but no body."

"That's—"

Amelia started to say that was impossible, but Aaron picked up where Nyla left off.

"We're not saying we don't believe you," he said quickly. "We do, completely. Everything you've told us is perfectly in line with what we already know."

"Which is what?" Sam cut in, speaking for the first time now that food was in front of him. Amelia snuck a cursory glance at him, which he avoided. Despite everything they'd been through and seen, she suspected Sam was coasting along on a bed of skepticism.

"The creature you saw last night is called the Chehwinoo," Nyla explained, dropping another round of pancakes into the skillet. "It's a monster from Native American mythology. It's born when an angry forest spirit possesses a human host, using the resulting vessel to go on a killing spree."

"Think of it as a sort of ice demon," Aaron added helpfully, "summoned when there's a substantial threat to its home."

"A *demon?*" Amelia repeated dubiously. "Like, Dante's *Inferno* demon?"

"More like *World of Warcraft*," he corrected her. Nyla snorted, rolling her eyes so hard that Amelia could see the action even though she was facing away from them. "The target becomes the creature, losing all sense of self. It only has one goal, and that's to wreak as much havoc as possible before it's killed."

"Sounds more like a werewolf," Sam argued. "Can it turn back, or—?"

"It's not a werewolf," Aaron said agitatedly. Again, Nyla snorted from across the kitchen.

"And it can't turn back," she clarified. Having finished cooking all of the pancake batter, Nyla joined them at the kitchen island. "The only way to get rid of the Chehwinoo is to kill it, but that's temporary. As we've just recently learned, the spirit will possess someone else if its first vessel is destroyed."

"But not just any vessel." Aaron slid the butter and syrup to the center of the island, waiting until Sam and Amelia had filled their plates before taking a pancake for himself. "We haven't figured out how it chooses, but there's some kind of selection process. After we killed the first creature in August, another one didn't pop up until Halloween."

"Halloween?" Amelia thought back to the research she'd done before their trip. Lots of articles speculated about the deaths in Somerton, but none had mentioned other incidents beyond the summer season. "Something happened over Halloween weekend?"

"You wouldn't have read about it," Aaron said, guessing at the source of her confusion. "There was a party at the Stamkos & Stein construction site, illegally of course. Nearly every attendee was killed, but the sheriff jumped on it before the media could get involved. That won't last, mind you. Leaks are already springing on social media. It's only a matter of time before the dam breaks."

"So, okay, wait," Amelia choked down a too-big bite of pancake. It was delicious, and the enjoyment must've registered on her face because Nyla lit up in response. "Start from the beginning. What happened over the summer?"

Nyla began the explanation, telling them about the missing hunters, her trouble with the sheriff's department, and an incident with a regular guest that prompted her to contact Aaron. Aaron picked up the story from there, detailing the more technical aspects of his involvement, the complications posed by his old team being assigned to the case, and their first encounter with the Chehwinoo. Amelia and Sam listened with rapt attention as Aaron and Nyla both described their battle with the creature in the Basin, the accidental death of Bill Hannaford, and their discovery of the monster's den. There, they paused, as if they were holding some information back and weren't sure if it was wise to share.

"I can't believe Ty didn't tell us about any of this," Sam muttered, crossing his arms over his chest, and leaning back in his chair as he digested both the story and the pancakes. Aaron smiled sympathetically.

"I'm sure he doubted you'd believe him if he did," he said gently. "Besides, the less people who know about this, the better. At best, most people wouldn't believe us, and we'd lose all credibility. At worst, cryptid enthusiasts would flock to Somerton and the Chehwinoo would have a field day."

"If it helps," Nyla added pointedly. "I haven't even told my best friend about this. Which is *killing me* by the way." The disgruntled mumble was directed at Aaron, who sighed wearily.

"With the way you and Clary gossip, if you told her in the morning, the entire town would know by noon."

"You're exaggerating."

"You're right, it would probably be closer to brunch."

"Let's say we believe all this," Amelia said, gesturing vaguely to the sky, "where does that leave us? Are you saying we need to find a way to kill this thing if we want to make it back to Philly in one piece?"

"Not at all." Aaron folded his hands in front of him on the counter. "You're free to book the next flight home. We told you the truth of the situation based on Pratt's vouching for you and Nyla's insistence after what you saw last night. We don't expect you to stay to deal with this. We've already killed one Chehwinoo, we can kill another one."

"Pratt's on his way back from Chicago now," Nyla said, shocking Amelia and Sam both. "Chia is fine. She has gestational diabetes, but she's stable now. He's coming back to clue up some things before he takes his leave early."

The way she said it made it seem like she was assuring them that they had all the help they needed, but Amelia caught the slight glint of mischief in Nyla's eye. She was baiting them, and not to leave. She was hoping that Tyler's involvement would get them to *stay*.

And damnit, she was right.

Amelia shared a look with Sam and knew he was thinking the same thing.

Nyla was growing on them.

"If Ty's involved, we're staying," Sam announced with finality. "He's our best friend, and he has a wife and soon to be two children to get home to. We're not letting him face this alone."

"We've been bailing each other out of ridiculous messes since junior high," Amelia said with a smirk. "We're not about to start now."

"This is a bit different than pulling a fire alarm to get someone out of detention," Aaron reminded them. Sam raised his eyebrows in surprise.

"You know about that?"

"He pulled the same stunt in the Academy," Aaron said. "We had an exam that he wasn't ready for. Told me he got the idea from you."

"Can't you get suspended for stuff like that?" Nyla flickered her attention between the two men, shock and amusement forming a wide-eyed smile on her face.

"Sam owed him," Amelia said. "Tyler was only in detention for taking the fall for something Sam did."

"Which was...?"

"Unimportant," Sam said quickly, waving a dismissive hand between them before Amelia could reveal the full story. "Stupid prank, nothing special."

Amelia caught Nyla's eye, silently conveying that she'd tell her about it later.

"If you're going to stay," Aaron began hesitantly. Amelia got the distinct impression that he was hoping they'd go home, but he'd have no such luck. With Tyler in trouble, Sam and Amelia weren't going anywhere. "We should go over some ground rules. Safety precautions, things like that."

"That's a great idea!" Nyla agreed suddenly, pushing herself up from her chair. "Suits? Why don't you take Sam and make sure the property is ready for nightfall. I'll stay here and go over what we know with Amelia."

Aaron seemed to pause at her enthusiasm, but after communicating silently for a moment, he relented. He stood, pressing a soft kiss to Nyla's forehead before nodding for Sam to follow him outside. Amelia watched them go and, as soon as the patio door shut behind them, turned an expectant eye to Nyla.

"Alright," Nyla said with a playful smile. "Now that the boys are out of the picture, I need your help."

Chapter Sixteen

SAM

"The main thing you need to worry about is keeping the doors and windows shut after dark," Aaron said, pushing on the bedroom windowpane. It creaked but held. "The Chehwinoo can't enter a closed dwelling, at least not that we can tell. The literature doesn't explain much either."

"I watched it sever a tree in half with one swipe and it can't bust down a door?" Sam was skeptical, he couldn't help it. Even after everything they'd seen, heard, and felt, he just couldn't bring himself to jump completely on board with the whole 'monster' schtick. Amelia could sense his reluctance, and he suspected that Aaron could too.

"I'm sure it could bust down a door if it tried," Aaron conceded. "The thing is, it won't try. No one has ever been attacked inside."

"You're basing this theory on a lack of murders?" Sam said dubiously. "That's not exactly confidence-inspiring."

Aaron carefully picked his way back through the tall shrubs surrounding the cabin. Back on level ground, he brushed the debris from his jacket.

"Look," his gaze traveled up and down over Sam with a calculating efficiency that made him want to squirm. Aaron was a different kind of authority than Sam was used to dealing with; he held himself with the surety of someone who *knew* they were in charge, not just someone who *wanted* to be. Despite his earlier sentiment, Sam guessed that Aaron could convince him the sky was green with only a firm tone and stern look. "I can appreciate that this is a strange situation for you. Trust me. I was introduced to the Chehwinoo in much the same way you were, and I know how badly you want to believe that there's a logical explanation for what you saw."

Sam dipped his chin in acknowledgment.

"I can't force you to listen to me. I can only tell you that this is *real*. It's real, and it's dangerous. Too dangerous for you to have an existential crisis if reality hits you in the middle of a confrontation with the creature." Aaron laid his hand on Sam's shoulder, holding his attention with unwavering eye contact. "Whatever mental journey you need to go on to accept that this is your life for the foreseeable future, do it on your own time. I risked my life every day for ten years on people who didn't take shit as seriously as they should've. I'm not risking Nyla's on you."

Indignation festered in Sam's chest, and Aaron must've seen it cross his face. He smirked humorlessly.

"Call me dramatic if you want," he said, shrugging one shoulder. Even the nonchalant movement looked refined and smooth. Sam resisted a grumble. "Call me an asshole, a prick, son of a bitch, I really don't care. My job is to keep as many people safe as I can. I can't do that if you're not all in on this."

They remained locked in a silent stare for another second, and then Aaron released Sam's shoulder and slid his hands into his jeans pockets.

"So, what'll it be, Samuel Peter Fisher?" Aaron asked, pausing to let the implications of him inexplicably knowing Sam's full name sink in. "Are you all in?"

Sam wrestled with his temper before he answered. He wanted to believe that Aaron was just being an arrogant dick, exerting his dominance because he got off on it, not because he had a point. He *wanted* to believe that.

The longer he regarded him, though, the harder it became to justify the thought. There was no malice, no enjoyment, no levity in Aaron's face or body language. He was completely, stonily, unshakably serious. His blunt words were a necessity, not because Aaron felt like he needed to be in charge, but because if he didn't say them, people could die. The woman he loved could die.

Which also meant that the woman *Sam* loved could die.

Realization hit him like a punch to the gut. Whatever was happening here, ancient mythological beings or otherwise, people were *dying*. It didn't matter what Sam believed. It only mattered that he was prepared to do whatever he had to do to keep everyone safe. To keep Amelia safe.

"I'm in," Sam said, setting his jaw. Aaron recognized the conviction either in his voice or in his expression because he immediately softened.

"Good," he said. "I hate being a hard-ass."

"So you say, but you've got the attitude down pat." Sam resumed walking, replicating what Aaron had been doing on the next window they passed. He pushed, feeling no give and assuming that was what he wanted. Aaron laughed behind him, waiting farther back on the lawn so he could survey the roof.

"I used to be Pratt's boss," he said with a sardonic grin. "How else was I going to get him to listen to me?"

"Point taken."

They made their way around the complete exterior of the property, pausing occasionally to check the locks on windows and doors. Sam showed Aaron the extensive security system his parents had installed, including the motion-sensing cameras. He was particularly interested in those. They had a recording function, but the clips weren't stored unless he changed the settings. Aaron requested that he do so. Anything they could learn about the Chehwinoo would be helpful.

"You'll feel a noticeable drop in temperature when it's around." They were back at the patio door now, examining the birdhouse that Amelia found on their first night. After inspecting it, Aaron suspected that the Chehwinoo had dislodged it from the tree on its way to the Bolt property up the road, which Sam had to ask for clarification on. He hadn't heard about the murders, and the thought that such a brutal killing happened so close to them set his teeth on edge. "It chills to freezing pretty quickly. Hard to miss. It's weak to fire, and it sounds like it can't pass through water. Nyla and I escaped it by hiding in a small, half-submerged cave, and from what you told us, it stopped chasing you once you were clear of the shore."

Sam remembered the Chehwinoo reaching for them as they sped away, its claws making a sizable rip in the hull.

"It's fast, but you should be able to hear it before it strikes," Aaron continued. "It makes a loud cracking sound when it attacks."

"Yeah, I remember," Sam said, speaking for the first time in a while. He was trying to process everything he was hearing, but he wasn't sure how successful he was. "What is that anyway? It's not its... voice. I heard it scream."

"The cracking comes from its jaw," Aaron said with a grimace. "When it opens, it's like the bones are made of ice. The sound is the ice breaking."

Sam stared blankly. He almost wished he hadn't asked.

"I think that about covers everything." Aaron looked over Sam's shoulder, through the glass patio doors. Whatever he saw had his face twisting in almost comical dread. Sam turned to see Amelia and Nyla engaged in enthusiastic conversation, huddled around something on Nyla's phone. Sam couldn't stop the smile that sprang to his face.

"That looks like trouble," he said, catching Aaron's eye. He shook his head in fond exasperation. "What do you think they're giggling about?"

"Whatever it is, I'm sure it's not good for my blood pressure." Aaron pinched the bridge of his nose between his thumb and forefinger, massaging gently. "Now I need to decide if I'm worried enough to ask."

Sam chuckled, turning to watch Amelia and Nyla through the glass again. Amelia made a sweeping gesture, mimicking something for the story she was telling. Nyla pulled a face of disgust before they both burst into laughter again. Sam's heart throbbed painfully in his chest.

"One last thing," Aaron said suddenly, striding up to the patio door and gripping the handle. With his other hand, he clapped Sam's shoulder, more pleasantly than the first time. "You should tell her."

Panic latched onto Sam's throat, making his voice come out strained.

"Tell her what?"

Aaron said nothing, giving him a disbelieving look that screamed 'are you fucking kidding me right now?' and hauling the door open before Sam could respond.

Chapter Seventeen

AMELIA

"Aaron's probably already figured out that I'm up to something, so we have to talk fast." Nyla pulled out her phone the second that Aaron and Sam disappeared out of view from the patio door, anxiously checking their progress through the windows as she spoke. "I'm going to show you a photo, then I need you to listen."

Amelia nodded, sitting up straighter. Listening to Nyla and Aaron's explanation had satisfied lingering doubts she didn't realize she had, and the relief was quickly morphing into excitement. The puzzle pieces she'd gathered were finally, *finally* fitting into place and things were beginning to make sense. Aaron and Nyla's involvement, the rabies bullshit, the FBI's intervention, everything. It was enough to make her almost forget the danger of the situation. Her instincts had been right all along. She pushed aside the sense of validation, focusing instead on the gravity of Nyla's voice.

"This," Nyla pointed her screen toward Amelia, "is the entrance of a cave. It's not too far from here, just on the other side of that big concrete slab the contractors laid last week."

She paused, allowing Amelia time to take in the picture. It was innocuous enough, more of a rough hole in the ground than a cave.

"Before I tell you about it, I need you to understand that there's no turning back from this point." Nyla dropped her voice to a whisper, still casting nervous glances at the doors and windows. "I know we haven't known each other long, but I'm serious. I'm about to share details that would have Aaron slamming his head against a stone pillar if he knew I was doing this. Can I keep going?"

The silence didn't stretch for long. Amelia liked Nyla, liked her openness, and admired her blind faith. She nodded, and she got the impression that Nyla's hesitance was more from obligation than actual distrust.

Trust was something Amelia had a tumultuous relationship with, and she'd worked hard over the years to get to a point where she wasn't outright hostile toward new people. She learned from a young age that she couldn't trust her parents, and that began a difficult journey of coping with her trauma. In high school, she was standoffish. In college, she was reclusive. Now, Amelia welcomed new people into her life with cautious enthusiasm, but her guard was never far from reach if she needed it. Most of her growth had simply been accepting her own instincts. For as much as she'd doubted them in the past, they'd never actually let her down.

Her gut had decided to trust Nyla after only their second meeting. Apparently, Nyla had made the same decision about Amelia. The difference was the lack of caution on Nyla's face. It made Amelia worry for her. She suspected that Nyla had the kind of trusting nature that would be easy to take advantage of, and Amelia felt a flicker of protectiveness in her chest.

"Keep going," she said firmly. "Whatever comes next, I'm in this for the long haul."

Nyla's face blinked into a dazzling smile, and Amelia couldn't hold back her own in return.

"You remember we told you Pratt was thrown out of the trap when we were fighting the creature?" Amelia nodded again. "Well, we left out some points. He *was* thrown out, but he didn't stay put. When he recovered from the blow to the head, he realized he couldn't get back through the fire and decided to do what he could from outside.

"See, we'd found this cave while we were setting up the trap." Nyla swiped to a new photo, showing a distanced view of the cave. Now, Amelia could see frost and melting snow on the surrounding foliage. "It's the Chehwinoo's nest. Or it *was* its nest. That's how we lured it into the clearing in the first place. We found the cave, and we set up nearby."

Amelia nodded along, concentrating hard. She didn't understand the signifi-cance of what Nyla was telling her yet, but she could feel the weight of it wavering in the air.

"After the Chehwinoo was dead, Aaron and I went looking for Pratt. He was in the cave when we found him, and he told us we needed to get down there ASAP. He'd found something, something really big."

Nyla raised her hand to swipe again but paused.

"Are you squeamish?"

Amelia shook her head.

"No, not at all. Why?"

"I've been calling this cave the Hovel of Horror. It's..." Nyla hesitated, working through something in her mind. Switching tact, she placed her phone carefully down on the countertop. "How much did you know about what happened this summer before we talked?"

"Not much," Amelia admitted. "I looked through a lot of articles online, but I couldn't find anything thorough."

"Right." Nyla bit her lip. "Okay. Well. Maybe that's a good place to start. After I called Aaron for help, we teamed up with a couple of locals I know and tried to piece together what kind of animal would do something like this. All of the bodies up until a certain point had gone missing, so the sheriff's office just assumed something was eating them. Then we found Leo, and things got more complicated."

A sadness draped over Nyla's posture, weighing her shoulders down.

"He was torn apart, but he was all... there. Nothing was missing, I guess is a better way to say it. That was the reason we thought it was a disease-driven rampage. No animal would kill that many targets and not, well, eat them."

"So, when you didn't have any bodies, you assumed it was eating its victims," Amelia summarized, organizing her thoughts. "But Leo proved that it wasn't. Which was weird."

"Exactly." Nyla picked up her phone again, encouraged by Amelia's compre-hension. "That presented a different problem, one we didn't really have time to worry about before. If the bodies weren't being eaten, then where were they?"

She met Amelia's gaze over the phone screen, stress creasing around the corners of her eyes. Amelia knew what she was about to show her before the phone turned.

"Pratt got our answer for us."

At first, Amelia couldn't make sense of the photo. It wasn't blurry, exactly, nor was it overly dark. The screen was splotched with all shades of brown and red, threaded with random pops of colours that were otherwise out of place. Amelia squinted, taking the phone from Nyla's hand, and bringing it closer to her. When the image finally broke through her fog of disbelief, Amelia was barely able to swallow her gasp.

Tyler had found the missing men, alright. He'd found a hell of a lot more than that too.

The first thing Amelia recognized was the ice that encased the cave. It looked like a giant worm had tunneled through the ground, leaving a round path through the dirt that formed a perfect circle of crystal-like ice. Dirt and rocks peppered the surface, muddling the otherwise shimmering blue-white of the cave. Long, finger-like icicles stretched from the ceiling, grasping for the ground below.

Then there were the bodies.

Amelia hadn't lied to Nyla when she said she wasn't squeamish, but her mind still rebelled at the scene in front of her. From the vantage the picture was taken, it was impossible to tell how many people were in there. Not that she could've pieced it together even if she was physically *there*. Limbs protruded from the ice like weeds poking through concrete, flesh black with frostbite, crusted with frost. After staring for far too long, Amelia determined that the large, misshapen patches of red-brown hovering beneath the surface of the ice were more body parts, eviscerated and frozen before the blood could leak onto the floor. Bones and hair completed the carnage, some frozen, some cracked, some loose and scattered across the floor.

It looked like the men had been ripped apart, tossed to the tides, and flash-frozen before the waves could crash onto the shore.

Hovel of Horror, indeed.

"It's hard to look at," Nyla said quietly, gingerly taking her phone back from Amelia. "As soon as we realized what we found, we called the fire department and Pratt's boss. With the Chehwinoo dead, the ice was melting really fast. The hunters... they were, um. Coming loose, I guess."

An image flashed in Amelia's mind of bloated, dismembered corpses breaking free from a quickly-melting slush, toppling to the ground with a nauseating splat. Her stomach churned.

"It wasn't until later that we realized we made a mistake," Nyla said, swiping through more photos. "If we'd just held off another few minutes, we wouldn't have called the authorities until we'd had a more thorough look. There was more in the cave than just the bodies—"

"The artifacts, right?" Amelia cut in, her mind clamoring for something to lessen the severity of what she'd seen. "The broken pots or whatever? I saw an interview."

"Yeah, that little detail wasn't supposed to get out," Nyla said, rolling her eyes. "But nobody tells Adrian Stamkos what he can or can't do."

The venom in Nyla's voice was palpable. The name Adrian Stamkos was familiar to Amelia even outside of this discussion, having popped up repeatedly in her research on Somerton. Adrian and his business partner, Quentin Stein, were co-founders of Stamkos & Stein Pharmaceuticals, but Adrian was clearly the figurehead. Amelia had stumbled across photo after photo of Adrian at press releases, charity events, fundraisers, dinners, and any manner of other public events. The only photo she'd found of Quentin was on his Wiki page and it was clearly a candid from the peripheral of a college lecture hall.

Amelia didn't like Adrian Stamkos. If his responsibility for the destruction of the Basin wasn't enough, his greasy, used-car-salesman attitude would've sealed his place among the people she wouldn't want to meet in a dark alley.

"We found some carvings, some in the wall and some on stones that looked like they may have been tools or containers at some point." Nyla pressed on, shaking off the lingering distaste in the air. "Whatever they were, they all had the same symbols somewhere on them."

She swiped again, and the new picture was of a curved piece of cracked stone with faint, rusty brown lines stretching in all directions. Amelia squinted at the angular pattern until something recognizable began to take shape. When it did, she gasped audibly this time.

It was the Chehwinoo.

A strong likeness to it, anyway. The crude drawing wasn't photorealistic by any means, but it was unmistakably the same creature. She blinked, trying to pick out the implications from the shock.

"These were all the pictures we managed to get," Nyla continued. "The ice was melting, things were... falling. And emergency services were already on their way. We were out of time. We managed to climb out of the cave before the FBI got there, but then we couldn't even get near it afterward. Crime scene cleanup took several days, then the area was warded off."

"Wait, why?" Amelia scrunched her nose, reeling back in confusion. "If the investigation was done, why did they seal off the place? The Basin is public property, isn't it?"

"Well, actually..." Nyla sighed, deflated. "The Basin is, yes, but that cave isn't anymore. That's the crux of the issue."

She shifted in her chair, gathering herself to say what she was about to say.

"With the new permit, the Hovel is now on Stamkos & Stein's private property." Amelia felt understanding bloom in her gut and, encouraged by her softening expression, Nyla trudged on. "They've set up a perimeter to keep people out. I know because Aaron and I tried to go back after the official investigation closed. With all of the bodies cleared out, we wanted to get a better look around. See if we couldn't dig up any answers. But they were waiting for us. I think George must've tipped them off."

At her questioning look, Nyla clarified that she was talking about Sheriff Mason.

"We can't get close to it, but it's our best chance to figure out what released this creature in the first place and how we can stop it."

"What makes you think there's more in the cave?" Amelia questioned, jumping in spite of herself as one of the bedroom windows rattled. Sam and Aaron must be testing the east side of the building. "I mean, maybe the Chehwinoo dug the cave and brought the artifacts with it?"

As soon as it left her mouth, Amelia knew the suggestion was stupid. Nyla was gracious enough not to point it out.

"It's not intelligent like we are," she said instead. "It has some sort of thought process; I can see that. But it doesn't reason like we do. I can't picture it bringing anything back to its home that wasn't necessary for one thing or another. And I doubt it dug the cave itself, at least not out of convenience. The Chehwinoo just so happens to dig into the ground and stumble across ancient stonework covered in pictures of itself? No way, that's too much of a coincidence. Either the cave was already there and it sniffed it out intentionally, or the Chehwinoo dug the cave in that specific spot for some instinctive reason.

"Which brings me to my problem. I've tried to sneak into the cave a few times, but they know my face. They also know Aaron's, and Pratt's. None of us can get close, and besides, they have it on record that we've been informed the cave is on public property. Getting caught there now would go on our criminal records, which isn't a big deal for me, but it is for Aaron and Pratt."

"So..." Amelia hedged, crossing her arms over her chest. "Where do I come into this?"

"Officially? You don't." Nyla shrugged. "I'm undeniably connected to Aaron, so if I get involved in anything illegal, tangentially or otherwise, it'll come back on him."

"Should we even be having this conversation then?"

"Hey, I'm just venting to my new friend about the hardships I've been dealing with as a business owner in the wake of this horrible tragedy." Nyla leaned back in her chair, hooking her arms behind her, and stretching with exaggerated casualness. "If said friend gets curious about the cave and decides they'd like to explore it in the early afternoon, say around break time for S&S's security detail which I've heard is at 1:25, and they then decide to take some souvenir pictures to share with certain parties after the fact, that's not on me. How would said friend *know* they were trespassing if there was no evidence of anyone telling them?"

The smirk that had been building in Amelia's expression finally broke free, mirroring Nyla's.

"We're going to get along just fine, I can tell."

"Good," Nyla said, laughing. "Now, we need to change the topic and fast. Aaron's like a bloodhound, except he sniffs out secrets instead of... whatever bloodhounds sniff out."

"Would it be too on the nose to say 'blood?'" Nyla's lips shrugged, conceding the point. "But yes, okay, topic change. What about—"

"What's the deal with you and Sam?" Nyla cut in suddenly, eagerly. "You're really not dating. Like, at all? Not even a little bit?"

"How do you date someone a little bit?" Amelia laughed, startled but not surprised. The abrupt change in atmosphere and topic released all of the nerves she'd been building with unexpected efficiency. The clock on the wall behind Nyla's head said that it was nearing noon. If her information was correct, Amelia and Sam would have to leave in no more than an hour to make it to the cave on time. Already, she had the basic framework of a plan taking shape in her head.

Nyla stared at her expectantly, fully trusting that Amelia had everything under control and having no qualms about changing the subject.

"How long were you waiting to spring that one?" Amelia taunted, retrieving a glass of water from the sink, and offering one to Nyla. "Was all that about the cave just to get my guard down so I'd be more likely to answer honestly?"

"I've literally been thinking about this since we left Tinny's," Nyla admitted, paying no heed to Amelia's veiled accusation. "I'm sorry, but there's no way nothing is going on between you two. And I've decided that we're friends now, which means you need to tell me about everything that's going on in your life so I can catch up."

"What about everything that's going on in *your* life?"

"We just spend the last twenty minutes going through that. Your turn."

Amelia raised an eyebrow, wanting to grumble but finding she was too charmed to be irritated.

"At least you're honest."

"My best friend says I'm unapologetically nosy," Nyla said proudly. "Now, spill it. You ever do it? Get drunk and feel each other up at a frat party? Book a hotel and 'oh no! There's only one bed!' and end up getting frisky in the middle of the night?"

"No to all of the above." Amelia laughed at Nyla's frustrated expression. "What?"

"*Something* must've happened," she pressed. "There's no way the man looks at you the way he does and isn't harboring some kind of feelings."

"How does he look at me?"

"Like you're the moon descended to Earth for his own personal viewing."

Amelia assumed that was an exaggeration, but she blushed nonetheless.

"We almost kissed once," she said after a while, not sure why she felt compelled to tell Nyla the truth. Maybe it was because her best friend was also Sam's sister, which meant that Amelia knew if Roxy got even a sniff of attraction between them, she'd run to tell Sam immediately. "But I don't count that."

"I KNEW IT!" Nyla pumped her fist triumphantly before registering what else Amelia had said. "Wait, why don't you count it?"

"Sam was completely shit-faced drunk and had just broken up with his night-mare of a girlfriend." Amelia couldn't stop the disgust from slipping into her expression. Dee, as she was referred to due to the unfortunate coincidence of her sharing Sam's mother's name, was never Amelia's favourite person. They were the same age and in many of the same classes in high school. During their teen years, they mostly avoided each other by running in different circles. There was no animosity or open dislike, merely a lack of friendship.

That changed when Dee and Sam got together. At first, like any good friend, Amelia did her best to be open and welcoming of his new girlfriend despite Dee's obvious distaste for Sam's unwavering friendship with her. Amelia could easily overlook the snide remarks, the veiled insults, and the blatant hostility when Sam wasn't around, but then she started to notice a change in Sam. He smiled less, laughed rarely, fought often, and began abandoning his responsibilities. Dee made him *miserable*, a shell of his former self. That was when Amelia stopped playing nice.

She was thrilled when Dee dumped him. Less thrilled when Roxy called her at three in the morning because Sam was drunk and stumbling through her dorm, grumbling that he couldn't find his way home. Getting his sloppy ass back to the apartment had been a herculean task, one that she only accomplished by sheer force of will and some strategically splashed ice water.

"I still think it counts," Nyla said. Amelia rolled her eyes, pressing her lips together to hide her smirk. Roxy also thought it counted, but she'd only seen a small sample of his state that night. Sam wasn't himself. Amelia couldn't justify holding the almost-kiss against him when he'd barely been conscious at the time, his lips searching for her even as he fought off sleep. A gentle shove on his chest was all it took for him to collapse back onto the blankets, snoring animatedly, his actions forgotten with the next morning's headache.

"Look, I get it," Amelia said with a sigh. "I understand why people think there's something between me and Sam. We've always been something more than just friends, not that I could tell you exactly *what* we are. But he's not interested."

Nyla's snort was loud and skeptical.

"Believe me or don't," Amelia said, shrugging. She ignored the twinge of hurt that came with the memory, hoping it didn't show on her face. "It's too much to get into now, but I have it on good authority that Sam doesn't want to be with me. It doesn't matter what I feel."

"What *do* you feel?" Nyla pressed, raising her eyebrow in suspicion. "Hypothetically, if Sam came to you and said something like 'My love, my darling, my goddess Amelia! I cut open my chest and present you with my still-beating heart! It belongs to you, my angel! Care for it well or stomp it into the dirt, it is yours to do with what you please—"

Amelia guffawed at Nyla's exaggerated declaration, tears collecting in her eyes as she continued to spout poetic, increasingly complicated confessions, waving her arms around in dramatic fashion and lowering her voice in an extremely poor imitation of Sam's timbre. When they'd both recovered from their giggling, Nyla planted her chin in her palm.

"Well? What would you say?"

"I'd probably ask him if he was on drugs."

"Seriously!" Nyla gave her a light smack on the shoulder. "Come on, would you consider it? Honestly?"

Amelia began to shake her head no, delivering her rehearsed answer with familiarity and exasperation.

"Would I consider dating a man that I regularly watch struggle to twist spaghetti noodles onto a fork without dropping it everywhere? What do you think?"

"I think, duh? Of course?"

"Exactly."

Wait— shit.

The words died in her throat as quickly as they'd come, her eyes rounding in panic.

No. Amelia's face fell instantly, her thoughts screeching to a jarring halt. She'd meant to say *no!* Could she salvage this? Was there a word she could utter after 'exactly' that would change the meaning of her answer? The longer she stayed quiet after she'd spoken the harder it would be to convince Nyla it had been a slip of the tongue.

Amelia risked a glance at her face, and she knew it was already too late.

Without warning, years of emotion that she'd pointedly and dedicatedly ignored clamored free from the recesses of her mind, seizing the chance to escape. Amelia pictured herself scrambling to catch them before they took flight, but she was too late. The butterflies that Sam conjured in her stomach, the same ones she'd refused to explore properly, fluttered through her chest, proving to her that her stubbornness hadn't diminished their strength. Nyla's almost supernatural ability to draw honesty from her had unleashed a torrent of things she'd long buried.

Shit, shit, shit. Not now. I can't think about this now!

Sensing that she'd just initiated some kind of inner turmoil, Nyla quickly came to her rescue as a peace offering.

"Oh! I just remembered! Clary sent me this picture of a guy she met on a dating app that looks like *Lynyrd Skynyrd*."

"Which one?" The relief she felt at having a lifeline made her sound more eager than she had any right to be, but Amelia clung to the offer with a death grip. She'd spent *years* refusing to think of Sam as anything other than her best friend, and she wasn't about to undo all of her hard work in the span of a single conversation.

The residual fluttering in her chest told her it was far too late for that, but Amelia focused on Nyla's confused expression instead.

"There's more than one?" Nyla looked up in surprise. "The music one."

"No," Amelia laughed. "*Lynyrd Skynyrd* is a band. Which member?"

"Uh..." Nyla frowned thoughtfully. "The... main... one?"

Amelia stifled a snort as Nyla showed her a photo of a guy who did admittedly look a lot like a younger Johnny Van Zant. She was thankful Sam wasn't here to witness this affront to music history. He'd have Nyla on a twelve-step rock education program before supper.

The patio door slid open, and the sound of Sam and Aaron's amicable chatter filled the room.

"Everything looks good," Aaron announced, striding across the room to lay his hand gently between Nyla's shoulder blades. "Did you cover the basics?"

"Yep," Nyla said, hopping up from her chair. "And now we need to go. I promised Clary I'd help her out at the spa for a few hours while Jessie is off sick."

"Call us if you need anything." Aaron extended his hand to Sam, who took it just a touch reluctantly. Amelia tilted her head in surprise. It wasn't like Sam to be hesitant around anyone, let alone people he should by all means be friendly with. "Anytime, alright?"

"Got it," Sam said. Amelia's confusion grew. He was gruffer than normal, too.

"Bye!" Nyla gave Amelia a quick, sudden hug before she could turn it down. She winced, but accepted the gesture as casually as she could. "Let me know if you get into trouble," Nyla whispered into her ear, low enough that no one else heard. Amelia nodded, giving her a gentle squeeze so that she understood. Satisfied, Nyla and Aaron made their exit while Sam stood at the window, watching the X5 drive away.

"Alright, what happened?" Amelia prodded as soon as it was safe to do so. Sam didn't look at her, but he scrunched his nose. "Why are you being all grumpy?"

"I don't know if I like that guy," he said, sounding so put out that Amelia couldn't help but laugh. "What? It's not funny. You don't even know why."

"Let me guess," Amelia folded her arms over her chest, "Aaron thought you weren't taking the situation seriously enough, so he intimidated you into listening?"

When Sam remained silent, Amelia only laughed harder.

"Christ, Sam," she said, shaking her head. "He's an *FBI agent*—"

"Former," Sam interjected bitterly.

"—he's just trying to make sure everyone stays safe. Including you, blockhead."

Her words clearly struck a sore spot, and Sam just grumbled. Amelia watched him for a moment, her lips pressed tightly together. She usually stopped herself from openly appreciating Sam's impressive stature, but her conversation with

Nyla had knocked her resolve loose. Even as she told herself not to, her attention caught on his wide shoulders and imposing muscle.

Shaking herself back into focus, she stood.

"You can mope later," she said, checking the time again. Amelia wasn't worried about getting Sam on board with her plan, a little trespassing was nothing they hadn't done before. All she needed to do was present her idea, and she was sure Sam would be more than willing. "Nyla asked us to help her out."

"Aaron didn't mention anything," Sam said questioningly.

"He doesn't know."

A satisfied smile spread across Sam's face.

"In that case, whatever it is, I'm in."

The Basin really was beautiful, when they weren't running for their lives from a nightmarish ice demon. Sam guided their way through the trees, but they hardly needed to stick together. With the ongoing construction rocking the very ground beneath their feet, stumbling onto the new Stamkos & Stein property wasn't a difficult feat.

They were dressed as hikers, carrying a day's worth of supplies in two backpacks to round out the illusion. Amelia sincerely doubted that, even if they were caught, someone would go through the trouble of searching their bags. Still, neither of them wanted to take the risk. This wasn't the first time they'd participated in less-than-legal activities together, and Amelia was sure it wouldn't be the last.

Sunlight shimmered through the trees overhead as they picked their way through the thickest part of the forest separating them from the Stamkos & Stein construction site. Amelia could make out the dull thrum of machinery and bored voices, loud enough to warn them when they were venturing too close to populated ground. They had a vague idea of where the cave was located, but they'd still ventured out exceedingly early to give themselves time for errors. It also meant that they weren't rushing through the path, prioritizing relative stealth over speed. Their slower pace combined with the moratorium on boisterous conversation left Amelia with far too much time to think.

Nyla had inadvertently opened Pandora's box, and Amelia couldn't figure out how to close it. Her question echoed in Amelia's mind, loud and demanding.

Would you consider it?

In truth? Yes. Absolutely, one hundred percent, without a doubt, no question. If Sam asked her out, she would accept. Happily. Eagerly. But she knew he wouldn't.

She'd always loved Sam. Some part of her heart belonged to him from the moment they met, his bright red dirt bike wheeling over her pavement-chalk masterpiece and ruining hours of dedicated work. She'd cried, he'd panicked, and the next thing she knew this random older kid was yanking a bubble-gum comic strip from his back pocket and reading it aloud to her to make her laugh. Roxy wheeled by not five minutes later, yelling at Sam for getting too far ahead, and the three of them spent the rest of the evening fixing the mess Sam made of her sidewalk art. From that moment on, they were inseparable.

But dating? No, that was never on the table. She didn't want it to be, not at first. As Roxy's older brother, Sam was implicitly off-limits despite the fact that they hadn't talked about it. Amelia had, of course, gone through her inevitable phase of crushing on him, how could she not? He was older, strong, thoughtful, and funny, and he always made her feel like she was the only person in the world worth paying attention to when she spoke. For Amelia, growing up in a home that robbed her of any voice she had, Sam's respect for her was a treasured gift. From the time she was old enough to know what a crush was to her first year of high school, Amelia nurtured that small piece of her heart that belonged to Sam. Then, he'd gotten a girlfriend, and she'd moved on.

It wasn't until a few years later that Amelia learned Sam had never been off-limits. Roxy was rooting for them to get together from day one, having convinced herself how awesome it would be to have a best friend for a sister-in-law. By the time they'd had *that* conversation, it was too late. Sam was with a new girl every other week, and Amelia was in the beginning stages of her relationship with Alex.

Thus began their decade-long period of near misses. Amelia dated Alex for six months, then broke up with him after he moved to Paraguay on an exchange program. Two weeks later, Sam was introduced to his coworker's new roommate, Sandra Brockwaller, aka Dee. They dated on and off for four years, with Sam dating Jayla somewhere in the middle of the Dee drama. Meanwhile, Amelia had taken a short break from dating to focus on gaining her independence after estranging herself from her family. Therapy and introspective healing took up far too much time to consider a relationship, and by the time she'd come to terms with the trajectory of her life, Sam was getting back together with Dee for the third time and Amelia was meeting Ben at the college library.

Ben. Amelia felt a surge of hatred in her chest as his name flitted through her mind. Trusting Sam not to lead them astray, she let herself simmer in that hatred in a way that she usually refused to. Her anger hadn't always been there. Until recently, memories of Ben were accompanied by regret and shame.

That had been more than just a simple breakup. She'd thought Ben was the one for a long time, almost the entire second half of their two-year-long relationship. Then she'd gotten pregnant.

The pregnancy in and of itself wasn't a problem. She didn't want kids, Ben did but wasn't ready. They both agreed that an abortion was the right thing to do, not just for themselves but for any potential child they brought into the world. She made the appointment, told him when it was, and thought that was the end of it until she arrived at the clinic and was told she couldn't drive herself home after the procedure. Amelia called Ben, only for it to go straight to voicemail. She tried again, then tried his work number. That was when his supervisor dropped the bomb on her that Ben had booked all of his vacation time and was already halfway across the Pacific, heading to Hawaii for a guy's golfing trip.

He was gone for a month.

Amelia remembered the panic and betrayal that she felt at that moment. She was always careful, so, so careful about whom she trusted. Nothing about Ben had given her any hint that he would do something like this, abandon her to deal with the aftermath of a mistake they'd both made. The clinic didn't care that she was in the middle of a crisis, though. They just needed to know she had a ride. Amelia didn't even think about it, she called Sam.

He didn't ask any questions until they were back in their apartment. When she told him what happened, Amelia could see the rage boiling inside him. With no immediate outlet, Sam had pushed aside his anger to take care of her. He took the weekend off work, almost getting fired in the process, and stayed by her side as she cried, threw up, went emotionally numb, and slept more than anyone had any reason to. Ben had shattered her far worse than her family ever had, convincing her that he was trustworthy and then proving that he wasn't in the worst way possible. Sam was the one to pick up the pieces, and that was when Amelia realized that her heart still belonged to him.

By the time Ben showed up at their apartment trying to act like nothing happened and Sam enthusiastically broke his nose in response, Amelia was helpless. To be fair, she'd tried to ensure Sam wasn't home when Ben stopped by. He was at work, not slated to come home for another few hours. Amelia planned to tell Ben where he could shove it, kick him out, and be done with it. Then he'd shown up, the picture of ease, and something inside her snapped. She screamed at him for hours, long enough for Sam to come home and throw Ben's ass out the front door.

She'd already decided to take a break from dating, both to recover from what Ben had done and to give herself a chance to sort out her feelings for Sam. It turned out to be a doomed effort. Shortly after Ben was forcefully ejected from her life with a severe nosebleed and bruised pride, she got word that her father died, and Sam proved all over again why he was the best person she's ever known.

She never had a chance. Amelia was always going to fall in love with Sam, whether he wanted her to or not.

As they came around the far corner of the concrete foundation, Amelia was so mentally exhausted that she'd almost forgotten why they were there. She felt raw and exposed, like the emotions she'd been suppressing for years had hit her all at once. She quickly tried to school her features before Sam turned to her, but she was just a fraction of a second too late. Sam caught the turmoil in her eyes, and he brought up solid.

"What's wrong?" He pulled her to the side, a little further from the construction site. They weren't close enough to be overheard anyway, but the distance was still comforting. "Are you okay?"

"I'm fine," she insisted, summoning her best game face. "Sorry. I was overthinking."

Sam nodded, accepting her answer at face value. It wasn't a lie, after all.

"I can see the security guys from here," he told her, gesturing through the trees. Amelia followed, spotting the two men with ease. They were too far back to make out details, but it was clear from their uniforms that they were guards. "What's the plan from here?"

"As soon as they clear the cave, we'll rush in along the treeline," Amelia pointed to their path. She didn't want to run out in the open in case they were spotted but making it to the cave was only step one. Their window was small, and they needed to infiltrate, document, and escape before the guards returned. "I think it'd be faster if you help me down. Then you can climb in after me."

"I'll help you rappel," Sam agreed, "then when you're clear, I can jump."

"Then we're just going to take as many pictures as we can."

"Take a video," Sam suggested instead. "I'll take pictures, you video."

"Got it."

Movement from the direction of the cave caught their attention, and Amelia glanced at her phone screen. It was 1:19.

"Looks like they might be slipping out early," Sam muttered under his breath, rolling up the sleeves of his shirt to bear his forearms. Amelia blinked her attention away from the flexing muscle, annoyance souring her tongue. What was *wrong* with her? She hadn't been this distracted by a guy since she was sixteen years old. It was as if her feelings for Sam were as boisterous and obnoxious as the man himself, demanding her attention at every opportunity now that they'd been unleashed.

Focus, Bradley. Crime now, hormones later.

"We'll need to be as quick as possible," she said, squinting at the guards as they continued to walk away from their post. "I'll go ahead of you and get into position."

"Go now." Sam placed his palms on her hips, guiding her around him and out of the underbrush. "They'll only be able to see you for another few steps. By the time you get in range, it'll be clear."

Amelia didn't hesitate, ducking out from under the trees and hurrying along the edge of the construction site. Her heart pumped faster the closer she got to the edge of the concrete structure, where there was a short span of open ground where she could be spotted before she reached the cover of the cave. The guards had rounded a stack of pallets and were no longer a concern, but that didn't mean no one else was watching.

Sam trailed a few steps behind her, his boots crunching softly in the dirt.

The cave was deceptively far from their hiding spot. Amelia felt a lurch in her chest as she realized they'd be exposed for at least a couple more seconds before they were in the clear, but it was too late to turn back now. Skidding to a stop and retreating would draw more attention.

A soft curse from behind told her that Sam had come to the same conclusion.

The packed dirt terrain slowly transitioned to moss, tree roots, and half-buried stones as they neared the edge of the trees again. Amelia hopped with as much care as she could, praying she didn't trip. With the cave in spitting distance, she only had to make it a few more steps—

A gust of relieved breath left her lungs as she slowed to a halt, quickly assessing the distance from the cave mouth to the ground. It wasn't impossible, but it wasn't easy, either. She turned, bracing one foot on the lip of the cave, as close as she could without risking dislodging the dirt she was standing on and falling back-first into the hole. Sam met her just as she was bracing her non-dominant leg, preparing to bear the weight of her descent as she led with her other leg.

Sam's hands gripped her forearms and Amelia mirrored him, locking their arms together. Sam placed one foot forward, sinking into a high squat, and then she was lowering herself into the lair of the Chehwinoo.

Amelia felt for purchase in the dirt, the toe of her shoe knocking detritus free from the uneven wall. There wasn't much to balance on, but she managed to get both of her legs halfway to the ground before she was forced to let gravity take over. Sam held her long enough for her to get oriented and then, with a quick nod, she was falling.

With a drop and a nauseating flip of her stomach, Amelia's feet thudded on the hard dirt. She shook off the aftershocks and stepped further into the darkness, making room for Sam to join her. His landing was steadier than hers, collecting himself almost as soon as he'd hit the ground.

"What are the chances we run into Mole People?" Sam flicked on his phone flashlight, wavering the beam to make the atmosphere more creepy. "Or those things from *The Descent*?"

"If we do, I'll make sure to trip you so I can escape," Amelia informed him. He scoffed, offended at the very suggestion.

"You wouldn't have to *trip* me, Amy Baby. I'd gladly lay down my life for you. As long as it's not Mole People. I don't trust anything with a nose that looks like an inversed scrotum."

"How chivalrous." Amelia found her own flashlight, directing it around the cave. "Now, come on. We don't have much time."

"Lead the way, boss."

Their descent into the Chehwinoo's old stomping grounds had been too rushed to feel any true fear, but now that they were encased in the palpable reality of the threat, Amelia felt a cold nugget of dread start to form in her stomach. The creature wasn't here, they knew that, but the possibility still flickered at the back of her mind like a candle flame in a frosted window.

The cave was smaller than she was expecting, only about the width of a bus stop and not quite as tall. The ground beneath their feet was hard and packed like it had been regularly walked on for years. The dirt walls were looser, and more ragged, though Amelia didn't know if that was natural or a result of the crime scene cleanup team.

"Okay Nyla," she whispered, opening the camera app on her phone. "Let's show you what we're seeing."

Amelia started a video, first aiming it at the opening of the cave, then panning to where she and Sam were standing.

"It's not that much colder in here," she said for the sake of the video, glancing up at the ceiling as she did. "It's chilly, but not freezing. I'd guess normal cave temperature."

"It's longer than it looks," Sam said, his voice revealing to her that he'd ventured farther into the cave. "Almost like a tunnel."

Amelia took care to slowly rove over every inch of the cave with her camera, recording as much as she could for Nyla's sake. She had to keep reminding herself to stop looking at her surroundings through the screen, knowing that her eyes picked up far more detail. Looking through the screen felt safer— she knew that the dark spots in the dirt couldn't be leftover blood from the carnage that used to be housed here, but her mind couldn't quite let go of the death that had once called this place home.

"I'd guess it's about... I don't know, 15 feet from beginning to end?" Sam said from somewhere ahead of her. Amelia hurried to catch up to him, a frown creasing her eyebrows.

"That's not right," she aimed the camera up, down, and to both sides, examining the image on her screen with growing confusion. "The pictures made it look way bigger. Which could be perspective, or maybe the ice, but—"

No, that wasn't it. Perspective was one thing, but something was definitely different about the space they were standing in. If anything, the ice would make the cave look *smaller* in pictures, not larger. It didn't match the Hovel in Nyla's photos, and not just because it wasn't covered in frozen carrion.

"I think you're right," Sam mused, stooping to take more photos. The soft flash of his phone camera had been going off consistently, like a slow strobe light. Amelia hoped it was still too bright outside for anyone to notice. "Look, this dirt isn't as packed as the rest."

Amelia stepped closed, dragging her light over every inch of the cave wall. Sam was spot on; the dirt and rocks comprising the rest of the cave, while not as well-traveled as the floor, were compacted and smooth, undisturbed except for the occasional bug or root. The back of the cave was different, loose and jagged, speckled with gravel and rocks that looked too clean to have been there for longer than a few months if that.

"This was sealed off," she said in a whisper, less for the video and more for her own thoughts. "Deliberately, do you think?"

"It's not a professional job," Sam concluded. "If it was done by contract workers, it would all be gravel or maybe sand. Could've been an accident, I suppose."

Amelia panned the camera around the cave again, slowly, lingering anywhere she thought she might've missed the first time around.

"I don't see anything else out of place," she said, looking back at Sam. "We should get out of here before the guards come back."

"Holy shit!"

Sam's sudden exclamation almost made her drop her phone.

"What? What is it?"

"Sorry," Sam winced, shaking himself, "I didn't mean to scare you, I just..."

He had his hand on the crumbled wall, staring at it with confusion and awe. Amelia looked from his face to his hand, waiting for him to explain. When he didn't, she mimicked him. As soon as her palm touched the rough stone, she knew what had surprised him.

The wall was *freezing*.

No actual ice could be seen threading through the dirt, but Amelia wouldn't have been the least bit shocked to find some. Just laying her hand on the surface had her shivering, all of the warmth zapped from her body in seconds.

"It's cold," she said aloud, realizing that Nyla couldn't feel the temperature through a screen. "Like, insanely cold. Way colder than it should be."

"Maybe it's deeper here than the rest of the cave?" Sam stood, scanning the ground for a distinct slope. "How cold does it get underground?"

"Not this cold this fast," Amelia argued, although she wasn't completely sure that was true. Something in her gut told her this wasn't a normal chill, and she'd already decided to let her gut handle most of her decisions for the rest of this adventure. It hadn't let her down yet when death was involved.

She checked the length of the recording, just past the fifteen-minute mark.

"Let's go," she said again, leaving no room for Sam to disagree. "They left early, they might come back early."

"Good point." Sam took a hearty step back from the wall, taking one final picture before pocketing his phone. "See you on the flip side, Nyla."

Amelia ended the video on the outdated slang, pocketing her phone too.

They moved swiftly to the entrance, where Sam automatically crouched to let her climb his shoulders. Amelia was about to suggest she take his backpack to give him more freedom to clamor up after her, but she froze with the words dancing on her tongue.

Voices. She heard voices.

And they were getting closer.

Chapter Eighteen

SAM

"Shit," Sam pressed himself flat against the dirt wall, tugging Amelia back with him. She followed wordlessly, snuffing the flashlight on her phone. "Short lunch break."

"Lift me", she whispered, jerking her chin upwards. "I'll see if I can spot them from here and we can time our exit."

"Any excuse to get between your legs." He waggled his eyebrows, ducking to wrap his arms around her thighs before she could chastise him for the ill-timed flirt. As stealthily as he could, he hoisted Amelia onto his shoulders, her legs on either side of his head as promised. "What's the view like up there?"

Amelia shimmied forward, gripping some errant roots protruding from the dirt, and carefully straightened her spine until she could just see over the lip of the cave entrance. She remained there for a moment, breath caught in her chest, and then she looked down at him again.

"They're by the treeline," she said. "Not paying attention, but I think they're getting ready to circle around. We need to move now."

"I'm going to boost you out," Sam readjusted his grip on her legs as he was speaking, making it clear that he wasn't waiting for an answer. Amelia braced herself, waiting for his cue. With a sharp exhale, Sam propelled her upwards. Amelia caught herself on the packed ground, locking her elbows and crawling forward until he couldn't see her anymore. Sam waited, listening for the okay, but it never came. He was about to call out to her when Amelia's voice covered the sound of his shuffling, much louder and higher pitched than it should be.

"Jesus! You guys scared me!"

"Fuck," Sam muttered, pressing himself against the wall again. The guards had spotted her.

"Ma'am, you can't be here." The voice was rough, almost bored. Sam pictured it belonging to the taller of the two guards, but he couldn't be sure without seeing them. Crunching underbrush met his ears, and Sam knew they were approaching. He all but stopped breathing. "This is private property."

"Oh shit, is it?" Amelia sounded genuinely bewildered. "I'm so sorry! I was with my friend, and we got separated and— you guys haven't seen anyone else around, have you? I was trying to go back to our car, but I think I went the wrong way. We're parked by some kind of... wilderness lodge, I guess?"

"You're going the wrong way alright," the other guard spoke up now, sounding friendlier than his coworker. Amelia was selling her story, and they didn't sound suspicious of her motives. Sam breathed a sigh of relief. "The Willow is the other way. Come on, we'll show you to the main road and point you in the right direction."

"Oh my God, that would be incredible, thank you so much!" Footsteps moved hurriedly away from him. Sam rolled his shoulders in preparation for a hurried vault out of the ground. "This place is huge! What are you building here, anyway? Some kind of factory?"

The answer was too quiet for Sam to hear, but Amelia's question served its purpose. He listened as the voices grew quieter, estimating when they were far enough away for him to make an unseen getaway. He waited an extra second or two, and then he lunged.

As athletic as Sam was, climbing never came naturally to him. He relied more on strength than finesse, jumping high enough to rely primarily on his upper body strength to drag him the rest of the way out. The light burned his eyes as they adjusted, the myriad of greens and yellows blinding in the afternoon sun. Sam shielded his brows, scanning the woods ahead for Amelia and the guards. They were at the edge of the construction site, just about to clear the trees. He moved quietly toward their previous hiding spot, which just so happened to bring him back into hearing range.

"You know, you shouldn't be out in the woods like this," the friendlier guard said, his tone honeyed and condescending, speaking down to Amelia like he would a naïve child. Sam bristled. "It's dangerous. You and your friend should be more careful."

"We weren't planning to go far," Amelia laughed softly, playing her part by breathing some light flirtation into her words. Sam felt a twinge of irritation, but he told himself to ignore it. It would be safer to meet Amelia back at the cabin. If he intervened now, it would just raise suspicion. Better to let her play out the lie she'd already sold. He knew she could handle herself. "We aren't used to the terrain around here. We got lost pretty much immediately."

"I'm not surprised," the same guard said in exaggerated sympathy. Sam noticed the other one was mostly silent, clearly not the people-person of the duo. He hurried toward the path that would lead him back to the cabin, pausing to make sure the guards weren't walking Amelia in a direction that would bring him into their line of sight. "The Basin isn't safe for a pretty little thing like you. All kinds of scary animals in these woods."

Okay, *Amelia* could handle herself, sure, but *Sam* was about to blow a gasket.

"This is only our first hike," she said demurely, and even though Sam knew she was playing a part, it still rankled his nerves to hear the almost sultry words leave her lips. "I don't think we'll be going on another one anytime soon."

"That's probably for the best," the guard said, so obviously pandering that even his partner snorted in disgust. "If you're interested in the woods, I'd be happy to show you around some of the easier trails. Maybe this weekend?"

His hand brushed Amelia's lower back, and suddenly Sam was changing course.

"Amy!" His relieved call startled all three of them, who turned as he broke into a jog. Amelia's expression registered confusion and warning in equal measures before she schooled her features into a mask of relief. "Thank God! I've been looking for you everywhere!"

He skidded to a stop in front of her, pulling her into a tight hug that had the added effect of yanking her out of the guard's reach. He looked disgruntled, swallowing whatever remark he wanted to make.

"Seth! You're okay!" Amelia injected the perfect amount of frantic relief into her voice, wavering it like she was about to burst into tears. "I tried to call you, but I couldn't get service! I thought for sure that you—"

"Hey, it's okay," he hushed, threading his fingers through her hair and pressing her face against his chest. They certainly *looked* like they'd been trekking through the wilderness for hours, covered in dirt and scrapes from their brief spelunking. Amelia shot him a venomous glare from the safety of his embrace, and he had to stop himself from smirking. Instead, he faked a few exhausted breaths, smoothing his hands over her as if to reassure himself that she was all there and in one piece. Finally, he turned his attention to the guards. "Thank you so much for this. I'm sorry we interrupted your work."

"We're not supposed to be here," Amelia said, lifting her face from his shirt to stare balefully up at him. Her expression pinched in concern. "There's construction going on. It's not safe."

"You're on private property," the gruff guard supplied, the friendlier of the two having decided he wasn't feeling so friendly anymore after Sam showed up. "Trespassing is a crime in this state. I need your ID."

Sam immediately felt the constricting grip of panic overtake his ability to speak, but Amelia rescued him, undeterred by the abrupt change in atmosphere now that she was no longer a damsel in distress that these men were saving. She swung her backpack off her shoulders, speaking in a low, appeasing tone.

"Of course, no problem," she said, rifling through the inner pockets of the main compartment. "We left the originals back at our rental just in case something happened, but I know I have copies here somewhere... aha!"

The folded printer paper depicted photocopied scans of two driver's licenses, one with a photo of Sam and one with a photo of Amelia. It was only when Sam caught the names that he noticed they were a forgery and not an actual copy of his ID.

The guards took the paper, scanning it for anything out of place. Amelia didn't look concerned, rocking back and forth on the balls of her feet with a polite impatience that perfectly suited the situation. Sam put his trust in her, looping his arm over her shoulders and subtly shifting his body language to match her energy.

"Alright then Ms. Bradshaw, Mr. F—" The guard paused, squinting at the paper. "Friis? That German or something?"

"Scandinavian," Sam answered helpfully, although he had no idea if that was true.

The guard grunted, handing the re-folded paper back to Amelia. "Just so you're aware, I'm adding your names to our internal database. If you're caught on the property again, we'll be getting the authorities involved. Understood?"

"Yes, thank you," Amelia rushed to say, nodding anxiously. "We're really sorry for the confusion. You'll never see us here again; you have our word."

"We appreciate your help, sirs," Sam gripped the man's hand, shaking it once. "Come on, Amy. Let's head home before it gets dark."

With his arm securely around her shoulders again, Sam led Amelia toward the main road. She stuffed the fake IDs for 'Seth Friis' and 'Amanda Bradshaw' in her back pocket, chatting jovially about nothing as they walked away. For a fleeting moment, Sam thought the guards would stop them. Anxiety filled his chest as they walked away, focusing on their next steps to keep his mind occupied. They'd double back around once they were clear of the build site. Each step he took felt both too slow and too fast, and suddenly he forgot how he normally walked. *Could* he walk suspiciously? Was that even possible? Would the guards somehow see the guilt in his gait and call them back? Thoughts along those lines swarmed Sam's mind until, at last, they were far enough away that, should the guards change their mind and come after them, they'd be home free before the sound of running footsteps reached their ears.

"What the hell is the matter with you?" Amelia demanded, turning to glare angrily at him. "Why didn't you go back to the cabin? If they stopped to think for even a second, they would've put two and two together."

"They would've figured out that we're secretly working for Nyla?" Sam said skeptically. It was the wrong thing to say, as Amelia's eyes narrowed.

"They would've figured out we were *in the cave*. Look at us!"

Sam noted the dirt again, realizing that, while it did support their story of being lost in the woods, it was *also* a dead giveaway that they'd been deliberately trespassing.

"Okay, but they didn't!" Sam argued. He didn't want to admit that hearing and seeing the guard flirt with her had ignited a flame of protective anger in him. She would never let him hear the end of it. "They would've seen me if I took the path back. I heard part of your story and figured it was less suspicious if I acted like I'd been looking for you."

Amelia made a face like she didn't quite believe him but couldn't prove that he was lying without going back to the construction site. Since that was out of the question, she huffed and kept walking.

Sam let out a soft sigh of relief, falling into step beside her and silently taking the win.

Amelia didn't need him to rescue her. He knew that. She'd been handling herself for far longer than he'd known her, and she'd survived things he could never understand. That didn't stop the raging need to swoop in whenever she was in trouble that consumed his every waking moment.

He'd acted without thinking, yes, but Sam was actually pretty proud of himself for keeping his cool. A few years ago, that guard would've ended up flat on his ass and Sam would've spent the night in a cell. It certainly wouldn't be the first time.

Sam spent a lot of time and energy in recent years reining in his temper. He wasn't an angry person and he never had been, but he *did* have a slight penchant for getting into fights whenever he was in a bad mood. Or when someone threatened the people he cared about. His freedom with his fists had gotten him into many sticky situations, more than a small number of which Amelia had bailed him out of. Nothing that landed permanently on his record, thankfully. He'd managed enough control to prevent that.

Barely.

Howard Bradley didn't make that any easier than Sam did. The man was determined to punish Sam and, by extension, Amelia for defying him. Sam lost track of all the avenues he'd tried to take, some more legitimate than others, but nothing that stuck. While Sam's parents didn't know the full extent of Amelia's home situation, Sam guessed they knew more than they were letting on. He'd consulted with his family's lawyer more than once, and yet he'd never gotten a bill.

It helped that Howard's fellow officers disliked him. Not enough to actually step in and do anything about his shitty behavior, but enough to avoid aiding him in any way.

It had been a long time since Sam got into a real fight. The closest he'd come was when that bastard Ben showed up at their apartment after the crap that he pulled with Am, but that hardly counted. It was a punch, not a fight. And Sam had every intention of keeping his record as clean as possible, especially if he was going to finally take the plunge with Amelia.

She deserved better than the punk-ass kid he'd been before he pulled his act together. Sam couldn't, in good conscience, offer himself to her if he wasn't proud of the person he was. Of the man he'd made himself into. He owed her that much.

Sam wanted to give her the world. She deserved the world, and everything in it. She deserved someone confident in who they were, someone who wouldn't make her worry about them, or her, or their future together. Someone she could depend on, rain or sleet or shine. He would never offer her anything less than a man who could lift her up, support her, and love her with everything that he had.

It took longer than he would've liked, but he was that man now.

His irresponsible habits were, mostly anyway, behind him. He had a stable job, good friends, and a strong future. Amelia didn't care about any of that, Sam knew, but *he* did. He had no more reservations, no more doubts about his ability to provide for her, both emotionally and in any other way she might need. Finances had never been an issue thanks to his family's legacy, but Amelia rarely let him dote on her like that. Sam doubted that would change if they started dating, but at least he could smother her ire with a myriad of tempting distractions.

His dick twitched, and he immediately put a stop to that line of thinking. They still had another 15 minutes of walking ahead of them, and Sam didn't love the thought of doing so with a raging hard-on.

Instead, he distracted himself with something a little more pressing. The murder-ice-demon had put a bit of a hold on his plans, but he hadn't abandoned them. Amelia said that they weren't meeting up with Nyla to go over the video until tomorrow. They had the entire evening to themselves.

He had to do it tonight.

Tonight, after the dust settled, Sam was going to do it.

He was finally going to tell Amelia that he loved her.

Chapter Nineteen

INTERLUDE

Nyla

As the afternoon faded into evening, Nyla couldn't decide if no news was good news or very bad news.

Her phone had been radio-silent for hours, no word from Amelia or Sam about the status of their recon mission. Nyla wouldn't dare text them first, she couldn't risk leaving any kind of paper trail. If she gave any inkling that she had prior knowledge to their escapade, her plausible deniability was out the window.

Truthfully, it didn't matter either way. If they got caught, Nyla couldn't bring herself to leave them high and dry. Still, she'd lay low as long as she could, hoping things went well and by the time Aaron discovered what she'd orchestrated, the deed would already be done.

They'd left Clary's spa less than an hour ago, rushing their goodbyes to beat the sunset. Spending the afternoon working with Clary had been a reprieve Nyla didn't know she needed; her days of late were consumed with death and darkness, neither of which could touch Clary in even her worst moods. Hanging out in the serenity of the spa, laughing and gossiping with Clary in between customers, had been healing for her. For both of them, really.

Nyla knew that Clary suspected something was going on. She wasn't an idiot, and she knew Nyla better than most. Which was also why Nyla knew that Clary wouldn't ask her about it, not until Nyla broached the topic herself. The benefit of sharing everything with her best friend meant that when she *did* need to keep a secret, it was taken very, very seriously.

A light snore interrupted her musing, and Nyla suppressed a smile.

Aaron wasn't much of a nap person, especially so late in the day. The fact that he'd fallen asleep while lounging on the couch in their joint cabin spoke to how exhausted he was.

Nyla felt a pang of fondness clench her heart, and she quietly put down her phone. Social media could wait; she wasn't really looking at it anyway.

For the first month of their relationship, Nyla was convinced that Aaron didn't sleep. He was often up later than she was, working silently on his phone or laptop, and he was *always* awake first. Nyla considered herself a morning person, but she had nothing on Aaron. Getting to see him asleep and vulnerable like this was a rarity.

She stood next to the couch, biting her lip to stop herself from grinning. Aaron hadn't even bothered to change out of his day clothes before passing out, managing to shed his jacket and unbutton his shirt and that was it. Nyla let her gaze travel appreciatively over his tawny skin, the recently permanent tension in his muscles nowhere to be seen. She glanced at the clock— just past seven— and determined that he'd be grumpy if she let him sleep any longer.

Since she rarely got to wake him, Nyla wanted to make this time count.

As carefully as she could, Nyla settled her knees on either side of Aaron's hips, gently sinking her weight onto him. He stirred but didn't wake. That surprised her more than anything else— in addition to rarely sleeping, Aaron was also a light sleeper. The slightest noise was usually more than enough to rouse him.

"Sleeping on the job," she murmured, smiling again as his breathing changed. "That's horribly unprofessional of you, Agent Klein."

Nyla slid her hands up his bare stomach, caressing his warm skin with her palms. Aaron smirked, his eyes still closed but definitely awake now.

"I'm entitled to a fifteen-minute break," he said, his voice muddled by sleep. "I might start taking more if it means I wake up to a gorgeous woman taking advantage of me."

"I didn't take you for a somnophilia enthusiast." Nyla leaned forward, peppering kisses along the planes of Aaron's chest. Still, his eyes remained closed. "Come on, *mi sol*, break's over. Time to get up or you'll be cranky at bedtime."

Aaron scoffed playfully.

"That's a new one," he said lazily, his words rolling from his tongue with languid ease, making his accent more noticeable. "What happened to 'Suits?'"

"Suits isn't going anywhere," Nyla promised, suckling the sensitive skin below his jaw. Aaron's breathing stuttered. "But I've been practising my Spanish."

"Without me?" Aaron rumbled. "I thought I was the only 'Spanish' you were practising?"

"If you think I need practise, then I've been underperforming."

Nyla silenced Aaron's laugh with a gentle scrape of her teeth over his pulse point.

"Come on," she urged again, slowly licking the shell of his ear before kissing the junction of his jaw and lobe. "Get up *mi sol*," she kissed his cheek, "*mi rey*," she kissed his throat, "*mi corazón*." Nyla paused, humming appreciatively at the growing hardness between her legs. "Well, part of you is up anyway, *mi patito*."

Aaron laughed fully this time, his eyes finally opening and gazing at her with both amusement and fondness.

"Did you just call me a duckling?" He chuckled, shaking his head when she nodded. "On purpose?"

"I got that one from Alma."

"Figures," Aaron said, rolling his eyes. "I think I prefer 'Suits.'"

"At least I didn't use your mom's suggestion," Nyla teased, bumping her nose against Aaron's. His blanching expression told her that he knew exactly what she was about to say before it left her lips. "My cute little *osito*— mmf!"

Nyla yelped as Aaron pounced, scooping her into his arms and flipping them in one fluid motion, pinning her beneath him on the couch. She laughed breathlessly, silenced by a searing kiss.

"If you think there's anything 'teddy bear like' about me, then *I've* been underperforming," he growled against her lips. Nyla shivered delightedly. "Do I need to prove myself?"

She was about to agree with a loud and resounding 'YES,' when Aaron's phone broke the air with a shrill ring.

They shifted apart, pulling themselves into seated positions in the middle of the couch. Aaron freed his phone from his pocket, frowning at the screen.

"Who is it?" Nyla asked, trying to glimpse the caller ID.

"Unknown number," Aaron said under his breath. With his thumb, he accepted the call. "Aaron Klein."

Silence, and then his expression lifted.

"Yeah, we're both here. Hang on."

Aaron held the phone aloft between them, tapping the speaker icon in the process.

"Alright, you're on speaker, Pratt."

"*That was quick.*" Pratt's voice crackled through the line. "*Don't tell me I interrupted sexy time?*"

"Who said anything about interrupting?" Nyla shot back, smirking at Aaron. "I'm perfectly content to keep going."

"*Please spare my ears,*" Pratt sighed dramatically, "*I've heard enough of Klein's yelling over the years.*"

"What do you want, Pratt?" Aaron prompted, exasperated already. "Where are you calling from?"

"*A gas station near the Somerton exit ramp.*" Background noise crackled through the line, punctuating his point. "*Look, I don't have long, and I can't be too specific, but I had to call.*"

Aaron and Nyla shared a worried look.

"*Kelley's been talking to Mason, and she's pissed. She knows you're still investigating, and she probably knows I've been helping you. Which means—*"

"Which means she's monitoring your phone," Aaron concluded with an aggravated huff. "Damnit."

"*I can't risk contacting you anymore, not about the case.*" Pratt sounded genuinely frustrated, which surprised Nyla. Even in the most dire of circumstances, she'd never heard Pratt be anything but cheerful. "*And I can't stay in Somerton. Chia...*"

"Don't," Aaron interrupted. "Your family comes first, Pratt. Do what you need to do here and get back to them. We'll manage."

"*Sam and Amelia can help.*" His voice was firm, certain. "*They can't get you the information that I have access to, but don't underestimate them. Especially Amelia. The woman is scary good at finding shit out.*"

"I'm counting on it," Nyla said without thinking, drawing a confused look from Aaron. She cleared her throat, ignoring him. "We've been talking to them. They're handling things like champs."

"*I'm not surprised*," Pratt said, and Nyla could hear the smile in his words. "*I'd trust either one of them with my life. I know you didn't want anyone else involved, Klein, but with Kelley on the offensive, you need allies. Sam and Am are good ones to have. They're not afraid to get their hands dirty.*"

"So I've learned," Nyla said, forgetting herself again. This time, Aaron looked at her in alarm. She was starting to wonder if she and Clary gossiped so much because they actually enjoyed it or because Nyla was simply incapable of keeping a secret.

"*I have to go, Kelley's expecting me at the motel soon.*" Pratt's voice moved away from the phone, speaking to someone else in the gas station. "*I do have a small parting gift. It'll be in your email by now. I told Chia to send it after I made it to Wisconsin.*"

"You're a lifesaver, Pratt." Aaron's mouth twisted into a small, sideways smile. "Good luck."

"*You'll need it more than me. Be careful, Klein. And Nyla? Make sure he doesn't get himself into too much trouble.*"

"I make no guarantees," she said. "Besides, out of the two of us, I'm far more likely to get into trouble."

"*Good point*," Pratt said with a chuckle. "*Klein? You're on your own.*"

With that, the line disconnected.

Nyla braced herself for Aaron to immediately bombard her with questions, but the promise of Pratt's information had taken precedence. Aaron opened the email app on his phone, scrolling through what looked like some kind of legal document. After reading for longer than Nyla was comfortable with, he pressed his lips into a thin line.

"He has a name."

Hope and dread flooded her in equal measures. She didn't need to ask whose name he was referring to.

Identifying the Chehwinoo was a controversial task, one that the three of them couldn't quite agree on the necessity of. Knowing who the Chehwinoo used to be didn't help them kill it, nor did it matter much in terms of resolution. They couldn't save the victim, they all knew that, so why bother finding out at all? Why risk discovering that it was someone they knew, a pillar of the community, or worse, someone they cared about? Nyla never liked James Carver, but she still remembered the punch to the gut of finding out that he was the unwilling perpetrator of so much death. Did she want to go through that again?

Pratt didn't think it was necessary, Aaron did, and Nyla was on the fence. Until they all agreed, they'd decided not to discuss it. Now, it seemed the answer had fallen into their laps whether they wanted it or not.

"All of the party-goers have been identified." Aaron glanced at her, waiting for her to object. When she didn't, he continued. "There's only one name missing from the list, both survivors and bodies. Do you know the name Malcolm Diamond?"

To her relief, the name was unfamiliar.

"It looks like Diamond organized the party," Aaron said, scrolling through the email again. "We've got text records and online messaging confirming his involvement. The handful of survivors also confirmed his presence, but he's been missing since the massacre. No body, no trace."

Nyla wasn't privy to all of the gory details of the party clean-up, but she knew enough. Bodies had been found mostly in parts, rarely all in one place, and some incomplete. Even those who were not fully accounted for had clearly suffered life-threatening injuries. Before Aaron moved them away from the crime scene at Kelley's insistence, Nyla even heard that one unfortunate man had to be identified by dental records from his bottom jaw, which happened to be the only part of him they found.

"Sounds like we have our ice demon," Nyla agreed, shuddering away the memory. "Was he involved in the demolition or something? Why did he turn?"

"He was a back-hoe operator for Blunden Construction. S&S hired them." Having gone through everything relevant in the email, Aaron slid his phone back into his pocket. "That's as good a link as anything I can think of."

"Okay, Malcolm Diamond is our Chehwinoo," Nyla repeated, chewing the inside of her cheek in thought. "And he was part of the construction crew. Does that mean there can only be one Chehwinoo active at once? The Basin has been swarming with workers, and I don't think anyone else has gone missing. Not... completely, anyway."

An image of the blood left behind by the construction worker Amelia and Sam had witnessed being killed flashed in her mind.

"It's looking that way," Aaron said hesitantly. "But I don't want to rule anything out. We should be careful to avoid assumptions. That's difficult when we don't have much else to work with, but we should try. Especially now that we won't be getting any help from Pratt."

Aaron fell silent so abruptly that Nyla thought he'd choked on his words. When she looked at him, she saw the almost pained expression on his face and knew he was thinking about his team.

Kelley's ire bothered Aaron more than he was willing to admit, but Nyla could see it in the way he tensed whenever the topic was brought up. He confessed to her that he'd been hoping Kelley would simply take him at his word like Clary had for Nyla, but things weren't that simple. Kelley refused to accept Aaron's ignorance at face value, and the rift it opened between them was growing with each passing day. It pained Nyla to see Aaron struggling like this, but nothing she said seemed to make anything easier. Whatever happened between Kelley and Aaron, they had to figure it out themselves.

Her phone buzzed, and Nyla whipped it out with more fervency than was warranted.

You'll never guess what Sam and I did today!

Amelia's short message sent floods of relief through her, and Nyla typed back excitedly.

I'll call you later to figure out when we can meet up tomorrow so you can tell me all about it!

She punctuated the text with three winking faces and turned triumphantly to Aaron.

"We may not have much to work with now, but I think that's about to change." She held up her phone and waggled it in the air. "We're meeting up with Sam and Amelia tomorrow. I *think* they have a video to show us that may give us the edge in this investigation."

"What video?"

Nyla paused, just long enough for Aaron to piece together that she was deciding how much to tell him, which meant that she knew more than she should.

"Nyla..." he began, his voice lowering in warning. "What video?"

"You know that tone doesn't work on me." She sniffed. "I like it too much."

"Don't try to distract me. What video?"

She pressed her lips together, refusing to answer. Aaron leveled her with his best glare, one that she'd seen reduce grown men to uncertain boys in the span of three seconds. It was intimidating, just not to her. She squared her shoulders, her mouth quirking in a defiant smirk.

"Have I ever told you how hot you look when you're mad?"

Exasperation flickered in Aaron's eyes, dispelling his gruff demeanor. He muttered something in Spanish, too quiet for her to decipher with her newly acquired and limited vocabulary.

"You're going to be the death of me, Nyla Leanne." Aaron huffed a sigh, crossing his arms over his chest. "Just tell me you didn't organize anything illegal?"

"I can neither confirm nor deny the legality of Sam and Amelia's actions," she recited carefully. "Plausible deniability. I wasn't there, so I don't know what happened."

"You do realize that in the four months since I met you, I've started sprouting grey hairs?"

"I've always liked the salt and pepper look."

He pinched the bridge of his nose between his thumb and forefinger, taking deep, measured breaths.

"I should've stayed in Chicago," he uttered. Nyla grinned, reaching for his arm and tugging him toward her.

"Let's not be hasty," Nyla said, sliding her hand up his arm and down his chest, teasing the waistband of his jeans. "My mouth is good for more than just aggravating you, you know."

And just like that, Aaron was laughing again.

Chapter Twenty

SAM

"This feels like something stupid people would do in a horror movie," Amelia said skeptically, planting her hands on her hips and staring at him from just beyond the doorway. "I have a rule about doing things stupid people would do in a horror movie."

Sam had the same rule, but he often didn't realize he'd broken it until far too late. This time, though, he was confident in his choices.

"Come on, Amy Baby," he cooed, hooking his arms over the edge of the hot tub and pouting at her. "Would I ever put you in danger?"

She raised her eyebrows at him, and a montage of sticky situations crossed his mind, all of which he was, in fact, responsible for. He shrugged, dismissing his own question.

"Aaron and I made sure every room was locked down tight," he tried instead, reaching for her hands. Amelia begrudgingly laid her fingers in his, letting him pull her closer to the edge of the tub. "We're safe as long as we stay inside the house. Besides, no ice demon could last more than two minutes in a hot tub."

"I'm pretty sure it could kill us in less than two minutes," she pointed out, but her resolve had broken. She bent to one side and removed her slippers one after the other, dropping them near the pile of towels Sam brought out for them. "Alright, move over Fisher. Your bulk is blocking my spot."

Sam smirked, knowing that already. He didn't move, forcing Amelia to shove him in exasperation when she was waist-deep in the bubbling water. He moved with her push, deliberately slow, until she laughed.

She'd forgiven him for the stunt at the cave, stomping away her anger on the long walk back to the cabin. Sam breathed a sigh of relief when they were safely inside, and she didn't immediately start peppering him with questions. He'd been trying to come up with an excuse that didn't involve him being an overprotective meathead since they left the construction site, but he'd come up blank. Better that she never asked at all, and he could pretend he was just making poor choices.

The hot tub wasn't a poor choice, at least.

It was located in what was essentially a sunroom at the back of the house, only accessible from inside. Even still, Sam could understand Amelia's concern. The room was almost entirely made up of windows.

The tiled floor blended into a matching tiled wall that stretched three feet up, and that was where all drywall disappeared. The room looked like it had a giant glass lid, sloping slightly at the roof to allow rain and snow to slide off easily. During the day, the room offered an unparalleled view of the outside. At night, the lack of outdoor lighting made the world beyond seem ominous and black.

For privacy reasons, Sam's parents had automatic blinds installed along each window, all of which he'd promptly closed as soon as he decided that he wanted to spend the rest of their evening in the hot tub. The only glass surface left uncovered was the roof, glazed over in places with steam.

Aaron and Nyla assured them that the creature couldn't or wouldn't break into a house. They were safe here; Sam was sure of it.

Amelia settled with the warmth as she sank further into the water, tipping her head back to rest against the exposed part of the seat. She took a deep breath, melting as she released it. Sam smiled, mimicking her position on his side of the hot tub.

"We should get a hot tub," Amelia mused, closing her eyes as she relaxed. "We could probably fit a small one in the living room."

"We could fill a storage bin with hot water and stick it on the balcony," Sam countered. Their 'balcony' hardly qualified as such, with only enough room for one of them to stand on it at a time. "Then we can just dump it over the railing when we're done. Water the flowers in the front yard while we're at it."

"Oh, I'm sure the building manager would *love* that." Amelia snorted, falling silent as the bubbles increased with the pre-programmed cycle. "Hey, Sam?"

"Yeah?"

"Things are going to turn out... okay, right?" She paused, considering her words. "Like... no one's going to... die or anything, right?"

Sam thought about it, staring up at the smudged stars.

"I don't know," he said honestly. He was still having trouble coming to terms with everything that was going on, but he couldn't deny that the danger in Somerton was very real, and they were throwing themselves into the thick of it with little warning or preparation. "Ty is going to be fine. He'll head home again and take care of Chia, and he'll be safe there."

"Nyla and Aaron are going to be fine, too," Amelia said with conviction. "They survived this once; they'll do it again."

"And so will you," Sam promised, lifting his head to find that Amelia's eyes were no longer closed. She was staring at the stars like he had been, a thoughtful expression on her face. "Whatever happens, I'm not going to let you get hurt, Am."

"You can't promise that," she said, smirking. Her eyes met his, her lips softening into a gentle smile. "But I know you'll still try. You always do."

"Of course," Sam shrugged, "who else is going to keep me in line? You think I can remember all of my important shit without you? I texted you last week to ask what year I *graduated,* Amy Baby. I can't let anything happen to you. I'd fall apart in every possible way."

He was teasing her, but it was also true. The thought of his life without Amelia pained him so much he could hardly breathe.

"I wrote all that stuff down ages ago," Amelia teased back. "You could replace me with the notebook in the kitchen junk drawer."

She laughed. Sam didn't.

He found her hand in the water, twining his fingers with hers and pulling her toward him. She looked at him in confusion but came willingly. When she was practically in his lap, Sam stopped, holding her gaze with unwavering determination.

"Nothing could *ever* replace you, Amelia." His voice cracked, trailing off in a harsh whisper. She blinked at him, surprised and uncertain. Eventually, when he didn't laugh or smile to undercut the seriousness of his tone, she nodded hesitantly.

"You're right," she said jokingly. "I *am* one of a kind."

Sam let himself smile this time, shifting them until she was tucked against his side, under his arm.

"The only one of you in the entire world," he agreed, leaning his head back against the tub again, resisting the urge to hum in pleasure as Amelia settled against him. "Which means I'm not letting you go any time soon. Sorry, you're stuck with me."

"Sam," Amelia said with a surprised laugh. "I've been stuck with you since second grade."

They lapsed into a comfortable silence, letting the sounds of churning water fill the air around them. Despite everything, it was peaceful. Too peaceful, really. It allowed Sam's mind to wander, reminding him sharply of the hulking elephant in the room.

Now. He should tell her now.

It occurred to Sam suddenly that this was the most exposed they'd ever been with each other. Sure, he slept without a shirt, but Amelia was his opposite in every way when it came to sleep habits. He'd go to bed naked if he could, and she slept fully clothed in a t-shirt and jogging pants. Now, he was lounging in what were essentially shorts and she was wearing the skimpiest excuse for a bikini he'd ever seen. It took every ounce of his self control to keep his eyes firmly above water level.

It didn't help that he'd pulled her over to him, making it impossible to hide his attraction should it decide to make an appearance. Am certainly wasn't helping matters.

She curled into his side, yawning, and Sam felt his body come to life at the touch of her bare skin on his. He had the jarring and terrifying thought that maybe Amelia wouldn't be so comfortable with him holding her like this if she knew how he felt. He should tell her, give her the chance to pull away if that's what she wanted. Or should he? Sam was affectionate with just about everyone, but Amelia didn't like physical contact with most other people. Would she resent him for taking away her only outlet? Would she resent him *more* for not? Would she even care?

Sam pumped the brakes on his whirling thoughts, taking a deep, steadying breath of chlorine-scented air. This always happened, whenever he prepared himself to confess his feelings. His thoughts would spiral out of control to the point that he couldn't think straight, and he didn't know what was right and wrong anymore. He wouldn't do that this time. For better or for worse, Sam was going to tell Amelia how he felt about her. Whatever the consequences were, he'd happily deal with whatever she could dish out if it meant keeping his best friend.

"Hey, Am?"

Sam's voice, despite his whisper, was far too loud.

"Mm?"

Amelia tilted her head up, but she was too close to see him properly. Sam fought back a smile as her sleepy movements brought her further into his embrace, practically nuzzling his neck. He sucked in a breath as her breasts pushed against his chest, barely covered by her bathing suit, the softness of her skin sending jolts of electricity through him.

Sweet Jesus Mary Mother of God—

Shaking his focus back into place, Sam cleared his throat.

"Listen," he began, wondering if he was really going to do this. Sam felt like he was on the precipice of a life-altering decision, which he supposed he was. "I know this trip hasn't exactly gone to plan, but there was something I wanted to talk to you about."

Amelia must've caught the uncertainty in his tone because she lifted her head to look at him properly.

"*Something* like you were tricked into investing in a pyramid scheme or *something* like you pissed off a high-ranking member of a drug cartel?"

He considered for a moment before answering.

"More like I gave my credit card information to a Nigerian prince who's definitely just some guy living in a basement in Ohio."

Amelia relaxed, giving him a small nod of approval.

"Complicated but not irreversible. Got it. My expectations have been set accordingly."

They weren't, but she had no way of knowing what he was about to do. *Christ*, he was really about to do this, wasn't he? Fear surged in Sam's chest, and the urge to backpedal nearly overwhelmed him. He couldn't, not this time. He'd broached the topic, and if nothing else, Amelia's curiosity would draw the truth out of him eventually. He'd made his bed and it was time to lie in it.

And hopefully bring her with him.

One step at a time, Fisher. Deal with the horny side of your brain later.

He took a breath, every rehearsed speech he'd practised promptly abandoning him. When Sam opened his mouth, he had no idea what was going to come out. He just had to trust himself to come up with something that made sense.

"Do you remember the night Dee and I broke up?"

What the fuck? Okay, clearly trusting himself was a mistake.

"Vividly," Amelia confirmed, shuddering at the memory. "What about it?"

He wished he knew.

"Uh," Sam rattled his brain, knowing he must've been going *somewhere* with that thought. A lightbulb blinked on just as he was about to jump ship, and he clung to it. "You asked me what I remembered from that night because I was acting weird, right? And I said I couldn't remember anything?"

"Sure," she said slowly. "Why? Don't tell me you just suddenly remembered? Sam, that was years ago!"

"Well, it's not exactly that I just remembered. I never forgot. I... I lied."

Amelia waited, giving no reaction. Sam took another breath. Suddenly, the hot tub water was too warm. He felt like his lungs couldn't get enough air.

"I lied and said I couldn't remember because I wasn't ready to explain myself. I mean, I should've been, probably, but the thought made me want to hurl. I still feel like I want to hurl. But I'm not going to!" He added the last part hastily as Amelia flinched away from him as if to avoid the oncoming vomit. "That's not the point. Uh..."

In all of his nightmares, he'd never imagined failing this hard at confessing to Amelia. He was talking about *vomit*. Who does that?!

"Okay, backtrack," he said hurriedly. "What I'm trying to say is that I've been wanting to tell you something for a really long time, but I never felt like it was the right moment, or I wasn't ready, or you weren't ready or... I don't know, I've probably convinced myself of every stupid reason in the world to keep this from you, but I've run out. I'm ready now, and I hope you'll be willing to hear me out."

Amelia's expression had grown wary, regarding him with an almost fear-like confusion. This wasn't going to plan.

"Amelia, I—" He stopped, swallowed, started again. "I've been hiding something from you for a really long time, and I don't want to hide it anymore. Whatever you choose to do with it is your decision, but... I want you to know."

This was it. No turning back.

"I love you, Amelia."

She stared at him, her expression completely blank.

"I mean I'm *in* love with you," he clarified, nervous energy making him fidget. "I've been in love with you for years. Ever since—"

"Senior year of high school, yeah I know."

Sam's words caught in his throat, stunning him violently into silence. Amelia was regarding him with anticipation, waiting for him to continue his speech like he hadn't just unlocked a vault of feelings he'd kept sealed in his heart for nearly fifteen years. His mouth fell open.

"How... you *know*? How do you know—?!"

"You told me."

Sam felt like his brain was short-circuiting. Every word from her mouth scrambled his senses beyond recognition.

"...excuse me?"

"You told me," she repeated. Her casual tone did nothing to soothe his bewilderment. "Multiple times now. I think... six, total? I can remember three specifically, but there's been more."

"I—" Of all the directions Sam predicted this conversation would go, he could never have guessed this one. "What— when? *How?*"

"Pretty much every time you got really, really drunk?" Amelia's attention shifted to the ceiling, thinking. "The first time was when you and Dee split. Then it was Tyler's bachelor party, then—"

"Wait, wait," Sam interrupted, his mind finally catching up to reality. He straightened, dislodging Amelia from his embrace. She looked put out but didn't try to come back to him either. "You *knew*. You knew this entire time and you never thought to bring it up?!"

"It's not like you were ever sober when you said it!" she defended hotly, crossing her arms over her chest. "I *tried* bringing it up when you weren't drinking, but you never took the bait. That's why I asked you about that night. I wanted to see if you would admit to it. For fuck's sake, Sam. You tried to *kiss* me! And then you went on and on about how you'd been wanting to for so long, but you couldn't and you wouldn't tell me why!"

Sam stared, his mind seeping out of his ears and into the bubbling water. He was broken, thoroughly broken.

"At first I didn't think you were serious," Amelia said, squirming uncomfortably. "After the first time, I just figured you were drunk and saying shit. Then it happened again, and again, and, I don't know, at some point I realized you weren't kidding. You just refused to talk about it when you weren't plastered, so I just assumed you didn't want to do anything about it."

Every nerve in Sam's body ignited at once with the instinct to refute her assumptions, but his mouth was still a little slow. She started speaking again before he could correct her.

"But thank you for telling me," she said, offering him a smile. "Getting it out in the open will probably help you get over it."

Get... over it?

With the shock ebbing, Sam finally registered the sadness in Amelia's eyes.

"I know it must've been hard for you, living with someone you liked while trying to move on. That's why I kept offering to put some distance between us, but you wouldn't hear it. I mean, I guess you know what you need better than anyone. I just know that my crush on you hasn't gone anywhere, so I figured it wouldn't hurt to try something different. Not that you ever let me get away with that."

She rolled her eyes at herself.

"I promise I'll let you say whatever you were going to say, but I want to make one thing clear first." Amelia met his stunned gaze with conviction. "I can't live my life without you, Sam. I need you with me, in whatever capacity you want.

Friend, boyfriend, occasional hookup, I'm willing to discuss just about anything as long as it means I won't lose you. I *can't* lose you."

"What do *you* want?" Sam asked, his voice strained. Amelia looked at him in surprise, not expecting him to speak yet.

"Does it matter?" She shrugged. "You don't need to worry about my feelings. I'll deal with whatever I have to. I don't want you to feel guilty for moving on just because I haven't."

"You haven't?"

"Of course not," she said with a sad smile. "I'll never stop loving you, Sam. You're everything to me."

The entire world could've erupted in bright green flames, a bubble-blowing dragon blotting out the moon with its neon wings, and Sam wouldn't have noticed or cared. His entire existence was fixated on the woman in front of him, saying things he never thought he'd have the privilege to hear.

"But that's my problem, not yours." Amelia took a steadying breath, resignation weighing her shoulders down. "I made my peace with this a long time ago. I don't need to know why you don't want anything to happen between us, but I can't say I'm not curious. Whatever it is, say what you're going to say. I'm ready."

Sam couldn't take it anymore. His body acted without instruction from his mind, reaching out and pulling Amelia into him for a fierce, desperate kiss.

She was surprised, jumping at the unexpected contact, but the surprise faded as quickly as it had come. As Sam kissed her, cradling the back of her neck in his palm, securing her to him with a hand on her lower back, Amelia melted against him. She met him kiss for kiss, breath for breath, wrapping her arms tightly around his shoulders and mimicking the movement with her legs and his hips. Her lips were soft, pillowy, and warm against his. If he didn't have something to say, Sam could've spent the rest of the night kissing her. He intended to when they'd both said their share.

"My future has always belonged to you," he whispered, resting his forehead against hers. With his eyes closed, Sam could almost convince himself he was dreaming. "*I* have always belonged to you."

"Why didn't you tell me before?" Amelia asked, tracing gentle circles across the back of his neck with her thumb. Delectable shivers rained down his spine, and he almost forgot she'd asked him a question.

"You want the honest truth?" He cracked an eye open to look at her, finding her watching him expectantly. "I've wanted to tell you so many times, but I kept finding excuses not to. After high school, I didn't think you'd take me seriously. Then you were with Alex, then I was with Jayla, then there was all that shit with school, and then the shit with your dad, then you were with Ben, and I was with Dee, and... I don't know, the timing was never right."

"Bullshit," Amelia said, scrunching her nose at him. "There were at least two years between Alex and Jayla. Why didn't you say anything then?"

"Early college years? No way," Sam scoffed. "I was a punk ass little shit in the first three years of college. You deserved so much better than that."

Outrage flashed across Amelia's face, and Sam only had a quarter of a second to brace for impact.

"You honestly think I cared about that?" she demanded, leaning away from him. Already Sam missed the contact. "Sam, are you fucking kidding me? You didn't say anything because you didn't think you were *good enough* for me?"

"I didn't *think*, I *know* I wasn't," he insisted. "For fuck's sake, Am. The bartender at Helly's used to keep a monthly tally of how many times he'd kicked me out. I almost flunked out of school every other semester. I had no idea what I was doing with my life, where I was going, what I wanted to be, nothing! The only future I could've offered you with any guarantee was a three-for-five beer every Thursday at the student bar."

"You really think any of that mattered to me, Sam?" She fully detangled herself from him now, her movements getting more and more agitated. "You have always been my person, from the very first day we met. Don't you *dare* sit there and sell yourself short. I won't hear it."

"That's exactly why I didn't tell you. You're too good for me, Am," she opened her mouth to berate him again, but he stopped her. "Wait, let me explain, alright? You wanna know when I realized I wanted to spend the rest of my life with you? I remember the exact date: August 21st, the summer after senior year. Derren Oliver's house party."

The look on her face told Sam that she remembered the party, but she didn't understand the relevance.

"The night you beat the shit out of my dad?" she said skeptically. "What did that have to do with anything?"

"Not that," he shook his head. "After. At the party. Pete dared us to do seven minutes in heaven, remember? We just hung out in the closet the entire time, but Kit was pissed when we came out."

He didn't need to elaborate on that, she definitely remembered. Amelia's ex had thrown a tantrum, not trusting her when she assured him nothing happened in the closet. They'd broken up that night, much to Sam's relief. He didn't like Kit. It gave him no small burst of satisfaction when Amelia, spiteful as she was, spent the rest of the party cuddled up to Sam to rub it in Kit's face.

Something changed that night, something intangible to everyone but them.

Sam recalled Derren asking him the next morning what specifically had been different about their behavior the night before, having heard that Am was out to spite Kit after he dumped her, and Sam didn't have a concrete answer aside from the fact that it was the first time they'd slept in the same bed, but that was mostly due to poor planning on the part of the party guests.

"That was the most fun I'd ever had at a party, and I realized it was because I was there with you. Not some other girl, or my sister, or the guys, just you. It felt right, like I was meant to be there with you, and I wondered why we hadn't been doing that all along. Except, when I thought about it, I was glad we weren't. It hit me that day that my crush on you was way, way bigger than a crush. I knew, even in my stupid teenage brain, that you were it for me. And the last thing I wanted to do was give you anything less than the best of me."

Sam gingerly pulled her back to him, smiling softly. The truth flowed easier now that he wasn't a nervous wreck. A decade's worth of confessions came out at once, releasing the tension in his soul.

"We were going to college, in another state, and I wasn't ready for a lifetime commitment. The problem was that I wouldn't settle for anything *less* than that with you. So, I decided I was going to work on myself. Figure out what I wanted to do, where my life was going, and when I felt like I had it under control, I'd tell you. When I was a man that you'd be proud to be with."

"I've always been proud of you, Sam," she murmured, nudging her nose against his. "Always."

"Maybe," he conceded, "but I wasn't."

There was a beat of silence, and then Amelia seemed to realize something. She leaned back again, staring at him in disbelief.

"Wait a minute," she blinked, "you were just going to go off and sow your oats and then *eventually* ask me out? What if I met someone else? What if *you* met someone else?"

"Well, I knew *I* wouldn't meet anyone," he said, looking at her like that much should be obvious. "As for you... yeah, it was a risk. I knew that. And I debated telling you for a long time because of it, but I just couldn't. If I told you before I was ready and we broke up, I don't think I'd ever recover. I needed to wait, to work on myself until I was confident with my ability to make you happy and give this my all.

"And sure, maybe that was stupid," he lifted a shoulder. He'd told himself as much many times over the years. "Maybe I was just looking for excuses because I was scared to tell you the truth, and I never should've waited for some mythical perfect moment that was never going to come. Nothing is ever perfect, even now. I can't say I ever pictured this moment taking place in the middle of a horror B-movie subplot.

"Maybe I was just sitting on the sidelines like a dumbass missing my chance to tell you how I feel. Maybe I would've waited too long and you ended up with someone else, but I could live with that. I could handle watching you meet someone, fall in love, get married, have kids, whatever you decided to do. I could deal with all that. But the one thing I could never do, Am, is lose you. You are so deeply ingrained in my life that I can't even begin to imagine what I'd do without you. Watching you fall in love with someone else would've been a lesser punishment than screwing up what we have because I was too impatient to wait."

"You really are an idiot," she chastised, a warm smile softening her words. "You could never lose me, Sam. You waited all these years for nothing."

"It worked, didn't it?"

"Only because Drunk Sam was looking out for you."

"I knew I kept that guy around for a reason."

As Amelia laughed at his cavalier attitude, Sam finally felt like he could breathe.

No, it was more than that. The tension constricting his chest had evaporated, yes, but that wasn't all. Something fundamental had shifted inside him, like a puzzle piece sliding into place. Amelia *loved* him. It was as though the universe granted him every wish he'd ever made all at once, blessing him with something he was sure would never happen. She loved him. She was finally his, and he was never going to let her go.

Sam slipped his palm around the back of her thigh, hoisting her effortlessly into his lap. Amelia was already shaking her head at him and smiling when he kissed her, still amazed that after all this time, he could do so freely.

Holding Amelia, kissing her, feeling her heartbeat quicken, it was more than Sam could've dared to hope for. Satisfaction simmered in his stomach, building rapidly until it twisted into urgency. By the time Amelia softly whispered his name, Sam's desire was alive and clamoring to be set free.

His lips found her neck, kissing and sucking on the soft skin there. Amelia tipped her head back, opening to him.

Then her gentle gasps were interrupted by a sharp inhale that had his entire body going cold.

"Sam."

Her spine stiffened under his touch, and he knew that something was wrong. This time, his name had left her lips in a hushed murmur, brittle with nerves. Sam pulled away, following her rapt attention to the roof.

The Chehwinoo stared back at him.

Sam cursed, tightening his grip on Amelia as he took in the sight. Despite the jarring image, he tried to remind himself that they were safe. The creature hovered over the glass, each of its clawed fingers gripping the iron frames securing the windows in place.

"It can't get in," Sam said aloud, unsure which of them he was convincing. "We're safe."

Amelia didn't look like she was listening to him, staring at the Chehwinoo in wary fascination. Luck permitting, this was the closest they'd ever get to the monster, and Amelia was taking advantage of the opportunity. Belatedly, Sam realized he should do the same.

"God, it's ugly, isn't it?" Amelia said out of the corner of her mouth, making him snort in an unexpected chuckle. As terrifying as the Chehwinoo was, it was equally disfigured. The more Sam stared at its sunken, skull-like face, the more he found wrong with it. All of the pieces were there— eyes, nose, mouth, teeth— and they were all roughly in the right place, but there was something off about the way it regarded them through the weeping tendrils of condensation and steam. Sam was struck with a memory of one of his student players who'd suffered a gnarly injury in a pre-season game. His helmet had been knocked off in a scrum, and in trying to retreat he'd been flipped face-first to the ground. He'd broken his nose, his cheekbone, his jaw, and lost three of his teeth. Combined with the bruising and dried blood, the kid looked like the poster child for an underground bare-knuckle boxing ring.

The Chehwinoo reminded him of that, without the worrying amount of swelling. It was disconcerting, trying to pick out recognizable features from the way its skin blended with the inky darkness of the sky.

"You know, I think it might be related to the guy that hit on me at the grocery store last week," Amelia said after a while. "They could be brothers."

Sam couldn't hold back his laugh, and in the time it took for him to recover from his brief outburst, the Chehwinoo was gone and the roof was coated in a thick, swirling layer of frost.

"Let's go towel off," he muttered, the water suddenly too hot and too cold at the same time. He pushed his fingers through his hair, shaking the droplets loose and finally prying his gaze away from the roof. "I don't think it'll come back, but... I'd rather not see it if it does."

"Agreed," Amelia said enthusiastically. She reached for the towels, handing him the larger of the two before quickly drying herself and following him into the security of the house.

Chapter Twenty-One

AMELIA

What in the ever-loving fuck just happened?

Amelia stared at herself in the fogged-over bathroom mirror, reeling from the aftershocks of what had transpired in the hot tub.

Not the Chehwinoo creeping on them like some kind of supernatural pervert, although that was unsettling in and of itself. No, before that. With Sam.

With her *new boyfriend*, Sam.

Maybe they hadn't explicitly stated that he was her boyfriend now, but he'd made it abundantly clear that he was in this for the long haul. Amelia was stuck grappling with the impossibility of that even now that she was inside, showered, and dressed in a pair of Sam's lounge pants and a tank top of her own.

She was reminded again of her conversation with Nyla, where she'd insisted Sam would never be interested in dating her. Amelia was eating her words now, though she was more than happy to, given the circumstances.

In her explanation to Sam, she'd low-balled the number of times he'd confessed to her. It had been happening nearly every time he was drunk enough to forget himself, and each time became a little harder for her to hear. Although the first time, after Dee broke up with him, remained the worst. Her feelings for him were still buried deep in her heart, and hearing Sam profess his love for her so casually had messed with her brain. Every subsequent confession had her chest twisting in on itself more and more. By the fifth incident and his continuing refusal to bring up the topic sober, she'd accepted that his feelings weren't something he wanted to act on, for whatever reason. She'd accepted that Sam didn't want to be with her, despite what he felt.

That hurt more than anything else, and *that* was why she didn't force the conversation when he wasn't drinking. It was one thing to hear him make a drunken confession, forget about it the next morning, and continue believing that he was just trying to work through an old crush. To hear him gently explain to her why he didn't want to date her, all the while being the kind, considerate Sam she knew and loved? Amelia didn't think she could handle that.

And all this time, she didn't have to.

Amelia cursed her own insecurity. If she'd just been honest with Sam, maybe not from the beginning but at least a few years ago, she could've saved herself a lot of confusing feelings.

But... was that really the right thing to do?

As flawed as Sam's plan had been, his approach wasn't without merit. Amelia never cared about his penchant for losing his temper with sleazeballs at the bar, nor did she care about his academic struggles. She meant what she said, she'd *always* been proud of Sam. Herself, on the other hand, was a different story.

Maybe, in taking the time to work on himself before taking the plunge on their relationship, Sam had inadvertently done her a favor, too. Amelia didn't always like the person that she was, particularly in high school and her first years away from her family. She overcompensated for her lack of freedom, behaving increasingly recklessly, and struggling with her crippled emotions. For as much as Sam insisted that he wasn't ready to commit to her before now, Amelia wondered if it wasn't *her* that really had work to do. Not that Sam would ever think so, but that didn't make it untrue.

And did any of it matter?

The how, why, and when of the circumstances that brought them together at last didn't matter anymore. They were *together*. Nothing was more important or precious to her than that simple fact.

So why was she still standing in the middle of the Fishers' ensuite, alone, like a lovestruck idiot?

When she emerged, Sam was lounging in the living room, freshly showered and shirtless, scrolling through his phone. It looked like work emails from her vantage point, but it could've been anything from the latest sports news to a random article that piqued his interest on social media. When she entered, he fixed her with a smile that made her stomach flip.

"You know," he said, dragging his gaze down her body. It wasn't the first time he'd appraised her like that, but this time was different. There was promise in his attention now, and it made her shiver. "I can't say I've ever been cock-blocked by an ice demon before. That's a new one."

"You really thought I'd have sex with you in a hot tub?" Amelia laughed, rounding the couch, and settling in Sam's lap without a second thought. She straddled him, noting with approval that he'd changed into sweatpants with acceptably thin, grey fabric. "Do you have any idea how much bacteria lives in that water? And don't even get me started on the whole 'water is as good as lube' thing. That's just objectively untrue."

"Water-based sex *is* much better in concept than in practice," he agreed, dropping his phone on the cushion next to him to slide his palms along her thighs. "Interestingly, there is currently no water to be found."

Amelia grinned, shaking her head.

"Are there condoms to be found?"

Sam's expression froze, then fell into a self-reprimanding string of curses.

"The *one time* I didn't think to pack any." He sighed, deflating into the couch. "Well, fuck me."

"Not without a condom, we *just* went over this."

He eyed her in exasperation. Amelia smirked playfully.

Sam leaned forward and captured her lips in a kiss, surprising her and taking her breath away. When they parted, they were both breathing a little heavier than before.

"I've waited this long," he murmured with a soft smile. "I think I can handle another night or two."

Amelia regarded him with interest.

"Not everything requires a condom, Samuel," she tutted, rolling her hips against his. He sucked in a gasp at the sudden friction, his grip on her tightening. "Don't tell me I have to teach you what a blow job is?"

He groaned, dropping his head back onto the couch cushion and huffing the air from his lungs.

"You're killing me, Am," he complained, and the answering pulse in his lap reiterated his struggle. "And believe me, it *really* isn't easy for me to say this, but I think we should wait. I'm... uh."

He released one of his hands from her hips, pushing it through his hair abashedly.

"I'm not exactly known for making smart decisions in the heat of the moment," he confessed. "If we're in the middle of things and you tell me to just forget about the condom, I will. I've done it before. And I know that's not what you want."

Amelia bit her lip to keep her amusement in check. She wasn't the least bit surprised that Sam was prone to lapses in judgement during sex. He was prone to lapses in judgement all the time, why would sex be any different?

"Then I guess it's a good thing for you that I'm much more disciplined," she told him, cupping his cheek and guiding his head toward her. She paused with her lips hovering against his, lightly brushing her nose with his. "Trust me. I won't ask you to do anything that either of us will regret."

Before she could seal her promise with a kiss, her phone began to ring from the coffee table. She glanced at the screen, even knowing she had no intention of answering.

"It's Nyla," she murmured, reading the name flashing across the screen. She picked up the phone and considered for a moment, thinking back to their texts from earlier.

"Is it important?" Sam's grip on her tightened, almost like holding her closer would give him the answer he wanted. She shook her head.

"She was going to call me to figure out the plan for tomorrow," with a quick swipe, she dismissed the call, "I can text her in the morning."

Less than five seconds after Amelia dismissed the call, she got a text.

Dead or banging?

Amelia laughed, pausing long enough to answer.

Not dead.

The message was read, and then the three dots indicating that Nyla was typing a reply appeared and vanished several times before another text came through.

Carry on!

Nyla's answer was punctuated with a haloed smile emoticon, which Amelia chose to ignore. She'd bring Nyla up to speed on all they'd learned in the morning; for now, her attention was elsewhere.

"Are you sure?" Sam pressed, although his body language was practically begging her to be sure. She didn't think he was aware of the gentle rocking of his hips into hers, reminding her of how aroused he already was. "If it's important—"

Amelia tossed her phone on the couch next to Sam's and silenced him with her mouth, kissing him with a ferocity that he was quick to match.

"If you're not careful, I'm going to think you don't want to do this," she said, trailing kisses along his throat. Sam grunted, shifting restlessly beneath her.

"Trust me, it's *not* that," he rasped. "I just..."

She knew.

"Sam," Amelia whispered the words against his skin, matching the slow rhythm of his grinding. "I want you. I want to touch you, and I want you to touch me. And if you don't start soon, I'm going to take care of things all by myself and punish you for it by making you watch."

"*Fuck,*" Sam fisted his hand in the hair at the base of her neck, pulling her up to kiss him. Amelia hummed in satisfaction, welcoming his tongue into her mouth with enthusiasm.

All Sam needed was to hear that she was doing this because she wanted to, not because she felt like she had to. Once he had that, Amelia felt him unravel and come to life beneath her.

She expected there to be an adjustment period where being with Sam like this felt weird to her. Amelia was prepared to talk herself through it, to trust in her feelings for him and believe that they'd find their flow with time. As it turned out, her fears were unfounded. Kissing Sam, touching him, it all felt like the most natural thing in the world, like it was the one thing that had been missing from their relationship but neither of them realized it before.

How in the hell had neither of them realized it before?

His touch was both gentle and demanding, desperate and controlled. Belatedly it occurred to her that Amelia had absolutely no idea what to expect from this side of Sam. She'd known the goofy, kind-hearted, lovable oaf side of him since they were children. This, however, was new, and the prospect of getting to know him all over again left her heart thumping excitedly in her chest.

But first she had a point to prove.

Breaking their kiss to allow Sam to lavish her neck with attention, Amelia steadied her breath.

"Sam?" He murmured a sound of response. "Do you happen to remember a rather bold claim you made recently?"

"I've made a lot of claims lately," Sam said with his lips against her skin. "All of them bold. You'll need to be more specific."

"I believe it was something about which one of us would tap out first," she purred, switching the direction of her hips as they continued in a slow circle. "You know, if we ever decided to sleep together."

"Sounds vaguely familiar." Sam hummed in thought. "I'm pretty sure I said I'd blow you out of the water though, if I had to guess."

Amelia smirked.

"How about we test your theory?"

Before Sam could respond, Amelia took control of the situation. She tangled her fingers in his hair, tugging his head back and exposing his throat. Sam grunted in approval, closing his eyes in pleasure as she kissed her way down his neck and chest.

"You won't hear any complaints from me," Sam said with a breathless chuckle, helping her as she slipped the waistband of his pants from underneath him. "Although I expect compensation when you lose."

"I think this counts as compensation," Amelia teased, dragging her hands in featherlight touches over his stomach and thighs. Sam squirmed beneath her, and she bit back a smile. Whatever bravado Sam held, they both knew who would win this war.

Her mouth roved over his skin everywhere but the twitching bulge in his boxers. Sam's breathing picked up the closer she got to tugging down his last remaining piece of clothing, giving way to frustrated sighs when she continued to ignore him. Amelia settled herself on her knees between his legs, taking her time getting comfortable, casually caressing Sam's inner thighs. When his chest was heaving and a thin sheen of sweat had formed on his forehead, Amelia relented and granted him the attention he craved.

Sam watched her take him into her mouth with an expression of pure adoration and relief, gently pushing his fingers through her damp hair and bunching his grip into a firm fist. She hummed in approval, taking satisfaction in the barely repressed grunts of pleasure that followed every stroke of her tongue.

Why Sam ever thought he'd be able to outlast her, Amelia couldn't guess. Either he'd made the joke knowing already that it was futile, or he'd underestimated her. Whatever the motive, Amelia was making him pay for it now. For every relief she gave him, she replaced with double the torments. Her hands found every sensitive span of skin she could reach, her lips and tongue gave him just enough pleasure to keep him on edge, never completely relenting to him. Sam's breath stuttered in his throat, coming out in tandem with low groans and murmured praise.

A surge of affection welled in the pit of Amelia's stomach. At last, when she could see the veins popping in the side of his neck, she swallowed him as deeply as she could, sucking and humming around his length. Sam went rigid, cursing and moaning her name on alternating exhales.

"Am, I'm—" he cut himself off on a harsh breath, his hips jerking uncontrollably. "Where?"

She released him with a wet pop, smiling wickedly.

"Wherever you want."

Sam cursed again through gritted teeth, tightening his fist in her hair. He didn't answer, but his attention dropped to her chest long enough to convey his desires. Biting her lip to suppress her grin, Amelia shed her shirt and wrapped her hand around the base of his twitching erection.

"Come for me, baby," she whispered, dragging her tongue along the length of his dick, mimicking the movement with her hand. Sam sucked in a sharp breath, letting his body take over and pumping into her grip until every muscle was taut, his climax crashing over him with an almost pained groan. Warmth spattered her neck and chest, and satisfaction coursed through Amelia's veins as Sam collected himself with a string of murmured affection for her.

"I think this might qualify as the best cabin trip ever," he said, sighing contentedly. Amelia laughed, sitting up a little straighter to give her spine a break.

Sam reached down and grabbed his discarded sweatpants, using them to gingerly and meticulously clean her skin. When he'd removed all that he could, he tucked himself back into his boxers and helped her stand, stealing a deep, passionate kiss. "Come on, I'll get a facecloth and take care of you properly."

"I hope that includes returning the favor," Amelia said, letting her hands fall to his hips and squeezing. She was teasing him, but at the same time, she couldn't help but wonder what the rest of their night would look like. Sam assuaged any doubt, slipping his palm to the swell of her ass and pinching, hard enough to make her jump into him.

"I said I was going to take care of you," Sam said. He pulled her along behind him, heading for the master bedroom and its ensuite. "Time for me to prove that I'm a man of my word."

Chapter Twenty-Two

SAM

The next morning, Sam woke with a smile.

He went to the bathroom with a smile. He made breakfast with a smile. He even took out the garbage with a smile. Sam didn't think he'd ever *stop* smiling, not after last night.

Amelia was his girlfriend.

It didn't feel real. He was more than a little afraid that he'd wake up in the morning to find the whole thing had been a dream, that he'd sunk so far into delusion that he'd made up the entire exchange. The relief that surged through him at finding Amelia curled in his arms, dressed only in his t-shirt and a pair of ruined underwear, was palpable. It was real. She was here. And she loved him.

The morning was spent reminding himself that they had bigger things to worry about. With the Chehwinoo lingering around the cabin, at least some of the time, he couldn't let himself get too distracted. That was difficult when Amelia had apparently decided that now that they'd fooled around a bit, pants were optional. Every time she bent over to grab something below hip-height, his dick was straining at the front of his jeans at the sight of her sinfully revealing panties.

He *really* needed to pick up some condoms. Today.

Satisfying his more carnal cravings would have to wait, though. Nyla called bright and early, and by the sound of her voice through the line, something was wrong.

She didn't give details, just said that she was on her way over to get them. No mention of Aaron, or the cave. Sam's happiness fell to the background of his mind as a solid knot of dread formed in the pit of his stomach. He hadn't known Nyla long, but he'd seen enough to know that she was talkative. If she wasn't giving details, that didn't bode well for whatever they were about to face.

He'd just managed to down half of a bottle of water when the sound of screeching tires echoed through the house. Amelia came running out of the bedroom, dressed in her own clothes and her hair pulled into a ponytail, and ripped the front door open just as Aaron's X5 rocked to a stop at the end of the driveway.

Before the vehicle settled, Nyla was bounding from the driver's seat.

"Big problem," Nyla panted, skidding to a stop on the brightly covered gravel. "Very big problem. We have to go, *now*."

Sam and Amelia didn't ask questions. They followed Nyla back to the X5 and barely managed to get their doors closed when the vehicle tore up the Fishers' driveway and back toward town.

"What the hell is all this?" Amelia asked uncertainly, shirking away from someone as they elbowed past her. Sam felt a twinge of annoyance, pulling her closer to his larger frame to shield her from the clamoring crowd. Nyla wasn't faring much better, standing a full head shorter than most of the assembly. Sam shuffled forward, shielding both of them as much as he could. "Are they protesting?"

Nyla had given them the run-down on the way over, and it was worse than Sam expected. Someone— likely a disgruntled relative— leaked the news about the Halloween party massacre. The anonymous party posted a scathing rant on social media, accusing Somerton law enforcement of prematurely declaring the 'rabid bear' problem solved, leading to a preventable tragedy. Sam was fully prepared for people to be angry, but he hadn't expected a mob.

From his vantage point, he could see Sheriff Mason approaching the front steps of the station. Aaron followed after him, arguing quietly. Even from here, Sam could see Aaron's careful composure only barely masking his fury. He was a force to be reckoned with, and Sheriff Mason was doing an admirable job of hiding the sweat under his collar. Sam grunted in begrudging respect.

"Aaron's trying to get him to reconsider," Nyla murmured, watching her boyfriend with a worried crease between her eyebrows. "George isn't listening."

"Reconsider what?" Amelia asked. Nyla shook her head.

"I don't know," she said under her breath, scanning the crowd. "As soon as we got the call from Pratt, I dropped Aaron off here and came to get you two."

"Tyler's here?" Sam craned his neck, searching for the bobbing blond head of his friend.

"He was," Nyla said. "He stopped by the station to talk to Kelley before he went back to Chicago, but then he overheard George talking about all this and he managed to get a call out to us before Kelley could stop him. I don't see either of them right now."

Aaron and Sheriff Mason's arguing grew louder the closer they got to the podium positioned at the top of the entrance staircase. By the time the sheriff was in position to address the crowd, Aaron had taken an aggravated step back and was watching with a hard, disapproving stare. By the time George began speaking, Aaron looked like he was about to start throwing punches.

Sam found he liked him a little better in that moment.

"Alright everyone, settle down," Sheriff Mason rumbled, sounding tired and stressed. Sam listened as the crowd shuffled into relative quiet. "I know you're all angry, and you have questions. I'm going to do my best to answer them now, but this is an ongoing investigation. I can't be completely transparent. I hope you understand that."

The answering roar told Sam that no, as a matter of fact, they did not understand.

"On August 10th, at 7:48am, the Somerton Sheriff's Department released a statement on the missing hunters. We reported that the remains of seven bodies had been found and were in the process of being identified. We also conferred with the Madison County Game & Wildlife Division and together we concluded that, based on the state of the remains, the killings had been committed by an adult brown bear with late-stage rabies.

"Rabies is a terminal condition. Our team, the FBI, and Madison Game and Wildlife coordinated a search for the infected animal, and we came up empty. Experts from Madison *and* Milwaukee determined that the timeframe of the killings indicated that the animal was either already dead or would be soon. In an abundance of caution, we held off on declaring the Basin safe again for another two weeks. When no further reports were made, the Basin was officially opened to the public on August 24th."

Agitated voices sounded off, some telling Sheriff Mason to get to the point, some telling him that he should've performed oral on the rabid bear in question.

"From August 24th to October 30th, the Basin was frequented without incident," Sheriff Mason said firmly, talking over the outbursts. "As you've been made aware by an anonymous text post shared in the early hours of the morning, an incident occurred on October 31st at the Stamkos & Stein construction site.

"Some young adults organized an illegal gathering and, unfortunately, were preyed on by another afflicted animal. Let me be clear, we here at the Somerton Sheriff's Department have *no reason* to believe that this is the same animal responsible for killing the hikers in August. We have been continuously consulting with the FBI and Madison County, and all of our experts agree that this is likely a different animal, one that possibly contracted rabies from the previous offender."

"WHY DIDN'T YOU WARN US?"

Sam tried to see who yelled, but the sudden uproar of agreement blocked any signs of the perpetrator.

"We made the decision to hold off on spreading our theory out of respect for the families of the victims," Sheriff Mason said, the rest of his sentence drowned out by outraged disagreement. "Now that the news has broken, I am coming to you today to ask for your help."

Nyla stiffened, her spine going ramrod straight. Sam felt a cold prickle on the back of his neck. Amelia gripped Nyla's arm.

"We are a community of wilderness survivalists," Mason boomed. "We know these woods better than anyone."

"George, don't," Nyla whispered.

"It is imperative that we contain this outbreak. We can't do that by sitting idly. The Basin is too large for our deputies to screen every acre, and that's where you all come in."

Sam felt the growing excitement of the crowd pulse through him like a war drum, each pang rattling his bones.

"The Sheriff's department is offering a $5000 reward for the capture and killing of any animal demonstrating the symptoms of rabies." Sheriff Mason held up a hand to quiet the crowd's anxious murmurs. "There are some rules, so I need you to pay attention.

"First, *every single member* of your hunting party must register with the Sheriff's department *before* you enter the forest. Second, you may only hunt in pairs or more, no solo parties. The reward money will be split evenly between members, and for groups of three or more, the reward total will be increased to $7000."

Sheriff Mason paused, assessing the reaction of the assembly. When no one openly complained, he continued.

"Understand that, should you turn up with an animal *not* afflicted with rabies OR your name isn't registered with the department, *you will not be eligible for the money*. Am I clear?"

A chorus of yeses echoed him.

"Good. The sign-up sheet will be posted here for the next three hours. If you fail to register in that time frame, you're shit out of luck."

Mason stepped back from the podium, and the crowd began to move. Sam grabbed both Amelia and Nyla, pulling them into him as people shoved and pushed their way to the front. Nyla turned to look at them, her eyes burning in anger.

"Come on, this way." She took hold of Amelia's other arm and Sam's hand that was on her shoulder, tugging them perpendicular to the flow of people. Nyla weaved a path through the crowd until they were clear, and then she dropped Sam and Amelia's hands to jog for a fire exit on the side of the building.

It wasn't locked, and soon they were striding purposefully down a cramped corridor, following the sounds of Aaron's angered accusations.

"It's the only option I had," Mason grunted, his words smothered by Aaron's fist slamming on the corner of his desk.

"It's a mass murder, that's what it is," he snapped, his frustration making his words sharp and cold. He barely regarded their group as they approached, and he didn't stop Nyla when she joined him in front of Mason's ornate desk. "You just dressed those men in spices and sent them to a buffet where *they're* the main course. You might as well have rung the dinner bell!"

"You're the sheriff," Nyla said, slapping her palms down on Mason's desk next to Aaron's closed fist. "*Make* another option!"

"I lost control of this situation the second that news leaked," Mason countered. He half-stood to level himself with Nyla in a posture that would've been intimidating if not for the wariness in his eyes. Aaron stepped aggressively forward, warning him against using such tactics with his girlfriend. "This town is out for blood. If I enacted a curfew, a ban, a neighborhood watch, whatever the hell soft-ass solution you're suggesting, at least two dozen men would tell me to fuck off and sneak into the Basin with a chip on their shoulder and a gun on their back."

"So, you're *encouraging* them instead?" Amelia interjected, disbelief and outrage loosening her tongue. Sam watched for signs that she wanted him to jump in, back her up, but she wasn't concerned with him. Her anger was taking hold, and Sam almost felt sorry for the sheriff. "Can't stop them, so to hell with it and condemn them all? Are all officers as considerate as you, or are the rest of them too busy knocking kids' ice cream cones out of their hands?"

"This is the best way for me to keep track of everyone," Mason said, yanking his desk drawer open and slamming a thick file in front of Nyla. "This contains information on every person at that damned party. There are people's sons and daughters in here, their nieces, nephews, grandsons, neighbors— hell, *I* know some of these kids! I can't stop their folks from going after the creature that killed their baby, but I can monitor them. If you have any better ideas, I'm all ears."

A moment of tense silence settled between Nyla, Mason, and Aaron. Sam and Amelia looked at each other, excluded from whatever history was binding the three of them at this instant. Finally, Mason sank back into his desk chair.

"I'm doing my best, Jameson. That's all I can do."

Nyla's lips tightened into a thin line. She straightened her shoulders, all of her animosity leaving her in less than a second. Her posture was rigid and cold, almost as clinical as Aaron's.

"Your best isn't enough, *George*." She turned on her heel, gently brushing Aaron's shoulder as she stalked toward the station door. The crowd had moved to the parking lot, passing the sign-up sheet around and using whatever surface available to them as a writing space. "People are going to die, and it's on your conscience. Not mine."

With an echoing slam, Nyla was gone.

Amelia stared at the gently vibrating door for only a moment before following.

"You can't afford to make enemies right now, Sheriff," Aaron reminded Mason, holding his stare. "You know as well as I do that we're your best chance at resolving this without any more bloodshed."

"Do I know that, Klein?" Mason quipped, his patience deteriorating by the second. "From where I'm sitting, you four have caused me nothing but trouble."

"Hey, I'm new to the party," Sam shrugged, "don't lump me in with the ruffians."

Aaron gave him a withering look.

"You told Nyla that you wanted the truth," Aaron pressed on, crossing his arms over his chest. The action wrinkled his suit jacket, revealing his holstered weapon. "She won't give it to you if you don't trust her. If you can't prove that *she* can trust *you*."

"What am I supposed to do?" Mason demanded, still sounding gruff despite the fact that his tone had dropped into resignation. "I've got 37 people dead, no leads, and an angry mob of locals one wrong move away from a witch hunt. I'm playing cards with half a deck and just praying there's still an ace in there."

"Your *ace* just walked out the front door," Aaron said. "And if you don't get her back on your side, an angry mob is going to be the least of your worries."

When it was clear that Mason had nothing more to say, Aaron strode over to Sam and laid a hand on his shoulder.

"Come on," he said under his breath. "There's nothing more we can do here."

Chapter Twenty-Three

AMELIA

She found Nyla sitting in the X5's driver's seat, her head angled back against the headrest, eyes closed, and her breathing measured. Wordlessly, Amelia slid into the passenger seat and waited.

After a minute or two of silence, Nyla sighed.

"You know what the worst part of being a woman is?" She opened her eyes, letting her head fall to the side to look at Amelia. "Working your ass off to earn just a mouse-fart's worth of respect and fighting tooth and nail to keep it, only to realize you never had it in the first place."

"The only mouse-fart around here is Mason," Amelia said with conviction. "Worse. He's mouse indigestion."

Nyla laughed, easing some of the tension from her shoulders.

"I wish it didn't bother me," she said quietly. "I don't hate my last name. I'm not ashamed of it or anything. It's just... I thought I was finally earning my place in this town. This feels like a step back."

Amelia remembered all of the vitriol posted online about Nyla. She hadn't had much of a chance to ask about it, given the circumstances. Now, the questions bubbled with equal amounts of curiosity and outrage on Nyla's behalf.

"What happened between you and the sheriff, anyway?" Amelia pressed. "I admit I did a bit of snooping and... let's just say it's pretty obvious the town doesn't like you."

Nyla laughed, her whole body shaking.

"That's an understatement." She sighed, collecting her thoughts. "I don't think it was anything specific. New people don't come to Somerton very often, so the townsfolk were already wary of me. Then I tried to change the way we do things here, and I kind of sealed my fate. I didn't realize how small towns work. To me, progress was only natural. Somerton has so much potential— I really believe this could turn into a safe haven for ecotourism without much effort. But... change is change. And people here don't like change."

Nyla smiled sadly at her.

"I represent change. So, they don't like me, either."

They were quiet for a time, letting Nyla's story settle.

"Then Bill didn't help things, basically elevating me from a thorn in his side to a threat to Somerton's way of life. He was the one who started calling me by my last name. It caught on with just about everyone except Clary and her family. They always had my back."

Amelia nodded, confusion flickering as the question sat half-answered in her mind.

"So, why *do* you hate being called Jameson so much? Is it just because someone you don't like started the trend?"

"Depends on who you ask," Nyla said, shrugging one shoulder. "Clary thinks that by calling me 'Jameson' instead of 'Nyla,' men are subconsciously trying to separate me from my femininity to make it easier to accept that I'm encroaching on their territory and doing it well enough to cause them problems, which my own subconscious picks up on and instinctively dislikes, causing me to react angrily."

Amelia blinked at her skeptically.

"Really it's just because I hate the whiskey."

They both laughed this time, collapsing into a fit of giggles that released the valve on the stress of the morning until tears were collecting in their eyes. Nyla recovered first, spinning in her seat to face Amelia properly.

"So..." she began, mischief twisting her smile into a smirk. "You weren't dead when I called last night. Does that mean you were...?"

When Amelia didn't answer, Nyla squealed.

"I knew it! I so knew it! How long has he been in love with you? Who confessed first? Is he big? Long? Girthy? Does he have any weird moles?"

Amelia coughed on her laughter, rescued from the onslaught of increasingly ridiculous questions by the arrival of Sam and Aaron. They slid into the back seat without complaint, Aaron's hand immediately finding Nyla's.

"Are you okay, *mi cielo?*" he asked, keeping his voice low. There was no doubt that Sam and Amelia could hear him, but they politely didn't comment.

"I'm fine, *mi sol,*" Nyla smiled, covering Aaron's hand with hers. Amelia caught the way Aaron's gaze darkened heatedly at the nickname, and suddenly she felt like she was witnessing something she shouldn't. Luckily, Nyla dispelled the charged atmosphere with a playful wink. "George will realize soon enough that he screwed up. In the meantime, we have work to do."

Nyla shared a look with Amelia, nodded so slightly that Amelia was sure the men missed it.

"Let's go to the Willow. I think Sam and Amelia have something to show us."

· · ·

Either Aaron had already guessed what Amelia and Nyla had concocted, or he was adept at hiding his surprise.

Amelia brought the video up on her phone, projecting it to the smart TV in the Willow's lobby. Sam was ready with his phone, too, scrolling through the photos he took to provide any needed context. They'd pulled the guest chairs as close to the screen as they could, keeping the lights in the lobby dim and the front door locked.

As the video played, none of them made a sound.

Until they reached the part about the frozen wall. Then, Nyla frowned and asked Amelia to pause the playback.

"Why would that be?" she pondered aloud, sharing a worried look with Aaron. "The Chehwinoo wasn't close, you would've noticed more signs. And there's no reason for the ground to be naturally frozen this early in the season."

"You said the Hovel was its den," Amelia said. "Maybe the prolonged exposure created a sort of permafrost?"

Nyla pressed her lips together, thinking.

"I don't think so," she said slowly. "Why would it only be frozen in that one place? No, I think... I think you were right about the cave being smaller. Can you rewind?"

She did, and they watched again. Nyla opened her original photos, comparing them to the video and Sam's pictures, her brow furrowing more and more.

"It's *definitely* smaller," she concluded. "There's gotta be something back there. Something that's keeping the ground frozen."

"Could it be Carver?" Sam suggested, hooking his arm around Amelia's shoulders. She took comfort in his warmth, the conversation making her feel chilled. "You said his body disappeared, right? What if it's back there?"

"It could be," Aaron agreed. "The real question is how did the wall get there? Was it deliberate? Or coincidence?"

"It could've collapsed with all the activity," Nyla said. She folded her legs beneath her in her chair. "Or it could've been thrown together. It's not a professional job, at least. I can tell that much."

"Whatever happened, that cave is important." Aaron crossed his arms, thinking. "There's a reason the Chehwinoo chose to nest there."

"Are there a lot of caves in the Basin?" Amelia asked Nyla. She nodded.

"All over the place. They're not official caves though, so most of them are undocumented."

"Could that be how the creature is moving around?" Aaron sat up, lacing his fingers together and resting his chin on his hands.

"What do you mean?"

"Nyla and I have mapped the attack locations to the best of our knowledge," Aaron said, reaching behind him to pull out a folded road map. He spread it on the floor before them, smoothing the creases and pointing out the marks he'd made in various colours of pen. "The Chehwinoo covers a lot of ground. Even with how quickly it moves, it would be difficult traveling only at night or in cloud cover. What if it's using the caves to travel in the daylight?"

"Jesus Christ," Sam uttered, "this is *The Descent*."

"I can dig around some spelunking forums, see if anyone has a rudimentary map." Nyla made a note on her phone. "If there's anything out there that will help us stop this thing, it's gotta be underground."

"Not to be a downer or anything," Sam said slowly, "but what makes you think it *can* be stopped? The spirit just found another host after Carver died, so why are you so sure there's something out there to find?"

"Sam's right," Amelia chimed in with a grimace. "You're making a lot of assumptions, aren't you?"

"Not as many as you'd think," Nyla said. "I've been researching the Chehwinoo since we killed the first one. I haven't found *too* much, but it's enough to give us a rough idea of what we're dealing with."

She pulled a notebook out of the pile of papers on the table beside her.

"It took me a while to figure out how to sift through the information I needed, but I got the hang of it after a while. The Chehwinoo has popped up in Somerton before, just not in our lifetimes. I started with weather reports for unusually long or cold winters, or random frosts that were out of season. Then I collected some books on local legends and matched up the dates wherever I could. I found a few Bigfoot-style accounts that lined up with one of the hard winter records. I also found some very old news articles referencing 'cold sickness' or 'cold curse.' Might be unrelated, but the dates also match up with one of the harder years, so I made a note of it."

She flipped through some of the pages.

"A lot of this information goes back over 100 years, so really all I have are fragments that I've pieced together. But I'm confident that this has happened before. Several times."

"Is there a pattern?" Amelia asked excitedly, leaning forward in her chair and disengaging from Sam. He let her, observing quietly. "Like, does it resurface every ten years or something like that?"

"I thought it might, but the dates are all over the place. Even accounting for huge margins of error, I can't come up with even a loose pattern that fits all the information we have."

"What about town development?" Amelia looked up at Nyla. "This has something to do with the S&S factory, right? Could it line up with other expansion projects in the area?"

"I haven't been able to get full access to those yet, so it's possible." Nyla put her notebook down. "Somerton's records are sealed going back 50 years. I requested access, but I haven't been approved. Probably George's doing."

"So, either this thing is very choosey about what constitutes an intervention-worth threat, or something is stopping it from running rampant. At least temporarily."

"Exactly," Nyla agreed with a smile. "That's where I'm at right now. Out of all the places in the Basin to hide out, it chose the Hovel for its den. That *has* to mean something."

"Does it though?" Sam piped up suddenly. "Can't it just be right-place-right-time? It needed a spot to hide, and it was close to that particular cave, so it made its nest there?"

"It could be, sure, but I don't think so. Not when you consider the stone carvings." Nyla paused, chewing on her bottom lip. "We can't know for sure until we figure out where Carver was when he turned. That could answer a lot of questions. If it was close to the cave, then yeah, it could be a coincidence. If it wasn't..."

"Then he deliberately sought it out, even in his corrupted mental state," Aaron concluded.

"Which means it's important." Nyla dipped her chin decidedly.

They fell silent, contemplating all that had been said. Amelia's mind raced as she tried to make sense of it all, searching for patterns or clues that would help them clean up this mess before anyone else got hurt.

"Do we know where Frosty the Snow-demon is nesting now?" Sam asked suddenly. Aaron gave him a half-smile, which Amelia took to be a sign that they were warming up to each other.

"No, but I've been working on that." Aaron pulled out another map, identical to the first except it was printed on nearly transparent paper. "I have a theory, and I'd like to run it by everyone."

He smoothed the new map out until it was matched with the one beneath it.

"This is the Basin. These red dots are known kill sites, and these yellow dots are reported sightings or attacks." Amelia immediately noticed that a marker had been added above Sam's cabin, accounting for the hot tub sighting she'd told Nyla about on the drive over. "If you connect the outermost dots, accounting for a few miles of variation, you get a rough idea of its hunting grounds."

Everyone leaned forward, scrutinizing the map. Amelia took a photo with her phone, and Sam did the same.

"In criminal investigations, this would be considered a comfort zone, either where the suspect lives or works. If the suspect is smart, they'll target victims outside of their comfort zone to throw off investigators. That's risky because they're deliberately entering an area that they're less familiar with and are more likely to make mistakes that get them caught. But it *is* a smart decision if they're trying to go undetected, which most criminals are."

Amelia glanced at both Nyla and Sam, confirming that they were both as confused as she was about where Aaron was going with this.

"Obviously, the Chehwinoo isn't a human. But it *used* to be. We've seen firsthand that their cognitive function and decision-making are largely impaired, overrun by the spirit of the creature. That means they wouldn't be thinking clearly enough to leave their comfort zone to conceal their location, but their instinct would still be to follow the basic principle. It would stand to reason then that this area," he traced the outline of a circle with his index finger, "is where the creature lives. Likely somewhere in the middle of the region, for convenience's sake."

"That checks out," Nyla said, nodding slowly. "Territorial animals behave the same way. Even if his human instincts aren't in the driver's seat, the animal instincts would lead him in the same direction."

"What are those numbers?" Amelia pointed to a series of digits dotting the map. Aaron followed her direction and straightened.

"Good question," he said approvingly. "I was curious, so I mapped both the first and second Chehwinoo on the same grid. The comfort zones line up perfectly, other than the fact that the first Chehwinoo's home base is closer to the edge of the comfort zone than the middle."

"Which lends viability to my theory." Nyla hummed in thought. "This area is important. The next logical step would be to search it."

"How long would it take to search an area like that?" Amelia asked uncertainly. "With only four of us?"

"Longer than we probably have," Nyla conceded. "But we actually have five of us."

"What?"

At that moment, almost as if she'd planned it, there was a knock on the front door. Belatedly, Amelia realized that Nyla probably *could* have planned it; she was sitting at the perfect angle to see the parking lot through the window.

She leapt to her feet, rushing to unlock the front door. When it swung open, Aaron's expression noticeably soured.

"Emmett!" Nyla greeted, hugging the absolute beast of a man that stood on the other side of the door. Amelia couldn't help but stare— the man, apparently named Emmett, stood roughly in line with Aaron in terms of height, taller than Sam by a few inches. He was *wide*, though, wider than Sam and *definitely* wider than Aaron. Part of that bulk came from the large work jacket he wore, but Amelia couldn't tell just how much.

"Nyla," he said with a grin, scooping her up in a swinging embrace. Aaron didn't look *angry* exactly, but Amelia didn't think she imagined the quick eyeroll that slipped out before he schooled his features into a polite smile. "Still getting into trouble?"

"Always," Nyla said cheekily. "Come on, I have people I want you to meet."

Nyla led Emmett to their group huddle, presenting him with a dramatic flourish.

"Sam, Amelia, this is my good friend and secret lover, Emmett."

"Only when Aaron is in Chicago," Emmett cut in with a sly grin. "I can never quite get her alone long enough when he's in town."

"Update your trade certification yet, Coady?" Aaron challenged drily. "If I remember correctly, it expires next month. Hate for your boss to have to kick you off the job over an administrative hiccup."

Despite the veiled threat, Emmett laughed.

"I welcome you to try, Klein." He extended his hand for a shake, which Aaron accepted with a wry smile. Amelia suspected that their relationship was a lot less hostile than they were making it seem. "Nice to meet you two, Amelia, Sam."

"Emmett is a local," Nyla explained. "And he's already up to date on our ice demon. I asked him if he'd be willing to lend a hand."

"Bricklaying isn't the most exciting occupation," he explained. "I'm overdue for a little thrill."

"Great," Nyla said, clapping her hands together definitively. "Let's get planning. I'll grab some popcorn."

Chapter Twenty-Four

INTERLUDE

Nyla

"I'd kill for a cigarette right now."

The first time Nyla and Aaron had sex, he'd been injured and considerably less mobile than normal. In light of his restricted performance, he'd made a promise to her at the time: when he was recovered, he'd make it up to her on every horizontal surface at the Willow, plus some of the vertical ones. Aaron had happily made good on his promise many times over, in varying degrees of creativity, but Nyla's favourite place to be with him was always the same: snuggled together in bed, naked and tangled in the afterglow of a good, hard romp.

"I didn't know you used to smoke," Aaron said, his voice rumbling against her ear. She counted the measure of his heartbeat as it slowed to a normal pace, his breathing following suit. Nyla's head was on his chest, her body stretched languidly beside his beneath the sheets.

Sam, Amelia, and Emmett left over an hour ago, having gone over the loose plan for searching the Basin and hammering out as many details as they could. It was too late in the day to start once they were all in agreement. The real work would begin the next day.

"I didn't," Nyla sighed, basking in the attention Aaron's hand was giving her jellied limbs. With slow, careful strokes, his palm smoothed over the skin of her arm, shoulder, and back, caressing her almost absently. "I don't know why but smoking a cigarette after good sex always seemed so satisfying to me."

Aaron laughed, stretching his free arm over to the nightstand to check his phone. Seeing nothing important, he dropped it again and folded his hand behind his head.

"How about something a little less carcinogenic?" Aaron nodded in the direction of the mini fridge, and Nyla hummed in agreement. With a quick kiss to her forehead, Aaron rose to retrieve two cans of beer.

Her sour mood had returned after the others left, following her to her cabin but not a step further. It was difficult to simmer when Aaron was around, her annoyance only ever lasting as long as it took them to find somewhere with some privacy and promptly shed their clothes. Now that she'd blown off some steam, as well as some other things, Nyla could think straight.

As angry as she was at George, she couldn't dwell on it. Whether he understood it or not, he was about to have another massacre on his hands. If they didn't do something soon, people were going to die. And despite what she'd said at the station, Nyla couldn't separate herself from that fact. She needed to try, vendetta or otherwise.

Aaron returned to the bed, handing her an open can from a local brewery she liked. Nyla sipped it thoughtfully, letting Aaron draw her into him as she slid into deep contemplation.

Finding the Chehwinoo was only one of their problems. They could kill it, but without further guidance, it would inevitably come back. More than that, they had to stop the hunting party from waltzing into the fire.

It was enough to give her a headache.

"You're thinking too hard," Aaron pointed out, pressing a firm kiss to her jaw. "Stop."

"If I could do that on command, I'd save myself a lot of sleepless nights," she said with a smirk. "Sorry. I know there's nothing we can do right now. I just don't like sitting here waiting."

"I know," he gathered her in his arms, soothing her with his presence. "Try to put those feelings aside for now, *mi tesoro*. You need to rest, too. All action isn't going to help us either."

"You're right," Nyla conceded, "but that doesn't mean I'm going to listen."

A knock on the cabin's door caught both their attention, giving confused looks in the direction of the porch and then at each other.

"Are you expecting anyone?" Aaron asked her, already reaching for his slacks. Nyla shook her head, sitting up in bed and wrapping the blanket tightly around her torso. Aaron's jaw clenched, cool professionalism taking over the warmth they'd shared. He holstered his handgun, which Nyla couldn't help but smirk at. Tall, muscled, and naked from the waist up, Aaron was plenty intimidating without his weapon. Adding it was a deliberate display of dominance that both soothed her anxiety and tempted her to pull him back into the bed and ignore their unwelcome visitor. Aaron noticed the quiet appraisal she gave him, his lips twitching in a barely-contained grin.

"Behave," he reminded her, pressing a gentle kiss to her forehead.

"Never," she said, biting her lip as he made his way to the front door. She leaned over far enough to grab the nearest article of clothing— an old high school t-shirt that had stretched and warped over the years until it fit her more like a shapeless minidress— and quickly slipped it over her head just as the sound of the door opening filled the cabin.

There was a slight pause, and from her vantage, Nyla could just make out the tension bunching Aaron's back. Whoever it was, he wasn't happy to see them.

"Can we help you?" If she wasn't sure before, Aaron's deadpan indifference confirmed that this was definitely an unwelcome guest. A flicker of panic sparked in her stomach, her mind conjuring images of repo men and debt collectors banging down her door. Nyla shoved those fears away. While it was true that she didn't have an income with the Willow indefinitely closed, she'd paid for the property in full. She had meager savings, but it was more than enough to last her another three months in terms of bills. Besides, she felt safe in knowing that *if* someone did come for her lodge, she wouldn't be alone in fighting to keep it. Aaron was more familiar with the law than she was; if he wasn't worried, then she shouldn't be. No one was coming to take her livelihood, not yet anyway.

So, who was at her door?

"Is Nyla here?"

"George?"

She was out of bed and standing next to Aaron in a few short strides, folding her arms over her chest. Aaron shifted enough to give her a proper view of Sheriff Mason, but not enough to remove himself as a physical buffer between them. George dipped his chin, having the decency to look embarrassed at interrupting them.

"What are you doing here?" Nyla tried to keep the trepidation from her voice, not sure if she succeeded.

"I was hoping we could talk," George said, shuffling his feet uncomfortably. He wouldn't quite meet her gaze, choosing instead to look at a spot on the doorframe that was far less interesting than he made it seem.

"If you're here to lay some bullshit charges on her, you can come back with a warrant," Aaron warned, his tone brokering no argument. "And you might as well bring a lawyer along. You'll need one."

"I'm not here to fight." George finally lifted his head to look at them, the worried crease in his brow giving away the gravity of his visit. Nyla straightened. "I need your help. Please."

"What kind of help?"

He produced a folded leaflet of paper from his jacket, handling it like an angry, venomous snake. As he smoothed it, Nyla recognized the sign-up sheet from the town meeting.

"I'm in over my head," he told them, gesturing hopelessly at the list of names. "More than half the town is going into the Basin, some of them as soon as tomorrow morning. That's too many people for me to follow up with. I know I was an ass back at the station," his gaze flickered to Nyla, "but I hope I didn't completely burn this bridge."

Aaron said nothing, waiting for Nyla to take the lead. She took a measured breath, considering.

"What exactly do you want, George?"

"Everything," he said, the words choking him like he had to force them from his tongue. "I'm all out of reasonable explanations for whatever plague is decimating my town. You know something, and I may not like what you have to say, but I'm ready to listen. I want you to tell me everything."

There was no mistaking the desperation in George's voice. He was at a breaking point, ready to accept whatever truth made even the tiniest bit of sense. He needed something to grab onto, something to make him feel like he could act. It was exactly the moment Nyla had been waiting for all these months, the moment she knew that if he was ever going to believe them, it would be now.

So, she told him. And, true to his word, Sheriff George Mason listened.

Chapter Twenty-Five

SAM

The plan wasn't *really* a plan, not in any way that Sam could follow. He'd tried to keep up with the technical jargon coming from Nyla and Emmett, failing miserably when the conversation turned to different altitudes and terrains. Sam simply informed them to point him in the right direction, and he'd do what he needed to do. The problem was that he didn't understand what it was he needed to do.

Thankfully, Amelia seemed to keep up with the conversation with more ease than he did. By the time they returned to the cabin, courtesy of Emmett, Amelia had compiled a thorough list of things they needed to prepare before the morning.

Spending their day trekking through the Basin, searching for signs of a rotting ice demon wasn't exactly Sam's idea of a fun vacation. He wouldn't argue, though. Whatever reservations he had, he wouldn't let Amelia walk into this nightmare alone. He was going to be right there with her.

Although, he wasn't overly reassured to hear that the last time Nyla, Aaron, and Emmett had led a group into the woods in search of this thing, both Tyler and Aaron had almost gotten themselves killed.

To be fair, they hadn't known then what they were dealing with. They still didn't, not as well as Sam would like.

He and Amelia had barely finished shoving some semblance of food in their mouths when they heard a vehicle coming down the gravel drive. They looked at each other in worry, both jumping to the conclusion that it was Nyla or Aaron, or maybe even the sheriff, and something was wrong. When Sam got to the front window, though, his nerves vanished.

Tyler quickly exited his sedan, striding purposefully to the front door and entering without knocking.

"Ty!" Amelia cried out in both relief and excitement. Sam skipped the greeting altogether, crossing the room in three steps and engulfing Tyler in a hug. "You're still here! How's Chia? When are you going back to Chicago? Do you need anything? Is everything okay?"

"She had her coffee late today," Sam said jokingly, interrupting Amelia's endless stream of questions. She scrunched her nose at him in agitation. "Just let her get her energy out and then you can talk to her normally."

"Shut up," Amelia said in an irritated huff. She elbowed Sam out of the way so she could hug Tyler too, squeezing him tighter than normal. "I was worried, okay?"

"When *aren't* you worried?" Tyler teased, ruffling her hair in the way she vocally hated, but secretly loved. At least, Sam assumed as much. She never stopped him or Tyler from doing it. "All is well, I promise. Chia is with her mom and the insulin is doing its work. I'm on my way home now, but I couldn't leave without checking in. You know, after everything."

Everything. That was a nice way of putting it.

Sam hadn't had much time to think on how he'd feel once he finally spoke to Ty again. There was a lingering hurt in knowing that his oldest friend had kept a secret from him, one that nearly ended up getting them killed. But there was also understanding. Some part of Sam expected him to be angry talking to Tyler, but now that they were here, face to face, he felt only relief.

"I should've told you guys," Tyler said anyway, as if reading Sam's mind. Maybe he just read his expression. "I just didn't think you'd really come all the way out here. If I'd known—"

"Stop," Amelia interrupted, giving him a stern frown. "If you'd told us over the phone that an ancient ice skeleton was murdering people in the woods, we would've thought you'd lost your mind. Everything worked out exactly as it needed to."

"Yeah, except for the part where you two are caught up in this mess." Tyler pushed a hand through his hair, revealing the dark roots buried beneath the blond. "I wish I could stay. Help. Something. With Kelley watching my phone, I can't even call Klein."

"What exactly is going on there?" Amelia asked, echoing Sam's thoughts. "Nyla said something about it, but she didn't give details. Kelley is your boss, right?"

Tyler nodded, providing a short overview of the complicated situation involving Aaron, who was the previous unit chief, and Kelley, who was the current.

"It's just one more hurdle we need to jump before we can clean up this mess," Tyler said, sighing. Sam clapped a hand on his shoulder encouragingly. "But that's neither here nor there. How are you? Both of you? How are you handling everything?"

"With grace and sex appeal." Sam grinned. Amelia rolled her eyes at him. "You know us, there isn't much we can't weasel our way out of."

"That's what I told Klein," Tyler said, returning Sam's grin.

"I'm surprised you can tell 'Klein' anything," Sam said, failing to keep the bitterness from his voice. "Dude's a corporate hard-ass if I've ever seen one."

Tyler furrowed his brow, the corners of his mouth lifting in a confused smile. Amelia shook her head, cutting in before Sam could explain.

"Ignore him. He's upset that Aaron called him on his bullshit."

"I hardly think questioning the sanity of two people blabbering on about an ice demon qualifies as 'bullshit.'" Sam sniffed.

"Maybe not if we hadn't just been *attacked* by said ice demon."

"Look," Sam said, shrugging, "all I know is that one minute, I'm fighting for my life against some deformed popsicle and the next, I'm being barked at by a CIA-flunky in an overpriced suit. I'm allowed to dislike the guy. Given the lack of sleep, he's lucky I didn't break his nose."

Tyler burst out laughing, sinking his hands into his pockets in a casual gesture.

"If you ever decide to try, *please* take a video." His laugh died to a chuckle, fixing Sam with a playful warning. "I've known both of you for years so trust me when I say, Klein may be a corporate hard-ass, but he'd knock you flat in less time than it takes you to blink. That guy is the only reason I passed my last physical."

A retort grumbled to Sam's lips, but Tyler held up a hand.

"Believe it or not, he was probably trying to protect you, not piss you off." At Sam's skepticism, Tyler continued. "Come on, Fisher. I know you. You're not exactly the pinnacle of reliability, and Klein's a hell of a lot more perceptive than the average guy. As uptight as he is, his Mama Bear override is *strong*. If he thought for even one second that your attitude would get you or anyone else hurt, I have no doubt that he would've given you an ultimatum. Am I right?"

Sam's petulant silence spoke volumes. Tyler only grinned.

"Fine," Sam huffed, "he's not an *arrogant* jerk. He's just a jerk."

"And one of the most dependable allies you'll ever have." Tyler swung himself into a bar stool, taking a deep swig from Sam's half-empty can of soda. "I actually think you guys will get along pretty well if you'd stop pouting."

"I'm not pouting!" Sam said, absolutely pouting.

"His ego is just bruised." Amelia laid her hand on his bicep, the warmth of her palm soothing him immediately. Sam felt a jolt of adrenaline at the impact of just that small touch. "He'll get over it, and then Aaron will wish he'd done more to piss him off just to get rid of him."

She was probably right. Sam was a bit childlike in that way, easily provoked and quick to forgive. He had no doubt that, at some point, he'd forget why he was ever bitter toward Aaron in the first place.

Just not yet.

"My ego is impervious to damage," he pronounced confidently. "Although I'd never turn down a little stroking."

He winked at Amelia, who rolled her eyes in exaggerated exasperation.

Whatever Tyler was about to say next was interrupted as his attention snagged on the dining room table. Sam knew what was there without looking.

"Is that our old bird house?"

He'd brought the splintered pieces inside, hoping there was enough structure left that he could cobble it together again. Unfortunately, the ice had demolished the little wooden house beyond repair, and Sam still didn't know what he wanted to do with the remains.

"Our frozen friend knocked it off its perch," Sam explained with a half-smile. "I was trying to fix it but, well, look at it."

Tyler nodded solemnly.

"Maybe we can make another one," he teased. "You think Mr. Albert still runs woodshop?"

"You think Mr. Albert would let us back *in* woodshop?" Amelia said with a disbelieving laugh. "Last I heard, they're still not allowed to have jigsaws on campus."

They all laughed then, nostalgic warmth spreading through the room. Sam was reminded of how grateful he was to have friends like this, knowing that no matter what— time, distance, work, family— their bond was there, ready to surge to the surface at the drop of a hat.

"I shouldn't stay too long," Tyler said after a comfortable silence. "I want to hit the road before it gets too late. Chia has been tapping out early lately, so if I'm much longer I won't get to see her before she goes to bed."

"Go," Amelia said, smiling. She didn't reach for another hug, her first one being more than enough to sate her. Sam suspected her enthusiastic greeting had more to do with an outpouring of relief than an actual desire to hug anyone. "We'll keep you updated on our end."

"You'd better." Tyler took her cue, settling for another brief hair tousle before enveloping Sam in a tight hug. "Behave, alright? Don't make me regret vouching for you."

"Never!" Sam gasped, affronted. He slapped Tyler on the back, ending the hug with a lingering squeeze. "Take care of your wife. And try not to pass on too many of your genes to that poor baby."

"Fuck off," Tyler said, laughing. He shoved Sam away from him, still chuckling. "If you guys change your mind about having kids, I'd be *way* more worried about passing on your genes, Fisher."

Sam's eyes narrowed at Tyler, wondering when he'd mentioned that he and Amelia were dating. He was pretty sure he hadn't. Tyler caught his questioning look and, with a smirk, tapped the side of his neck knowingly.

"Pretty weird place for a bruise," he said nonchalantly. Sam cupped his hand around his neck, knowing he couldn't feel the hickey but needing to search for it anyway. "I'm texting Roxy on the way home. She's going to be *livid*."

Far too cheery at the prospect of dealing with Sam's fireball of a sister, Tyler sauntered out the front door, waving over his shoulder like everything was finally right with the world.

Chapter Twenty-Six

AMELIA

Tyler's visit had given them the dose of normalcy needed to finish getting through the day.

Amelia didn't love the thought of spending several hours searching the Basin Forest for the Chehwinoo, but what choice did she have? She'd seen the destruction the creature wrought with her own eyes. Knowing that she could help and had chosen not to wasn't something she could live with.

Besides, she liked Nyla and Aaron. She didn't *want* to abandon them, death-hike, or no death-hike.

The remainder of their evening was spent packing. Neither of them was particularly wilderness-savvy, but some strategic internet searches and a heaping dose of common sense helped them piece together a rough list of essentials. Well, helped *Amelia* piece together a rough list of essentials. Sam was there for moral support and retrieving things as directed. By the time darkness fell, the only thing left for them to do was get a good night's rest.

Except that was about as likely as the sky falling down around them.

"I can think of a few things that would tire us out," Sam suggested with raised eyebrows. Amelia glared at him.

"Did you remember to buy condoms?"

His expression fell guiltily.

"Yeah, that's what I thought."

She busied herself going over the map that Aaron had let them borrow. Nyla was familiar enough with the layout of the Basin that she didn't need a pre-hike study session, and Aaron wouldn't willingly leave her side, so the map went to

Sam and Amelia for the night. She knew she couldn't memorize the entire thing in a matter of hours, but she could try. The problem was that the more she stared at the map, the more overwhelming their task became.

How the hell were they supposed to find this thing in the middle of... all that?

"You're overthinking again," Sam said from his spot on the couch. Amelia sat cross-legged on the floor, poring over the map that dwarfed their coffee table.

"When am I *not* overthinking?"

"Good point." Sam shifted behind her, and she knew before his hands found her waist that she was about to be disturbed from her perusal. With a swift tug, Sam pulled Amelia from the floor and onto the couch with him, holding her captive as he shuffled into a horizontal position. When he was settled, stretched across the full length of the couch, he tucked her securely against his chest, his palm on the back of her head, pressing her cheek against his heart.

"Sam—!" Amelia pushed against him, but his arms were like steel around her. Sam grunted, and she angled her neck to look up at him only to find he already had his eyes closed. "Would you let go?"

"Shh," he murmured sleepily, trapping one of her legs between his thighs. Amelia struggled in his grip, exasperated. "Sleep."

"I can't sleep," she complained. Sam's other hand grabbed her forearm, pulling her arm around his torso and pinning her between the couch cushion and his body. With one arm and one leg immobilized, Amelia knew she wasn't freeing herself any time soon.

"The map will be there in the morning," he said, his words slurring. Sam could sleep under just about any circumstance, and Amelia always envied that about him. "Save the others from the torture of spending time with you when you're sleep-deprived and cranky."

"You're such a dick," she uttered into his shirt, the words coming out muffled. Sam shook with a soft chuckle, and then the hand on her head drifted down her spine, soothing her tensed muscles. For a moment, Amelia actually believed she might fall asleep.

Then a piercing wail sliced through the silence.

She sat bolt upright, using Sam's shock to shake off his grip. The sound echoed, hollow and chilling through the night air.

"What the hell was that?" Sam muttered, pushing himself up onto his elbows. Amelia scrambled from his lap, rushing to the window, and yanking the curtains back.

It was quiet again, but it wasn't peaceful. Amelia stared hard into the inky darkness beyond the glass, fear inching up her spine. As she watched, tiny fractals of ice began to form in the corners of the pane.

A chorus of shrieks shook the air, followed by a series of gunshots.

"The hunting party," she whispered in horror. "They went out tonight."

That wasn't supposed to happen. Nyla told them that hunters typically set out in the early morning, before dawn. While the lack of light could cause problems, they weren't expecting too much trouble. The Chehwinoo would likely be hunkering down for the day at that point, and the hunters wouldn't be in much danger. It would've given them a solid 7 or 8 hours of daylight to find the creature and take care of it before anyone else got hurt.

They never guessed the hunting party would leave *tonight*.

By the time Amelia recovered from her shock, the screams had turned to whimpers and then to eerie silence. More screams, closer this time, began to tremor through the leaves.

"Sam, it's the hunting party!" Amelia slammed the curtains closed, muffling the sounds. If she listened to them much longer, she'd be frozen in place for the rest of the night. "We have to do something!"

"What?" Sam's startled voice followed her as she spun on her heel, reaching for her boots. He caught her arm, pulling her to an abrupt halt. "Are you insane? You're not going out there! You'll be killed!"

"I can't just sit here and do nothing!" Amelia argued, shrugging out of his grip, and frantically searching for her hoodie. "Those men are dying! We have to help them."

"What are you planning to do?" Sam demanded, physically blocking her from the door. Amelia tried to duck around him, but his frame was too bulky. She crossed her arms over her chest instead, refraining from stomping her foot indignantly. "Am, we've both seen what this thing can do. How are we supposed to help?"

"We have a cabin the size of a small country!" Amelia snapped, waving her arms around her to illustrate her point. "The Chehwinoo can't come inside, right? We can get our asses out there and guide the hunters to safety! All we have to do is avoid the cold. It's not like we won't know when it's coming!"

"And what do we do when it's coming?" Sam shot back. "The thing's faster than a teenage boy's first handy. You gonna outrun it?"

"We'll get something to slow it down." Amelia whirled, calculating the most effective means of fending off the creature. Strategies sprouted in her mind like wild daisies, none of which she could accomplish with the things currently at her disposal. She turned to Sam again. "We need some kind of weapon. Maybe—"

"Amelia, *stop*. This isn't happening!" Sam pleaded, desperate. Amelia wouldn't back down— *couldn't* back down. Not now. Not when people were in danger. "We're not equipped to handle this, alright? We don't even have a gun!"

That gave her pause, but only for a second. They *did* have a gun, and Sam realized it at the same moment that she did.

"No," he interrupted her thought process before it could go any further. "Absolutely not. You're staying put, and that's not up for debate."

"You're choosing *now* to put your foot down?" Amelia snapped, all but begging him to relent. "Since when do you ever shy away from trouble?"

"Don't act like this is comparable to a B&E," Sam said. "My first and only priority is keeping you safe. If I think for even a single second that I can't do that, whatever the situation, it's. Not. Happening. I don't know that I can keep you safe if we go out there right now. So, we're not."

His tone was aggravated but final. Amelia glared up at him, challenging his steely resolve with an unabashedly low blow.

"What if Tyler's out there?"

She saw the hit land as uncertainty briefly flashed across Sam's face. Tyler wasn't out there. They both *knew* that Tyler wasn't out there. He'd left for Chicago hours ago. He was probably in bed with Chia, soothing her through her pregnancy pains. But he hadn't texted them to say as much, so the possibility was there. Amelia tracked Sam's thoughts as they surfaced.

Tyler is in Chicago.

He didn't text or call us to confirm he's in Chicago.

He might have been called in to help with the hunting party.

He could be out there right now.

He wasn't. Amelia was sure enough to bet money on the fact that he wasn't. But it was *possible*, and that's all she needed to steer Sam over to her side.

While he was still wavering, Amelia darted around Sam and ripped the front door open just as chaos crashed through the trees. Weapon or no weapon, she was going to do whatever she could to help.

She looked up in time to see a man, a hunter in army green and neon orange, thundering through the underbrush with pale, unfiltered terror on his sweat-drenched face. He was far, but not too far. If he sprinted, he could make it to the safety of the house before the creature was on top of him. Amelia ran out onto the porch, waving her arms in the air to grab the man's attention.

"OVER HERE!" she cried, her heart hammering in her chest. She wasn't expecting the fear that solidified in her stomach the moment she was outside, but she fought through it. Panic had long since lost the ability to paralyze her. "GET INSIDE! QUICK!"

The man faltered, tripping over a discarded branch that had splintered from its parent tree. Amelia froze, her breath stilling in her chest as the man tried to catch his balance and keep running. Something was moving through the trees behind him, bringing with it a deathly chill in the air. The Chehwinoo was coming, and it was coming fast.

In a blur, Sam lunged from the back porch and sprinted at the man, skidding to a stop just in front of him, his sneakers sliding in the mud. Amelia screamed at them to *move*, and in the next second, Sam had an iron grip on the man's jacket and was hauling him to his feet, dragging him to the safety of the cabin. The trees were shaking violently now, frost beginning to spread across the grass at an alarming rate. Amelia's heart felt like a jackrabbit thrashing against her ribcage, pushing air from her lungs and making her want to run. She fought the urge to leave the porch, holding the door open for Sam and the hunter as they barreled toward safety.

With a crash, the Chehwinoo burst into the yard.

Amelia screamed again, incoherent in the face of the snarling creature. It looked worse than when she'd seen it before, and she briefly wondered if some of the hunters' shots had landed. It roared in anger, its golden yellow eyes homing in on Sam and the hunter, jerking its fractured limbs into a canter. Sam shoved the man ahead of him as they reached the edge of the porch. He stumbled over the doorstep, careening to the floor, and sliding to a stop against the kitchen island. Sam was only a few feet behind him, but it felt like miles as the Chehwinoo continued to gain ground. Amelia started to search for something to defend him with— a broom, a fire extinguisher, *anything*— when she was struck hard in the chest. She fell backward with Sam, who'd tackled her back into the cabin just as the frost clutched at the wood beneath her feet. With a violent kick, Amelia slammed the cabin door on the Chehwinoo's infuriated screeching.

Sprawled across the floor of the cabin, the three of them struggled to catch their breath.

"I hate you so much," Sam panted, dropping his head back onto the tile with a hard thud. "Seriously. You're so lucky you're hot."

She barked a short laugh, quickly pushing herself into a seated position.

"You're the one that ran out there like a lunatic," she chastised. "I was just holding the door."

Sam muttered something unintelligible, but Amelia's attention had already shifted to the man. He was huddled against the kitchen island, breathing in shallow, rattling gasps. He looked unharmed, just in a state of shock. Amelia scrambled over to him, crouching in his line of sight.

"Hey, can you hear me?" When he nodded, she kept going. "How many people are out there? Do you know?"

The man shook his head.

"Were you with anyone?"

He nodded and held up a single finger. Amelia shared a look with Sam, but before she could press for further information, the man's tongue loosened.

"My buddy, Jack," he rasped. "He— it—"

They didn't need to ask for more. It was clear from the look on the man's face that there was no rescuing Jack.

"We need the gun," Amelia announced, getting shakily to her feet. The Chehwinoo, with so much prey readily available, hadn't lingered. She could already feel the warmth returning to the air. "There have to be more men out there. We can try to guide them back."

"I'm not going to convince you out of this, am I?" Sam said in resignation, not really posing it as a question. "Call Nyla. Let's see if we can't rescue some of these idiots."

◈

The hunter, whose name turned out to be Kliff, had lost his rifle in his escape. That left them with only Mr. Fisher's old Remington 700 as their means of damaging the creature. Amelia toyed with the idea of unraveling the garden hose, but she wasn't yet able to determine if the Chehwinoo was *weak* to water, or if it simply had an aversion.

Unfortunately for them, Kliff was too traumatized to be of much help. He gave them the general direction he'd come from, guessed at the number of men he'd crossed paths with, and then fell into a series of nervous mumblings that neither she nor Sam could pick out.

They were on their own.

Making the dash from the front door to the rental truck was the hardest part. Taking the first step into the night, willingly, knowing she was leaving the safety of the cabin proved to be a bigger mental block than Amelia was ready for. With a deep breath and a tight grip on Sam's hand, they'd sprinted to the vehicle and fumbled with the automatic lock for a heart-stopping second. By the time they were seated inside, they were both panting heavily from the adrenaline alone.

"Okay, now what?" Sam asked, pressing the keyless start button and adjusting every setting he could reasonably reach. It was a nervous tic, one that Amelia dutifully ignored.

"We should pull the truck out onto the road," she said, thinking out loud. "It's more open than the driveway. We'll be exposed, but the creature will have less cover. And the hunters might be able to see us better. If we can get their attention, maybe we can get them into the truck and back to the cabin. We could fit five or six people in here, right?"

Sam glanced at the back seat, calculating.

"If we cram them, yes." He shook his head. "Do we know if a vehicle counts as 'inside?' Have Nyla and Aaron tested that?"

"I don't know," Amelia bit her lip, looking down at her phone, "I still haven't heard back."

She'd called Nyla immediately after Sam left to search for the Remington, getting only her voicemail. She left a frantic message with as much detail as she could provide, then sent a series of texts for good measure. Her phone remained despairingly quiet.

"Well, it's the best shot we have right now." Sam lurched the truck into gear, peeling down the driveway with unnecessary volume. "If they don't see the headlights, maybe they'll hear us."

He revved the motor, honking at uneven intervals. Amelia fought back the instinct to tell him to be quiet; if the men were near enough to hear them, the creature was too. They couldn't attract the attention of one and not the other, not with any plan she could come up with.

When the truck settled in the middle of the cabin road, the Basin was still silent.

For a tense moment, Amelia didn't know if she was relieved or disappointed. No movement meant no life, for better or for worse, which also meant no imminent danger. Whether that was because the hunting party had already been wiped out, or because they were too far from the cabin to reach them, she had no way of knowing.

Sam laid on the horn again, the tenor echoing through the trees and disturbing the silence. Amelia stared through the window, waiting for signs of anyone or anything crashing through the woods. When a young maple buckled just beyond the reach of their headlights, she registered what it meant before Sam did.

The prospect of someone in danger pushed all hesitation from Amelia's mind. She shoved the truck door open, jogging into the path of the headlights and waving, watching her shadow's fingertips rustle the shivering leaves.

"Is someone out there?" she called, cupping her mouth with her hands. An answering shout carried on the breeze, directly in front of her. Sam was out of the truck now too, rifle poised and balanced on the hood. With clumsy unfamiliar movements, he removed the safety and leveled the scope with his right eye. Sam wasn't a hunter, but Mr. Fisher had shown them both the basics of gun safety on the off chance they needed to handle one— thinking back on it, he probably meant in case a bear wandered onto the property. Amelia guessed that a life-or-death fight with an ice demon wasn't on his radar at the time.

Sam's finger hovered outside the trigger, like they'd been taught.

Amelia held her breath, waiting. The noises grew closer, and she was able to pick out at least two people. The wind shifted, bringing with it an icy chill. Two people, and one Chehwinoo.

The trees crackled and splintered, releasing the creature before the men. It leapt from the sea of evergreens and crashed gracelessly onto the stretch of road between Amelia, Sam, and the escaping hunters. Gravel and dirt sprayed in wide arcs where its disjointed limbs plucked its spindly body from the ground, crackling and hissing with unnatural strength. The Chehwinoo let loose an inhuman shriek, thick globules of slush spattering from its knife-sharp fangs and colouring the dirt with melting ice. From back on, Amelia could see the uneven pulse of its lungs beneath its papery skin, suctioned onto its ribs like latex.

The hunters tumbled into the street, and Sam shot.

The bullet glanced off the Chehwinoo's shoulder, splintering its arm from its body. Sam quickly reloaded as Amelia dashed to the other side of the truck, away from the monster and into the hunters' field of vision. She whistled around her index finger and thumb, the piercing note grabbing their scattered attention with more efficiency than her voice ever could've. They saw her, hope lighting their features, and scrambled to reach the safety of the truck.

Another shot sounded off, followed by more cracks and screeches. Amelia chanced a look at the Chehwinoo, howling in fury at Sam as he leveled the rifle for another shot. Faster than she could blink, the creature swiped its horrifically long claws in a wide arc, clipping the front bumper of the rental and knocking Sam to the ground. The rifle skittered to a stop just out of his reach. Amelia didn't think— she rushed forward to grab the gun, but her movement drew the Chehwinoo to her. It lunged, snapping its broken jaws, reaching for her with its remaining arm. She faltered, sliding to her knees and letting the gravel take her the extra foot she needed to clear its grip.

"Am, watch out!"

Sam's bark warned her in just enough time to dodge the Chehwinoo's back-swing, the cold bite of its claws nicking Amelia's sleeve and tearing it straight down the length of her arm. She huddled behind the front tire of the truck, catching her breath, assessing. The rifle was closer to Sam now, and the creature was closer to her. No, not to her. To—

The Chehwinoo belted a roar of agony, galloping at full speed toward the hunters. They froze, caught between making a final dash for the truck or returning to the cover of the trees. Their indecision only lasted half a breath, but it was enough. The Chehwinoo's teeth squelched through both of them in a single snap, piercing one man through the shoulder and the other through the chest, shaking its head violently until their bodies were flung from the confines of its teeth. Amelia screamed, clamping her hand over her mouth a fraction too late.

Crimson blood dripped from the Chehwinoo's gaunt skull, collecting in shallow pools in the gravel. It heaved deep, shuddering breaths, as if scenting its successful kill. With a jittery, almost hesitant gait, it reached for its severed arm. Amelia watched in shock as it jammed the twitching limb back into place, grinding its bones together until they fused. The sound made her want to retch. She waited for it to turn on them with the same frightening speed that it had used to target the hunters, but it remained in place, breathing heavily, letting the blood and slush ooze from its mouth.

By the time Amelia had collected herself, Sam had the rifle. He inched around the truck, taking advantage of the Chehwinoo's momentary lapse. When he reached her, Sam tugged Amelia behind him, shielding her from the guttural moans emanating from the creature's throat.

She wanted to ask what it was doing. She wanted to see, she wanted to look away, she wanted to understand, and she wanted to never speak of this again. In the absence of clarity, Amelia chose to face the demon head on.

Sam raised the rifle, and the Chehwinoo moved.

Like lightning, the demon batted the Remington from Sam's grip just as a bullet pierced the air. It missed its target, lodging somewhere in the trees. Gathering itself to its full height, the Chehwinoo eyed them with its cold glare, cracking its maw open and loosing a tremoring scream.

Amelia ducked behind Sam's bulk, covering her head, bracing for impact, but it never came. She heard the roar of an engine, squealing tires, and suddenly the gravel was illuminated with the bouncing beams of headlights.

"Jesus!" Sam cursed, shoving Amelia backward. They both tumbled to the ground just as the Chehwinoo turned to face this new arrival, its scream cut horrendously short as a blast of controlled flame struck it in the mouth. The creature writhed in pain, screeching in outrage, and then it tore off through the trees after less difficult marks.

"Are you guys okay?"

The familiar voice preceded the thump of boots in the dirt and then Nyla appeared, circling the truck as it rolled to a stop. She shouldered the nozzle of a weapon that looked like it was plucked straight from a Michael Bay film.

"Nyla?" Amelia questioned, looking warily at the futuristic apparatus. "What... what is that?"

"Flamethrower," she answered easily, offering Amelia her hand to help her up. Sam was brushing the dirt from his jeans when the truck's driver appeared, and Amelia recognized Emmett. "Well, this went to hell faster than expected, didn't it?"

Her voice was far too calm for the situation, Amelia thought. Then again, maybe staying calm was what had helped them survive the first creature.

"Stupid men and their stupid egos and their stupid lack of common sense," Nyla muttered under her breath. "They shouldn't be out here. Not now."

"Tell that to them," Emmett grunted, jerking his chin in the direction of the two bodies the Chehwinoo had left behind. Nyla's expression darkened for just a moment, and then she was shrugging off the dread. Amelia only wished she could compartmentalize like that. Maybe it had something to do with her dating a retired Fed.

"What are we dealing with?" Nyla asked them, turning deliberately so she couldn't see the bodies. Amelia turned with her, keeping her back to them, too. "How many?"

"You know as well as we do," Sam said with a grimace. "There's one traumatized hunter back at my place, and these two. It seems like there're noises coming from every direction. It's impossible to pinpoint where they're coming from."

"Not for us," Nyla said with conviction. "Em?"

Emmett pulled a crumpled map from his tattered army green jacket, smoothing it over the hood of his truck.

"We're here," he pointed, "and the hunting party would've started somewhere around here. It's the only safe place to enter the Basin at night."

"Safe being the operative word," Sam interjected.

"The fucker ran this way," Emmett continued like Sam hadn't said anything. "Which means..."

They all fell silent, listening. When Nyla and Emmett straightened suddenly in response to some sound Amelia missed, they shared a discreet nod.

"Northwest," Nyla muttered under her breath. "Not good. It's moving toward the highway."

"Let's focus on getting as many people inside as we can," Emmett said, reassuring her. "You guys said one was in your cabin? Can we fit more?"

"It's not so much a cabin as it is a McMansion." Nyla smirked.

"We can definitely fit a mildly out-of-control frat party in there," Sam agreed, nodding sagely. Emmett scrunched his brows a little at the comparison, but it served its purpose.

"Alright," Nyla said with a deep breath. "Let's go. The night is, unfortunately, very young. If anyone is going to make it to dawn, we need to hurry."

Chapter Twenty-Seven

INTERLUDE

Aaron

Aaron didn't think it was possible for his headache to get worse. He was never one to have headaches at all, and he was glad for it now. The pulsing pain behind his eyes distracted him from the array of documents spread out across ex-sheriff Bill Hannaford's abandoned desk.

After speaking to George at length, Aaron had accompanied him back to the station to try to fill some of the gaps in their theory. To his credit, George had accepted the Chehwinoo mythos with little resistance— Aaron suspected that they had small-town superstition to thank for that. Or the desperation of a man who was decidedly out of options. Whatever the reason, Aaron was more than a little relieved that he didn't have to fight with George to get him on their side. It was a small blessing that he didn't take lightly.

A blessing he *had* taken lightly was the Bureau's exhaustive efforts to digitize every physical file in their repertoire. What he wouldn't give for a real-life CTRL+F function to sort through the stack of papers in front of him with any kind of efficiency.

George wasn't much help. Having only recently been brought up to speed with the situation, he didn't know what he was looking for. Any effort he made to skim documents simply resulted in him repeatedly asking Aaron if minute details were relevant, taking both of them twice as long to get through a single page. Eventually, Aaron told him to focus on his normal work for the sake of his sanity.

Nyla opted to remain at the Willow with Emmett. Aaron tamped down the spark of jealousy that fizzed in his gut at the memory. He trusted Nyla without question, and Emmett was proving to be a reliable friend. His instinct to rebel at the idea of his girlfriend spending time alone with another man came from a place of insecurity he'd long buried. The echoes of youth-fueled temper rarely disturbed him as an adult, but tonight he was on edge. Too much stress, too little sleep.

He pulled his phone from his pocket, illuminating the home screen where he'd featured a candid photo of Nyla, stretched precariously against the trunk of a leaning birch tree, reaching for an abandoned bird nest she wanted to display at the lodge. Aaron smiled, reassured, and turned back to his work.

It was a quiet night at the station, which was ominous in and of itself. Much like an emergency room, a quiet night in law enforcement was almost always a precursor to chaos. Aaron ignored the nugget of apprehension at the base of his skull for as long as he could, but when the front door opened and the sound of determined steps in practical heels approached them, he knew his peace was about to be shattered.

"Sheriff Mason," Kelley's voice broke the silence, crisp and authoritative. Aaron would've smiled if he wasn't so exhausted. When he'd first met Kelley, her confidence in speaking to people outside their unit had been shaky. Now, she commanded a room with ease. "I need to speak to you—"

Her words clipped as she rounded the hall into George's office and her attention landed on Aaron. She was stunned for only a second, and then hard anger took over her expression.

"Klein," she said sharply. "What—?"

She stopped herself, taking in the scene before her. Kelley was smart and capable, it was why Aaron named her chief in his absence. It also meant that she put two-and-two together much faster than either he or George could come up with an excuse for him being there. When Kelley realized that Aaron had formed yet another allegiance, her gaze darkened.

"You've got to be kidding me," she muttered, collecting herself before speaking again. She lifted her head with bitter judgment. "Sheriff Mason, you *are* aware that Mr. Klein is not a member of the FBI, correct?"

"Agent Kelley," George began, standing uncertainly. "I was just conferring with—"

"I don't care what you're doing," she interrupted. "This is a federal investigation. You are not permitted to share confidential information with contractors."

George hesitated, looking to Aaron for guidance. Aaron sighed, nodding his chin as subtly as possible toward the door, trying to convey to George that he should leave. While George didn't pick up on the cue, Kelley did.

Bristling with annoyance, Kelley stepped aside.

"Your front desk phone is ringing," she snapped at George. The sheriff looked quickly between Aaron and Kelley, finally accepting the not-so-subtle hint. Without further delay, he ushered himself out the office. As soon as he was out of sight, Kelley whirled on Aaron.

"Do I have to arrest you to get you out of my hair?" she demanded, striding purposefully across the room toward where Aaron sat. He stood in response, knowing full well that she wasn't trying to intimidate him with her proximity. Kelley knew that Aaron wasn't easily cowed. She was trying to see what he was working on but covering her snooping with her aggressive body language.

"You can't arrest me for doing my job," he argued. Anger flared in her eyes.

"You're not *doing your job*," she corrected, "you're making mine harder."

Aaron didn't want to fight about this. Not again.

"Pay me no mind," he said as casually as he could manage. "There's no reason we can't work independently on the same case."

"Oh, bullshit." Kelley folded her arms over her chest, regarding him with skepticism. "You ruined any illusion of collaboration when you *lied to me*."

"Which time?" Aaron retorted. It was a low blow, but his patience was quickly splintering. His shot landed, and Kelley's anger hardened into scorn.

"Get out," she commanded. "If I see you anywhere near this station, I'll have your ass in jail so fast your ears will still be ringing with your Miranda Rights when I lock the cell."

Kelley turned on her heel, stomping for the door, and that's when Aaron decided he was done.

"Why can't you trust me on this?" he said, huffing in irritation. "All the years we've worked together and now, when I need your faith the most, you're choosing to be stubborn."

"*Stubborn?*" Kelley stopped dead in her tracks, cold fury replaced with white-hot rage. "What do you *want* from me, Aaron? I spent the weekend slicing through red tape with a clerical machete to get Wildlife down here ASAP and I come back to find half the Basin on fire, Bill Hannaford dead, James Carver missing, a corporate political scandal that's *way* above my paygrade, Pratt with a *concussion* and the three of you babbling about a chemical explosion and a sick bear that apparently hired *Ed fucking Gein* to be its interior decorator!"

Kelley paused, breathing hard, as her words hung in the air between them.

"And you know what the worst part is?" She sighed, pushing her fingers through her blonde locks. "Even though your story was *obviously* crap, I busted my ass pushing it through. Do you have any idea how many favors I had to call in to cover this shit up? How many people I had to negotiate with? How many rules I had to break? And I did every single bit of it without hesitation because *that's what you would do*."

Aaron didn't interrupt her, letting the hurt and betrayal flow freely in the room.

"You were the kind of boss I always wanted to be," Kelley muttered. "You were strict but fair, and you had our backs first. It didn't matter what kind of trouble we got ourselves into; you'd defend us tooth and nail and then tear strips off us later, when it was just the team. You'd accept whatever ridiculous lies we fed you because you knew that if we weren't telling you the truth, it was because we *couldn't,* and as soon as we *could,* we would. You trusted us unshakably, so we trusted you.

"So, here I am, having accepted your lie thinking you'd eventually trust me with the truth." Kelley was quickly losing steam, anger fading to confusion and pain. "And the truth isn't coming. I can see it on your face, Klein. You have no intention of telling me what's going on here. What conclusion am I left with other than that you don't trust me?"

Silence followed her question. Aaron swallowed, pushing aside his headache, his sleep deprivation, and his stress. Kelley deserved his full attention, and he was going to do his best to give it to her.

"How many times have I lied to you, Kelley?" he asked. She paused, taken aback, before answering.

"Including this mess? Twice."

The answer surprised him, until he realized she was talking about his reason for leaving the team. Aaron took a steadying breath. He couldn't part with two truths today, but he could part with one.

"You're right," he said, resigned. "That's two too many, but I can only fix one right now."

Kelley's eyebrows drew together.

"I left the team because someone asked me if I always wanted to be an FBI agent," Aaron explained, "and I realized that I'd *never* wanted to be an FBI agent."

Kelley opened her mouth, found no words, and closed it again. Aaron waited for his confession to sink in before continuing.

"It's stupid, right?" He raised an eyebrow at her. "That's why I didn't tell you. All my life, I've done whatever made my parents happy. When I excelled in school, they encouraged me, so I kept excelling in school. When I took a career aptitude test and law enforcement was at the top of my list, my parents were thrilled, so I studied law enforcement. I chose this life because I was good at it, not because it was what I wanted. I just didn't realize that until Izzy asked me if I'd always wanted to be in the FBI."

At Kelley's surprised expression, Aaron coughed a laugh.

"Yeah, a two-year-old caused my midlife crisis. Talk about adding insult to injury."

He crossed his arms, leaning against George's desk.

"Why didn't you just tell us that you didn't want to be a Fed anymore?" Kelley asked in bewilderment, momentarily distracted from her ire. "I mean, I guess you did. But you didn't *explain*."

"Kelley, I handpicked every single person on our team to be the most efficient unit in the department," Aaron said. "You all worked your asses off for me. You dedicated your careers to working *for me*. How was I supposed to tell you all that I was done because I never got the chance to choose what I wanted to be when I grew up? I couldn't disrespect you like that. You all deserved better. I didn't have better, so you got the best I could do."

A begrudging understanding passed between them, quickly replaced by agitation as Kelley found the thread of her betrayal again.

"That doesn't even matter now," she quipped. "Don't think I'll give you a pass because you told me one of your secrets. I risked my job for you, Klein. And you can't even summon the decency to tell me why you can't be honest."

"I did," Aaron said insistently. "You weren't listening. *I handpicked every single person on our team.* That includes *you*, Rebecca. I know you, better than most. I know your skill, your capabilities, your strengths, your weaknesses, everything. I know you're a damn good agent. I also know that, above all else, you're pragmatic. Logical. You won't believe a single word of what is happening here. Don't you think I want to tell you? Don't you think I realized how wild our story was? I knew you'd have questions, and I knew it would be a pain in the ass to hide the truth from you. For fuck's sake, Kelley. This isn't easy for me either. But I know you won't be able to accept what happened out there—"

"Try. Me."

"*Listen to me,*" Aaron growled. "I don't need to try you. I know. I worked with you for ten years, Kelley. That wasn't for nothing."

"Don't act like you know what's best for me. You don't get to decide what I'm ready to hear."

"In this case, I do." Aaron took a deep breath, emotions tumbling over one another in his gut. "I don't want secrets, I don't want lies, but I don't have a choice. It's like the potato salad."

Whatever Kelley had been about to say died on her tongue. She scrunched her face in blunt confusion, trying and failing to make sense of his words.

"The... potato salad?"

"Last Christmas," Aaron said dismissively, waving his hand in the air. "German brought in his grandmother's potato salad to the potluck."

"Right..." Kelley trailed, still not following.

"Pratt loved it, remember? Ate half the bowl. He asked German for the recipe so he could make it at home, but we all told him it was better if he didn't know. I offered to give the recipe directly to Chia so Pratt wouldn't see what was in it."

"Eggs," Kelley said, her eyes lighting in recognition. "The salad had crushed hard-boiled eggs."

For as long as Aaron had known him, Pratt insisted that he hated eggs. All kinds of eggs. However, Aaron knew that the hatred was purely mental. He often saw

Pratt digging into dishes with eggs as a component and, as long as he didn't *know* the eggs were in there, he thoroughly enjoyed himself. As a result, no one told Pratt if there were eggs in a recipe.

At the Christmas party, Pratt insisted that he could handle it. He'd long since figured out that people were hiding the presence of eggs from him, and he suspected that was the reason for the potato salad recipe gatekeeping. He'd given a long speech about how he was an adult, and he could handle knowing that something he liked included eggs. He insisted that he could still enjoy the food if he knew.

In the end, German gave him the recipe. To prove his point, Pratt took a huge spoonful of the potato salad. He promptly threw up into the nearest trash bin.

"Pratt likes eggs, as long as he doesn't know they're there." Aaron caught Kelley's eye. "We keep it from him because we know how he'll react, and knowing will just ruin the experience for him. Rebecca, I'm doing the same thing.

"I know this is hard to take, but there's no doubt in my mind that you *won't accept* what's really going on here. You can't. It's not in your scope of reality. If I tell you, I know exactly what's going to happen. You won't accept it because you can't justify your beliefs with the facts. You'll drive yourself insane, and you'll have all of us committed. You might even have *yourself* committed. I won't do that to you. If you being eternally pissed at me is the price I have to pay for protecting your sanity, I'll pay it. I'm not claiming I know what's best for you, but in this one instance, I wholeheartedly believe that keeping the truth from you is the right thing to do."

Aaron softened, appealing now to his friend, Rebecca, not his successor, Agent Kelley.

"You trusted me once," he reminded her. "Draw on that trust, please. Have faith that I'm doing this for a reason. A really fucking good one."

The room settled. Kelley and Aaron remained frozen, staring at each other, unwavering. After far too long, Kelley sighed, averting her gaze.

"I'm telling the team about Izzy," she said under her breath. "They deserve to laugh at the fact that a toddler made you question your life decisions."

For the first time in too long, Aaron grinned.

"Aaron—!" Sheriff Mason skidded to a stop upon seeing Kelley still in his office, his expression faltering. Aaron could see the clear panic on his face, but with Kelley in the room, he couldn't speak openly. "There's... there's a situation."

At the same time, Kelley's phone began to buzz repeatedly. She held up her smartwatch, her brows furrowing more and more with each word she read.

"What the hell..." she whispered, glancing sharply up at Sheriff Mason. "You wanna tell me why I just got notice of nine emergency calls in the last five minutes, every single one of them in your jurisdiction?"

"It's the hunting party," George explained, his eyes pleading with Aaron to understand the parts he wasn't voicing. "They left tonight. I didn't realize— I didn't think—"

George paused, collecting himself.

"Someone was attacked," he said. "The whole operation is falling apart. Fast."

Aaron whipped out his phone to see texts from Nyla, telling him that she was with Sam and Amelia, doing whatever they could to help, and that he should meet them at Sam's cabin. Fear gripped him, and he hastily tried to call her. No answer.

Kelley was quiet for a moment, thinking hard. Eventually, she grabbed Aaron's shoulder and met his gaze with fire.

"You were never here," she said quietly. "If anyone asks me, I haven't seen you since the press conference. When I got to the station, the only people around were Sheriff Mason and the receptionist."

Aaron nodded once in understanding.

"Don't make me regret this, Klein," Kelley pleaded. "Do whatever you have to, just make sure you come back alive."

Chapter Twenty-Eight

SAM

With Nyla and Emmett helping, they'd managed to save a handful of hunters.

After the first few fumbling attempts, they'd worked out an effective system. Nyla and Emmett, wielding the flamethrower and the Remington, positioned themselves in the truck bed, keeping the creature from getting too close. Sam drove the Tacoma along the cabin road, directed by Emmett, stopping whenever they heard signs of trouble. At that point, Amelia and Sam would hoist a flare each and try to guide the men to safety, dropping them off at the cabin before going out again to continue their search.

It was working well until they came across a group of hunters too large to transport in one trip.

Once they realized they couldn't possibly fit all the men into the truck, even cramming some in the open bed with Nyla and Emmett, panic had taken over the hunters. They fought viciously, throwing each other to the ground and clamoring for a spot in the vehicle. Sam and Emmett wedged themselves in the middle of the scuffle, calling for order, but the adrenaline was too high for reason. When the temperature dipped, the arguing turned into a frenzy of desperation and fear.

Sam had one man by the arms, locked behind his back, while Emmett held two more by the chest when Nyla stood in the truck bed and blasted flame into the air.

"Emmett! Take the rifle and bring as many men as you can to your dad's truck," she commanded, firing the flamethrower again when the hunters began to push back. "Amelia, climb up here with me. Sam, drive. All of you shut the *fuck up* and let us help!"

The momentary shock of Nyla's firm orders wore off quickly. Emmett grabbed as many men as he could, tearing off in the direction of his vehicle. Sam dropped the man he was restraining, who collapsed to the ground in a disgruntled heap. Amelia had one foot on the tailgate, her left hand clutched in Nyla's as she helped her up when one of the hunters let his temper flare.

"Why should we listen to *you*, Jameson!?" He lunged into the truck bed with Nyla and Amelia, spitting his words in Nyla's face. "Don't act like you know better than us!"

"Hey, back off, asshole!" Amelia elbowed her way in front of Nyla, glaring at the hunter. Sam saw her fist clench, knowing she was getting ready to throw a punch if necessary. "We're trying to *help* you, you ungrateful shit."

"We wouldn't need help if it wasn't for *you!*" The hunter ignored Amelia, cursing at Nyla. Amelia drew herself taller, but Nyla laid an appeasing hand on her shoulder. "I don't know what the fuck you did, but I'd bet my left nut that all of this is your fault!"

"Seriously, Warren? You're going to pick a fight with me *now?*" Nyla jerked the flamethrower's nozzle toward the trees, which were shaking violently in the distance. "We don't have time for this! Get your ass in the truck!"

"How about you give me the flamethrower, and I'll get my ass *home!*" Warren made a grab for the nozzle, crowding Nyla's space until the backs of her knees collided with the edge of the truck bed. Amelia steadied her, and Sam prepared to leap into the bed to their defense, but he didn't need to. Suddenly, Warren was jerked backward by his collar, hitting the ground with a decisive thud that knocked the air from his lungs.

"Listen to the woman or we'll leave you here as an appetizer," Aaron snarled, shoving his hand into Warren's shoulder blades as he released him. Warren pushed himself onto his elbows, gasping for breath, while Aaron turned to the others. "Anyone else want to test me tonight?"

Wordlessly, the remaining men crowded into the truck.

"Good timing, Suits," Nyla said with a smile, hopping down from the truck bed and wrapping her arms tightly around Aaron. He breathed a sigh of relief into her hair, and Sam was caught between giving them a moment of privacy and urging them to hurry. Before he could turn his head, they separated. "I didn't even hear you pull up."

None of them had. Aaron's X5 was mere meters away, and they'd all been too busy shouting over the panicking hunters that they hadn't noticed.

"How many do we have accounted for?" Aaron demanded, winded.

"Five in Sam's cabin," Amelia answered him, nodding in the general direction of the cabin. "Six more in the truck now. Three went with Emmett. At least seven dead, but there's probably more."

"Alright." Aaron squeezed his eyes shut, pinching the bridge of his nose. "Kelley and her team are going to be on the way soon. George is organizing his men, but we have to try to take care of this before they get here. Obviously, our original plan is out. We need to try to corral it somehow, get a shot through its chest. The Chehwinoo is fast, but it has too many moving targets. It can't possibly get to everyone. We need to draw its attention this way, and then we can hold it off until we can limit its movements. Then we can— is that a flamethrower?"

Aaron's speech came to a screeching halt as he finally registered the dystopian-looking monstrosity in his girlfriend's grip. She shrugged casually, hoisting the nozzle for his inspection.

"I called in a favor," she said less than helpfully. Aaron blinked, a stunned expression on his face.

"Three more at the cabin!" Emmett's call brought their attention to the road, where he was jogging down the gravel drive with the rifle strapped to his back and a flare held high above his head. "How many are left?"

"At least thirty," Aaron said with a grimace, recovering from the momentary shock. "George is hoping that most of them are on the other side of the river, away from immediate danger. But we don't know for sure."

A chill swept through the air, and all five of them flinched.

"Get inside," Aaron uttered under his breath, swinging open the driver's side door of his BMW. "Quickly."

They did as they were instructed, Nyla sliding into the front seat with the flamethrower laid across her lap, nozzle pointing at the door. Sam held the back driver's side door for Amelia, who hastily scrambled into the safety of the vehicle, meeting Emmett face-to-face as he climbed in from the opposite side. Once everyone was seated and the doors closed, Aaron turned around to speak to them again.

"Can we all agree that the Chehwinoo will probably go after the largest group?" He paused to give them time to disagree. When no one did, he continued. "According to George's manifest, the vast majority of hunters were heading for the Willow, where Leo disappeared."

"They've scattered," Nyla said, biting her lip in thought as she scanned the manifest. It was discarded on Aaron's middle console; Sam hadn't bothered to look at it, knowing his input wouldn't be helpful in this regard. "At least two of these guys are among the ones we've rescued. That's a long way from the Willow."

"Damn," Aaron said, sighing and ruffling his hair in frustration. "We need to track it down. We can't do anything until we know where it is, and we don't have a lot of time. Kelley is covering for us, but even if everything goes our way, reinforcements will be here by midnight. This is already a slaughter. It's about to turn into a massacre."

"Kelley?" Nyla questioned, looking at Aaron hopefully. "She's on board?"

"We hashed some things out," Aaron admitted, twining his fingers with Nyla's. She squeezed them reassuringly. "What we need right now is a miracle."

"Is there no way we can enact the original plan?" Emmett pleaded. Sam had been quiet up until this point, but his exasperation boiled over now.

"We're missing half the ingredients of the original plan," he huffed. After finding the Chehwinoo's lair, the strategy had been to light the entire place on fire, with Emmett, Nyla, and Aaron ready and armed with rifles should the creature make an escape. With no lair, no accelerant, and one rifle, Sam guessed that Emmett knew as well as they all did that their plan was useless. He was as desperate for a solution as the rest of them were. "It's the middle of the night, we don't have anything prepared, and there are about 40 lives on the line. I think we're past the point of planning."

"Sam's right," Amelia said, leaning forward. She pressed her leg against his in the process, silently lending him her support. The pressure soothed him. "We don't have the time or resources to go about this the way we want to."

"So, what," Emmett said, "we give up?"

"We need a new idea," Amelia corrected. "Something we can pull off with the things we have available to us right now. Time limit included."

"I have an idea!" Nyla ignored Aaron's curious stare, instead making eye contact with Amelia. The two women shared some kind of unspoken agreement that made Sam nervous. From the way Aaron's jaw twitched, he was sensing it too.

"Is it a stupid idea?" Amelia asked with lifted brows. Nyla smirked.

"I've had worse."

"Count me in."

"Hold on," Aaron interjected quickly, echoing Sam's panic. "What idea? Nyla—"

"Amelia and I have got this handled," she assured him, doing absolutely nothing to spark confidence. "I just need everyone to be at the right place at the right time, and we'll put this fucker down before the clock strikes twelve."

A beat of silence was all they had to decide if they were going to trust Nyla's plan. Aaron looked at Sam, who shrugged, and then at Emmett, who held up his hands as if to say 'not my girlfriend, not my call.' When Aaron's shoulders sagged in resignation, Sam summoned every ounce of optimism in his body.

"Alright then, evil stepsisters," he said, addressing both Amelia and Nyla. "We've got two hours before this carriage turns back into a pumpkin. What do you want us to do?"

Chapter Twenty-Nine

AMELIA

"I'll have you know that every bone in my body is screaming that this is a terrible idea."

Nyla paused in her movement to look back at Amelia, a sheepish grin on her face.

"I never said it was a *good* idea, just that I've had worse."

"I'm starting to think that discrepancy is smaller than I thought it was."

They were skirting the edge of the cabin road, crouch-walking through the dense underbrush toward the Fishers' property. This felt to Amelia like the last place they should be, but Nyla insisted that she had it covered. The fact that she had her flamethrower poised and ready to fire at the slightest hint of trouble did make Amelia feel marginally better.

After discussing the plan in depth, Nyla gave everyone their assignments and they split up soundlessly. Aaron took the BMW ahead, Sam drove the rental truck packed with hunters back to the cabin, and Emmett set out to bring his father's truck closer to the lake, preparing himself as a failsafe. Amelia wasn't sure what that meant exactly, but Emmett seemed to so she trusted that everyone was where they needed to be. She had to, otherwise she'd have a panic attack before the stressful part of her night even started.

Nyla instructed her to be quiet, which was almost more worrying than if she'd told her to draw attention to herself. Amelia measured her breath and placed careful steps, slinking through the dark until the harsh white cast of the cabin's porch lights flickered through the tree branches. Here, Nyla paused, holding out her arm for Amelia to pause with her.

They weren't hidden well. The underbrush here wasn't overly thick, and they weren't in the most inconspicuous place, but that didn't matter for their purposes. Nyla nodded to Amelia, leaning back against the trunk of an evergreen to wait. Amelia chose to remain upright, watching the scene unfold with morbid fascination.

This is a bad idea. This is such *a bad idea.*

Amelia hushed the voice in her head repeating her reluctance to stay put. For better or worse, she trusted Nyla. She agreed to this plan. She was going to see it through.

In less than a minute, the Fishers' backyard was teeming with shivering hunters.

Aaron strode brusquely to the center of the yard, stepping onto the edge of the stone fire pit to grab everyone's attention. He didn't need to— he was easily the tallest person present— but the act made him a more prominent target and seemed to settle the men.

Amelia counted. From her vantage, it seemed like nearly everyone had agreed to their plan or, more likely, Aaron hadn't told them the plan and convinced them to leave the safety of the cabin with a series of charming lies. She prayed they wouldn't regret that decision later; the last thing Amelia wanted was unwitting blood on her hands.

Nyla remained deceptively relaxed, her muscles poised and ready to spring to action at a moment's notice despite her casual posture. Amelia hoisted the Remington, hoping she wouldn't have to use it. She'd shot a handgun before, but it was many years ago. Rifles were another story, one that she didn't want to end with undue maiming. Just when she was second-guessing herself on the correct position of the safety mechanism, Aaron began speaking.

"I need you all to form into groups," he said with authority, directing the men into several trios. At his command, the men shuffled into the positions he dictated, stirring uncomfortably. At first, Amelia thought Aaron was making nonsensical demands to buy time, but she quickly realized that every move was calculated. By the time Aaron was done rearranging the traumatized hunters, they were in a formation that would provide the quickest retreat into the cabin with minimal bottle-necking. If everything went awry, Aaron was preparing to save as many men as he could, leaving himself the most exposed.

"What are we doing out here?" One of the hunters asked, nervous energy shaking his voice. Aaron answered with an appeasing, polite smile.

"This is just temporary," Aaron assured them. "I'll get you all back inside as fast as I can. First, I need names. Yours, and anyone you know is missing. Look around, take stock of who's standing next to you, who's in another group, and who you don't see."

"You brought us out here for a head count? You said you were getting us home!" Someone else shouted, aghast. Aaron addressed him with calm certainty.

"The FBI is on scene and we're working on arranging appropriate transportation, but there are more of you to rescue. We need to find them, and right now, you're our only resource."

"We could've done this inside where it's safe!" The same man argued.

"I know you're frightened," Aaron said gently. "But we were already struggling to breathe in there. I asked three different people for a total count, and I got three different answers."

The assembled men mumbled uncertainly.

"We can't afford to miscount and have agents risking their lives looking for people who don't need to be found. This night has seen enough death," Aaron said firmly. "Now, please do as I asked and make sure that we know who's present and who's missing, and then we can all get out of this unscathed."

"A head count?" Amelia whispered in shocked awe to Nyla. "*That's* the excuse he went with?"

"What did you expect him to say?" Nyla shrugged. "'Hey, I need you guys to be live bait for a hot sec?'"

She had a point, but Amelia was more surprised that the head count excuse worked. Nyla must've seen her disbelief because she added:

"Aaron is very persuasive."

As the muttered counting of the assembled hunters rustled through the air, Amelia and Nyla settled in to wait. The idea had been to draw the Chehwinoo to them by presenting a more appealing target than the scattered men remaining in the woods, playing into its prey drive instinct. Live bait was a crude way of putting it, but it wasn't inaccurate.

Amelia just prayed that their risk paid off.

Her skin was hyper-sensitive to any shift in temperature, so much so that Amelia was afraid she'd miss it when the actual Chehwinoo showed itself. *If it showed itself.* For all they knew, another group of hunters had banded together and formed a much more appetizing meal for the creature. She soon realized that she shouldn't have worried— the air chilled so suddenly that it felt like someone had opened a freezer behind her. Amelia and Nyla both stiffened, scanning the clearing for the source of the terror snaking through the crowd.

Aaron sensed the shift at the same time they did, his hand slowly drifting to the gun holster on his hip. The assembled men, whether consciously or not Amelia couldn't tell, quieted and began to shift restlessly. The creature was here, but they'd yet to determine where.

That didn't bode well. Amelia hadn't seen the creature as much as some of the others, but in her experience, stealth wasn't its favourite tactic when prey was readily available.

"Come out, you son of a bitch," Nyla uttered under her breath, clutching the flamethrower tightly. Amelia held her position, forcing herself not to move.

Branches rustled overhead, twigs snapped, and still they waited.

Something caught her attention near the cabin, though Amelia couldn't put her finger on exactly what it was. Never one to ignore her instincts, she glanced over and scanned the shadows. Nothing appeared, so she was about to return her gaze to the crowd when her vision snagged on a ripple in the darkness. Her heart hammered as she processed what she was seeing, drowning out all other sound.

"Nyla," Amelia rasped, staring wide-eyed at the misshapen mass undulating over the cabin. "It's on the—"

"*Aaron! THE ROOF!*"

Nyla was already moving when Amelia snapped into gear, erupting from the thicket just as Aaron spotted the Chehwinoo lurking atop the shingles. He barked at the men to get inside, pulling his gun and firing into the creature in one fluid movement. The bullet struck the Chehwinoo in the shoulder, just north of its heart. It screeched, reeling back, its claws gripping the roof tiles to keep itself upright. The men surged toward the back door, clamoring and shouting as they rushed to safety before the creature regained its balance. Aaron's forethought did its job— while there was some struggling and bumping, the majority of the hunters were safely inside before the Chehwinoo leapt from the roof to the ground.

Aaron shot it again, striking its stomach. The Chehwinoo recoiled, its high-pitched wailing piercing the air sharply. There were five hunters still fighting to get to safety.

"Get its attention," Nyla instructed Amelia, finger on the flamethrower's trigger. She knew that the flame would be useless at this distance, so Amelia lifted the rifle and did her best to aim.

"Over here, motherfucker!" Amelia yelled, firing in blind faith. The Chehwinoo whipped its head around, the bullet tearing through the top half of its skull. Shards of glass-like ice and viscous darkness exploded from the impact, hollow, earth-shaking roars trembling through the air as the creature writhed in pain. Amelia stared in shock at the carnage she'd wrought.

"Nice shot," Nyla said out of the side of her mouth, giving her an approving nod.

"Would you believe it was luck?"

"Absolutely." Nyla grabbed the sleeve of Amelia's sweater, tightening her grip in a solid fist. "Now, let's hope you didn't use up all of it. Run!"

Amelia didn't have to be told twice.

The two women took off at break-neck speeds, traversing the loose gravel with little regard for balance or twisted ankles. The night was inky around them, the visibility so low that Amelia had to trust her muscle memory to guide her down the familiar road. The Chehwinoo recovered from its injury, crashing after them over a chorus of shouts from Aaron directing the remaining men back inside and telling Nyla and Amelia to be careful.

The lake had never felt so far away.

Amelia swung the rifle over her shoulder and against her spine, freeing her hands to clear low-hanging branches from their path. Nyla lagged a little behind her, suddenly skidding to a stop and whipping around to face their pursuer. Amelia cried out and turned on her brakes, but Nyla snapped at her.

"Keep going!" She raised the flamethrower, igniting a blaze of targeted heat five feet long and billowing in the biting wind. In the light of the flame, Amelia was shocked to see the Chehwinoo emerge from the darkness practically on top of them, jaws snapping relentlessly. It recoiled from the fire, screaming in fury at Nyla. "Amelia, *now!*"

Against her better judgement, she kept running.

Amelia's own breathing smothered out most other sounds. She thought she heard Nyla coming after her, but she couldn't be sure without stopping to look. The creature's anguished screeching followed her through the trees, getting farther away before getting louder again as it resumed chase. Amelia tried not to think about how close it had gotten before, trusting Nyla to keep it at bay long enough for them to get to their destination.

The pier was close, Amelia could feel the shift in the breeze as it kissed the water's surface.

Another blast of orange light. Nyla was fending the creature off again, keeping it in line as best she could with the flamethrower. Amelia couldn't stop now, couldn't slow. She needed to get to the lake.

Legs burning, pain lancing through her chest, for one striking moment Amelia felt like she was going to collapse before she made it. Then, blessedly, a break in the thicket.

Basin Lake swelled into view, glorious and intimidating in the cover of night.

Amelia stumbled to a stop at the edge of the water, whipping around to search for Nyla. She was nowhere to be seen, but she could hear her. The creature was snarling and snapping, crunching through the forest at an uneven pace. The staggered burst of orange flames was the only indication of where Nyla was. Amelia tensed, ready to run back to help, but it wasn't necessary. With a monstrous crash, the Chehwinoo tumbled through the trees and onto the shore.

Her sneakers sank into the icy water's edge, soaking up to her ankles. Amelia sucked in a sharp breath at the unexpected shock of cold, holding herself steady. Nyla circled the creature, maintaining a steady stream of flame to keep it at a distance. The Chehwinoo's body was slick with melted ice, coating its blackened skin with a glistening cloak that made it look like it was dripping in oil. It screamed relentlessly, swiping and gnashing its jaws at Nyla with palpable hatred. When Amelia stomped in the shallow water, the Chehwinoo turned its glowing topaz eyes on her, all but freezing her in place.

"Want an easier target, you ugly bastard?" Amelia taunted, splashing more. The Chehwinoo hissed, crouching to spring at her. She knew it could reach her from here, but she trusted Nyla's plan. It had worked so far, they just needed a few more seconds of luck. "Come on, how do you feel about a little skinny dipping?"

Nyla blasted the creature again, jolting it into motion.

It faltered on unsteady limbs, scrambling toward Amelia with more speed than she was ready for. She stumbled backward, the sole of her sneaker landing squarely on a rounded stone slick with algae. A second before it happened, Amelia knew she was falling. It happened in slow motion, her brain processing the danger before she was fully seated in the shallows of Basin Lake, the water soaking through her jeans and the sleeves of her sweater up to her mid-forearms. Nyla's expression froze in panic, and she rushed forward with the flamethrower to help, but she was too far away. She'd never get there in time.

Fortunately, they had a little bit of luck left on their side.

The grinding of rubber on gravel filled the air, accompanied by the rev of an engine. Amelia, Nyla, and the Chehwinoo were all drawn to the source of the noise mere seconds before Sam crashed the rental Tacoma into the creature's lanky body.

The Chehwinoo didn't have time to scream before the truck barreled over the uneven wooden pier and launched into the lake, the creature clawing at the truck's body as it tried to escape. The driver's side door opened and slammed, but it was too dark to see Sam's escape from the runaway vehicle. From the lack of splash, he'd at least avoided the lake.

When the Chehwinoo's legs hit the water, propelled by the careening truck, the angered screeching turned to anguished fury, shattering the air at inhuman decibels.

Amelia scrambled to her feet, racing to the pier with Nyla hot on her heels. The Chehwinoo clamored to get on top of the truck, to get away from the water that was slowly turning to ice around the point of impact. The truck continued to sink, weighed down by the creature.

"Rifle," Nyla demanded, all but snatching the gun from Amelia's grip as she removed it from her back. It took Nyla three whole seconds to aim, and then the night was pierced by the crisp, echoing sound of a gunshot and Amelia watched as a gaping hole appeared in the Chehwinoo's chest. It froze, its claws outstretched, and then it fell backwards with a shudder and a splash, disappearing into the black depths as an ice sheet continued to spread across the center of the lake.

They stared, catching their breath, waiting for it to remerge. When it didn't, Amelia's posture sagged in relief, turning to the beach with a smile, searching for Sam. When she didn't see him, a knot of fear formed in her stomach.

"Where's Sam?" Her voice was quiet, uncertain, like she didn't want the answer. "He jumped out at the edge of the pier, right?"

She took a step in the direction of the incline that loosely connected the cabin road to the pier, where the truck initially collided with the Chehwinoo and the plan instructed Sam to leap from the truck to the safety of the pebbled sand. He wasn't there, and Amelia didn't see any evidence that he had been.

The door had opened. She *knew* the truck door opened. She heard it.

"Did you see Sam jump out?" She didn't wait for Nyla to answer, the look on her face was enough. Amelia realized with dawning horror that Sam, despite what she'd heard, was still inside the truck.

The truck that was currently trapped with its front end submerged beneath a foot of solid ice.

"SAM!" Her feet were moving before her brain, stumbling in the dirt as Amelia whirled toward the lake. Thankfully, Nyla's brain was working for her. She grabbed Amelia's arm, yanking her to a sudden halt.

"Amelia, *wait!*" Nyla jogged ahead, waving her arms high above her head at something Amelia couldn't see. "EMMETT!"

"On it!"

The answering call brought Amelia's attention to the far shore of the lake, where Sam's motorboat roared to life with Emmett at the helm. He crashed through the edge of the ice sheet, getting as close to the protruding tail end of the Tacoma as he could before the ice became too strong to break with sheer force. He left the boat running, launched himself from the vessel, and slid to his knees approximately where the truck's back window would be. Amelia watched, her heart a hard, painful lump in her chest, as Emmett took the blunt end of the oar and drove it repeatedly into the ice.

"Come on, come on, come on," Nyla muttered beside her. Amelia hadn't noticed her return to her side, now clutching her hands as if both of their lives depended on it. Amelia returned her grip, watching unblinkingly as Emmett finally reached the unfrozen lake water below. The ice fractured into large, disjointed pieces, bobbing on the surface. Emmett kicked them aside to give himself room, and then he plunged his upper body into the churning depths. Nyla gasped, echoing Amelia's fear that he was going to dive fully into the lake himself. He didn't, anchoring his lower half on the solid ice below him. An agonizing ten seconds later, Emmett was pulling a shivering Sam through the hole in the sheet.

Relief surged through Amelia's entire body, bringing tears and anger to the forefront. She wanted to scream, cry, collapse, all of the above. But she couldn't, because in the next second Nyla's gasp turned into a panicked yell. They weren't out of the woods yet.

"Emmett! The ice!"

Amelia saw it now. The edges of the sheet were shrinking, melting as rapidly as it had formed now that the Chehwinoo was dead. Emmett caught on immediately, hooking his arms underneath Sam's and hauling him to his feet.

"The boat," he huffed, his voice carrying in the unnatural silence. "We need to get to the boat!"

Amelia never wanted to feel like this again. Standing on the side of the lake, watching from a distance, helpless, was the most soul-crushing thing she'd ever experienced. She couldn't do anything but wait and hope that Emmett and Sam made it back to them in one piece.

Echoing cracks filled the air as the ice deteriorated. Sam was slow on his feet, dragged down by the chilled water clinging to his clothes and the lingering daze of the crash. Emmett was compensating as best he could, but the ice was melting too quickly. They wouldn't make it. Amelia could tell from here that they wouldn't make it. Sam had already been in the water too long— another dip could kill him. Emmett wouldn't fare much better with his upper half drenched from rescuing Sam. Even if they managed to get back into the boat from the water, it might be too late to save them from the frigid temperatures.

"*Move!*"

Amelia and Nyla only had a split second to react before Aaron bolted past them and onto the pier, shedding his jacket as he ran. Nyla yelped in fear as she realized what he was about to do, flinching as if to run after him and only stopping herself at the last moment. In an impressively long leap, he stumbled onto the very edge of the stable ice, catching himself on one knee and slipping forward with his momentum. He clamored upright, reaching Emmett and Sam in the span of a single breath. Between Aaron and Emmett, they managed to hoist Sam into the boat just as the ice buckled beneath their feet. Emmett caught himself on the side of the boat, his torso balancing the weight of his legs over the edge of the hull. He flopped into the boat, lunging to grab Aaron, who was rapidly sinking into the slush. By the time all three men were safely into the boat, everyone was sufficiently wet and shaking.

But they were alive.

"Jesus Christ," Amelia muttered, racing after Nyla to the pier where Emmett was steering the boat in preparation for docking. Nyla snatched the discarded rope and looped it over her arm, ready to throw it once they were in range. After some cursing, lots of complaints, and a bumped knee or two, everyone was safely back on dry land.

While the men caught their breath, Nyla ran to retrieve Aaron's BMW. Emmett sank to the ground, falling back against the pier's post and letting out his breath in a huge rush. Aaron paced a loose circle, walking off the jarring impact of jumping onto something as solid as ice from a distance. Sam was the worst of the three, collapsing flat onto his back and panting heavily. Amelia fell to her knees next to him, shedding her sweater and draping the dry portion over his torso.

"You're such a *moron!*" she snapped, panic-driven fury bubbling in her throat. "You were supposed to jump out of the truck!"

"I tried," Sam coughed a laugh, shaking his head in disbelief. "The airbag went off when I hit Mr. Freeze."

"Mr. Freeze?" Amelia repeated in a monotone. "Is that really the best you can do?"

"You're right," Sam said, ashamed. "That's weak material. I'll get back to you after I can feel my limbs again."

"How did you get out?" Amelia's anger had settled, and now she was in full problem-solving mode. She smoothed the wet hair from Sam's face, collecting his hands in hers and gently warming his fingers between her palms.

"I cut myself loose," he said, his voice wavering as shivers rocketed through him. "If I didn't have Nyla's pocketknife, I'd probably still be down there."

"Her foresight is scary sometimes," Aaron agreed, shaking the dirt from his jacket, and shoving his arms into it. He turned to Emmett. "Was it her idea to prepare the boat, or yours?"

Emmett grinned.

"What do you think?"

Aaron smiled back, suddenly illuminated by headlights. As if summoned, Nyla peeled off onto the side of the road in Aaron's BMW, sending a spray of gravel in her wake. She left the vehicle running, opening the back door so the four of them left standing could help Sam into the warmth of the SUV. With that done, everyone else piled in, Nyla taking the driver's seat from Aaron with a glare that could stop traffic, and they headed back to the Fishers' cabin.

Chapter Thirty

SAM

Sam thought he knew what cold was. He'd grown up in Illinois. He'd played in the snow without a jacket. He'd lived through a power outage in a snowstorm. After nearly drowning in a frozen lake, Sam now understood that he'd never known cold. Not like this.

He wasn't going to die, he was confident in that at least. There was a moment, between the airbag deploying and the first frigid laps of lake water at his ankles, that he was absolutely certain he *was* going to die. Only a few seconds elapsed from the time he hit the water to the time he freed himself from the truck, but it was enough to convince him that he wasn't getting out of this alive. His seatbelt jammed, the airbag was suffocating him, the window was only halfway down, and he was losing oxygen. Quickly. It was pure luck that his struggling drove the handle of Nyla's pocketknife into his thigh and sparked a moment of clarity.

If it wasn't for that knife, he'd be dead.

If it wasn't for him, they'd all be dead.

Sam was getting really tired of life-or-death stakes.

The remaining hunters were still gathered in the cabin when they returned. Nyla and Emmett set to work reassuring them and sending them along to the sheriff's station; Aaron wanted to help, but Nyla insisted that since she and Emmett were locals, they'd listen better to them. With the group heading either home or to see George Mason, the five of them breathed a collective sigh.

There was still much to be done, but for now, they could rest. That included getting both warm and dry.

Emmett and Aaron declined a hot shower, accepting some clean towels and freshly laundered clothes. Emmett was slightly bigger than Sam, and Aaron was slightly slimmer, so his clothes wouldn't fit either of them perfectly. They fit well enough to carry them through the rest of the night, though.

Amelia joined Sam in the bathroom while he cleaned himself up and dressed. She said she didn't trust him not to do something stupid and shock his heart, but he could tell that she was worried about him. The thought warmed him and made it incredibly difficult to keep his hands to himself.

When her tentative touch met the still-shivering skin of his back, Sam couldn't resist anymore. He abandoned the shirt he was unfolding and turned to wrap her in his arms.

"What are you doing?" she hissed, resisting for only a moment before his desperation registered. Amelia bit off the rest of her complaints, returning his embrace and rubbing gentle circles along his back.

"I thought life was supposed to be *less* exciting in your thirties," he mumbled into her hair. Amelia laughed, squeezing him. "Let's not take any more vacations for a while, alright?"

"Sounds like a plan to me," she said, and Sam could hear the smile in her voice. "I'm even starting to miss Mrs. Schwartz. At least her crabby attitude is predictable."

"If Mrs. Schwartz walked through that door right now and complained about how much noise we were making, I think I'd kiss her full on the mouth." Sam gave a bone-weary sigh. "With tongue."

"Ew," Amelia said, giggling. "That's an image I *really* didn't need."

"You think she's been reading our mail while we're gone? I subscribed to some questionable newsletters just to spice up her morning snooping."

"I guess we'll know if there's a bunch of church pamphlets shoved under our door when we get back."

Silence fell between them, heavy with a truth that neither of them wanted to admit to. Amelia broke first, tilting her head back to look at him.

"We're not going home until this is over." It wasn't a question. Sam nodded slowly.

"We can't."

Not when their friends needed them.

When they emerged from the bathroom, clean and dry, they found Emmett, Aaron, and Nyla in the living room. Emmett had taken up residency in the lounge chair, fully reclined with his baseball cap over his face, covered in a throw blanket from the waist down. Light snores were rumbling through his chest. Nyla and Aaron were on the loveseat, Aaron with one arm hooked over the back of the sofa, his other hand holding his phone in a loose grip. Nyla was curled against his side, her head tucked into the crook of his neck, her fingers splayed out over his heart.

Aaron was the first to notice their return, nodding silently in greeting. He pressed a gentle kiss to Nyla's head, waking her from her half-sleep.

"Feeling better?" she asked once she spotted Sam and Amelia, who'd made their way over to the opposite couch and folded themselves into the plush cushions. Sam pulled Amelia's legs over his, resting his hands on her shin and thigh. He grinned in answer to Nyla's question.

"Feeling like if I was ever planning to do a polar plunge in my lifetime, I'm not now."

Amelia rolled her eyes, lightly shoving his shoulder.

"Have you heard from Ty?" she asked Aaron. He raised his phone and waggled it in confirmation.

"He only made it about halfway home before Chia made him turn around," he said with a fond smile. "Apparently, he wouldn't shut up about how worried he was, and Chia didn't have the patience to deal with him fretting all night. He's back at the station now. He'll head home when this is all cleaned up."

"That doesn't surprise me," Amelia said. "Ty always was a bit of a drama queen."

"I managed to convince him to stick around Mason for now," Aaron explained. "Kelley wanted to book it over here, but I told her we had it handled, and we'd meet them at the station as soon as we could."

"Which is... in the morning?" Sam asked hopefully. Aaron's grimace told him that his hopes were unfounded.

"Try in an hour," he said apologetically. "That's all I could get us. We're lucky it's that much."

With that encouraging thought, Sam took Emmett's cue and tilted his head back on the couch cushion, trying for twenty minutes of peace before he had to face this kerfuffle all over again.

"Is it possible to have a stress headache so bad it gives you an aneurysm?"

Tyler all but collapsed into the desk chair opposite Sheriff Mason, dropping his head back so far that his hair flopped back off his forehead and curled upright. Sam clapped him on the shoulder, smirking.

"Look at lil' miss princess over here," he taunted. "Try almost drowning in a frozen lake and then you can complain."

Tyler cracked an eye open, scowling at Sam.

"Tell me again why you aren't going back to Philly?"

"And deprive you of my revered company? Of course not."

"It's rare that I get to see karma play out in real-time," Aaron mused, crossing his arms over his chest and smiling smugly at Tyler. "It's like looking at a caricature of my life working with you."

"Eat a dick, Klein."

"Are you offering?" Sam jumped in, wiggling his eyebrows suggestively at Tyler. He glowered, resuming his half-nap as Aaron continued to smile like he was having the time of his life.

The sheriff station was cleared out now, the last of the hunters having been sent home to get some rest after giving their statements. Kelley was still in the interrogation room with Sheriff Mason, discussing final touches and the next steps. The rest of her team had been sent back to their hotel in Hatfield, something none of them were particularly happy about. Kelley kept the peace by giving them all clear instructions for what she needed them to do, making the order seem less like a deliberate exclusion and more like a necessary division of labor.

Sam wasn't sure if it worked to soothe their agitation, but it did get them out of the station with little argument.

Everyone present was more or less in the know. Aaron had instructed them not to be too detailed with Kelley. She was supportive, but she didn't know the specifics of what was going on. Sam decided to keep his commentary to a minimum when she was around— he put his foot in his mouth at the best of times. Discretion was never his strong suit.

After far too long of nothing happening, the sounds of Kelley and Mason approaching was a welcome reprieve.

"Alright, I have good news and bad news." Kelley's voice preceded her, exhausted but authoritative. Sam even thought he could see some of Aaron's mannerisms in her posture.

"Start with the good," Nyla insisted. "I need something to soften the blow."

"Wildlife has agreed to quarantine the Basin," Kelley explained, to sighs of relief all around. "Obviously we can't have agents positioned around the entire perimeter, but we're placing them at all the major entry and exit points. That would be Lichen House, the Willow, and Cabin County."

"You should set up a roadblock off of route 57 too," Nyla said, approaching Kelley to show her on the map still strewn across an abandoned desk. "There's a turnaround here that people have been using as a starting point for the trails. It's not an official marker, but enough people know about it that it's become a bit of a hotspot."

"Thanks, I'll add that to the list." Kelley made a note on her phone. "I can't guarantee that this will completely stop people from venturing into the woods, but it will hopefully deter them. I've got media liaisons preparing press releases about a huge rabies outbreak and warning the public to stay away due to the risk of infection."

"That's more than we could've hoped for," Aaron said. "Thanks, Rebecca."

Kelley nodded brusquely, brushing off Aaron's thanks with an uncomfortable shake.

"I've also," she continued, tapping on her phone screen a couple of times, "gotten clearance passes for everyone in this room. It wasn't easy, so do *not* give me a reason to revoke them. I had to falsify some of your backgrounds for this. My job is on the line too."

Kelley walked up to Nyla, showing her the pass on the screen.

"You're the only one I didn't have to mess around with," she told Nyla with a half-smile. "As far as the board is concerned, you're our local guide and consult."

She moved on to Aaron.

"Your story is basically the same. You're private sector, invited by the FBI to assist in the investigation."

Emmett was next, standing up a bit straighter.

"Here's where things start to get a little less... truthful." Kelley frowned, showing Emmett the screen. "If anyone asks, you work with Nyla now."

"Got it," Emmett said with a decisive nod. Appeased, Kelley turned to Amelia and Sam.

"You two were the hardest to clear," Kelley said with a sigh. "I couldn't figure out how to justify an admissions counselor and an athletics trainer in a wildlife investigation."

Amelia gave her a shrugging smile.

"Luckily," Kelley said, eyeing Sam. "It seems like the Fishers are pretty influential people in Illinois. I was able to get these without fabricating some clearly fake story. But," Kelley interrupted Sam before he could speak, "that also means these are the weakest of the passes. They won't hold up to *any kind* of scrutiny, so you need to stay well under the radar. Are we understood? Do not give anyone a reason to look into why you're here."

"Yes ma'am," Amelia promised on both of their behalf, guessing that Sam would forget this conversation happened the moment it was convenient. She wasn't wrong.

"That's it for the good news," Kelley said, back to face the entire group. "Now for the bad. Wildlife wants this cleaned up fast. I won't be able to stop them from intervening for long. Whatever you lot are planning to do, you need to do it sooner rather than later. They already don't trust the local police to handle it, and pushback from the federal branches is ramping up. It won't take much for them to get fed up and bowl over my authority."

"How much time can you give us?" Aaron asked. Kelley gave a noncommittal shrug.

"A week, maybe. More if no one else turns up dead. Less if they do."

One week. It wasn't enough time, but it was all they had. Sam felt unease spread throughout the room like a creeping chill.

"I wish I could do more," Kelley said sympathetically. "But I'm already on thin ice with this whole situation. I'm lucky they haven't removed me from the case altogether."

"You've done more than enough," Aaron reassured her. "We'll take it from here. Thank you."

Kelley nodded again, sensing that the conversation was about to turn in a direction she couldn't follow. She started to leave when Sam stopped her.

"Not to overstep," he began slowly, in a tone of voice that told Amelia and Tyler he was definitely going to overstep, "but does the FBI have a budget for like... property damage?"

Kelley narrowed her eyes at him.

"Why?"

"Hypothetically," Sam said, "if your investigation led to... say... vehicular trauma, would your department pay for that?"

Kelley blinked, silent.

"Sam drove his rental into Basin Lake," Amelia supplied with a deadpan expression. Sam looked affronted.

"Out of necessity!" He turned pleading eyes to Kelley. "Is there any way that we could write this off under FBI casualties?"

"I'll see what I can do," Kelley said, leaving abruptly before anyone else could burden her with additional stress.

"I wouldn't get your hopes up," Tyler stage-whispered to Sam, "that's Kelley-speak for no fucking chance."

The front door opened, which seemed to surprise Aaron, Tyler, and Nyla. Sam didn't understand why until he realized that Kelley had left through the back entrance, meaning there was someone else here. From the look on Mason's face, it was someone uninvited.

"Well, this does make my life a bit easier, doesn't it?"

The voice echoed through the station, grabbing the attention of their little group with ease. Sam recognized the lilt as a soft New York accent, like the speaker had lived there as a child but moved before reaching adulthood, or vice versa. They turned as a unit, catching sight of the intruder immediately.

He was average in height, carrying himself with the haughtiness of a much taller man. Thick, golden-brown hair swirled on the top of his head, speckled tastefully with flashes of grey. He was clean-shaven, sporting a fine-tailored navy suit jacket with off-white slacks underneath. He looked like the owner of a yacht club, if not for the shoes. They were clearly business loafers, shined to perfection.

"Can I help you?" George asked, trying to take control of the room with the deep gravitas of his voice. It failed, all the authority gravitating toward the newcomer. He shot them a casually friendly smile, too perfect to be genuine.

"I certainly hope so, Sheriff Mason," the man drawled, all but stalking across the room toward them. There was something predatory in the way he moved, completely at odds with his pleasant expression. "I have a feeling this is the little motley crew of ruffians that's been causing a great deal of distress in my office. I thought it was about time I had a gentle chat with you all, see if we can't clear up our misunderstanding."

Sam had never seen this man before, but it didn't take long for the gears to click into place in his mind. A light of recognition sparked in him, spreading through their assembly like wildfire in a dry thicket. Somerton's Sheriff Station dropped sharply in temperature, mimicking the cold, appraising attitude of the man standing in their midst. They may have conquered yet another Chehwinoo, but a different breed of ice demon was now extending a hand toward them for a crisp, firm shake.

Adrian Stamkos had finally come to Somerton.

EPILOGUE: CALLIE

Hatfield, Wisconsin

"Why exactly did Nyla need a flamethrower?"

Callie ignored the irritation in Orville's question, answering as honestly as she could.

"She didn't say. Just that she'd have it back to you by next week."

If her own irritation showed, Orville didn't acknowledge it. Callie wasn't surprised; he rarely acknowledged her anyway.

She was a law school graduate, but no one would ever guess that based on the way Orville Guttenberg treated her. He was a man in his late 60s, clinging to the ownership of a small claims law firm in the middle of butt-fuck-nowhere Wisconsin. His partners had long abandoned him, his wife left him more than thirty years ago, and his children refused to speak to him outside of the mandatory holiday phone calls. In short, Orville was a crotchety old man married to his work, and Callie was the only one who could put up with him for more than a few hours at a time.

It wasn't easy. Orville did everything he could to undermine her intelligence, but with the other three employees at Guttenberg Law on a rotating schedule, Callie was the sole person able to keep accurate information on the company's daily routine. As much as Orville hated it, the firm wouldn't run without Callie's interference.

And soon, it wouldn't run without her, period.

"I don't like doing favors for your friends," Orville grouched, lumbering down the hall toward his office. Callie almost snapped back that Nyla wasn't her friend, but she stopped herself. For one, Orville wouldn't care either way. For another, she wasn't sure that was actually true.

Were she and Nyla friends?

Callie wasn't used to having friends. Law school and the subsequent grunt work for Orville kept her too busy to socialize in any capacity. Dating, friendship, hobbies, all were off the table since the day she moved to Hatfield. Callie couldn't remember the last person she'd had a non-work-related conversation with.

Aside from Nyla.

It's not that Callie didn't like Nyla. On the contrary, she liked her a lot. Nyla was outgoing and resourceful in ways Callie wasn't. Callie had a lot of respect for the lodge owner, especially in the face of all the harsh criticism she endured from Somerton's residents. Callie considered herself to be a confident person, but she doubted even she'd be able to handle all of the abuse Nyla took on simply for existing in a town that didn't want her.

Callie could never forget the day they met. When Nyla had dropped by the office last year, requesting Orville represent her in a disagreement with town management, he'd turned her down in the most brutal, Orville-like fashion. With her small stature and cute, feminine features, Callie expected Nyla to burst into tears at the hateful words coming out of her boss's mouth. To her surprise, Nyla had completely ignored Orville's outburst and instead turned to Callie with an expression like a tired mom dealing with a tantruming toddler.

Callie couldn't legally represent Nyla at the time, but she did help her draft the petition she needed. Ever since, they spoke on an occasional basis.

Those occasions had increased recently, suddenly and without explanation. Nyla reached out to Callie several times over the last three months, asking for increasingly obscure documents with complicated and restricted access. When the request to borrow Orville's flamethrower came up, Callie couldn't deny her curiosity any longer. She wanted to ask Nyla outright, but how was she supposed to bring it up? After weeks of no-questions-asked, Callie wasn't sure how to transition to lots-of-questions-asked without sounding suspicious and nosy. Besides, if Nyla was involved in anything she shouldn't be, Callie would be in a difficult position with her boss.

It occurred to her suddenly that Nyla was likely keeping her in the dark on purpose, having realized the same thing Callie just did. Nyla was more perceptive than people gave her credit for. Her decision to keep her correspondence with Callie as vague as possible was surely deliberate. As lawyers, she couldn't exactly hide any illegal activity from Orville, especially when she'd essentially made them accomplices by aiding Nyla without question. Nyla, one of the most talkative people Callie knew, was probably conducting some untoward business and deliberately keeping Callie in the dark to protect her from Orville's legendary wrath. Something a friend would do.

Callie smiled to herself. Yes, she supposed Nyla was her friend. The realization sparked a pang of regret that she *hadn't* asked more questions. If Nyla was involved with anything dangerous, Callie wanted to help if she could. She'd just have to keep it a secret from Orville.

Soon enough, that wouldn't be an issue.

Orville was going to retire. He'd said as much for the last five years, but it was really happening this time. He'd had three surgeries in the past six months, and it was getting difficult for him to read court transcripts without his thick, bottlecap spectacles. He was old, and he couldn't keep going like this. When he left the firm, Callie was going to take over. She had no concern over whether or not Orville would appoint someone else in his stead— there was no one else *to* appoint.

Callie had big plans for this place. Starting with convincing some of the old attorneys to come back. Three had already agreed, given Orville was no longer in the picture. Small claims were just a temporary steppingstone for Guttenberg Law— soon to be Quinn & Associates. Once Callie got some prosecutors on her payroll, her dreams would really take root.

First, though, she needed to secure the Lichen House contract.

It was a silly, nonsensical hurdle that Orville threw at her in the last month. He was feeling particularly vindictive and made a lot of pomp and circumstance about refusing to retire before that contract was settled. Lichen House had been in corporate ownership limbo for years now, stuck between new management that wanted to turn the place into a tourist trap and government regulations that wanted to preserve the property as a historical landmark. There was no reason they couldn't accomplish both, but getting all relevant parties in the same place at the same time to negotiate was proving to be difficult, especially with Mayor Carver MIA.

Before their little firm could slip out from under the thumb of Orville's stubborn habits, Callie needed to make headway on Lichen House and now

Somerton's resident pariah and Callie's newly realized friend Nyla Jameson had inadvertently given her the perfect opportunity to do just that.

"Orville?" Callie stood up from her desk, determination singing in her blood. "Are you taking the company vehicle to New York?"

He grunted a series of noncommittal phrases, none of which answered her question. It didn't matter; Callie knew that Orville hated driving. He wouldn't take the company vehicle unless he had no other choice.

"I'm going to head over to Somerton for the week," she announced to the empty hall. As much as Orville liked to pretend that he had hearing loss when he didn't like what was being said, Callie had seen his medical reports. He had perfect hearing, he just used it whenever it suited him. "I was going to drop into Lichen House to speak to Ephraim Coady anyway. I'll pick up your flamethrower while I'm there."

Another series of grunts, which sounded vaguely optimistic. Callie smiled. She always felt her best when she was doing something productive, and the coming week was shaping up to be one of the most productive she'd had in a while. Callie could negotiate the Lichen House contract with Ephraim, find out why Nyla needed access to Somerton archives stretching back a full century and what on Earth any of it had to do with a flamethrower, and be back in Hatfield all before Orville returned from his conference.

Somerton wasn't her favourite place to be, but at least she'd get out of drinking Orville's disgustingly watered-down coffee for a few days. That fact alone made the trip more than worth her while.

ACKNOWLEDGEMENTS

I can't believe we're here again already! My third book! Holy shitballs (pardon my French). As always, I wouldn't be here without my amazing support group. My husband, Patrick, you're one of the most kind, incredible people I know and as often as you tell me you're proud of me, it's never as proud as I am of you. My friends/beta readers (because you're both), thank you for helping me hash out this mess of a plot into something legible. And, of course, my readers. Thank you for making this entire thing possible and supporting me in any way that you can. I appreciate each and every one of you more than you know.

ABOUT THE AUTHOR

Victoria Jayne Saunders is an author of new adult horror, romance, thriller, and fantasy. She lives in Newfoundland, Canada, with her husband, three cats, two dogs, and one very cranky lizard. She graduated from the Memorial University of Newfoundland in 2016 with a BA in English Language and Literature. She loves DIY, reading, writing, and forgetting to eat when she's playing too many farming/life sims.

ALSO BY VICTORIA JAYNE SAUNDERS

Deus

A society of were-sharks accidentally dissolves a human trafficking ring to rescue a hapless college student. Also, Greece.

Ebook and paperback available here (Amazon, if you're reading this as a physical copy)

Kill Bite: Book One of the Topaz Trilogy

Find out how we got here if you haven't already (in which case... why did you read this?) Follow Nyla and Aaron as they discover the truth behind the disappearances that started it all.

Ebook, paperback, and hardcover available here (Amazon, if you're reading this as a physical copy)

CAMOUFLAGE

Catch the epic conclusion of the Topaz Trilogy

Coming 2024

www.ingramcontent.com/pod-product-compliance
Lightning Source LLC
Chambersburg PA
CBHW011938210726
48290CB00011BA/2836